Praise for *The Prometheus Man*

'A debut thriller that succeeds . . . Many high-octane action scenes Reardon executes with skill.' *Kirkus Reviews*

'Reardon shows admirable skill at keeping his readers on the edge of their seats and making them think too.' *Shots*

'A winning international thriller that is as smart as it is suspenseful. Part Robert Ludlum, part Michael Crichton, with a contemporary spin all Scott Reardon's own.'
Christopher Reich, *New York Times* bestselling author of *Rules of Deception*

'*The Prometheus Man* is a bullet-paced thriller that provokes fear, anger, and sympathy simultaneously, and makes us ho e the world never lets this particular fiction turn into reality.'
' homas Perry, Edgar Award winner and bestselling author of *The Informant*

'A henomenal debut, full of non-stop action and thrills. With this bi engineered twist on Jason Bourne, Reardon offers a dark vision covert work that may be closer to the present than we think.'
M thew Quirk, bestselling author of *The 500* and *Cold Barrel Zero*

' are find in the reading landscape: a fast-paced techno-thriller h well-realized characters and a beating heart. A lot of people running around claiming to be the next Michael Crichton. cott Reardon actually has the writing chops to pull it off.'
rad Parks, Shamus Award-winning author of *Say Nothing*

THE PROMETHEUS MAN

SCOTT REARDON

MULHOLLAND
BOOKS
HODDER

First published in Great Britain in 2017 by Mulholland Books
An imprint of Hodder & Stoughton
An Hachette UK company

This paperback edition published in 2018

1

A CIP catalogue record for this title is available from the British Library

Paperback ISBN 978 1 473 62902 8
eBook ISBN 978 1 473 62901 1

Printed and bound in Great Britain by Clays Ltd, Elcograf S.p.A.

Hodder & Stoughton policy is to use papers that are natural,
renewable and recyclable products and made from wood grown in
sustainable forests. The logging and manufacturing processes are expected
to conform to the environmental regulations of the country of origin.

Hodder & Stoughton Ltd
Carmelite House
50 Victoria Embankment
London EC4Y 0DZ

www.hodder.co.uk

To my wife, Lindsay
To anyone who has a brother and to John, my brother

FACT:

May 8, 2001: Researchers inject aging mice with human stem cells. Almost immediately the mice begin scoring better on the Morris water maze, a test of cognitive function.

June 20, 2006: Doctors at Johns Hopkins inject stem cells from mouse embryos into paralyzed mice. Within a week, the mice recover significant motor activity.

November 10, 2010: Scientists at the University of Colorado injure the limbs of lab mice and then inject them with stem cells. Within days, the injuries heal. There is, however, an unanticipated side effect. The treated muscles nearly double in size and strength.

Let justice be done, though the world perish.
                                        — *King Ferdinand*

THE
PROMETHEUS
MAN

CHAPTER 1

"YOU NEED to come in."

The words came out so low and fast Karl wasn't sure he'd heard them.

He rolled over in the bed. "Who is this?" Then he remembered he was on a cell phone and the line wasn't secure. "Wait. Say again."

"You need to come here. Right now."

His feet were already on the floor the moment he recognized the voice. There were questions on the tip of his tongue, but the circumstances answered them before he could speak.

Did something happen at the lab?

—Of course something happened at the lab.

Are the police there?

—He wouldn't tell you if they were.

"Fifty minutes," he said and hung up.

He was actually only twenty minutes away, but Weaver—the voice on the phone—didn't know just how frequently he switched hotels. Within minutes, he was out of Paris proper and heading for the lab. It was that hour of night when so much of the world was at rest that it became a sort of death. He sped across silent streets and empty highways, a world without people, until he reached the forest outside Versailles.

He pulled onto a service road. Once he reached a redundant power station, he skidded to a stop. The wind whistled across his windows and bent the trees in his headlights. He sat there for a minute, knowing he ought to call this in to Langley, ultimately deciding he wasn't going to do that.

He drove around the power station and took the road another half mile to a warehouse whose only color came from ancient scabs of red paint.

The stars were out. Karl could see Weaver sitting on a cinder block surrounded by black leafless trees.

Weaver had always reminded Karl of Renfield, the attorney Dracula turned into his houseboy. He was short, severe-looking, and had the kind of temper that flares only when a back is turned. Weaver said nothing as Karl approached. His eyes were fixed on the horizon, though in the woods there is no horizon.

Without looking in Karl's direction, he stood up and led the way to the lab. The entrance to it was inside the warehouse, which wasn't actually a warehouse. And that was the idea. No road crew or stray backpacker could ever know what was here.

Inside, the lab was dark. It wasn't supposed to be. Weaver flipped the switch to a light by the door.

And there was blood.

It was streaked over the plexiglass wall that divided the lab from the rest of the building. Where it wasn't streaked, it was sprayed.

Karl saw a handprint in it.

"I locked them in," Weaver said. "I had to."

He stood waiting for the reaction, the explosion at what he had done. But Karl just turned and stared at him.

"One of them got loose," Weaver said. "It was waiting for us."

Karl glanced at Weaver's jacket pockets, looking for the bulge of a weapon.

"I got out first and used the override. By the time I got back, it had dragged Dr. Feld to the door."

"What override?"

"It was holding him against the glass." Weaver closed his eyes. "I couldn't see what it was doing to him, but he was still alive."

Karl looked at the plexiglass. There were other partial handprints and, between them, runny smears where someone had tried over and over to wipe away the blood. Which would have been difficult, like scraping egg yolk off a plate after it's congealed.

"It was keeping him alive on purpose." Weaver pulled out another cigarette. "It was torturing him."

"'Animals don't torture other living things.' Your words, Dr. Weaver. And please don't smoke in here."

Weaver turned on him. The expression on his face was hard to look at. "You don't get it. The code. It knew he had the code to get out."

Then Karl understood the purpose behind the wiping. The last one alive would have tried to clear the blood off the glass, so he could see Weaver. Plead with him.

"Unlock the door," he said.

Weaver grimaced like this was a sick joke.

"They could still be alive. Unlock the door."

"But by now the rest of the sample could be loose too. I'm not going to—"

Karl shoved Weaver back against the wall and pressed his forearm into his neck. Weaver choked in silence, in acceptance.

"You override the override," Karl said, "or whatever the hell it is you have to do to get that door open."

Weaver worked on the door while Karl went into the woods. At the base of a little tree, he dug up the Sig compact he'd buried in a plastic shopping bag. When he got back, he found Weaver standing across the entrance from the lab door.

They hit the fluorescents inside, but only a few came on. The rest dangled by their wiring. The alarm system went off, but since they'd disabled the sirens long ago, the blue lights spun in silence, whipping shadows around the room. Through the strobing, Karl could see Dr. Feld. He was right by the door, right where Weaver had last seen him.

Deep gouges had been cut into his skin, splitting it wide along his legs, back, and sides. His foot, still encased in its Rockport orthopedic walking shoe, lay several feet from his body. His face wasn't on right: something powerful had gripped it and twisted.

Feld's assistant was stretched along the floor nearby, facedown, with one arm extended overhead. Patches of hair and scalp were missing from the back of his head. The other arm was so dislocated from its socket that the wrist rested on the back of his skull. Karl didn't see Eric Reese, the youngest member of Project Prometheus and the only one he really knew.

With his weapon raised, Karl crept through the door. The spinning lights made it seem like in every corner of the room something was moving. He listened as hard as he ever had in his life. As he scanned the room for bodies, dead or alive, his eyes stopped on something else.

He didn't recognize it at first—it looked so different from the way it had looked the last time he'd seen it and so different from the way it was supposed to look. Only its height was the same: four feet. The largest members of the species, Karl had been told, weighed 110 pounds. This one must have weighed twice that. Its hands had thickened, and the skin on them looked chunky, like raw hamburger microwaved gray. The musculature was all wrong. It was thick like a man's, not lengthy like a chimpanzee's.

The chimp was propped up against a desk with its hands in its lap, like a child being read a story. There was blood pooled under its body and a hollow space where its throat had been. Skin hung in rags under its fingernails. Though he would never admit it to anyone, though it wouldn't go in any report, Karl knew its wounds had been self-inflicted. He knelt down and gently cupped the back of its head. Then he looked at Dr. Feld and his assistant and tried to imagine scenarios in which they bled out fast. He stayed there until Weaver came up to him.

"Contact Dr. Nast," Karl said. "Tell him everything's on hold."

When he looked up, Weaver was staring at him. "I thought you knew." He almost sounded sad.

"Knew what?"

Weaver hesitated.

"Knew what?"

"Dr. Nast got the go-ahead."

"The go-ahead for what?"

"To start the next trial. They injected the first volunteer two days ago."

Karl burned the lab that night. He didn't wait for instruction. That would only provide them with an excuse to talk him out of it. And he'd already decided to strangle what they were doing in its crib. Because the people he worked for would never stop otherwise. Because, in a way, the chimp had done exactly what it was supposed to do.

Some things don't burn right, and the lab burned like the whole world was on fire. Everything twisted in agony—the flames inflicting the damage and the structure suffering it. Blue-black smoke blotted out the moon and ruined the sky.

Karl stood deep in the woods in case anyone came. But no one ever did.

CHAPTER 2

(Three years later)

WHEN TOM turned onto Antoine Street, he almost did something that would get him killed. He almost stopped walking.

Forty yards ahead, the man he was following had frozen again. Like the last time, Benjamin Kotesh had turned and was looking up at the rooftops—just staring. Unlike the last time, he had the look an animal gets when it hears something, feels its mortality.

Antoine Street was a narrow passage between two rows of buildings that rose up like oil tankers about to converge. It was a tight place, and the prostitutes and addicts orbiting Moulin Rouge gave it a tight feeling. No one, however, had accosted Kotesh on the way over. No one asked him for money. No one offered him a room. People can sense another person's criminality only when it exceeds their own. And even the Albanian pimps leaning on SUVs seemed to sense that as the man in the gray suit passed, something in the area was worse than they were.

Kotesh still hadn't moved. There were no alleys to step into, so he had no choice but to keep walking up to the one person he didn't want to see him. But Kotesh's eyes never came down to street level, even as he started turning around and around.

He thinks someone is following him from the rooftops.

Which was impossible—the alleys that split through the neighborhood were at least thirty feet across.

Tom didn't look up. Didn't do anything to draw attention. He

8

couldn't risk it. He was by himself, and no one knew he was here. Two hours ago he'd been in his office at the US embassy in Paris. Then he'd walked out the door to hunt down a French citizen, thereby breaking the laws of both countries.

Kotesh pulled the duffel bag he was carrying tight against his body and put his hand inside his jacket, right where a gun would be. Then he was moving again. When the neighborhood began to get expensive, Kotesh started raising a cell phone to his ear and lowering it, over and over. Whoever was supposed to be on the other end wasn't picking up.

After four calls went unanswered, he gave up on the phone and pushed through a glass door into the marbled lobby of his building. From a shadow between the streetlights, Tom stared at the windows on the fifth floor. He had followed Kotesh here yesterday. It had taken him three years to get to yesterday.

Now he stood, waiting for the lights to go on. Five minutes passed. Yesterday it had only taken two.

In one window, light flashed. A muzzle flash could look like so many things that Tom wasn't sure what he'd seen. But he had a couple seconds to decide whether to do something about it. Fact: Kotesh had to lead him to the other men. This wasn't a hope or a wish or a plan. This was a need.

He did something.

If there were others in the apartment with Kotesh, he needed to know. So he crossed the street and rang Kotesh's buzzer several times—long rings, urgent—and shouted into the intercom, *"Police. Ouvrez."*

He darted back across the street and watched Kotesh's apartment from the shadows. No one came to the windows. No lights came on.

Now he had a choice. But it was one he'd made three years ago.

There were two security cameras in the lobby, so he scanned the side of the building. His eyes stopped on the fire escape, the bottom of which hung fifteen feet off the ground, one and a half times the height of a basketball hoop.

He could make that.

He looked around to make sure no one was watching, then sprinted at the building. He ran two steps up the side of it before he was close enough to lunge for the fire escape. His fingertips caught the bottom rung. He pulled himself up and waited for his breath to slow. Then he put on thin leather gloves and climbed through the window to the stairwell.

At Kotesh's door, he turned the knob. To his surprise—and then concern—the door smoothed inward. He stared into the spaceless murk beyond it.

He slipped inside before there was time to think about what he was doing. And as he did, his skin crawled from his ankles to the back of his skull. He waited for his eyes to adjust. One second of silence stretched into two. Two into four.

He listened into the silence, felt into the emptiness. And for a moment, nothing else about him existed: the family he once had, his odds of survival, his anger, his sadness.

From the foyer, he could see every room in the apartment was clear except the bedroom—it loomed unknown behind its closed door. He eased the door open. An orange haze emanated in from the streetlight outside.

The room had been decorated to conceal the identity of its true occupants. Along the walls hung framed photos of a newlywed couple hugging in various rain forests, beaches, and ski slopes. They did not live here.

On the floor in a loose pile were the bodies of seven men.

The blood curdling out of their nostrils and caked to their clothes was dry. They'd been dead for hours before Kotesh rushed back to join them. One man was staring in his direction, not seeming dead so much as paused, as if at any moment he would snap eyes on Tom and grin.

There were bullet holes in some of the bodies, but the rest looked like they'd been crash-tested. Limbs were bent unnaturally. Joints had succumbed to the random cruelty of momentum. Whoever had murdered a roomful of men who were themselves murderers had shot some and beaten the rest to death. And whoever it was, he must have come and gone through the roof—just like Kotesh thought.

The window facing the alley was open, and the breeze made the curtains rise and fall in little breaths. Tom stuck his head out and saw fifteen feet of brick in every direction. There was no way someone could have come and gone through this window.

Yet someone had.

He searched the pile of bodies and found Kotesh. The forces that had powered Kotesh's face, lighting up his eyes, giving him expression, had quit. Like a vacuum cleaner that exceeded the length of its cord.

He grabbed both of Kotesh's hands and checked them. His own hands shook a little as he did this. But there were no scars on Kotesh. This wasn't the man he really wanted. Or at least not the one he wanted most of all.

Without Kotesh, he had nothing. Tom stared at him, unable to accept what this meant: the truth about someone decent and kind had died with a man who was neither.

Three years ago, Tom had flown to Paris to visit his brother. Eric had been working for a pharmaceutical company. The offer from the firm had been too good to refuse. What little they'd inherited from their parents was going fast, and Eric was determined to lift them out of the middle-class poverty they were shocked to find themselves in. Eric was like that. There was nothing he wouldn't eagerly endure in the name of responsibility. And even now, as Tom remembered this about his brother, it filled him with the warming pride that makes people cry at college graduations.

The day before he flew home, he and Eric had gone out for

beers. Tom remembered nothing about the rest of the night. The next morning, Eric said they'd had too much to drink, but there was something he wasn't telling him. When Tom left for the airport, he paused outside the apartment door like he always did when he didn't want to leave a place, and he thought he heard Eric crying. He stood there for almost a minute, telling himself: *Go in. Come on. It's your brother. What if he needs you?* But he was late for his plane, and the taxi outside was honking.

Three weeks later, Eric disappeared, and all traces that he'd ever existed went with him. Six months after that, his body was found in Tangier.

That was when the changes started. Tom felt different. Then he was different. He was stronger, faster. The changes were small at first. But they grew bigger. Then they grew worse.

Now he stood over the bodies of seven men, hoping the answer to what happened to him would also be the answer to what happened to Eric. He searched the apartment and the men's bodies. Only one had anything on his phone. He'd mapped an address: JN, 55 Rue de Verdun, Saint-Cloud.

Someone coughed.

In the silence, it was an explosion of sound. Tom lurched back, almost tripping over the leg of a table. He felt something heavy shift on top of it and turned in time to stop a lamp from toppling over.

It took him a moment to identify the new sound in the room: the wet suck of oxygen. He followed it through the darkness back to Kotesh's body.

The little muscles around Kotesh's trachea were straining to pull breath into his throat. All it would take was a few pounds of pressure on either side of the airway. He stared at Kotesh's throat longer than he should have.

Gently he turned Kotesh's head to face him. When he saw Kotesh's eyes were still open, he slapped him lightly on the cheek.

"Ben. Ben Kotesh. Can you hear me?"

No response.

"Can you hear me?"

Kotesh moved his head.

"Ben, I'm going to help you, but you need to answer my questions."

Kotesh's eyes moved around the room without seeming to lock on any part of it. He couldn't talk—probably couldn't hear either—so Tom needed to think. The bodies could be here for four or five days before the smell reached the neighbors. Kotesh would bleed out long before then, and Tom had a week at most before the CIA figured out what he was up to.

Another option came to him.

He walked out of the apartment, and as he left the building, he pulled the fire alarm. He didn't know the exact sequence this would set in motion, but he had an idea. Once news of what happened to Kotesh hit the wires, the CIA would launch an investigation—and he would find a way to become a part of it.

As he turned onto Avenue of Martyrs, something else dawned on him. Whoever had been in Kotesh's apartment had followed him yesterday to find it.

In that case he didn't have a week after all.

CHAPTER 3

WHEN KARL landed at Charles de Gaulle Airport at 10:00 PM, he lurched awake and looked around the cabin trying to remember where he was.

Sixteen hours earlier he'd been on Fort Irwin, in the armpit of the California desert, getting drunk and gorging on discount items from a Walgreens after-holiday candy dump. On his tiny television, there was an infomercial for something called the Juice Tiger, which featured a ferocious eighty-year-old in a tracksuit who, every time the host asked him if juicing really worked, would start doing abdominal crunches and angrily ask, "Does it work? *Does this look like it's working, Dave?*" Then three enlisted guys barged into the empty barracks where he'd been kept isolated for months. They told him he had to be on a transport *right now.*

This is it, he thought. *They're finally taking you to jail.*

But the aircraft, a cavernous C-17 Globemaster he sat in the back of all alone, had taken him to Dulles. Once there, he'd been given a Delta Air Lines ticket to the spot he was now: Paris.

A little girl in a "Juicy" T-shirt was standing in the aisle, picking her nose rhythmically and staring up at the overhead bin. When Karl popped it open, he found a gigantic stuffed rabbit with a demented, crack-cocaine expression on its face and tried to hand it to her. The girl glanced at the rabbit, glanced at him, then wiped the finger that had been in her nose up to the knuckle across his duffel bag. As he stood there wondering how exactly he felt about this, the girl's mother took the rabbit out of his hand, giving him a look like they were in her daughter's bedroom and she'd just caught him sneaking in the window. He told himself he ought to be used to this. He was six-four, and he had the kind of face that made people think, *Axe murderer.*

While he waited, dehydrated and thirsty, to get off the plane, the girl's mother turned around, and he noticed a juice box on the little girl's meal tray. He took it. The girl watched in quiet awe as he punched the straw in and sucked until the empty box made a slurping sound.

As she started to voice the beginnings of an objection, he pointed at her. "We're even."

Inside the terminal, flat-screen TVs showed gorgeous newspeople standing urgently outside a Paris apartment building, where the bodies of six men had been found in a "human pile." Travelers huddled under the screens in groups, and strangers looked at each other and shook their heads as if to say: *Why does the world have to be this way?*

Past security, Karl noticed a young man stop and look at him, then approach tentatively.

"Mr. Lyons?"

Karl looked him over. "They know not to send anyone."

The young guy smiled, shy but good-natured. "Well, you know how they can be."

On the drive over, he kept eyeing Karl but didn't say anything until they hit the Arc de Triomphe.

"I'm Tom Blake, by the way."

He looked like something out of a college brochure. Not like the eunuch they always put on the cover, who if he were any more intellectually stimulated would be running naked through wheat. No, he looked like the kid on the edge of the picture, who's just been yanked out from beneath miles of thought and who stares at the camera just a little too long and a little too hard.

Karl simply nodded, and they drove the rest of the way in silence.

With its upper floors hidden by trees, the US embassy in Paris was a fortress you couldn't quite see. Perimeter security was two tiered. The outer tier featured two-foot-thick concrete cones that could stop anything short of a large and persistent tank. The inner tier consisted of a spiked black fence with guard stations that looked like telephone booths. The outer ring kept vehicles out. The inner ring kept people out. Tom stopped at the gates to show his ID. Thick cylinders—bollard barriers—sucked into the ground, allowing them to pass.

Inside the building, Karl was struck by how busy it was—both for 10:30 at night and for Paris. There were senior men and women making phone calls in the lobby, young people in wrinkled suits getting out of the elevator, and still others trying to get in.

That was when Marty Litvak entered through the lobby. A five-foot space of no-man's-land formed around him.

It may have been the only US intelligence agency that existed outside of presidential control, but the CIA crawled with politics. French Revolution politics. And after decades of hearings and purges and survivors floating around in bureaucratic stasis, everyone beamed with the morbid curiosity that went with it: *Will Martin Litvak remain head of a major desk or will his head wind up on one?*

Officially, the CIA had no rank structure. There were no lieutenants, no special agents in charge. Instead the hierarchy went by pay grade. And by that standard, Marty was the richest man in the building.

Karl watched as Marty walked into the elevator, and six people efficiently shifted to the other half of it.

* * *

Marty was holding a slim phone to his ear when Karl opened the door to Marty's office. He motioned Karl into the CEO-size suite, which was fitted with the trim furniture Karl associated with London bankers who only ate sushi. The office was dark except for a desk lamp. The late hour didn't show on Marty. He was one of those people who becomes timeless in an office.

Karl stood, fingering his luggage. Although Marty was almost sixty, he'd always reminded him of the young men in black-and-white photographs. His eyes held a work ethic and an acceptance of responsibility that people said didn't exist anymore.

When Marty finally hung up, he inspected Karl head to toe. Then frowned. "You're still dressing like an autistic person."

Karl glanced down at the olive-drab pants he'd found on the base. They looked like he'd slept in them. Or like Dom DeLuise had slept in them, and then died in them.

They eyed each other, grinning. Then Marty gestured to a chair as if just remembering. Karl dropped his stuff on the floor except for his computer bag, which he slid on Marty's desk, displacing a marble ball held up by expensive-looking twigs.

"So how's the diet?" Karl said.

"It's not a diet, Karl."

Marty practiced CRON—Calorie Restriction with Optimal Nutrition—in the hope that by consuming 30 percent fewer calories, he would live 30 percent longer.

"Why am I here?" Karl said.

"Well, you're no longer welcome at Bragg. Or Little Creek."

Marty opened a file.

"The CO there made you move into a"—Marty flipped the page, smiled—"a Super 8 motel. Tell me, did they leave the light on for you?"

"That's Motel 6."

"I beg your pardon?"

"Motel 6 leaves the light on for you."

"What does Super 8 do for you?"

"Super 8 doesn't do shit, Marty. It's like a Denny's with beds and people crying at night in Spanish. Now what the hell do you want?"

Marty took a breath and pressed both palms against the top of his desk. For a second exhaustion hung on his face. "We need a go-to. Notwithstanding what happened in Canada and your subsequent behavior, some people still think you're one of ours. Including me."

Karl watched Marty. For them to bring him back, something must have scared them pretty bad.

Marty pushed a photo into the glow of the lamp. "Paris police got a call this morning. This is what they found."

The photo was of a pile of bodies. One man's forearm jutted at an off angle from his elbow, held in place only by skin. Another's jaw had collapsed on one side.

"One of them survived," Marty said, "the person we think was the actual target."

"What is this? Why am I here?"

"The sole survivor is Benjamin Kotesh."

Three years ago they'd used Kotesh to help them move materials for Project Prometheus. He was a corrupt corporate security professional, which was why they used him.

"Kotesh's right hand was crushed," Marty said. "He'll probably lose it. He was interrogated before he was shot, so the shooter may have only had time to fire once. That shot, by the way, was to the head. It's a miracle Kotesh survived."

"Interesting choice of words."

Marty retracted the photo and made it disappear into a drawer in the desk. His eyes flicked back to the computer bag on his desk. Marty had a mild case of OCD—which was why Karl put it there.

"Where's Kotesh now?" Karl said.

"The French won't tell us. They've actually got something for the first time since World War II. I suppose they want to make it last."

"That will take diplomacy. You don't need me for that."

Marty produced a second photo. His face was obscured in shadow, but Karl could see the fear in it.

"This is why you're here," Marty said. "It was taken the same night."

He pushed the photo over. It was grainy, obviously from a security camera that pointed down a narrow street. The lens was so wide the roofs of the buildings on each side of the street were visible.

Marty pointed to a black speck on the roof. "Langley thinks— and I agree—that this is a boot." There were motion lines around it, but Karl could make out the heel. It was cocked back as though whoever it was had just jumped from one roof to the other. "And that's a thirty-four-foot jump. The world record is twenty-nine and change."

Karl picked up the photo and stared at the boot. There was only one person in the world it could belong to.

He noticed his fingers were shaking. Marty noticed too. They both stared at them, agreeing with them.

"Marty, you told me—you *assured* me—he died two and a half years ago. Medullary thyroid cancer, wasn't it? You actually went to the trouble to make that up."

"We lost him."

For a moment Karl couldn't speak. He stared at Marty's lapels, wanting to grab him by them.

The man who they'd lost was Ian Bogasian, the first and last human test subject of Prometheus. Considering what happened with the chimpanzee outside Paris, what they did to him never should have been done at all.

"You *lost* him?" Karl said. "How do you *lose* him? He weighs 270 pounds."

"We set up a new program. We were trying to...manage his symptoms. At times we allowed him to leave the facility—monitored, of course. A couple months ago, he just disconnected."

"My god, you're crazy."

Marty didn't say anything.

"Tell me the truth or I'll walk. Was he running ops?"

Marty folded his hands, unfolded them.

And Karl had his answer. He flashed on Sammy Badis, a Harvard-educated heroin dealer who'd made a foray into machine-gunning American oil workers in Algeria. A year ago they'd found his body at a resort in Morocco where one of the Kardashians was supposedly staying. His chest had been crushed, and so had his hand—which was strange because there was no bruising on the outside. Nobody could figure this out, because how do you break the large bones in someone's hand without using something hard, like a hammer?

There were others on the kill list who'd died under odd circumstances. Many, many of them.

The official term for someone like Bogasian was NOC, non-official cover operative. That's what Karl had been for the past decade. He'd started in the army where he'd been just another piece of meat from the hills. Then he'd worked his way to the teams and from there to the CIA. But Bogasian represented the next generation of people like Karl. Or at least that had been the idea once.

Karl stared at Marty. "Why would Bogasian kill someone associated with Prometheus three years after the fact?"

"I don't know."

"Is he coming after us?"

"I don't think so. I believe someone else found out about him and is running him, and they've figured out how to treat his symptoms, keep him online. But I don't know why he'd go after Kotesh. Kotesh's involvement ended three years ago. He's irrelevant."

That only makes it worse, Karl thought, *Bogasian killing without any seeming point.*

"How do you know Bogasian's even working for someone?" he asked.

"I'm assuming he's working for someone else because I'm assuming the worst, of course."

"Is that the worst? Imagine him out there, totally unchecked. I still think of those women in St. Petersburg."

"We agreed never to speak of that."

Neither one of them said anything.

"When this massacre came in, it went straight up the line. And now our own people think we have the largest technology gap our country has faced since the Russians shot Yuri Gagarin into space. They're shitting themselves."

"Imagine what they'll do to you when they find out you're the one who made him—and then lost him."

"Well, I really couldn't have done it without you, Karl. Please don't forget that. I know I haven't."

Another silence.

Marty tapped the photo of the boot. "That brings me to what we need you to do."

"I know what you need me to do."

"You can't kill Bogasian until we've found out who's running him. That's priority one."

"I liked him, you know. Before everything tipped over."

"I know that. You don't need to tell me that."

"None of this is his fault. He's sick."

"Then it's a mercy."

Marty watched him for a moment.

"No one can ever make a man do an evil thing," he said. "They can only appeal to what was always there."

Karl didn't say anything.

"There are already three official investigations going. Some of us want our own snake eater working in parallel. Now with your cooperation—your *full* cooperation—a certain investigation by the inspector general, into you soiling yourself in Canada last year, will not make its way to Justice next month. And will not ever."

"And the field?" The words came out funny, high-pitched, like a boy's. Karl smiled, embarrassed by the need within his request. And Marty smiled back, equally aware of this need.

Marty continued as though he'd never stopped. "Furthermore you would then be eligible to return to...real work. No more bunking with trigger-pullers in the bush."

Karl could feel inside himself a desperate stupid hope, which always meant one thing: walk away. Generosity from a man like Marty came with strings attached, and those strings led places.

But then he thought of Fort Irwin, where he'd spent the past six months. Time had stretched out in front of him until he couldn't see it, couldn't feel it pass. Time put him in its infinite white space. A couple times a month, he'd find himself in the shower with no memory of how long he'd been there or what body part he'd just been washing.

"I imagined by this point in the conversation, you'd have a very different expression on your face," Marty said.

"I'm thinking."

"Alex is dead. Your parents are dead. You never had children, and you have a sister in South Dakota who doesn't return your phone calls. It isn't my place to say it, but where else do you really have to be?"

Karl looked at the floor, then the windows—anywhere but Marty's eyes.

"If I accept," he said finally, "there will be nothing that affects any innocent third parties without my knowledge. Promise me."

Marty leaned forward with the perfect stillness of a man whose anger has crowded out all other impulse. "When you do what we do, when you break the rules of civilization in order to save it, there's always blowback. And you know it."

Neither one of them moved.

Finally Marty stood up. "We're not reporting your presence here to French intelligence, so if you're caught, the determination of your diplomatic status could go either way. FYI."

"The French are a mild, rational people. I'm sure they'll understand."

"No one else is officially on this. You are not to discuss the photo I showed you with your staff—who by the way are not your staff but are serving you in an advisory capacity only."

Marty opened the door and motioned to his assistant.

Karl stepped into the waiting area and turned around. "This doesn't mean I'm your hatchet man. I hope that's clear."

"There's one other thing." Marty picked up an empty plastic cup off a table and held it up like it contained a fine wine. "We're going to need you to piss in this. I hear you've been hitting the bottle pretty hard." Marty's eyes twinkled like he was smiling even though he wasn't. "You know, Aldrich Ames was an alcoholic too."

Karl stared at the cup, wanting to slap it out of Marty's hand with all his might. *Welcome back, Karl. Now if you don't mind, we're going to need you to get on all fours and lift your hind leg and pee in this cup. It's only a formality, as is this rolled-up newspaper I'm prepared to spank your nose with.*

"So what do you say?" Marty held out the cup.

Karl slowly took it.

Marty smiled. "Your team is already waiting for you. We thought you might say yes."

So that was that. Karl could hunt down a man he once liked and respected but who was now too dangerous to live. Or he could go to a supermax prison for the next ten to fifteen years, assuming he behaved himself and became a role model to his rapist/murderer peers.

Even though he wasn't sure he'd ever believed in God, he said a prayer for the good and decent man Bogasian had once been. And he apologized to that man, because he would still exist if Bogasian had never met Karl one afternoon three years ago. Then he walked down the hall and wondered what it'd be like to kill a man for doing exactly what you'd created him to do.

CHAPTER 4

THE WAR room was stocked with human resources. Some people picked at their hands. Others chugged coffee. As Karl walked in, they all swiveled in their chairs and pointed blank faces at him.

The support people lined the walls while the two analysts, James and Henry, sat front and center. They were both around thirty, dressed in business casual, both made plain by careers where success was achieved not through brilliance but by not screwing up.

Karl walked to the front of the room and used the laptop on the podium to log in to the system. For all forty-one years of his life, he'd always felt like a small man in a large man's body, and even now he couldn't stand upright. He always stooped, always minimized.

While he waited for the computer to load, his thoughts turned to that pile of bodies and the man who put them there.

You could kill any person anywhere in the world with someone like that. You could take control of a nuclear submarine or a battleship, maybe even a third world country.

And if you figured out how to make more of him, you could be a nation of one—someone with the power of a government and the anonymity of an individual.

On the seventy-inch wall screen, he brought up a picture of Benjamin Kotesh, his ex-associate.

"Give me the financials," he said to no one in particular.

James and Henry powered to life.

"Two known accounts for Ben Kotesh," Henry said. "One at Deutsche Bank in Paris, another at Banc Commercial in Berlin."

"You can tell that already?" Karl said.

"The file on him is pretty decent."

"Find out the balances on those two accounts."

Karl heard the door open. Tom, his ride from the airport, walked in and hovered with his back to the wall.

Karl motioned him over to a corner while everyone worked.

"Did Marty send you earlier today?" he asked.

Tom's expression didn't change. Not that Karl expected it to.

"You lied to me."

"In as limited a way as possible, sir. I wanted to make my case for joining your team, but..."

"But what?"

"You didn't seem to want to talk."

"How'd you find out I was arriving?"

Tom looked around to make sure no one was watching them. "This room was supposed to be ready at 11:00 PM, which meant you were landing around 10:00. When I walked by Director Litvak's office to request to join this operation, his assistant wasn't there but had left the Delta home page up on his computer monitor. Your name was with security. And around 10:00 PM, at the Delta terminal, one flight landed from the United States. Thirty men came out, and the only one who didn't have a suit on or anyone with him answered to 'Lyons.'"

Karl noticed that he didn't smile as he spoke. This would have been a very stupid time to smile.

"I want on this, sir."

"I thought people lied to get less work, not more."

Tom glanced at the others again. "Give me forty-eight hours to add value. If I don't, you won't even have to say anything. I'll fire myself."

Henry interrupted them.

"Sir? There's no money left in Deutsche Bank and nothing in Commercial."

Karl thought a moment. The room got quieter.

"Highest balance in the last year?" he asked.

"$550,000 in Deutsche Bank and $550,000 in Commercial. $1.1 million total. Commercial was closed out a couple of days ago. Deutsche Bank two weeks ago."

"Where did it come from?"

Karl looked over, surprised it was Tom who asked this. It always impressed him to see a shy person forced out of his shyness by ambition. It was painful and wonderful—all at the same time.

"Same source," Henry said. "Gallen Bancshares. Swiss bank."

There were sighs. They were premature.

Swiss bank secrecy was a lie—always had been. If there was evidence of a crime, the Swiss would play ball. Kotesh's money would have been "laddered" through at least three tax havens, including one that wasn't even a tax haven, just wasn't on good terms with the US, like Guatemala. It was a lawyer tactic: if you can't hide your guilt, at least make it too mind-numbingly awful to prove.

"When was the $1.1 million transferred to Deutsche and Commercial from the Gallen?" Karl asked.

"April 4."

"Do we have access to Gallen's accounts?"

"Yes."

"Okay. Check for any transfer of approximately $1.2 million *to* a Gallen account on April 3, any Gallen account."

There were skeptical looks.

"Any Gallen account, sir?" Henry asked.

"Yeah."

"May I ask why—"

"The money would have gone into a main account and then been transferred to the account that sent the money wire to

Deutsche Bank and Commercial. That way, the main account number stays a secret, even from Deutsche Bank and Commercial."

"But, sir," James said, "the total amount was $1.1 million, right on the nose. If we can't match the amount, we have nothing."

"The money was just passing through. And I bet about 10 percent went to private client fees. Someone at these banks knows what's going on. They take their pound of flesh."

Eyes tilted back down to the screens. James and Henry called out account numbers for people to search.

The bank records they were accessing came from "cooperating" financial institutions. There were two types. The first type employed an asset who gave the CIA account access usually on a voluntary basis but sometimes simply by being a sucker for phishing emails or other types of "social engineering." The second type was less of an actual friend and more like the sweet, trusting girl on Lifetime who just wants to fall in love but winds up with the panty-sniffing sociopath masquerading as a pediatric cancer specialist. They thought they were in a relationship with RKO Hamilton, a respected cross-border accounting firm. They were actually involved with a CIA front company.

The relationship was abusive. The US government saw to that.

Karl turned to Tom and lowered his voice. "Fine. You have forty-eight hours, but you go under the needle tonight."

"A polygraph?"

"All these other people have just taken one." He stared at Tom until he nodded.

James's head popped up. "There's a transfer that matches the date and the approximate amount. Very approximate. Name on the account: Alan Sarmad."

Karl froze.

Sarmad was another name from Prometheus he thought he'd never hear again. Sarmad was a partner in a private shipping company that made the bulk of its money transporting black-market product for organized crime in Europe and Russia. Sarmad had contacts across the Mediterranean, and he could move absolutely anything without questions—from Ukrainian girls who'd answered an ad for modeling work abroad to the human embryos and fetuses that Prometheus required by the pound.

Sarmad had died three years ago—according to Marty.

He'd worked with Kotesh. They knew each other but not that well. So why would Sarmad transfer more than a million dollars to Kotesh now, three years after these two had lost any reason to stay in touch?

"Get an address," Karl said.

Henry looked surprised. "We already have a file on him."

People exchanged glances. This was a coincidence, and they had been trained not to like those.

"Then maybe we got our guy," Karl said, trying to play it down. "What project is he under?"

James looked at his screen. "Project name is…blank. And we have no address for him."

This was odd.

The entire reason they'd used Sarmad and Kotesh on Prometheus was because nobody would believe the US government would ever have anything to do with men like them. As a further precaution, Marty made sure Kotesh and Sarmad had never been entered into any database. Which meant even the CIA couldn't connect them to the CIA. And yet someone here had recently created a file on them.

Karl scanned every face in the room. "Find Alan Sarmad. Now. I can guarantee Interpol is connecting this guy as we speak."

CHAPTER 5

TOM PUSHED through the door to the basement lab. He couldn't believe he'd pulled it off and gotten on Karl's team. He felt like he'd just run several miles—sprinted for his life over those miles. It was sticky where his sweat had dried, and his body was coasting on adrenaline. But he understood: this was the only chance he'd ever get to find out what the CIA knew about Kotesh.

Still, in solving one problem, he'd created another. Karl was suspicious, and he'd be checking Tom's personnel file soon, if he wasn't already. When he did that, he'd find that Agent Tom Blake was twenty-five years old, proficient in Russian, and had graduated from Georgetown magna cum laude. There was just one problem.

Tom was not Tom Blake.

He was Tom Reese. And Tom Reese was nobody really. He'd stolen Agent Blake's identity two months ago, shortly after Agent Blake left the country. Now he was taking his best chance to investigate his brother's death before the CIA discovered Blake was in two places at the same time. But Karl's suspicion—and now the polygraph—meant his time as a CIA agent was accelerating toward its expiration date. And so now it was a question of two things: when the hit would come and whether he'd flinch before it did.

His body said, *Run*. His mind said, *You have nothing to run to*. His body said, *It's not too late*. His mind said, *You knew what would happen the day you walked in the door*.

The only person in the lab was the tech, who hadn't heard him come in and continued typing on his computer. Typically a European embassy had zero need for a specialist with a biometrics background. But France was importing a large, increasingly pissed-off Muslim population to replenish its rapidly aging workforce, and the CIA was looking to exchange DNA evidence with French intelligence—of which there were about thirty different agencies to deal with.

The tech was still typing when Tom stopped behind him and slid a two-inch-thick file of names and addresses onto his desk.

The tech glanced at it and sighed. "Not tonight."

"Not tonight," Tom said. "Now."

The tech muttered something. Then as Tom turned for the door, he said, "More reports arrived today."

Tom spun back. "Any matches?"

"None yet."

"Let me know when there are."

"You're full of it tonight."

"Maybe I feel lucky."

The tech chuckled. "Napoleon used to ask his generals if they were lucky or not. So what about you? Are you a lucky person?"

"I used to think so."

Tom sat in his office, staring at the white walls, gently rocking in his chair. Several weeks ago he'd brought the flannel shirt Eric had died in to the tech. When the tech saw all the blood, he asked who the shirt belonged to. Tom had said that man wasn't important. It was the others he wanted.

Together they found the DNA of four other men on the shirt. Tom believed these were the men who killed his brother—or were involved enough to leave their DNA on the shirt he died in. The location and type of DNA told him something about each man. One had left sweat around the collar where he'd gripped and re-gripped it. Another left a two-inch patch of spit on the chest. The more Tom learned, the more he wanted to know.

Finding these men was something they had no authority to be doing. Not that the tech knew that. He was carrying around a secret he didn't know was a secret. Tom had decided to say nothing and assume he wouldn't talk to anyone rather than ask for discretion and risk suspicion. As far as Tom could tell, the tech's social life took place outside the office—online. So that was where Tom placed his bet: on modern social isolation. But all it would take was one wrong comment. And for the past two months, he thought about it every morning, first when he woke up with his heart slamming in his chest and then an hour later when he walked into the embassy and felt every eye see him for his crime.

To find out the identities of these four men, he and the tech had started checking the DNA they'd left on the shirt against DNA samples from Interpol and various police departments across Europe. It was a system Tom had lifted from the British police. Hardly anyone knew it, but the British had revolutionized the science of criminal investigation. In the UK, almost everyone who was arrested had to provide a DNA sample, and within a few years the British had amassed the largest DNA database in the world.

That database and others like it were so large that Tom and the tech had to confine their DNA requests to educated people with dual citizenship, which Tom believed his brother's killers to be. He was sure Eric's death had something to do with the research job he'd taken in Paris. It was slow going at first—people needed assurances—but it was amazing, and disturbing, how helpful people became when you were calling from a US embassy.

Tom typed in Sarmad's name and brought up his profile.

Name: Alan Cagan Sarmad
Aliases: --
Place of birth: Munich, Germany (not verified)

University: Paris-Sorbonne; Russian University for the Friendship of Peoples

Current residence: --
Known addresses: --
Past residence(s): Nice, France; Genoa, Italy; St. Petersburg, Russia

Case officer: [redacted]
Dates Active: [redacted]
Project(s): [redacted]

Tom clicked on the past residences. A message popped up: *Access restricted.* Then when he tried to click on the case officer, another one appeared: *System administrator notified.*

Sarmad's contacts—at least some of them—were listed, so he printed them out.

His phone rang.

"Am I speaking to Agent Blake?"

"...Yes..."

"This is Eugene Carlson. I'm ready for you in Conference Room B on the second floor."

"Excuse me?"

Hesitation. "I was told you'd be expecting my call."

The lie detector. Two seconds passed, and Tom was aware he was supposed to be saying something.

"I'm going to need to reschedule," he said. "I'm on something time-sensitive."

More hesitation on the other end. "Agent Lyons was pretty specific about the timing here—with both of us, from what I understand."

"How long will this take?"

"Well, that really depends on you."

"I'll be right down." Tom hung up.

He would never be able to beat a lie detector. They would ask—extensively—about his interest in the case, and he could never lie well about that. The hopelessness he felt as he stood up was almost out-of-body. At the stairs, he thought once again about running out of the building. His forehead was moist, and he'd pitted out his shirt. He even looked guilty.

When he walked into Conference Room B, there was an exceptionally thin middle-aged man carefully eating an apple, and Tom noticed the wrappers from his dinner were folded symmetrically in a takeout container. The apple, Tom realized in mild horror, was what this man had saved for the treat at the end of his meal. For him, this actually passed for dessert. He was the absolute last person Tom wanted giving him a polygraph. He looked like the most thorough, pleasure-deferring human being Tom had ever seen in his life.

"Please sit down," Carlson said.

Tom took the chair closest to the door and noticed every light was on and the air-conditioning was turned off. Even on the level of sound, all privacy had been drained from the room.

Carlson slid a napkin onto the table, placed his half-eaten apple on it, and opened his laptop. They began as soon as he had Tom hooked up to the computer, facing him.

"What's your name?" Carlson asked.

"Thomas Blake."

"Just try to relax. What city are we in?"

"Paris." There was a little drop of sweat right under Tom's hairline. It was stuck there, tingling against the skin, itching it.

"What's your name?"

"Thomas Blake."

"Okay. I need you to *calm down*."

"This really isn't a good time."

Tom turned his head a couple degrees to hide the sweat from Carlson. All he wanted to do was wipe it off, but that would only draw attention to it.

"Please face me," Carlson said.

Tom turned back slightly, complying as little as possible. He could feel his heart beating in his chest. He took quick breaths, not to slow it down but to make it beat faster. From what he knew about polygraphs, the test would involve at least some questions everyone lied about. *(Have you ever used drugs? Have you ever lied to someone in a position of authority?)* His physiological response to those would set a baseline, and if his physiological response to the real questions was higher than the baseline, they'd know he was lying. If he could keep himself amped up enough, it might raise his baseline and mask the lies with it.

But, of course, this was exactly what they'd expect a guilty person to do.

"You have to try to relax."

Carlson waited ten seconds. The room was so quiet that every time Tom shifted in his chair, the sound announced his discomfort throughout the room.

"What city were you born in?" Carlson asked.

"Louisville, Kentucky."

"Have you ever stolen anything?"

"No."

"Have you ever lied to a coworker?"

"No."

"Did you meet Agent Lyons at the airport without authorization?"

"Yes."

The sweat drop ran down his face and disappeared into his collar. Tom waited for the next question, but Carlson didn't say anything. Instead he picked up the phone and muttered something into it.

Tom turned to him. Smiled. "I'm trying to relax."

Carlson just kept glancing into the hallway. Tom turned and saw a man with an earpiece appear at the end of it.

"You're off the charts here," Carlson said. "I cannot test you like this because I cannot get a baseline, you understand that?"

"Yes."

"If I asked you to take your shoes off, would I find a tack in them or something?"

"Excuse me?"

"Are you trying to throw this test?"

"Look, I—"

"Answer the question, Agent Blake."

"Right before you called, I'd just gotten something—"

"If you don't answer my question, this test is over."

"Would you just listen—"

Carlson slapped the laptop closed and stood up and started walking out of the room.

"Hey, just wait a minute, okay?"

Carlson paused in the doorway.

"Right before you called, I'd just gotten a list of men who could be involved in what happened to Benjamin Kotesh. You've heard about all the bodies they found in his apartment? Well, I might have to go check one of these guys out...on my own, and I may have let Agent Lyons think I've had more time in the field than I really do. I'm just kind of freaking out a little, okay?"

He laughed nervously at himself and then looked at Carlson like he was hoping he'd say something nice. Meanwhile he prayed that what someone once told him about lying was true: the most believable lie is the one that makes *you* look bad.

Carlson leaned over and tapped the tabletop with one reedy little finger. "You think you can calm down in another hour or so?"

"I don't think so."

"Okay, then tomorrow we do this first thing." Carlson started to unhook him.

"Sorry. I hope I'm not getting you in trouble or anything."

Carlson waved him off. "It happens. If nobody oversold themselves every now and then, we'd all be stuck in a cubicle somewhere wondering why the phone doesn't ring. You really need to deal with all that stress, though. You were all over the place on the machine. According to both readings, you were lying when you said your name was Thomas Blake."

Carlson stared at him.

Then he laughed.

Tom laughed back.

He waited for Carlson to begin packing his things, then stood up and checked his phone. Almost 1:00 AM. He'd only bought himself eight hours. But as he walked past the man guarding the stairs, it felt like all the time in the world.

When he got back to his office, the red button was flashing on his phone. The voicemail was from the tech. Within minutes, he was back in the lab, list in hand, thinking, *Please have something, please have something.*

The tech said, "We got a partial."

"What does it work out to?"

"The DNA we just received matches the DNA from the shirt you gave me about 99.9 percent. In other words, we've found the first cousin of one of the guys you're looking for."

"What's his name, the cousin?"

"Samuel Nast."

Tom opened up the file he'd dropped on the desk earlier. It contained brief dossiers on the men whose DNA they'd been able to get their hands on. Samuel Nast had been pulled over in Manchester with a car he'd borrowed from a friend, and the police had collected his DNA. Now an analysis of it had made its way to them.

Nast probably had no idea one of his cousins was a murderer, just as he probably had no idea his own DNA could prove his cousin's guilt.

An exact match would have been easier—then they'd have their man, and there'd be no need to investigate any relatives. But the odds of that were low. A partial match—that was the name of the game. A partial match meant they had a relative of one of his brother's murderers, and once they had that, most of the work was done. Within any given family tree, the kind of person Tom was looking for stuck out like piss in your Cheerios.

Tom said, "Pull up Samuel Nast on the system. Let's check out the relatives."

The tech read off the computer screen. "We got one. He's an insurance agent of some kind in Hong Kong."

"Has he traveled to Europe in the past year?"

"Nope."

"Our guy travels."

"Jonathan Nast is one of his cousins," the technician read off the screen.

The address from the phone in Kotesh's apartment listed a JN.

"In the last two months, he traveled to Berlin, London, Madrid, New York, and Tangier." He scrolled down. "Works for Schroder-Sands. It's a huge pharma company."

A pharma company. Eric had worked for a pharma company.

"Known contacts?" Tom asked.

The technician started rattling off names.

"What about Alan Sarmad?"

The tech looked up after a moment. "There he is." He started to say something else.

But Tom was already walking out.

The first man they'd matched was Alan Sarmad, but he had been impossible to find. So Tom had focused on the second match, Benjamin Kotesh. But by the time he'd made it into

Kotesh's apartment, six of Kotesh's men were dead and so was Kotesh for all intents and purposes. So the first man didn't seem to exist, and the second one had turned up half-dead. Now he had only one lead left: Jonathan Nast.

But that wasn't all. Someone else was trying to find these men too.

Someone had followed him to Kotesh's apartment, which meant this someone was probably still following him.

Who?

Who would possibly want these men dead at the exact same time you're finding out who they are?

And what, other than the fact they murdered Eric, connects them?

He realized he was holding his breath and reminded himself to breathe. Once a week, he'd get this feeling of being overwhelmed by what he'd done, and he'd wonder whether he had taken everything he'd been given in life—the advantages he'd been born with, the love he'd once received—and flushed it all down the toilet.

But then he'd think about things Eric loved to do—like go on walks. Eric had a senior citizen's affinity for strolling around the neighborhood, speculating as to the various perversions taking place behind closed doors and chatting with the neighbors about their wayward children as though he had raised three or four himself. Tom wondered what the people who'd killed him loved to do. He would imagine them—faceless, always faceless—with a moment to themselves, finishing a beer, noticing a sunset, taking in one of life's small pleasures.

It was simple really.

He wanted them to no longer be doing those things.

As soon as he left the embassy, Tom got in his car and drove straight to the address for JN, 55 Verdun. He crawled past the dark house, then reversed and parked right across the street. He sat, watching the front windows, wanting to hurl himself through one of them and go hunting for Nast.

He could barely keep his eyes open. His adrenaline had dumped, and suddenly it was work not to fall asleep where he sat. He didn't realize he'd already nodded off until headlights startled him. A taxi. It slowed in front of Nast's house.

No one got out.

There was the silhouette of a woman in the backseat. She was looking at the house, trying to decide something. She dialed a cell phone. The dead-blue light lit up the bottom of her jaw and the delicate muscles around her neck, and turned something sleek and beautiful into something strange and demonic. No one answered her call. She got out of the car and started walking to the front door, then stopped suddenly. She was upset, he could tell somehow. She stood there, all done up in heels and a little dress, swaying slightly without meaning to, and he got the sense she'd just come from a club. She scribbled something on a piece of paper and placed it in the mailbox in the same weak, careful way that people put flowers on a grave.

She dropped herself back into the cab. As she leaned toward the driver, headlights from another car splashed light across her face. She squinted, and then as if sensing she was being watched, her eyes locked for a half-second on Tom. Some women had stares that could shrink a room down to their eyes, and it became almost impossible to look away. He held hers and then realized he hadn't really seen her face.

The back of the car went dark. And in an instant, the cab had pulled away.

As Tom got out of his car, he looked around. The wind was blowing, and the rushes of air made the leaves hiss. A dog barked. Far away, a car alarm went off. There was no one on the street, and no more cars came. He bent down to see if there was a figure sitting in one of the parked cars lining the street. Then he went straight to the mailbox. Her note sat on top of yesterday's mail. He took it back to the car and unfolded it:

> *Your phone's been off. Now it says your number is out of service. I'm kind of freaking out. Can you please let us know you're okay?*
>
> *Love,*
> *S*

He went to rip up the note, but suddenly he didn't want to touch it. He hated it, the thought that there were people out there who could care this much for someone like Jonathan Nast. It was one of those thoughts that grew, though you wished it wouldn't, into a truth about the world. And truths like that only came late at night, only when they could make you the most alone.

He sat there for a few minutes, getting himself straight, and then started to get out of his car. He froze. There was movement in the rearview mirror. Another car crawling past the street he was on.

Its lights were off.

He pried the plastic paneling off the frame of the car door and grabbed the Glock he'd hidden against the metal frame inside. He cut across Nast's lawn and peered in the windows. A light was on in the hallway, but otherwise the house was dark. This might be his only chance to find Sarmad. He decided to go in off the cuff, which was desperate and stupid, but then these were the qualities that had gotten him this far.

He stuck a tension wrench he'd made from a windshield wiper blade into the keyhole of the front door and twisted it slightly, creating a ledge in the tumbler. With his pick, he pushed up the pins inside the lock until they cleared the tumbler and, as a result of the ledge, couldn't fall back in. The lock twisted.

He pushed the door open a foot, letting in as little street light as possible, and slid inside. Equal parts fear, excitement, and hatred pumped through his veins. He stood, listening, trying to decipher each of the little noises that fill a house. He made his way to the kitchen, then to the darkened bedrooms. The beds were all empty.

In an office, there was a metal box with a padlock. He returned to the kitchen, emptied out a beer can, and cut a tear-shaped shim out of it with a butcher knife. As he yanked on the padlock, he worked the shim deeper and deeper into the space between the shackle and the lock until the lock sprang. When he opened the box, there was nothing inside.

He turned and looked at the black file cabinets in the office. These had radial locks, which he didn't have time to deal with, so he tipped the cabinets over and hacked out the backs of them with the butcher knife. They were also empty.

Was this guy going somewhere or had he already gone?

He pushed the file cabinets back against the wall. As he left, a cell phone started ringing. He froze. The phone went to voicemail. He kept waiting. Still no one came for it.

The phone was sitting on the kitchen counter. He went over and saw it had a protective case. Probably wasn't a drop phone. Which meant Nast might not have left for good yet.

Outside Tom got in his car and waited. He'd give it until morning. If Nast hadn't appeared by then, he'd bring Karl here and see what the CIA knew. He now had—what?—seven more hours as Agent Blake. Then they'd know the truth, and he'd become one of those people you see on the evening news who are so screwed, you kind of hate them for it.

With his hands still on the wheel, he slumped against his knuckles, exhausted. He thought of his brother, and the thought made his heart a drain that nothing would ever fill.

He was sixteen at the time. His brother was a senior in college.

A few hours after their parents' car collided with an eighteen-wheeler on Interstate 90 outside Billings, Montana, a police officer had come to the house. He told them what happened and stood there waiting for them to cry. But there was no way either one of them was ever going to do that in front of him.

"Is he okay?" the officer asked Eric, looking at Tom. "Doesn't he speak?" Tom's eyes were fixed on some trees at the edge of their property. He couldn't bring himself to meet the officer's gaze.

"I don't think he's there yet, Officer."

"You're not his legal guardian. He's going to have to speak to someone."

Eric could tell all his brother wanted was to be alone, just the two of them.

"It's just that..." Eric lowered his voice. "He's special, Officer."

The officer made one of those surprised O's with his mouth, and Eric touched Tom on the head as if to say, *See, the poor thing's so special he doesn't even know we're talking about him.* And so Tom was spared, at least that night, from some stranger's questions and sad smiles and sympathetic looks.

That was Eric. He was the broker between Tom and the rest of the world. He was the one who gave everyone else the energy and the curiosity to know Tom, who was, as their father put it, "this ghost of a little boy." All brothers share a connection because they are versions of each other. And Tom's version needed Eric— though Eric's probably hadn't needed his.

That summer Eric was a rising senior at Johns Hopkins. In August he moved them in with friends living off-campus. He was methodical about creating a life for them that was theirs alone. They would go to dinner, just the two of them, at least four nights a week. Eric got a car and came up with ridiculously time-consuming errands for them to run together all over Baltimore. Somehow he'd pay for trips home on holidays, even though it felt less like home each time.

First, they stopped seeing their aunt when they visited. Then they stopped seeing their parents' friends. Everyone just ran out of things to say. They still hung out with their old friends, but without the adults, there was no connection to the past. And since he and Eric weren't moving back, there was no connection to the future either. So they just floated from party to party, basement to basement, moving like a hole in time.

At the end of the night, when everyone else went home, they'd go back to their motel. They'd both lie there, arms folded behind their heads, and talk about things they couldn't tell anyone else. Or they'd watch TV and crack themselves up making comments about doomed attempts by drivers to escape the police ("The alley has fooled no one! *We're watching you on Skycam!*") or about the dialogue in '80s horror movies:

Girl: *Stop it, Charlie.*
Charlie: *Jeez, babe, I only want to show how much I love you.*

Other than blood, Tom didn't know what the difference was between a brother and a friend. He didn't know why the word "brother" felt so fragile in his throat. But he knew, from the way Eric would always find an excuse to pat him on the back as they got ready for bed, that these nights meant everything to him too. And that not having these nights, not having this place to go together, would mean not having anything.

It was a pretty good life for an orphan. For anyone.

Then Eric left for Europe.

CHAPTER 6

KARL WAS asleep, or at least he was supposed to be. Marty had given him the key card to a room at the Hotel Lotti, and he'd come to lie down. He rolled onto his side, looked at the comforter, and thought about all those news reports revealing that hotel rooms were the fire hydrants of the human world: not one stick of furniture in most of them had been spared the mark of the beast in the form of some man's semen. In some rooms, under UV light, it looked like a goddamn crime scene.

One week ago to the day, his sister had tracked him down. He only answered the call because it was from a South Dakota area code. As soon as Tabby heard his voice, she started crying and said, *Dad's dead.*

He asked when.

Three weeks ago. I called and called. I needed you.

Tabby was his kid sister. It was easy to imagine her at the funeral home, already overwhelmed into submission, having to pick out the right casket while quietly calculating whether her credit card company would decline the transaction. Like Tabby, his father was someone he'd always been uniquely connected to. Unlike Tabby, his father was connected to him because everyone else was a little scared of the old man.

Their family was a squad of undomesticated Irish homesteaders with a few grubby fingers on the white picket fence and, should one of those digits slip, a short fall back down into the great white trash. Every civilized thing his aunts, uncles, and cousins did, they did with irony. *Hey, honey, looka me, I'm usin' a friggin' napkin.* They were like dogs that had learned to walk and talk but still carried around a touchy pride about their origins as dogs.

Two hours into Karl's sixteenth birthday party, his father had come into the backyard streaking like a comet past the guests and the mismatched lawn furniture and then stood there smirking, barely contained, all potential energy about to go kinetic. He handed his son the keys to a fifteen-year-old Honda, and then—the big reveal—a six-pack and crash helmet. And he roared something. Three words.

Let her rip.

Everyone burst out laughing. But through the laughter and the screwed-up faces, Karl and his dad stared at each other, and they weren't laughing. Because they both understood what his father really meant: *Take it while the taking's good because you're like me and maybe you'll crash, and maybe you'll burn, and maybe you'll wind up selling tires for a guy you used to know in high school too.*

And Karl had done pretty much just that. Shortly after setting fire to a $10 million lab outside Paris, he'd been arrested crossing the Canadian border with a man taped to the interior of his trunk. The guy dealt in cubes of uranium deuteride, and Karl had it on good authority—if the dregs of humanity the CIA called sources could be called that—that the cubes were destined for Europe, then Hong Kong, and ultimately for Iran. Which made sense. Smugglers liked to work their way down the border-security food chain.

And Karl hadn't phoned it in, because the ship with the cubes had been about to leave port, and he found out the guy had a girl with him, one he didn't treat like a daughter.

But that wasn't what kept Karl up at night. That wasn't a pimple on the ass of what kept him up at night.

*   *   *

Phase one of Prometheus started with mice.

Marty had read an obscure paper in the *Journal of Regenerative Medicine* about a stem cell experiment that had created "super-rodents," and the potential applications of this technology were so obvious that Marty was worried another nation might get there first. Physically augmenting an operator was the answer to the problems that assassinations inevitably caused. It wasn't just Executive Order 11905, which outlawed "political assassinations," or the UN Charter, which made them illegal anyway. It was the fact that it was extremely difficult to kill someone in a way where you'd never get fingered for it.

Actually it went beyond that. Since Korea, warfare had changed. It wasn't enough to win wars. You had to win cleanly. Targeted killing—that was the future of warfare in an age when the whole world was watching, and some people were beginning to realize America's military technology had gone in the wrong direction. Everything was casualty-happy, designed for the battlefield, not the streets. No civilization since the dawn of man had ever maintained its dominance in the face of a major change in military tactics. No one had been able to let go of what had served them so well. The Assyrian chariot got trampled by the Scythian warhorse. The Greek phalanx fell to the Roman legion.

Maybe, Marty said, they could change all that.

Ian Mesrop Bogasian was born in nowhere, Ohio, to Armenian carpet importers. He was the embodiment of a fading American ideal: the kid without perfect grades or some freakish athletic talent who inches his way up in the world the unglamorous way—with his eyes to the sky and his nose to the grindstone.

Bogasian joined the army on the G.I. Bill, becoming the first person in his family to go to college. After graduation, he re-upped for military service, this time to become a Green Beret. Two years later, when Karl made his approach, he was a rising star and a strong candidate for Delta Force.

For a certain type of young person, there was nothing in this world as disappointing as the realization that adult life wasn't filled with feats of strength or tests of character but with procedure and paperwork and the kind of compromise that grinds big ideas to dust. So when someone like Karl showed up, representing an elite within an elite, and asked guys like Bogasian whether they really wanted to be all that they could be, they tended to say: *Fuck. Yes.*

They met outside a roadside diner, facing the hundred-year-old tombstones at a Presbyterian church.

"Know why you're here?" Karl said.

"No. Colonel McVries said to come meet a guy."

"He tell you anything else?"

"He said you were a liar and an alcoholic. He also said that he wished that you were a member of a protected group because he'd like to commit a hate crime against you."

Karl didn't smile. "That's very funny. Tell him he's buying tonight. I work for the CIA."

Bogasian nodded. Guys on the teams were known for their titanic egos. Bogasian seemed different. He wasn't eager to be flattered by all this.

"I want you to apply for a new initiative that's about to go live," Karl said. "It's an experimental program to enhance the human body."

"If you don't mind me saying, what the hell does that mean?"

"We're going to sever the nerves in your back, then the nerves in your arms and legs. Then we'll go to work on your musculature. We're going to hurt you. Very badly. Then we're going to heal you. That process will turn you into something very unique."

"And after that?"

"Well, this is where I'm supposed to tell you we're looking for a new type of operator. But that term doesn't begin to describe this role, what it means, what it will cost you." Karl leaned forward almost imperceptibly. "You want to know what we're looking for? We're looking for a criminal."

Bogasian didn't say anything.

Karl leaned back and stared at the dilapidated gravestones. "We want someone who's willing to break every major law of every country he steps foot in."

"That what you do?"

"Yes. And let me tell you what that means. People will hate you if they find out what you've done, even the people you're helping. Laws exist to legitimize violence against you, and conventional morality will say that you're disgusting, that you've lost any claim to being a good person. You'll be alone. In every way."

Karl handed him a card.

"Call that number if you're interested. You have three days."

It was customary for military personnel to transfer to civilian status before working for the CIA, thus severing the connection between them and any US government body. But they weren't hiring someone for the CIA. In fact Bogasian's transfer wouldn't be a transfer at all. It was an honorary discharge.

Two months later.

A warehouse outside Paris.

Someone read the risk factors to Bogasian, and he listened to them like they were something out of a cell phone contract and not the verbatim autopsy results of the dead mouse twenty feet from him. Within a few weeks they started "traumatizing" his muscle tissue and various parts of his nervous system. They did this for a very specific reason. Stem cells were special. They could turn into any type of cell in the human body, even cells that weren't human. They could become part of a fingernail or a lung or a muscle. The scientists used the damage to attract the stem cells and in effect tell them what to turn into. But they weren't using the body's repair mechanism to heal. They were using it to enhance.

Some of the stem cells they put into Bogasian came from his own body. Some they took out and used to grow more stem cells, which was horrifying for Karl to think about. The cells had the power not only to perpetuate life but to create it. Eric Reese, a young scientist on the project, once asked him, *What do you call the cell that can make anything?* He smiled. *The God cell.*

But what they were doing was experimental. A lot of cells would be wasted, which meant they needed volume—but of a certain type. Benjamin Kotesh got them the bodies. He stole them from the morgues at French hospitals. Alan Sarmad arranged their delivery. And so Bogasian had the cells from at least ten human embryos—ten would-be people—pumped into him. His brain and spinal cord were juiced. His fast-twitch muscle mass was increased 100 percent. The size of his adrenal glands was doubled.

He got everything the chimpanzees got before one of them tore two people apart outside Paris.

"Hello?"

Karl was vaguely aware he'd answered the phone. He prayed the call would offer something to occupy his mind. His thoughts were racing again, and he was sweating, and all he wanted was for them to stop.

"Karl, it's Tom. I've got something for you."

A half hour later, as day was about to break, Karl's taxi dropped him off several blocks from a house in Saint-Cloud. It was one of the wealthiest areas around Paris. Some houses even had their own tiny yards. People would have worked for years to afford those yards.

Karl found Tom down the street in a Ford coupe. These little Fords were everywhere, which was a strange sight for Paris, and

Karl kept looking at them, half expecting to see a Virginia license plate or a red-blooded-American bumper sticker (MY KID KICKED YOUR HONOR STUDENT'S ASS).

"So what exactly do we have here?" Karl asked as he plopped into the passenger seat.

"I found this guy Jonathan Nast on Alan Sarmad's contact list and decided to check it out."

It took Karl every ounce of his being not to react. Nast. It was another familiar name from Prometheus. Dr. Alexander Nast had been the lead doctor on Prometheus. Were he and this Jonathan Nast related or was it one of those coincidences he'd been trained not to like?

"When did you find this?" he asked.

"An hour ago."

"You haven't attempted to make contact?"

"I just got here." He pointed at Nast's mailbox. "Yesterday's mail is still in there, by the way."

Karl grinned. "So either no one is home or we're going to walk in on someone who may have just massacred seven men and is disciplined enough to never go outside."

"I can live with that."

"Screw it," Karl said. "Me too."

At six in the morning, the neighborhood looked empty, but Tom and Karl made their way to the backyard like they owned it in case someone was watching. They pulled on latex gloves. Then Karl tried the back door. As soon as his fingers touched the knob, the whole mechanism fell out of the doorframe. He froze, listening for two things: the sound it would make on the pavement and the response it would provoke inside the house.

But somehow Tom was already down on a knee in front of him. He caught the doorknob with one hand. When the other pieces of the lock hit the concrete and came up ringing, he silenced them with the other.

They waited. But it remained quiet in the house.

Karl realized he was staring at Tom and turned his eyes back to the door. He tried not to think about how quickly—almost instantly—Tom had reacted when the doorknob fell out. It reminded him of something. Someone.

He pulled out two Sig pistols, both very small and very illegal. He handed one to Tom as they slipped through the door and swept the western side of the house.

The place was decorated for a life lived after dark: a lot of black wood, Japanese screens, and pop art. There was a photograph of an eyeball and another of an emaciated teenage girl squatting over a neatly folded American flag. When the sun went down, the house probably looked nice the way a nightclub can look nice. But in the morning light, it was a place you woke up in and knew that somewhere out there, if she knew what you'd been up to, your mother's heart was breaking. And Karl had a feeling the owner was the kind of person he would see on the street and vaguely want to hurt.

In the living room, there were plastic takeout containers full of half-eaten food, and in the kitchen there were dirty dishes piled in the sink. It seemed like Jonathan Nast had been holing up in here for the last week or two. An empty SKYY vodka bottle sat on the carpet as though it'd been dropped there. Karl and Tom moved toward the hallway to the bedrooms.

A clock radio went off.

They spread to opposite sides of the hall and waited for someone to turn it off. When no one did, they followed the sound to the master bedroom. The pop song on the radio tinkled through the door. A young man sang that he was young and beautiful and he was going to shine so bright he would set the whole world on fire.

The door was ajar. Karl eased it open and stood back. The door yawned on a master-bedroom suite with three door-size mirrors, two seventy-inch flat-screens, and an unmade bed with silk sheets.

Karl left the music on and moved around the bed to open the curtains.

Then he saw the body.

The man was on the floor hidden behind the bed. There was blood around his mouth, and Karl didn't have to touch it to know it was still slick.

He knelt down. The man's collar was messed up, and there was the beginning of a hand-size bruise on the side of his head. He must have died only a few hours ago. As soon as Karl got closer, he smelled something acidic and noticed the urine stains that had spread out like the wings of a butterfly down the insides of the man's khakis.

The voice on the radio sang about how even though youth fades, beauty never dies.

Tom showed no reaction as he knelt over the man and stared into his face. He did this longer than he needed to before he felt the pockets and fished out a wallet. The ID inside confirmed it was Jonathan Nast. Tom slid the wallet back.

Then for some reason he grabbed each of Nast's hands and turned them over, examining them. When he was done, he continued staring at the body. Karl watched him.

"We have work to do," he said finally.

The computer in the home office down the hall was still on. Tom went over and nudged the mouse. A password prompt appeared.

"I think I can get in here," Tom said.

"Five minutes. Then we're gone."

Tom tried a bunch of common passwords: *123456, password,* Nast's last name. Nothing worked.

Karl looked around the office. "How old is this guy?"

"Late thirties," Tom said.

Karl reached into the desk drawer, rummaged around, and

came out with a Post-it note with a number on it. Tom typed it in, and Microsoft Windows slowly began to load.

Tom gave him a look.

Karl shrugged. "It's a generation thing."

Tom went to My Documents. There were only two folders. Tom opened all the files and clicked through them. Nothing jumped out. Next he went to My Pictures. He stopped on a file labeled "Materials."

"Click on that," Karl said.

The screen froze as a huge file loaded.

Tom cocked his head. "You hear that?"

It took Karl a few seconds. Then he heard a distant siren.

Tom grabbed the mouse, steadied his hand as much as he could manage, and started closing all the files as fast as possible.

"Just take the hard drive," Karl said.

Tom reached down to unlock it. He stopped. "They'll know someone showed up after the fact and took it."

"What?"

"The computer's still connected to the internet. The service provider will know when it stopped sending a signal, and they'll know that happened hours after the time of death."

"So what?"

"When the police figure out it was someone else besides the killer who took it, their interest in the case is going to skyrocket."

"Shit."

Karl needed a minute to think. The siren got closer.

"I don't suppose there's any way to stop that from happening."

"No, it's already happened."

"The hell with it. Take it anyway."

Tom disconnected the computer and picked it up. Then they left the house and did their best to stroll casually across the lawn. The sirens were close now. They were opening the doors of the Ford when two police cars peeled around the corner.

They drove right past the Ford and continued past Nast's house, lights flashing.

Karl started laughing. "What're the odds? I mean what the hell kind of criminal commits a crime at six o'clock in the morning? At that point you may as well just get a job." He glanced at Tom and laughed. "You should see the look on your face."

He hit Tom on the arm and took a big healthy breath.

"God, I haven't had this much fun since we killed bin Laden and found porn on the fucker's computer."

CHAPTER 7

ON THE drive back to the embassy, Karl was secretly pleased when Tom in his shy, indirect way inquired as to the nature and intensity of Osama bin Laden's pornography. Out of respect for the dead, Karl told him he didn't really want to get into it, but suffice to say in one of the brief clips he'd seen, there was a blonde wearing chaps and a World War II gas mask.

Tom gave him the horrified, vindicated look everyone got when they heard this. It was part *Really?* and part *I always fucking knew it.*

Karl grinned. "Wait, you know about the sex tape, don't you?"

"I'm sorry?"

"You heard me."

"Uh, no, I don't believe—"

"The agency considered staging an Osama bin Laden gay sex tape and one for Saddam too."

Tom just stared at him.

"Think about it: what better way to discredit a man in the Muslim world. Osama, they decided, was a top. You know, proud guy like that. *It fits.* But Saddam has those roomy hips." Karl leaned in and lowered his voice. "So they were going to make him a power bottom."

Tom looked horrified—and yet fascinated. "So what stopped them?"

"Well, the gay agents thought it was brilliant. But the straight ones thought it was just too bigoted."

They both started laughing, Karl loudly and Tom almost silently. Then they drove a few blocks without a word.

"Hey," Karl said. "I'm making you second chair."

Tom looked like he was trying not to seem as pleased as he actually was about this.

"What?" Karl said.

"May I ask why?"

"Why?" Karl shrugged. "Because I find people assigned to you by your boss don't work for you, they work for your boss. And in this case those two people remind me of Ken dolls."

"You mean Henry and James?"

"They look like they have that odd, little plastic mound between their legs, is what I'm saying."

Tom made a right on Victor Hugo. Outside, the sky was overcast, and people moved like they didn't want to be on the street. A homeless man sat under a poster of a woman about to dab herself with L'Oréal anti-aging skin cream. He stared up at the sky and either started laughing or crying.

"You got any family back home?" Karl asked.

Tom nodded, but his eyes turned inward. "You?"

"I had a wife once."

"What happened?"

The question surprised Karl. Most people didn't ask.

"She died," Karl said. "Cancer."

"What was it like?" Tom said. "Being married."

"It was good."

At first Karl thought he was going to leave it at that. He stared at his palms, noticed the lines on them for the first time in years.

"What? You really want to know?" he said.

Tom nodded.

"You ever see the movie *Network*?"

Tom nodded again.

"Okay, there's this scene where William Holden's wife is yelling at him for cheating on her—you know, fist raised." Karl raised his fist and shook it like he was wielding a rolling pin. "And the last thing she says is 'And if you can't work up a winter passion for me, the least I require is respect and allegiance. I'm your *wife,* damn it.' And the way she says 'wife'...you get the idea this lady's not describing their relationship, she's standing up for her motherfucking *rights.* That was how my wife said it. The way you tell other people they're on your property." Karl laughed once, shook his head. "It was the best four years of my life."

Karl looked at Tom, and Tom nodded, like he couldn't quite understand but he was eager to. They drove in silence for a while.

"My brother was obsessed with *Network,*" Tom said.

"So he was a real pervert, is what you're saying?"

Tom turned and just looked at him.

"Only someone with a twisted mind, a real sicko, could love that movie," Karl said. "Let me ask you something: does he smoke menthols and drink Tab?"

"In his mind, it's only a matter of time before we all wind up on the sex offender registry."

Karl burst out laughing. "This brother of yours is a goddamn prophet. What is he, a defense attorney or a gynecologist or something?"

"He's in medicine."

Karl stopped smiling. "What do you mean he *was* obsessed with *Network*?"

Tom took a second too long to answer. "He lives in Phoenix with his wife and kid. Doesn't have much time for movies anymore is all."

Something about how Tom phrased his response seemed off to Karl, but he couldn't put his finger on it.

The embassy came into view. As soon as they parked, Tom

looked over at him. "Karl, thank you. For the promotion. And for telling me about, you know, your wife and everything."

Karl gave him a nod and got out of the car. He realized he was smiling.

Back in the war room, the first thing Karl did was look up Alexander Nast, the doctor from Prometheus. He wanted to see if Dr. Nast had a son named Jonathan. He prayed not. From what he'd been told, Nast had known nothing about the chimps outside Paris. In fact he thought he was working to save the life of Karl's volunteer, a man named Ian Bogasian. They'd told him Bogasian was terminally ill with some neuromuscular disease Karl couldn't even pronounce the name of. Nast was the perfect asset. When he heard about Bogasian's diagnosis, he was the one rushing them.

The system said there was no file for a Dr. Alexander Nast. Either it had never been made in the first place or someone had deleted it.

As Tom went through Jonathan Nast's hard drive, Karl got up and went over to the window. The streets outside were empty. Gray clouds expanded in the sky. It was late morning, and already the city existed only in shadow. Even the daylight was too dark.

"Karl."

It took a moment for the sound of his own name to pull him out of his thoughts. "Yeah?"

"You should see this."

On the screen, there was a picture of a black hood, the kind you put over a prisoner's face. It was pointed at the top like a Ku Klux Klan mask.

"I found this in his download history. Even if you delete your browser history, sometimes things you look at online get saved in Windows Photo Gallery."

"So he didn't take the picture?"

"No, but there's more." Tom kept scrolling. "I think he was looking at buying them." The variety was horrifying. Each hood had its own personality somehow, the same way jack-o'-lanterns do.

Tom kept going through the pictures Nast hadn't known to delete. There were images from banner ads and photos of other products he'd considered buying. Tom stopped on a picture of two brass rods. He sat there, looking at them.

"What is that?" Karl said.

"If I'm not mistaken, those are brass contact points." Tom looked over. "I think he was building some kind of cattle prod."

Karl barged into Marty's office, told his assistant there was no need to announce him, he'd just let himself in, and shut the door behind him. Marty was sitting at the table by the window, looking outside and sipping what smelled like a particularly healthful green tea.

Karl walked over and put a printout of the hoods and the brass contact points on the table. "We just pulled these off the computer of a guy named Jonathan Nast."

Marty leafed through the photos. "Jesus Christ." He stopped on the brass contact points. "What are those?"

"We think they're the contact points for a stun gun of some kind."

Blood drained from Marty's face. He started to say something, then looked out the window suddenly. "Any idea what for?" he asked finally.

"No."

"Do you have him? Jonathan Nast?"

"He's dead."

Marty looked up.

"Don't look at me. I didn't do it," Karl said. "What do you know about Jonathan Nast?"

"What do you mean?"

"Whenever you ask something, and someone says 'What do you mean?' that tells you they know exactly what you mean."

Marty stared at him for a moment. "Really you're asking two questions, and the answer is yes—to both of them. Yes, Jonathan Nast is Dr. Alexander Nast's son, and yes, I know who Jonathan Nast is. In fact you might even say I know more about him than his own father does."

"And why the hell is that?"

"Jonathan is a bad apple, or at least he was. It's sad really. He fell in with an Albanian network—you know, the half-Muslim kind who hate the white man but who run drugs and teenage prostitutes and honor-kill their wives. I had him hired three years ago through a proxy to do some work for us on Prometheus. Small stuff, but the little weasel turned out to be good at it."

"Why?"

"Because he was Dr. Nast's son, and Dr. Nast knew a lot about us. Know how the Chinese ensure someone's compliance? They give his relatives a job, and the message is clear: *We know how to help you, but we also know where to hurt you.*"

"Do you know how we found Nast's son? We connected him to Alan Sarmad."

Karl waited for a reaction. Three years ago Marty had told him Alan Sarmad was dead, murdered by some associates of his in the shipping business. Marty had lied about Bogasian and now Sarmad, and Karl wanted to know why.

Marty dabbed his mouth and set his teacup on the saucer so carefully it didn't make a sound. "I saw you went with someone else over the people I provided you. How's he working out?"

"He's fine."

Marty rocked gently in his chair and nodded.

"How come you never told me Alan Sarmad is still alive?" Karl asked.

For a moment Marty didn't seem like he was going to respond. "It appears he survived the hunting accident, Karl."

"And you didn't think that warranted an update—"

"And I wrote it off, because that's what you do. If I had to go around Europe killing everyone who knew something about us, then I'd kill the number of people usually required to take office in a small African country. Besides, Sarmad isn't exactly an easy man to get to."

"Sarmad is dangerous. He knows all the wrong people. And you owe me an answer."

"He's a non-issue. If he gets picked up and starts talking, he knows what will happen. Once his silent partners get word of his loose lips, they'll kill his wife and his parents and sell his children to a nice man in Dubai who pays in ounces of gold."

Karl started to say something.

"But"—Marty smiled—"I promise you that if he's involved in what's going on with Bogasian, I will happily turn you loose on him—with a smile in my heart and a song on my lips."

Karl had always respected the way Marty found an almost Christian joy in the rare times when bad things actually happened to bad people. But he didn't smile back.

"I thought I told you, I'm not your hatchet man," he said.

"Then what are you?"

They watched each other.

Finally Karl said, "Listen, there are files here on Alan Sarmad and on Benjamin Kotesh. Someone's put them together, and they're not sharing. I need access to everything."

"Your clearance was just reinstated. Now you want it upped?"

"See, I think what we have here is a cockroach-in-the-kitchen situation. You've already told me two lies. Now I'd like to turn on the light and see what else is crawling in its own filth on the floor."

"You're like one of those fat children from the Stanford

marshmallow test. If you don't eat the marshmallow, you can have another one later. But if you just stuff it down your throat, you only get type 2 diabetes. I can't do it."

"But I believe in you, Marty. I believe you can do anything you put your mind to."

"It shines a spotlight on the very thing we want left in the dark."

Karl gave him a sympathetic look, the evil of which got him to stop rocking. "Maybe this should go to committee."

Marty's thin, birdlike lips pressed together.

Anything that went to committee would eventually get to the director of the CIA and from there to the White House. And at that point the politicians would have it in their orbit. As a matter of sacred personal policy, Marty only made the politicians aware of the issues he already had an answer to. Once there was consensus on the importance of the issue, Marty waited until there was urgency. And once he had that, he provided the answer. Then he got his hand shaken. Then he returned to work that actually had a point.

"Your job is to investigate whoever's running Bogasian," Marty said, "not the CIA." He stared at Karl for a few seconds. "Perhaps we need to find somebody else for this assignment."

Karl hadn't been planning to investigate the CIA, just free-ride off work that had already been done. But hearing Marty put it like this gave him an idea. The CIA could track its agents' phones, even in another country. He could check who'd been by Nast's home in the last twenty-four hours.

"Look," Karl said. "I appreciate what you're doing for me. I was…out of line."

Marty sighed. "No, you weren't. There's something I've been meaning to say. You worked for me for eight years, and I was never much of a mentor to you. You did a lot of things you weren't comfortable with, and I never honored you for that. Instead I kept you in the dark. I hope you can forgive me."

Karl was speechless. They both sat still, looking anywhere but at each other.

"Okay," Marty said finally. "I won't up your clearance, but I'll do you one better. Off the books, right after Bogasian disappeared, I used an asset to try to locate Benjamin Kotesh and Jonathan Nast. We couldn't find them, but maybe there's something there."

"Why didn't you tell me?"

"Because it's evidence I know who they are. I only had hard copy files made. They're with the original Prometheus documents, so it'll take me a couple hours to get you everything." He raised a finger before Karl could say anything. "If you settle down, I'm prepared to share."

"What do you think these people are really up to?"

"There's only one reason someone would steal Bogasian from us." Marty was quiet a moment. "Obviously they plan to kill a lot of people with him."

CHAPTER 8

TOM AND Karl were in the war room together later that morning when Tom's cell phone rang for the third time. It was Carlson again, calling about the lie detector. Tom muted the ringing. A second later, his phone vibrated. New voicemail. The messages had been getting increasingly threatening—until this one. Carlson's voice had been eerily calm: "We're searching the building for you right now."

Tom figured he had maybe another hour before they found him.

He knew now that Nast was already dead by the time he'd first gone into the house. He'd looked at the beds but hadn't thought to check the floor beside them. In fact Nast was probably in the process of dying as he was checking the street. Like before, whoever had followed him there hadn't wavered. He just broke in and took someone's life without hesitation.

Now the files Karl was getting were all Tom had.

Karl stood in front of the computer. He kept waving his right arm around, emphasizing his points with the Snickers bar he held at the end of it.

"We lost the spy game to the Russians because they got us to doubt our own agents," he said. "We spent more energy ferreting out moles than we did gathering intel. Now we've swung in the opposite direction. Our agents can do no wrong. And if they do, nobody wants to hear about it."

At first Tom hadn't known why Karl had summoned him to the war room. He was starting to get an idea.

Karl touched a piece of paper. "Why do you think in an agency this computerized so many people communicate on the material easiest to get rid of?"

Tom nodded. "How many of your communications were hard copy only?"

Karl froze.

"I meant, when you were—"

Karl raised his hand to stop him, then tossed the half-eaten candy bar on the desk. "So you know about me?"

"I just heard you'd been...out of commission."

Karl laughed a little in the direction of the floor. "Yeah..."

"Was it really that bad?"

"I got arrested trying to cross the Canadian border with a guy taped up in my trunk."

Tom was quiet for a moment. Then: "What kind of tape did you use?"

"Excuse me?"

"You use duct tape?"

Karl grinned. "Well, that was my first choice naturally. But the thing was: I ran out. So I found some blue painter's tape."

"That stuff tears so easily."

"Ah, but what I lacked in quality, I made up for in quantity. You should have seen the freaking guy. He looked like a frightened Easter egg."

"Karl, I hope I wasn't out of line earlier—"

"Forget it. And, look, if you ever have a question about anything here, you can—" Karl shrugged. "Well, you know."

When Karl looked at him, Tom's eyes shifted automatically a couple of inches off his.

What would your family think of this? he wondered. *Of what you're about to do to a man who just wants to help you?*

The phone rang.

Karl snatched the receiver. "Lyons."

Tom heard someone talking on the other end.

"No, we'll come by and get them." Karl hung up. "Our files have arrived. They're with Marty's assistant."

Tom nodded, thinking, as Karl sat down and started typing at the computer. He needed to get those files now.

"Agents aren't supposed to turn off their cell phones, as you know," Karl said as he loaded a map of Paris on the big screen in the front of the room. "We have a tracking package for our agents' phones, and talking with Director Litvak gave me an idea." Karl smiled. "I had the package enabled just a few moments ago."

Red dots started populating the map. The dots, representing agents, moved along the screen. One of them stopped near another dot where Nast's home was.

"Well, holy shit." Karl turned to Tom. "I was just checking to see if someone had been snooping on any of these guys behind my back, but this is right around Nast's time of death."

Tom nodded, like he was impressed.

The dot proceeded to move from the street across the lawn. It paused outside the house for a moment.

Karl stared it in disbelief. "He's going into the house..." He clicked on the dot. An image loaded.

When it appeared on the screen, he didn't seem to understand what he was seeing. But there was Tom. His photo and profile, right beside the map that showed Nast's home.

Karl turned and started to lunge for something in his desk. He didn't see Tom's face at first. Just the gun.

Neither spoke. Karl made no attempt to get out of his chair. He just kept staring at Tom, like his mind was stuck on a continuous loop of not believing what he was seeing, then accepting it, then not believing again.

Tom had never pointed a gun at another person before. The grip felt too warm on his palm, and he could feel it slipping a little—*wanting* to slip—and every time Karl glanced at it, Tom wanted to look down and make sure the Sig did not in fact have a safety he'd forgotten to switch off.

Once, he'd seen an interview with a New York police officer who said you can tell a lot about a person by how high he holds his hands when a gun is on him. The kind of person who doesn't want trouble reaches for the sky. Karl's hands hadn't gone up an inch.

"I never liked that you picked me up at the airport," Karl said.

Tom managed not to take his eyes off him as he reached down and ripped an Ethernet cable from the wall.

"Who else are you going to kill?" Karl said.

"I didn't kill anyone."

I just led the person who killed Nast there before I could get my hands on him myself.

Karl just smiled.

Tom went across the room and ripped another Ethernet cable out of the wall.

"Is someone making you do this?" Karl said. "Look, you know me. I might understand."

"I'm sorry I got you involved." Tom dropped a phone jack on the floor—crushed it. "I need your phone."

"I'm giving you a chance here."

"I need your phone."

"I think you know what happens after that."

Tom took a big breath, so there wouldn't be any waver in his voice. "Karl, your phone. Please."

"But I could be in here for hours."

"You're stalling."

"Am not."

Tom sighed and raised the gun, but he had to lower it again

because his hand was shaking. He looked back at Karl, who was staring at his hand. He'd noticed.

"I'm trying to talk to you," Karl said as he made a little show of the inconvenience of digging his phone out of his pocket. He held it out for Tom to come get it.

"Slide it over."

Karl put it down and kicked it. "Why are you doing this?"

"I can't tell you that. You'd only use it to find me."

Karl frowned. "They're going to do a lot more than find you."

Tom pocketed the phone, punched in the exit code on the door, and backed through.

Karl leaned forward. His expression was sad almost. "Wait. Just come back in here and talk to me. Please."

The change in Karl's tone was so startling Tom didn't move.

"You know what I do here, right?"

Tom didn't say anything.

"If you close that door, you'll be completing an act of espionage against the United States of America, and then it's just a matter of time and a little hard work before I watch the lights go out in your eyes."

Tom could only stand there with his feet planted on the carpet. It was fascinating how calmly—almost reassuringly—Karl said this.

"Goodbye, Karl." Tom started to turn around.

"Do you know how the first people hunted animals that were bigger than they were? They chased them for miles and miles and then they ran them down. Imagine for a moment how that'd feel. You're a mastodon the size of a school bus, and no matter how fast you run, there's always someone on the horizon who just won't stop coming. I bet by the time those people stabbed that mastodon to death, in a sense it was already dead. It just didn't want to run anymore."

Tom said nothing.

"Don't make me do that. Don't make me *want* to do that. You're not the kind of person I want to *hunt*, for Christ's sake. So talk to me. Make me understand. And don't be a mastodon, Tom. Choose life."

The only thing Tom was sure of at that moment was that he could not stay in this room for another second. He closed the door behind him and gripped the doorknob. It took all his strength, and the knob bit into his palm, but then the metal began to pop and lengthen. He bent the doorknob down and sealed Karl inside.

Karl was at the door immediately.

First he tried the knob. Then he tried locking and unlocking the bolt. The door wouldn't open.

He went to his desk and felt around until his hand touched the Sig he'd taped to the top of the drawer. He turned and fired into the lock over and over, then hurled himself against the door. He spilled out on the floor of the hallway along with bits of door. Then he bear-crawled through the pieces to get to his feet and ran to the nearest office. There was a guy blowing on his coffee. Once he noticed the gun, he raised his hands.

"Your radio!" Karl said.

The man cocked his head and gave this some thought.

"Now, motherfucker!"

The man reached into his desk and threw it to him. Karl ran out of the office to look for a floor plan as he tuned to the emergency band.

"Station Chief, this is Karl Lyons."

There was a pause.

"Authenticate," the chief said.

"6149-Yankee."

The radio crackled softly as they ran his response to the coded challenge.

"Proceed, sir."

"We got a blow drill." Karl walked to a window and checked to make sure Tom wasn't on the fire escape. "I'm calling it."

Another crackle. "Engagement is level 5. Is that a go?"

"That's a go."

In about ten seconds, the downstairs would turn into a kennel. Marines—the ones who pined away for this sort of thing—would be going in all directions, arming up, shouting instructions. Level 5 was the most "assaultive" end of the Continuum of Force in the close combat manual, and they would be pretty excited about that.

"Do we have a location for the hostile, sir?" the chief said.

"No."

"What was his one?"

"The war room on the second floor."

"How long ago?"

"Three minutes ago."

"What's his two?"

Karl was about to say anywhere outside the walls of the embassy, outside of US jurisdiction. Then he remembered the files. Tom had worked hard to lie his way onto the investigation—so there was something here he needed.

"Martin Litvak's office," Karl said. "And his three will be anywhere outside the building."

"Name, description?"

Karl turned the corner and ripped an emergency exit floor plan off the wall. "Tom Blake."

They ran the name.

Now the station chief hesitated. "Sir, you are aware—"

"Yes, I know who he is. And full engagement protocol is authorized."

"Sir, the Rules of Engagement provide—"

"You have your orders, Station Chief. If you can't catch him, kill him."

*   *   *

Tom did his best to walk normally down the hallway. He passed an acquaintance and nodded hello.

Once he got to Martin Litvak's waiting area, he went up to Marty's assistant.

"I'm Tom Blake. You have files for Agent Lyons and me."

The assistant didn't move.

"The need-to-know only includes Agent Lyons," he said.

Tom looked around the room. "Are they even here yet?"

"Obviously I can't—"

"Look, just let me know when they get here."

"This—"

"This is a waste of time," Tom said, noticing the man flinch each time he cut him off. "I'm assisting Agent Lyons. Are you sure my name isn't on there?"

"I can assure you that once Agent Lyons—"

"Okay, fine. Just call him when they actually arrive."

The man blinked something back. "Look, that isn't the issue, as I explained."

"What have you explained?"

Tom was watching his eyes. The temptation had to be powerful. Then the assistant's eyes ticked over to the corner of the room, where there was a thin metal briefcase.

"If you just *listened*," the assistant said, "you would realize I cannot release them to—"

Tom was already moving around the desk. The assistant didn't even have time to raise his hands in defense. Tom grabbed him, wrapped one arm around his neck in a sleeper hold, and squeezed. If the man's carotid arteries were a garden hose, Tom had just stomped on them.

The assistant went limp, but he'd be back up in thirty seconds. Tom propped him against the wall, so the blood wouldn't pool in his head. He stashed his gun in the briefcase, because in a minute or two the Marines would be involved and he might be tempted to use it. He snapped the lid shut and hit the hallway.

You don't betray your country without good reason, and he was holding his. He hefted the case: weird that something so significant could weigh so little. He turned down the hallway to the emergency exit on the northwest corner of the building. The exit was unguarded, seldom referenced—a security afterthought.

He could see the double doors seventy yards ahead. The hallway was so white and bare it offered no sense of his progress. He didn't seem to be getting any closer to the doors until suddenly he was right up against them.

He pushed on one of the double doors. The handle went in, but the door didn't budge. He tried the other door. It was locked too. He put down the briefcase and pushed with both hands, putting all his weight into it. Still no give. Suddenly he understood. It was too late—he was screwed—but he understood. They were locking down the building.

He turned around and pressed his back against the doors. He could hear his heartbeat thudding in his ears. He surveyed the hallways, each of which would lead to a different fate. He hadn't planned to actually be in a US government building when the US government discovered what he'd been up to. He had to think.

Boyd cycle.

John Boyd was the military strategist who figured out why during the Korean War the US's F-86 achieved an unheard-of 10:1 kill ratio against the faster, more nimble MiG-15 used by the North Koreans. (Answer: unlike the MiG, the F-86 had greater visibility due to its large canopy as well as the ability to multitask.) His broader conclusion, though, was that whichever combatant could repeat the cycle of observing and reacting the fastest would gain a step, then another, and eventually overcome.

So if he wanted to live, he had to react more quickly to each phase of the embassy's response than the embassy could to each phase of his escape.

Well, John, that's beautiful and all, but it's kind of a tall order.

Tom forced himself to imagine the first response. No alarm would sound. The CIA did little with that much ceremony, and despite what the Marines thought, the CIA ran the building. The passport office would shut first. They'd expect him to mix in with the crowd because the security cameras would find him anywhere else. He glanced up at the camera watching him now and saw his reflection in its dead eye.

Plan B: an exit on the north side of the building. It had a relatively light security presence.

He neared the hall to the exit. A man in a wrinkled suit passed him going the other way. They nodded to each other professionally. Tom stepped around the corner—

And wished he could take it back.

For a second, his calm nearly dissolved into the animal urge to bolt. The long hallway led to a gated exit, which was guarded, as he'd known it would be. But the security presence had been doubled. An icy feeling crept up the back of his skull and threatened to become articulate. Through a window on the other side of the gate, he saw a woman with a baby stroller duck her head in the rain and run for cover.

Two guards perked up as he came into view. Their gaze went from his eyes to the case, then back to his eyes.

Run.

The urge came to him so softly he wasn't sure he'd felt it. He started to shake a little. He pretended to wipe something off his cuff to channel the shaking into something that didn't flash: *Alert. I am behaving strangely. Stop me to find out why.*

He took a deep breath, let it out slowly. Then he observed the situation.

—Three guards at the station, twenty feet ahead.

—A fourth guard at the end of the hallway, fifty feet away.

—A fifth guard, a floater, probably on patrol somewhere nearby.

There were only three escape routes: two connecting hallways and a doorway with a stairwell sign above it. The hallway he was in now was not only long but narrow. The Marines could just shoot in his general direction and let the ricochet do the rest.

Tom did his best imitation of a calm man. When he was close, two guards exchanged glances. One sort of smiled. The other sort of frowned. A third glanced at Tom and stopped tapping his pen. Every little thing they did dripped with meaning.

Run.

The word hung on him. It was still just a whisper—he could ignore it.

He didn't slow down. The exit was still too far away, and none of the guards had taken a contrary move. He focused on the paint strokes on the wall, trying to appreciate the uniqueness of each one while he watched the guards out of the corner of his eye.

Movement at the end of the hallway.

Tom looked up and saw the floater. He was looking in Tom's general direction. It was too far to tell what he was looking at, but he wasn't moving.

He knows.

Tom felt sweat in his armpits. His face was reddening—he could feel heat rolling off it. He forced himself to nod hello at the guards as he passed—just as he usually would. One nodded back. The other guard was still eyeballing him. Tom glanced over at their security monitors: Marines were running down a hallway. The guard watching the screen frowned and turned toward him—

A door burst open behind him.

Tom whirled around and saw Karl. The guards turned too.

When Tom turned back, the Marine by the door was turning a key in the wall near the exit. The gate began to close.

Karl was shouting and pointing. But the hallway was too long for anyone to understand him. One of the guards stood up, looked at Karl, and pointed at himself: *Are-you-talking-to-me?*

A voice said, *Run. Running is your only chance.*

Tom ignored it. Running was death. The gate was within spitting distance, and it still had ten feet before it closed. Tom nodded at the guard by the gate. The guard nodded back. Tom lifted the briefcase and tapped it as if to say: *Special delivery.* The guard frowned. Tom gripped the case, ready to swing it.

"Freeze."

A Marine, twenty feet to his right. Tom could practically feel the sights of the rifle on the side of his neck. He didn't look over. Didn't need to.

He braced himself and dove toward the stairwell. The M-16 fired a maiming round, not a "kill" round. The nerves on his back were pressed against his skin, waiting for the maiming—eager for it.

But the next thing he knew his hand was closing around the metal doorknob. He swung the door open, then slammed it behind him.

The hallway shook with a cracking sound.

As he crashed down the stairs, he checked himself for blood. After two flights, he still hadn't found any.

He pictured the building in detail. The alleys would be watched. He'd never make it to the roof. And the stairwell only went down.

The boiler room.

He'd done his research, even ventured down there several times. The basement was viable. He flew down the stairs and burst through the hall door.

Three Marines spun on him.

There was no escape. He had to fight. The moment all other possibilities caved to this absolute, his body got tight. When he moved, it was no longer the product of his intentions. It was the discharge of something so powerful it was inevitable. He couldn't control it, only direct it, delay it. He stopped thinking—his thoughts were already movements.

He was so close that the first Marine didn't even try to fire on him. He just reached out to grab him by his shirt. Tom ducked, grabbed the Marine by the waist, and spun him like a Tilt-a-Whirl headfirst into the tile floor. The man hit, and his limbs spread like a broken toy.

The second Marine shouldered his M-16 and swung it on him. Tom closed in, banking on the unwieldiness of the M-16, which was longer than the other Marine's M4 and required greater stand-off to fire. Tom feinted right. The M-16 swiveled and obliterated the wall he would have been in front of. He lunged left, right under the M-16 barrel, and felt it swing overhead, scraping his scalp. He grabbed the barrel, which burned his hand, and ripped the rifle out of the Marine's grasp. With his free hand, he cracked the man across the side of his face.

Then he swung the stock of the rifle into the Marine's jaw so hard the skin did a quick, ugly ripple across the outline of his skull. Tom drove his fist into the Marine's chest, and the man shot back and slapped against the wall.

The only reason the third Marine hadn't fired was Tom's proximity to the other two—that and he seemed confused by Tom on a profound philosophical level. As Tom bum-rushed him, the Marine's eye dropped to his sights.

He fired.

Tom ducked.

He fell to his knees and slid right into the Marine's legs. The barrel was already descending as he hammer-fisted the Marine in the stomach. The man doubled over, and Tom popped up to his feet. He let the M-16 he was still holding slip farther down in his hand, lengthening his club, and brought it down on the man's head. The man's legs stiffened, and his torso balanced on two inanimate pegs. Tom grabbed him and eased his body to the floor.

A door banged open, and a fourth Marine popped into the hall, moving fast like he'd heard something and come running.

He turned on Tom and three unconscious men, one of whom Tom was ballroom-dipping to the floor. The Marine leveled his rifle. There was a burst as Tom took a step and flattened himself behind the corner of the hallway.

A bullet hit the man on the ground. His leg twitched, and the backside of his pants exploded like a small firecracker had gone off inside them. But the fourth Marine was still firing.

Keeping as much of his body safe behind the corner as he could, Tom reached around with the rifle to shield the downed Marine's head. He had just lowered the M-16's stock in front of the man's face when the rifle spun out of his hands.

As it rattled on the floor, he saw the split polymer on the stock. The firing stopped, and Tom slipped back around the corner. He could hear the fourth Marine yelling their location into his radio. There was another stairwell off a second hallway. Leaping down another flight of stairs, he finally reached the boiler room. The door was locked. He kicked it open and closed the door behind him. Then he gripped the doorknob and bent it against the frame like he'd done with the door to the war room.

He knew the Paris underground was a giant honeycomb, and only 170 miles of those tunnels, caves, and catacombs were charted. The rest of it was so vast and forgotten that, just last month, Paris police had discovered an underground restaurant, complete with electricity, phone lines, and motion-triggered barking to keep the mole people away.

In this particular section, there was an extensive sewer system that emptied into the Seine River. The embassy at one point had multiple entrances to this part, but they'd since been sealed for security reasons.

Tom was looking to open one of them back up.

There was a metro stop directly east of the embassy. For safety reasons, the large drainage tunnels were unlikely to be near subway lines. So he went to the west wall and found the section where a door had been bricked over. He ripped a fire axe off the wall and swung at the brick until the only thing he could feel was the vibration in his arms.

Eventually the brick spread. He pulled down a large section of the wall and found the door. He hacked at the door's lock until he could push it open. He stuck his head through. There was just enough light from the boiler room to make out a round tunnel. He climbed in and went right—away from the Seine.

Using the light from his cell phone, and praying he was too far underground for the phone to transmit his location, he followed the tunnel to a large cavern. It was the nexus of forty-odd crudded pipes and passages spewing dark liquid. Water dripped, flowed, and crashed. The sounds converged into a single overwhelming roar. It smelled like filth that was still alive.

All the water shot into one large canal. And flowing through it was a river of blackish chum that rushed into a massive mouth-like opening that was stretched wide to suck it all in.

There was a heavy metal door on the other side of the water, the kind with bolts in the frame. The kind he could maybe—maybe not—get through somehow. The walls were slick. He looked up. The ceiling was a large dome with a network of piping running across the whole thing.

He took off his belt, looped it through the handle of the metal case, and improvised a shoulder pack. Then he jumped and grabbed a pipe. He used it to pull himself up the slope of the ceiling. By the time he was forty feet high, almost halfway across, his hands were useless with slime. He looked down. The black water rushed below him.

When he got to the top, the piping ended abruptly. There was a gap in it. He looked around frantically for some way across, and as he stopped and rested both hands and feet on a pipe, they started to slip. Every few seconds, he had to re-grip just to stay in place.

Shadows hid most of the other side of the dome, but he thought he could see another pipe.

And what if there was nothing but smooth ceiling?

He looked down at the water, calculated his odds of drowning.

Carefully he rocked his weight back and forth, then launched himself across to the other side of the dome. He stretched out, his fingers disappearing into the shadows. He clawed at the wall for a half-second before his hands closed around a pipe. He tried to grip it as hard as he could, but as the rest of his body swung below him, his momentum unbalanced him.

The pipe shot out of his grip.

As he fell, he clawed at the wall again. One moment, he felt nothing but air. Then the tips of his fingers found something. And just as he realized he was safely hanging by one arm, he also became aware that his other arm, which was supposed to be securing the case, had been whipped away from his side. He felt the weight of the case dig once before it slipped off his shoulder.

He couldn't really see the loop on the case, only the motion of it, but he shot his right arm out and somehow stabbed two fingertips through the belt loop. On instinct, they curled around the leather.

He dangled, wincing as his body rotated and torqued his other arm. Then he pulled himself up and reattached himself to the wall. He was reaching for the next hold—

There was a *ping* against the pipe.

Karl watched the pipe vomit up a wall of dirty water over Tom's face. After the initial geyser, the pipe continued trickling water, forcing Tom to squint through it. Two Marines flanked Karl. Both had flashlights attached to their rifles. The lights never left Tom's face and hands.

"Agent Blake," Karl yelled—he could barely hear himself over the crashing water—"stand down or we will shoot you down."

Tom didn't move. He put a hand up to block the lights on his face.

"Whatever you're doing, you're about to die for it."

Tom shifted along the ceiling, and Karl and the Marines all started screaming over one another.

"Keep your hands in view."

"Stay where you are."

Tom froze.

Karl: "You have ten seconds to start climbing down. Then we're going to engage."

Tom shifted again, and this time Karl thought he was going to climb down. But instead Tom paused. His eyes moved around the cavern. There were two ways out as far as Karl could tell: a bolted door on the other side of the water, which Tom couldn't reach, and the way he'd come, which was where Karl stood. "The only reason I haven't fired is because I want those files," Karl said. When Tom didn't do anything, Karl turned to the Marines and nodded.

Tom's eyes dropped down to the water rushing below him. When he looked up, he stared at Karl for a moment.

Then he let go.

As he hit the river, the water parted and came back together with a slurp. The first Marine shook his head and was saying under his breath *Jesus fucking Christ* over and over.

Karl walked to the river and peered into the water. "Where does this drain?"

"Probably directly into the Seine, sir," the second Marine said. "But it's a quarter mile away."

Karl watched the water. He'd never seen anything so black and lifeless. He didn't even want to put his hand in it.

"Get me a diver."

"A diver?" The Marine paused, thought about how to put what he had to say. "We don't have a diver. This is France, sir."

"Go find Martin Litvak and tell him to get me a diver. He can *rent* the equipment if he has to."

"Sir, you're aware there might be an issue on account of the Seine River being smack in the middle of Paris?"

When Karl turned and stared at him, the Marine took one look at his face, then disappeared back up the tunnel toward the boiler room.

Karl turned to the water. It was rushing at twenty miles per hour at least. He couldn't get the look on Tom's face out of his mind—it made him think of something D. H. Lawrence had written a long time ago: "I never saw a wild thing sorry for itself. A small bird will drop frozen dead from a bough. Without ever having felt sorry for itself."

Karl thought maybe he had just watched a young man do the same thing.

CHAPTER 9

THE PIPE didn't run straight. It split and twisted. A mile as the crow flies became four as the shit flowed. Tom tried to force his head upward—or at least in the direction that felt upward. But there was no way to tell what was up and what was down because there was no light. His head bounced off the pipe walls, and his lungs shrieked until his eyeballs shook. When he did get his face into the air trapped above, he sucked a mixture of water and oxygen. Then he did everything in his power not to do anything that might make him take a breath underwater, like cough.

The goal was simple. Air pocket to air pocket. Gulp air and brown water in one pocket. Exhale and maybe puke in the next. Make it for thirty seconds—until the next pocket. It didn't matter where the pipe led or even if it ever stopped. He just wanted those thirty seconds.

The pipe split, and the back of his shirt caught on the bottom. He forced his eyes open. Pitch black. Nothing to see, just the sting of water running over his eyes.

The realization came to him like underwater scream bubbles in a horror movie. *Trapped. Underwater. In the dark.*

He scrambled in every direction, but he was caught like a child hung by the back of his belt on a coat hook. The current was so fast his arms were pinned to his sides.

He was going to take a breath.

Already the need was there. He started shaking his head from the pain. With all his strength, he reached forward through the current. His hand brushed something round. It skipped through his fingers, and the current powered his arms back to his sides. He started shaking his head harder.

He wanted to scream. His face contorted, letting water leak into his mouth. He raised one arm—raising both was too hard—and using his other hand, he lunged off the bottom, tearing himself free. The round thing hit him in the forearm, and he grasped it and pulled himself up. He felt the surface tension of the water break over his face. There were five inches of air at the top of the tunnel.

He hung there in a chin-up position, gasping into darkness.

Part of him wanted to hang there forever, just cling to the iron rod until his arms gave out. He looked around for a ledge or a passageway. He didn't care if it led anywhere so long as it allowed him to never go back in the water again.

He laughed mutely at himself.

Yeah, that's it. Maybe you can make a home down here and live like that freak in Phantom of the Opera. *You can eat trash. And as for water, well, you are practically drowning in it, now aren't you?*

But the only way out of the pipe was to go back in it. Once he stopped shaking, he let go.

When he was finally dumped into the Seine, he opened his eyes. There were shards of light in the water. Air bubbles passed in front of his face.

They were descending.

Which didn't make sense. Air bubbles ascend, move toward the surface. It was basic physics: the air is less dense than the water—

He was swimming distance from the surface, but he wouldn't reach it because he didn't know which goddamn direction it was.

Then the obvious occurred to him: he was just upside down.

He rolled over and started swimming down into the depths, or what felt like down into the depths. Twenty seconds later he was in daylight, sucking oxygen like a newborn, so happy he thought he might cry.

Exhausted, he dog-paddled to a pier. As soon as he pulled himself up and rolled onto it, he threw up: brownish water teeming with little brown solids. He waited on his hands and knees until he was functional.

He knew the embassy would be moving to phase two. And, whatever that entailed, he wasn't ready for it now that he realized he'd gotten out of his depth somewhere back in the computer room, when he pulled a gun on a man who'd killed so many people that his life had maybe collapsed under the weight of all their souls.

The briefcase.

He looked over at his shoulder and saw the briefcase pinned by the belt against his body. And now that he had it, the words came that every freak with a dream in a basement somewhere never imagines he'll say and really believe:

You're actually pulling this off...

Those words got him up off the dock. The plan had been to piggyback off the CIA until the end, take the ride from Kotesh to Nast to Sarmad, get the whole network, and find the last man. Of course the plan was also stupid and arrogant, and he was lucky to have survived it. But you work with what you have, and up until he'd gotten the briefcase, what he had was squat.

As he jogged down the pier, water ran off his shoes like he was in an unusually gradual process of pissing his pants. A man painting a picture stared at him in horror. Tom's brain was still about ten seconds behind his body. He realized he was listening for a siren and had to remind himself that whoever was coming for him now would not be announcing themselves with one of those.

He remembered his cell phone and took it out and pitched it in the water. Then he turned down a side street. As he passed parked cars, he tried the driver's-side doors. Fifteen cars later, he found an unlocked old orange-brown Citroën and slid behind the wheel. He flipped the visor down. No keys. He looked under the seat. He got out and checked behind the tires. Nothing. So he tore the cover off the steering column with one swipe.

And froze.

His ability to do this so easily surprised him, even now. His hands were shaking, something they were doing more and more often. He took deep breaths until his hands were still enough to open the glove box.

There were four wires running up the steering column: two red, one brown, one green. He stripped the reds with his fingernails, stabbed them with the tip of a pen from the glove box, and tore them each apart. Then he twisted their wiring together. The lights on the dash came on: he had power. He stripped the brown wire and touched it to the two reds until the engine shook.

He pulled onto another side street, opened the briefcase, and started flipping through files. Alternating his attention between the road and the file, he went through the addresses. He had maybe another forty-five minutes in Paris, and he wasn't coming back.

Silvana Nast.

His eyes paused on her picture. This was the woman he'd seen outside Jonathan Nast's house. He wasn't 100 percent on that, but he sensed it somehow. She was Nast's sister, and for a moment he realized she probably didn't know yet that her brother was dead.

She had just graduated from Skema Business School with a bachelor's in marketing and had interned with Ogilvy & Mather. No full-time job was listed, so like millions of young French people in the current economy, she was probably unemployed and still desperately looking for something entry level. There were records of all her travel in the last three years, including one trip with her brother to Nice.

Someone had been keeping track of her.

Under "Suspected Contacts," Tom found what he was looking for: Alan Sarmad. Nice was one of the three cities Sarmad was known to operate out of. Silvana and her brother might have met Sarmad there. Which meant she might know where to find him.

He checked her address. She lived in the Latin Quarter—only ten minutes away.

Karl slipped two divers into the Seine and stood thinking up an explanation in case the cops came and wanted to know why two men who didn't speak a lick of French were bobbing around in the middle of Paris with thirty pounds of scuba gear.

It was a stupid thing to do, but he had to check the immediate area. A fugitive's odds of escape increased the farther he traveled. Unfortunately the water turned out to be too dirty to see anything, so the divers were basically feeling around the drainage gates to see if Tom's body was trapped against them.

Karl pulled out his phone and dialed Marty.

"Yes?" Marty said.

"Was there someone in those files with a Paris address?"

"Are you on a *cell* phone?"

"We have one shot at this, Marty."

"If he goes to an address in Paris, he's either very smart or very dumb."

"Tell me you have another copy of those files."

"No, I'm afraid you actually caught me telling the truth about that."

"I'm going to be researching this myself. Am I going to find an address for anyone who could be even accidentally connected here? Tell me now."

Marty hesitated. "Nast has a sister in the city. Her address would've been logged when we ran a utilities search."

"I need your response team."

Marty was silent. Using a quick response team would result in a detailed report.

"What do you have in mind?" Marty said.

"Locals." Using assets rather than agency personnel meant they could keep this off the books.

"Are you sure about this? Paris, Karl, Paris."

"He just escaped a lockdown. He has the only set of Prometheus files in existence, and he hustled his way onto the investigation of a crime he himself committed."

"It'll be tough to black-bag him. They may have to go all the way."

"I can live with that."

The line went dead.

Tom drove by Silvana's street once to see if anything looked funny. This was cursory and sloppy, but he was on the clock. There was no one sitting in the parked cars that lined both sides of the street. No one walking outside. Compared to the rest of the neighborhood, the street looked deserted.

He left the Citroën running in a no-parking zone. As he got out, water that had pooled on the seat spattered onto the pavement. He went to Silvana's building and hit the buzzers to the other apartments until he pissed off one of the tenants enough to buzz him in just to get him to stop. He went up to Silvana's floor and knocked on the door. No answer. He dropped to the floor and waited for a shadow to move past the strip of light under the door. But there was nothing, and he didn't hear anything in the apartment. He decided she wasn't home and went back outside.

When he reached his car, he noticed a van double-parked at the mouth of an alley. No one was inside, but the engine was running. He walked to the intersection and looked down the alley.

Two men were struggling with a woman.

Tom ran toward them. The men didn't see or hear him because the woman was kicking and screaming.

"You're not police!" She sucked in air, about to yell louder.

The first man covered her mouth while the second uncapped a syringe. The woman froze, eyelids squeezed shut.

Tom grabbed the hand with the needle and pulled the man's arm back until there was the sound celery makes when it snaps in half. He palmed the man's skull and accelerated it into the alley wall. The man's head hit the brick and bounced off it.

Tom spun on the second man, whose arm was elbow-deep in his jacket. He started to pull out a gun. Tom kicked him in the knee, hyper-extending so far it bent backward like a dog's. As the man fell, Tom swung his fist into his temple.

With both men on the pavement, Tom looked around. They were alone.

He turned back to the woman, who'd been thrown to the ground and was picking herself up. She was wearing a fitted flannel shirt and skin-tight jeans with designer rips in the thighs. Even with her hair matted to her face, he could tell she was attractive. She was one of those people you knew was going to be great-looking even if you only saw them from behind.

She seemed to sense someone was standing there.

"I haven't seen your faces," she said. "Just go."

"Are you Silvana?"

She looked down at the two men on the ground. All she said was, "Oh. Nice."

"Is your name Silvana?"

She didn't say no.

"We need to get out of here."

She pointed at the men. "Wait, did you do this? For me?"

"Yes—"

"Thank you," she said, still dazed. "That was so nice."

Gently he took her arm, and she followed him back to his car. When he opened the door for her, she planted her feet.

"More of those men will be here soon." He tilted his head toward the alley. When she didn't say anything, he reached for her arm.

She jerked away. "I'm thinking!"

Two Peugeots peeled around the corner. Silvana looked at the cars, then at him, said, *"Shit, shit,"* and pushed past him into the car, giving him a look that said: *And why the fuck are you just STANDING there?*

The Peugeots spread out, trying to block them in.

Tom dropped into the driver's seat, twisted the wheel, and stomped the accelerator. The wheels spun so fast they couldn't grip the pavement. The Citroën floated away from the curb and through a 180-degree turn on liquefied rubber. When it hit a parked car on the other side of the street, the tires caught, and they shot forward, scraping between the Peugeots.

Tom turned onto another street, then another, trying to put a maze between them and him. That worked for maybe twenty seconds. Then both cars streaked into his rearview mirror.

He dropped a foot on the accelerator and fishtailed badly around a rotary. His car swung toward a crepe stand. There was a moment when the momentum almost had them. But then the tires caught, and the car slingshot down a narrow side street.

The first Peugeot negotiated the turn low and even. In fact, it gained on them. The other spun out completely. Its flank slapped the curb, popping the rear tire.

The remaining car grew bigger until it filled Tom's rearview mirror.

Then its grille disappeared from view, and it collided with the back of his car. The Citroën slid around on its cheap suspension. Tom took another turn into an alley. The right side of the car dipped a foot as the left side rose up. It was like driving a water bed.

They were coming up at a ninety-degree angle on a wide street ahead. The road was clear except for a row of cars sitting in the rightmost lane—the one they were approaching at fifty miles per hour.

Tom saw a space between two stopped cars. Maybe four feet apart.

The Peugeot was coming back at them. Tom accelerated, aiming his car for the little sliver of open real estate. Out of the corner of his eye, he saw Silvana look at the space he was aiming for, then at him. Her mouth formed an O, and she reached up for what his uncle used to call the "oh shit" handle.

As they shot the gap, they struck the cars on either side of them. The cars' bumpers cut into the side of the Citroën and scraped along it like knives.

Their car shot across the street.

A stone wall loomed just thirty feet ahead.

Tom hit the brakes and spun the wheel, but the car slid out and side-swiped the wall. Silvana's window was down. Her hand came off the handle and was gouged by something. She cried out. When Tom looked over, she was sucking on the edge of her palm.

He accelerated down the street and merged onto the E50 highway. He was trying to figure out what he should say to her, when the driver of the Peugeot pressed the nose of his car against the back of theirs and accelerated. Their car surged forward like it had caught a wave. As they passed ninety miles per hour, the engine of the other car got louder. Both cars kept accelerating together.

At 120 mph, it felt like they were in a free fall.

Tom could feel the tires start to slip. If he turned the wheel, he'd flip the car. They started passing cars so fast the cars almost looked stationary.

A little blue Renault hatchback came into view. Then they were colliding with the back of it.

The impact launched Tom and Silvana at the windshield, but their seatbelts saved their faces from the glass. The little Renault shot forward diagonally, out of the way, and Tom saw its entire back side had caved in.

The Peugeot behind them hadn't slowed. It kept forcing them forward. That was when Tom saw the turn ahead. There was a guardrail running alongside the highway, and he realized the other driver intended to spear them into it.

Both cars were still picking up speed as they went into the rail. Right before impact, Tom turned the wheel to hit it at a glancing angle. The left headlight popped on the steel barrier, and the car rocked side-to-side with all its weight. For a moment it almost slid out of his control.

They careened back into traffic. Tom waited until the Peugeot tried to ram them again. Then he swerved hard to the right lane. The Peugeot's momentum carried it forward, alongside their car.

Tom twisted the steering wheel left, pushing the Peugeot across the breakdown lane and pinning it against the rail. Sparks flew up in a seven-foot rooster tail of light. The driver shielded his face with one hand and steered with the other. It took him a few attempts, but then he used the greater weight of his car to push them back into a center lane.

They were approaching an overpass, and for a brief moment, neither of them tried to maneuver against the other. Tom glanced at the driver, who stared back at him with eerie neutrality. Tom noticed the man's hands flex around the steering wheel. His body tensed.

And Tom knew what he had to do.

He took his foot off the accelerator. At 130 miles per hour, the car lost speed like he'd just tapped the brakes. His front bumper fell back next to the Peugeot's rear bumper. They were reaching the top of the overpass. The other man jerked the wheel toward Tom, and Tom did the same toward him. The front of the Peugeot went right, the back went left, and the Peugeot helicoptered off the road.

As it mowed through the guardrail, the posts anchoring the rail ripped out of the ground. The Peugeot kept spinning, tires screaming, and vanished as it fell off the side of the overpass.

Tom couldn't believe how perfectly the guardrail had failed to do its job.

He glanced at Silvana. She was staring at him like she'd been about to ask a question and gotten stuck.

"What is it?" he said.

"Who the fuck *are* you?"

CHAPTER 10

BOGASIAN'S EYES shot open. He sat up in bed and looked around.

Once he'd showered, he ate and got dressed. Afterward he sat on the couch. Sounds of traffic came in through the window. A woman with a little boy in the next room was shouting at someone about how honesty was the only thing separating mankind from the animals. Her voice, like the traffic outside, came in suffocated through the walls. Eventually her words turned to sobs, and then there was the sound of someone laughing.

Bogasian listened quietly for almost two hours. Then it was time.

The lab was in a high-rise filled with doctors' offices. Bogasian took the service elevator and waited by the back door until one of the doctors let him in. Bogasian didn't look at the man or say anything to him. He went to the examination room, took off his shirt, and sat on the exam table without moving for twenty minutes until another doctor came in.

Bogasian reclined on the table. The doctor moved carefully around him as he swabbed his neck. Then he inserted the needle.

Bogasian shot upright.

The doctor was studying his face. They always looked at him, waiting for him to wince when they went in deep. The doctor kept watching him as he put more weight on the needle to push it deeper. Bogasian turned and stared at him, and the man's eyes skipped over to the heart-rate monitor.

When the doctor removed the needle, Bogasian opened the bag he'd brought and grabbed his laptop. Then he stared at the doctor until the man let himself out of the room. Bogasian went to the web page of a shipping company and clicked on a translucent icon that wasn't visible unless you were looking for it. The screen went black. Then words appeared:

—*Are you ready for tasking?*

Bogasian typed: *Yes.*

Five hours later he arrived at Jonathan Nast's home. Police cars were parked scattershot around the lawn. Caution tape was strewn over everything. Men and women in uniform roamed the property.

Bogasian got out of his sedan.

As he lifted the caution tape, he flashed his Interpol ID, and an officer waved him through. The front door was closed, and because no one had dusted it for fingerprints yet, he went around back. Two techs were dusting the door to the rear entrance but didn't seem to be finding much of anything. As Bogasian slipped past them, he noticed the pieces of the lock mechanism. There would be no fingerprints on those either.

Inside, another officer stopped him. While Bogasian showed his ID, he stared at a vent in the living room. They hadn't thought to look there yet, and he didn't plan to be around when they did.

He slipped into Nast's office, where a woman was taking photographs. Bogasian waited in the doorway until she noticed him and then tipped his head toward the door. She gave him a look and stood there, fingering her camera. He waited, staring at her, until she spread herself against the wall and squeezed past him.

He closed the door behind her. As quietly as possible, he opened the closet. The little laptop and the equipment attached to it were still running.

He could see the cops in the living room on one screen and more cops in the front yard on another. He'd found the equipment last night—Nast had a thing about self-surveillance—but he had left it to see what it had to tell him. He went to the folder with the last twenty-four hours of recorded surveillance and copied it to his thumb drive before deleting it. He then copied twenty-four hours of recorded surveillance from a couple weeks ago—twenty-four hours of an empty house—and pasted it into the same folder. Then he stepped out and closed the closet door.

Back at the hotel room, he fast-forwarded the video file on his thumb drive until a figure appeared on Nast's front yard at 2:00 AM the day before. That was two minutes after he'd killed Jonathan Nast. He watched the figure grow larger in the screen as the person floated up to the window, right up against another camera. Bogasian paused the footage, took a screen capture, and hit PLAY again.

This was the young man he'd followed to Benjamin Kotesh and later to Jonathan Nast.

Bogasian had been trailing him for over a week, but he'd never seen him this close. He stared at the young man's face for a long time. Then he hit PRINT and tossed the printout on top of his other file—the one with a picture of Silvana Nast paper-clipped to the front.

For the next four hours, Bogasian sat on the edge of the bed, perfectly still and silent. It was dark in the hotel room now, the way he preferred it. He'd always been able to see well in the dark. Despite everything they'd done to him, that never changed. But he had another reason for keeping the lights off: the dull ache they caused around his eyeballs.

It wasn't light sources themselves that did it. It was reflected light. The sun's reflection off a car or track lighting reflected in buffed floors. It seeped into his eyes, and he saw things no person should ever have to see. If he could, he just avoided the light altogether.

Finally it was time. He sat at his laptop, went to the shipping company website, and scrolled across the screen until he found the tiny, nearly invisible link. When he clicked on it, the screen once again went black.

He waited, perfectly still, perfectly patient. Now that he was at the computer, everything felt so easy and cool and good.

The screen cast a green pall over the room. For a second, he thought it might be one of those nights where he waited on one end of the line with no one on the other end. He imagined on those nights his only connection with the world was a computer blinking in the dark office of an empty building.

But little white words materialized:

—*Has the target been located?*
—*No.*

A pause. Whoever was on the other side was thinking.

—*Re-task.*

The cursor pulsed while he waited.

—*New target: 100 Boulevard Gén Leclerc, 6th floor. Police guard.*
—*Name?*
—*Benjamin Kotesh.*
—*Shape the scene?*
—*No need.*
—*And afterward?*
—*Resume initial task.*

CHAPTER 11

SOMETHING IN the backseat was exerting a gravitational pull on Silvana's eyes. She twisted around, peering back there for the third time.

After going a hundred miles per hour, going twenty felt so boring it was like slipping backward in reverse. Tom was able to take his eyes off the road long enough to turn around. The backseat was caked with papers and food wrappers in various stages of biodegradation. Every surface looked sticky. Bodily fluid sticky. The thing looked like something had just been born in it.

Silvana eyed his wet clothes and copped the plaster smile people use when a social situation does not allow them to avert their eyes or gasp. She gave a long look at the door handle and turned to him.

"This is really quite a nice vintage car. How long have you owned it?"

He braked at a stop sign and stared at her. She tried to hold his stare but gave up, probably on the theory that maintaining eye contact with anyone who lived like this could only result in violence.

As he drove on, he motioned for her purse.

She looked at the handbag like it was a small animal and she was worried for it.

"There's a phone in your purse," he said.

"So?"

"Give it to me." He thought a moment. "How much money do you have?"

She considered this and started shaking her head like she'd come to a decision and it was irrevocable. "I can't give you money."

"We're going to need it."

"*We're* going to need it? Are you *trying* to scare the living shit out of me?"

"Look, I'm not a threat to you. I just want some information."

"Who are you?" She was shouting now. "Who were those men? What the hell is going on here?"

"Those men worked for the CIA."

"Oh, of course. And where are you taking me, huh? *To a bunker? Are you one of those bunker people?*"

"They're going to a lot of trouble for you. You need to give me that phone right now."

When she didn't move, Tom leaned over to grab the phone out of her purse. She jerked the purse up to her chest, taking his arm with it. The back of his hand grazed her breast.

Silvana gasped, and for a split second Tom could see the terror in her eyes. They both froze, watching each other.

Tom fixed his eyes on her. "Your phone is broadcasting a signal to at least—"

"What are you doing?"

"Right now your phone is broadcasting to at least one radio tower and probably more, which means your position can be tri-angulated—"

"If you ever try to touch me again, I will open this car door and *throw* myself on the street."

Tom slammed on the brakes.

Silvana got very still—right before she bolted for the door. Tom reached across her and held it closed. She fell back in her seat. They sat about a foot apart, exhaling into each other's faces.

Tom extended his hand. The way he did it felt like a threat, even to him. She opened her mouth to say something, scream it—her eyes were wild—and he thought she was going to hit him.

"Your phone," Tom said. "Please."

She forked it over. He flicked it out his window and kept driving.

It got hot in the car as he merged onto the A86 to double back around Paris. He turned on the AC.

"Look, thank you for saving me from those guys," she said. "Now I would appreciate it if you told me who you are."

"Why were those men after you?"

"I asked you a question."

They stopped at a light. She glared at him.

Five lights later, she sighed. "I don't know why they were after me, okay?"

"You know someone they're after."

"I don't."

"Then it must be you they want." He knew this wasn't true, but her reaction would tell him more than her answer. He shook his head. "Maybe I shouldn't be helping you."

"Maybe you shouldn't," she said.

"Now what makes you say that?"

Silvana looked like she was about to say something, but then she reached into her purse.

"Keep your hands where I can see them," he said.

She flipped her hands up away from the purse, and he checked the rearview mirror. There was no sign of anyone. He snagged the briefcase from the backseat and pulled out the gun. He was going to put it in his waistband when Silvana's hands shot up like she was under arrest.

"Whoa, whoa," she said. "You're American, right?"

The way he looked at her must have given her her answer.

"I'm not a threat or anything, okay? I love America," she said, nodding to emphasize the last part, to show he could really take that one to the bank. "'Great faces. Great places.' Great *people*, actually—okay, most of the people. Not the enormous ones in jean shorts and Nike sandals who walk around Paris eating and pointing at everything. Perhaps you've seen one? Or ridden one?" She laughed. "This whole thing is a misunderstanding. I'm not a threat, okay? I'm not anything."

He glanced over. She looked like she just wanted to get a smile out of him. He was about to give her one when she swung the purse into his face.

She clawed at the door handle again, and this time her fingers snagged the latch. The car door burst open. Somehow she'd already slipped her seatbelt. She was half out of the car when he caught her wrist. Even then she tried to fight free. But he yanked her back into the car. She dug her fingernails into the back of his hand, curling her lip as she did. Blood welled up out of the scratches. He let her dig until she lost her enthusiasm for it.

"Please close the door," he said.

She pulled it closed as he hauled her the rest of the way back into her seat. He indicated the seatbelt, and she strapped it across her body. He didn't let go until he heard it click.

As they drove, Tom considered what he knew about her. The first thing he'd noticed was her English—she was well-educated and spoke with no accent. She dressed like someone with money or someone who came from money. And she must have spent a decent amount of time in the States. "Great faces. Great places" was a reference to Mount Rushmore.

She must have been too preoccupied to notice, but her hand was bleeding badly. Tom handed her some tissues from his back pocket that had dried into a fuzzy mass. She stared at it, seemed to consider its sterility, then dabbed at her wound.

"Apply pressure," he said.

"I know what to do."

"More pressure than that."

"I said I know what to do."

It got quiet again. Silvana already had a routine: she would look at him like something was on the tip of her tongue, then at the last second look away, exhale, and start picking at the vinyl on the dashboard. A minute later she'd be looking at him again, and the cycle would repeat.

"My brother," she said after another stretch of silence.

"What about him?"

"There's no other reason those men would even know my address."

"What's his name?"

"I'm not going to tell you that."

"You know why the CIA would be interested in your brother, don't you?"

She didn't say anything.

"I know you know because you say I'm kidnapping you, and yet you don't seem that interested in talking to the police. They know who your brother is. They probably know who you are too. And they don't want either of you in their country, do they?"

She looked down sadly at her fingers.

"Your brother is Jonathan Nast."

She did a remarkably good job of not reacting.

"I don't know where he is or what he does anymore." She said it like people came by asking about her brother every week.

"You took a trip with him to Nice last year."

She froze, but in a dynamic way, like someone about to throw a punch. "First of all, fuck you for even knowing something like that. Second of all, a lot can happen in a year."

"You went to Nice with your brother last year. Why?"

The little muscles around her eyes tightened, as if the topic of her brother and their trip together was a wound that, touched too hard, would split wide-open. When she finally spoke, her voice sounded funny, like she was crying even though she wasn't. "It was just a long weekend I planned for us."

Tom opened his mouth to say something, but she beat him to it.

"You say those men back there were American," she said. "You're an American. Why would Americans fight each other over me?"

Maybe she was smarter than he thought.

"Let me guess," she said, "you work for the American State Department, but you don't really." She started shaking her head. "No, that's not right. If you worked for the American government, you'd need permission from the French government to be here, and there's no way they'd give you permission to do what you just did. Which means you're here on your own. You're just some guy. Aren't you?"

A lot smarter than he thought. He wondered whether that was a very good thing or a very bad thing.

"And what if I am?" he said. "Just some guy?"

"Well, then I think I'm pretty much screwed."

"I can help you, if you help me."

"And what does that involve?"

"Telling me what you know."

She looked outside, at an empty field next to the highway. "What if I wanted you to get me somewhere? Could I count on you to do that?"

"Yes."

"Of course I can't really trust you, can I?"

"No, but think of it this way. I just saved you from two men trying to drug you and stick you in their van. How much worse could I really be?"

"No, see, what you were supposed to say was 'You can't really trust me' and leave it at that. Then I'd at least know you were somewhat honest. Instead you were clever. And a woman should never trust a clever man."

"So she should trust one who's not clever, who's a moron?"

She didn't say anything.

"You know, anyone who's motivated enough to do what those men almost did is motivated enough to keep trying."

"Berlin," she said softly. "Would you take me that far?"

Tom sat in the car. They'd stopped at a roadside café. Once Silvana went inside, Tom alternately watched her from the car and read the files he'd taken. From what he could put together, the files pertained to a project referred to only as "Prometheus." But there was no description of it. He couldn't even tell what the project's purpose was.

He noticed another man sitting in his car, a Citroën. The man wasn't on the phone or eating, just sitting there. Tom watched him for a minute. *It's nothing*, he told himself. The two cars chasing them had crashed. Nobody could have caught up to them yet.

Are you sure there were only two cars?

He pulled out the file on Silvana again. There were three known associates for her: her brother Jonathan Nast, Alan Sarmad, and her father, Dr. Alexander Nast. The tech had matched Jonathan Nast and Alan Sarmad to Eric's shirt. But there was still one last man who'd never been identified.

Could it be her father?

The tech had told him that the DNA they'd gotten off the shirt from the last man had been more damaged than the others. It had been harder to match against their samples. They'd never considered that two of the men could be related to each other.

Tom pulled the file on Dr. Nast. It was too large to go through in detail now, but flipping through, he found reports written by Nast and information about relatives in non-US countries. Still nothing to indicate his role in whatever was going on.

He checked Nast's travel in the past year. There was nothing, just empty space on the page. He went further back, but there wasn't anything until August three years ago. Before that date, there was information about every trip Nast had taken since he'd gotten his doctorate. But from that point on, not a thing.

He'd disappeared.

Right around the same time Eric had.

Tom put the files back in the briefcase and sat thinking. He didn't know what this amounted to, just that it amounted to something.

For now he decided to focus on Alan Sarmad—because while Silvana's father was a question mark, Sarmad wasn't. Sarmad's DNA was on Eric's shirt. That was a fact. But eventually Tom would need to know about her father. And he had to be careful how he went about it. Like most things involving the human heart, like the heart itself, it was something that could be found only indirectly. On this, the rules were iron: the less you asked, the more you were told.

Through the windshield, he looked at Silvana sitting by herself in the café booth. Her hands were placed delicately on the table. One hand was clamping a tissue on the other. And the way she sat there, so softly she almost didn't exist, made him wonder whether, by taking someone who was probably innocent in all of this, he'd done a terrible thing.

He sat watching her. Everything about her told him to let his guard down. She was about his age. She said whatever popped into her mind, which made her a bad liar. And then there was her smile. It was a winking smile that said, *Maybe we can be friends.* It was the smile of someone who had done wild, exciting things, and if this smile greeted something you said or did, then it had the power to make you exciting too. But worst of all, she was attractive. Attractive in a way he found devastating somehow. Her irises were a faded shade of blue, yet they were heavy, holding something sad, something she'd never share. Their contrast with her jet-black hair only enhanced the effect.

But her brother had left saliva on the front of Eric's shirt. He'd spit on him.

And in the end, it took only one thought for Tom's guard to return to a standing position: Silvana was far more likely to get him killed than the other way around.

When Tom got out of the car, he noticed the man sitting in the Citroën was still there. He looked like he was texting.

He thought back to Karl in the war room: *They're going to do a lot more than find you.*

He went into the café and slid into the booth across from Silvana. They didn't talk. She fidgeted with some sugar packets, and once her coffee was refilled, she poured sugar into it until the mixture was, by his estimate, 50 percent sugar and 50 percent coffee.

"So…" she said.

It took him a moment to realize she was waiting for him to say something. He watched her.

"You know, we're not terrorists just because we're a quarter Lebanese," she said.

"I never said anyone was a terrorist."

"And yet here we are."

"You don't look Middle Eastern."

Her lips curved into a smile. "I know. I don't look angry enough."

"There's a file on you. They wouldn't have created it without a reason."

"I don't—"

"If I don't believe you, I'm not motivated to help you."

She swiped some sugar off the table. "I don't know what you want," she said.

"They're going to keep looking for you, you know."

"Just tell me what you want."

"Your brother."

Her face tightened, and she looked down at her hands. The left one was picking at the right, which squirmed like it didn't like it. She crossed her arms over her breasts, holding herself, and looked him in the eye.

"I have nothing to say about my brother," she said.

"Then tell me about you. Why did you go to Nice with him?"

"I wanted us to do a weekend together, you know, like families do." The little muscles around her eyes tensed like they had in the car. "He said he'd be willing to go to Nice, so I spent all this time planning our trip because I'm an idiot, and then when it came time to fly down, he actually showed up. We arrived and were actually talking for the first time in years, and everything was going so well, and then I heard him on the phone say he was there with his sister, and he laughed. And the way he did it was...I knew what it meant." She looked down, exhaled. "He only went because he had business down there."

"Is Alan Sarmad in Nice?"

She paused. "I don't know who that is."

Tom patted the file he'd purposefully left on the table. "That's not what my file says."

"Well, can I see it? It might be—"

"No." He left the file within reach, but she didn't go for it.

"I should have the right to—"

"This isn't a courtroom. I saved you, remember, from two guys trying to give you an injection in an alley."

He'd raised his voice. A woman at a nearby table turned to look at him. He stared back at her until she looked away.

"Why are you doing all this?" Silvana said.

"That's not important."

"Of course it is."

Tom glanced out the window and then looked back at her. "I'm investigating a murder."

She didn't have to say what she was thinking. He could see it in her eyes: *Was it someone close to you?*

She looked down and stared into her coffee.

"My brother dropped something off at his place. I only waited outside in the car," she said. "But believe me, you don't want anything to do with Alan Sarmad."

For the first time since she'd seen the gun, she actually looked scared.

CHAPTER 12

THE QUICK response team had been a disaster. They'd done something worse than failing—they'd created a scene. There were already Facebook posts and tweets about the car chase and the accident it had resulted in. People were even discussing it in chat rooms. Other than the lonely perverts on *Dateline*'s *To Catch a Predator,* Karl hadn't even known people still used chat rooms.

What he needed right now was to find out as much as possible about the person whose address Tom had gone to. He walked into the war room and stood over James, one of the analysts he'd been given but hadn't really wanted.

"What did they say?" Karl said.

James swiveled to face him. "Agent Blake was observed at the address with Jonathan Nast's sister."

"She involved in any of this?"

"Director Litvak said there was no evidence one way or another. They ran analytics on her and staked out her place for a while in case her brother came by. He never did, but the address was logged according to protocol. Want to see a photo of her?"

James handed Karl the printout. The woman was young, pretty, in an ageless kind of way. Could have been twenty—or thirty-five.

If she wasn't involved, why would Tom take her?

"What do we know about her?"

James swiveled back to his computer and read off the screen,

"Born in New York. Lived with family in Hungary, Germany, and the UK. She graduated college in Paris. Still unemployed. No political activity. Doubt she knows who the prime minister of France is."

"What about personal activity?"

"She almost flunked out of school once. She's visibly drunk in a third of her pictures on social media. Other than two friends, there's a pretty big cast of characters rotating in and out of her life. And there are no photos of her with family in years. Not a one."

"What's she think of her shit-bag brother?"

"She writes seven emails for every one of his. Seems he didn't want much to do with her."

Karl stared at a picture of her standing by herself on a hiking trail. "So what's she into?"

"You mean besides sitting in cafés and not working?"

"Everybody loves something."

"Youth unemployment here is 25 percent. There's a whole generation of people like this. She's floating."

"Well, she's just landed on our chessboard, and now she's up to her neck in shit."

"Wait, are we treating her as a source, or a target?"

"Go to her apartment and see what you can find."

James nodded, and Karl walked into his office.

He sat there for a few minutes, sucking coffee through a hole in the plastic lid and thinking about the look on Tom's face right before he'd hit the water. There was this . . . acceptance in it. And that was odd because it just didn't feel to him like the look of a traitor. Aldrich Ames was an alcoholic who sold his country out for the money. Robert Hanssen did it for the feeling of superiority— aided by a general whack-job quality Karl could never put his finger on. Traitors were just like most criminals. They were shallow. They hurt other people casually because it made their lives easier, and that meant they weren't the type to willingly face drowning to death 200 feet underground.

So the question Karl kept coming back to was one of origin: *What possesses someone who would do this to join the CIA in the first place?*

The fact that Tom had joined the Special Activities Division instead of becoming an analyst told him a lot. As far as everyone in SAD was concerned, SAD *was* the CIA. In their estimation, the rest of the place was pretty much just churning out intel that was so meaningless, so devoid of any possible significance, that you had to laugh at it or you'd cry.

—*What? India may pass an initiative reducing its civil service staff? You wake the president, I'll brief his college roommate's brother's wife and tell her little Sanjay is going to need a new job!*

It was an irony the American people had never seemed to understand: the most useful place within an organization whose stated purpose was to gather information was not in actual intelligence gathering. It was in operations.

So why would a young man sign up for this—the real this?

It was the way Tom stared into Nast's dead eyes and found something he didn't exactly hate in what he saw. It was a look Karl recognized. The work appealed to something Old Testament in a person. And if it offered job satisfaction, it was a blunt-force-trauma kind of job satisfaction. It was waving and smiling to some tyrant who didn't realize he was walking onto train tracks. It was waiting patiently as the train swung into view.

It was the fact that when you were operating solo, without a friend in the world, you got to be the smile. And the train.

Karl had no idea what Tom was after. But whatever it was, it had engaged him on a moral level.

He started reviewing security camera footage of Tom's escape. It made him uneasy how young Tom looked. That face belonged under a baseball cap, not on his to-do list. Karl put another disc into the player. He fast-forwarded to Tom's fight with the Marines. The camera was far away and at an awkward angle, but Karl saw a door bang open and Tom come through it. Three Marines turned on him in unison. Tom grabbed the first one—big guy, over 200 pounds—picked him up like it was the most natural thing in the world, and slammed him into the floor so hard the others froze.

Karl hit PAUSE.

His armpits were hot with the moisture that forms right before you break into an actual sweat. He didn't move for almost a minute. Then he hit PLAY and watched Tom dodge between two armed men trying to sight him. He moved like his world was subject to different laws than theirs. Within five seconds they were unconscious on the ground, and one had been thrown ten feet across a hallway.

A moment ago, with absolute certainty, Karl had known of only one man in the world who could move like that. Now, he knew, there was another.

And he realized, with a growing sick feeling, that now they had two men to find, both of whom had been augmented and were running loose around Europe with an illegal stem cell technology in their heads.

But how did Tom Blake get augmented in the first place?

He needed a clue, something to start with. He thought about everything Tom had said, everything he'd been weirdly quiet about, every gesture. He remembered their conversations—and regretted telling Tom about his wife. It was weird and awful to realize that the first person you'd had a real conversation with in twelve months had just been waiting to fuck you over.

Karl picked up his phone. Marty didn't answer until the fourth ring.

"Tom's been augmented," Karl said.

"How do you know that?"

"I just watched what he did to the blow team."

Marty didn't say anything.

"We have to disclose Prometheus to the DoD and the president."

The silence between them grew.

"This man infiltrated our *embassy.* Our entire defense apparatus needs to be put on notice."

"I think you know that isn't going to happen."

Karl was quiet for a moment.

"Fine," Karl said. "I'll put him down. Then I'm going to find the people who made him, and I'm going to put them down." He paused. "And if you use this as an excuse to reopen the program, Marty, I'm going to put you down too."

He sensed Marty's smile through the phone line.

"Welcome to the game, Karl," Marty said.

Then he hung up.

Karl watched the rest of the tape. Shots rang out from off-camera. Tom darted behind a doorway and darted back out to shove a rifle stock in front of a downed Marine's head. Almost instantly the rifle jumped out of Tom's hands as a bullet hit it.

This wasn't in the report.

Karl had to rewind it and watch a second time. Tom had saved the man's life. It didn't make sense. Traitors were like sex addicts: eventually they all lost their standards. But in the middle of betraying his country, Tom had stopped to save one of its grunts.

What difference does it make?

He's like Bogasian. He's too dangerous to live.

The air in the room suddenly felt shared. Karl glanced up and saw James standing in the doorway.

"Did you find anything at her place?"

"The cops were there. Apparently somebody saw us trying to take her." He paused. "There's something you need to see."

"Now?"

James just nodded.

They went to Tom's office, which was lit up like the set of a photo shoot. Techs were pulling fingerprints off every surface they could. People were going through files with gloved hands.

A woman, whose resemblance to Large Marge in *Pee-wee's Big Adventure* was kind of astonishing, looked up when they walked in.

James gestured toward Karl. "Tell him."

"Sir," the woman said. "We've only found one set of fingerprints in this office."

Karl shrugged. "So?"

"So they're not Agent Blake's."

Whatever anyone in the room was doing, they stopped and stared at Karl.

"That's not possible," Karl said.

"That's a fact."

"So whose are they?"

"The prints don't match any employee of the CIA. They don't match anything in the FBI database or any other database we can access."

Karl stood there blinking, then said in a low voice, "So you're telling me the chipper young man who's been coming to work here every morning, getting to know everyone while he accesses and steals our nation's secrets, is actually *not* an employee of the Central Intelligence Agency. He's a John Doe, and one we have absolutely no way to identify. Is that correct or have I perhaps missed the pony in this pile of manure?"

No one said anything.

"Where is the real Agent Blake? *Is* there even an Agent Blake?"

"He's in Africa," James said. "There's nothing in the system because his assignment was non-official. But the home office confirmed it—he's been in Djibouti for the last three months."

CHAPTER 13

AN IDENTIFICATION. That, Tom knew, was the key for any person on the move. But there was a circular logic to all forms of ID. To do anything in this day and age—get a job, rent a car, make a large purchase on credit—you needed a photo ID. Yet applying for a photo ID didn't itself require a photo ID because if you already had one, why would you need one? So the system relied on place of birth, date of birth, mother's maiden name, etc., for the application process. As a result, if you knew these things about another person, then as far as the government was concerned, you *were* this person.

This was what allowed Tom to do something that on paper sounded impossible: steal the identity of a CIA agent. But crazier things had happened, he figured: you just had to be desperate enough to try.

When he was researching the CIA, the Valerie Plame scandal had shown him the extent to which the CIA used front companies to place agents. Plame was a Beltway energy analyst and mother of two who'd been outed as a non-official cover CIA agent by a member of the White House staff. In the resulting media furor, a huge amount of information about the way the CIA operated was disclosed—for those willing to read between the lines. Allegedly, hundreds of agents had used the same company that Plame had as a cover: Brewster Jennings & Associates. What Tom couldn't believe was how thin Brewster's veneer as a real operating company was. It was basically an address, a phone number, and a Dun & Bradstreet credit report. After the scandal, an anonymous source even commented on this, noting that Plame only used Brewster as part of her cover while in the United States. When she was abroad, she used something "more viable." Tom realized that this change from shallow front to something "more viable" was the point of transition where he could insert himself.

He'd been living alone in a studio apartment off Wisconsin Avenue in Washington, DC, for nine months at that point. Two weeks earlier, an idea—the idea—had come to him: he could bring the men who killed Eric to justice, and he could stop whoever had augmented him from ever doing it to anyone else again. Other than a clerk at Safeway and an eighty-five-year-old neighbor whose evening walks sometimes coincided with his own, Tom hadn't spoken to another person in at least a month. *Is this totally insane?* he wondered. *Have I finally gone crazy?* But then another thought came to him:

Where else do you really have to be?

He'd been working sporadically—temp jobs, catering. He even did a little work on construction sites where he was the only white guy and the others stared at him with looks that said, *And where did you go wrong?* The money covered rent most of the time. His expenses beyond that were minimal. For food, he ate whatever was cheapest per calorie: peanut butter, lots of peanut butter, ground beef, potato chips, white bread, vegetables (on manager's special). He had $80,000 in the bank from his parents, which he hated to touch. It was one of the only possessions of theirs that he'd hung on to. The other three being: his mother's wedding ring, every scrap of paper he'd ever found with his parents' handwriting, and a plastic butter tub from the 1960s. It was funny how only the most everyday objects remained static-clung to a person's memories. The tub belonged to their dad, and Tom had a ridiculous affection for the thing. Their dad kept cornstarch in it, which he used to powder his crotch with a little mitt after every shower. It was something Tom and his brother found so bizarre as kids that they'd crawl, giggling, into the bedroom to watch. And this practice stopped only when, one day, their dad spun on them, brandishing the mitt like a butcher knife, and chased them through the house, insisting everyone pull down their pants and "freshen up."

Tom knew he could go back to college, get a good job. He was smart, and he'd always been able to teach himself anything. An autodidact, that was what his teachers said he was. But when he projected himself ten years into the future, sitting in an office somewhere, he still saw himself alone. An impressive job could fulfill his every material need, but not do what he really wanted. It could never give his life meaning. Never give him the people who made that meaning possible, and then kept it alive in you. And so the question never went away: *Where else do you really have to be?*

Everything he needed to learn came from the internet. What he couldn't find on the internet itself, he learned from people he met on it. For $100, an ex-thief taught him how to pick just about every kind of lock there was, even the new ones with security pins that took twenty seconds to open instead of ten. "Locks," the man explained, "exist to keep honest people from temptation. You need to start thinking of them as purely symbolic."

Tom contacted a frequent commenter on a gun-talk forum, a fifty-seven-year-old ex-Marine whose wife had died recently and who was more than happy to teach Tom to shoot so long as they could talk for an hour afterward in the parking lot about the man's daughter ("A woman should never marry a man more than 30 percent dumber than she is."), Obamacare ("If Obamacare was a physical object, it'd be a fist colliding with my perianal area as my mother-in-law force-feeds me broccoli"), and Tom's marital status

("A quiet guy like you needs a good woman or you're going to wind up in a bell tower, sighting civilians").

The internet connected Tom to all the lonely people who saw a young man without a family and were eager to help. Individually their knowledge was valuable. Collectively it could have brought down a government.

First he camped out on Dolley Madison Boulevard until he found men who resembled him driving from the direction of the George Bush Center for Intelligence. Then he broke into their homes, learned their names, and narrowed his candidates down to those who were listed as officers of companies registered in Delaware. These were the agents who'd be using a company for cover. When one of them—an agent with the same first name as his—didn't come home for a week, Tom broke into his apartment a second time.

He found a social security card, a utility bill, and information that led him to the agent's mother and ultimately via Facebook to her maiden name. Now he had what he needed to get a birth certificate. The first three digits of a social security number are determined by the zip code of the applicant's mailing address. So the social security card told him what state the agent was born in and thus where to apply. He used the birth certificate to get a driver's license. And once he had that, he was able to get a passport for Tom Blake—but with his own picture. He didn't know how long Agent Blake would be gone, but he was fairly certain that if Blake was traveling undercover, it would be known only to his immediate superiors, and for security reasons it wouldn't be input into any central database. That meant he could be this man until someone realized there were two Tom Blakes in an organization with more than twenty thousand employees.

When he arrived in France as Tom Blake, he'd already called ahead to let the embassy know he was coming. He showed them his ID, and after they'd confirmed his identity and established he wouldn't be running any ops in-country, they honored his request for an office to use for a few weeks. Three days after that, he'd connected with the lab tech and stolen his log-in and password.

He'd known it was only a matter of time before he got caught, which meant he'd need yet another identity. So on the corner of Clauzel and Martyrs, he found Adrien Michel, a homeless man about his age. Posing as a UN employee gathering demographic information, Tom got a birth date, place of birth, full name at birth, mother's maiden name, everything he needed to send to the Office of La Mairie for a birth certificate. Tom didn't even need to go to the office himself. Despite their reputation for customer service, the French really couldn't have made the whole process more pleasant. And because he felt bad about taking advantage of a drug addict, he atoned by repairing Michel's credit history, which had been wrecked by a Banana Republic charge marked 1,875 days late.

As a backup in case the CIA figured out the Michel identity— and they would eventually—Tom found a student at the Sorbonne who also looked like him. He followed him home, waited until he went out for a jog, then picked the lock on his door with a bump key and stole his ID card and passport.

"Credit card, please."

There was the impatience in the first syllable of something repeated for a second time. Tom looked up and handed the motel clerk Adrien Michel's ID and the credit card he'd opened in Michel's name. After leaving the café, he and Silvana had driven a few more hours and then stopped at a motel, the kind that wouldn't have security cameras. The wallpaper behind the clerk was peeling. The rust stain underneath it looked like a gunshot wound.

"How many is this for?" she said.

"Two."

The clerk looked at the ID, which had Tom's picture on it. She started typing.

"I have a non-smoking king," she said.

"We'd like something with two beds."

More typing on the computer. "Sorry, that's all we have."

"What about a cot?"

Tom looked out the window at Silvana waiting in the car. She seemed small and somehow blank, the way a law-abiding person looks when he's just been arrested. He turned back when he realized the clerk had said something.

"I'm sorry?" he said.

"*Just* gave out my last cot. Lot of families tonight."

"Okay."

When he opened the car door, he interrupted Silvana dabbing at her eyes. He keyed the ignition, and there was a moment where it might have been okay to say something. But he couldn't think of anything.

He drove around to the rear parking lot and parked front end out. Once he got the door to their room open, Silvana rushed past him and disappeared into the bathroom.

He heard the faucet.

"Are you okay?" he called out.

No response.

Eventually the door swung open a few degrees. Silvana pulled back the tissues on her hand and showed him a long, smiling gash. As soon as she took the pressure off, the wound grinned up blood all over her hand.

"I'll be right back," he said.

He went down the hall, but the first-aid kit in the janitor's closet was empty. He looked around for anything else he could use. When he reappeared in the bathroom doorway, he held up a roll of duct tape. Silvana's mouth fell open.

"I think I need to go to a hospital," she said.

He didn't even need to say anything. She could tell just by looking at him that wasn't going to happen. Finally she sighed and held out her hand. He removed the tissues and examined the cut, then unwrapped a bar of soap and handed it to her.

"Work up a lather and wash the area." He turned on the faucet for her.

She eyed the soap. "But that's going to hurt."

"Yes."

"Like...a lot."

"Yes."

She waited for him to elaborate, and when he didn't, she started washing the wound. She didn't make a sound. She didn't even make a face.

"I have to make sure there's nothing in it," he said. "Otherwise it won't heal."

"Okay..."

"I'm going to have to pull it apart to see in—"

"But that's going to *really* hurt."

"Probably."

"That doesn't sound like—is that what they do in the ER?"

"Basically."

"*Basically?* Now there's a level of certainty you pretty much never want used in reference to your body."

"In the ER, they'd irrigate the cut with saline solution and apply some antibiotic, but only after making sure there's nothing lodged in there."

"And where did you learn that?"

"Boy Scouts."

"You were a Boy Scout?" She laughed. "What was your den number?"

"That's Webelos."

"What's Webelos?"

"Webelos are what kids are before they become Boy Scouts. Webelos are in a den. Boy Scouts are in a troop."

"Ah."

Tom put her hand in his. Her skin was soft and cool, and it was nice touching it. He pulled the cut open, ran it under the faucet, and looked inside. She sighed in pain.

Now that he was closer to her, he could smell the lemon scent from whatever she'd washed her hair with that morning. As he rinsed her cut again, he glanced at her. A few tiny droplets of sweat had broken out on her nose. She looked at him, then quickly away.

"What is it with men and duct tape?" she said finally.

"What do you mean?"

"You're all obsessed with it."

"You can fix everything with duct tape."

"Everything?"

"That's right."

She smiled. "Not, you know, *everything?*"

"Sure. Tools, cars, plumbing...acquaintances."

"'Acquaintances'?"

"Yes, you take a piece, and you put it over your new friend's mouth. Peace and quiet ensues."

She just looked at him.

He held up the duct tape and unrolled a strip. "You can also tape your new friend's wrists to the armrests, so she can't jump out of a car going thirty miles per hour."

"Are you making *fun* of me?"

"It's a three-hour drive to Nice tomorrow. You better hope so."

Her jaw dropped a little, like she couldn't believe what she'd just heard. She cocked her head, studying him from a different perspective. "Wow," she said, "it has a sense of humor. I was beginning to think you were born of a jackal or something."

He put some Kleenex between the duct tape and the cut and then used the tape to pull the two sides of the wound together.

"I mean, this is progress," she said. "Shit, I'd hug you if I weren't afraid to touch you."

Then she flashed him a crooked little smile. He noticed her lateral incisor was twisted out of position. It was the kind of little imperfection that took ordinary plastic beauty and elevated it from something in a magazine into something real, into something you couldn't know you wanted until you saw it.

"What?" she said.

He shook his head, and as he stepped back, he watched the tension release from her body.

"You sure you want me to take you to Berlin?" he said.

"Uh-huh."

"What's in Berlin?"

"Someplace I know I'll be safe."

Who's there?

"I hope it's a good friend," he said.

"It's not important."

Is it your father?

He waited for her to elaborate, but she didn't. He smiled and said, "Okay, but just to be clear, if I take you all the way to an address there and it turns out to be a day spa or something, we're going to have a problem."

She didn't take the bait. Just grinned. "You bastard. I have never been to a *day spa* in my life. What makes you think I'm that kind of girl anyway?"

"I was kidding."

"Oh no, see, that's one of those things you actually mean but you say is a joke when the other person calls you out."

"You're calling me out?"

"Oh, I'm calling you out, fucker."

"Okay. You know what gave you away? Your purse. It's huge. That's *never* a good sign. At first I thought you were one of those women who keeps a little dog in it."

She shook her head gently at him. "You know, I'd slap you, but it probably wouldn't do anything except make you angry."

"Once you show me Sarmad's house, I'll take you to Berlin. Deal?"

At the word "Sarmad," the smile on her face died. Finally she nodded. "Deal."

CHAPTER 14

KARL WAS still in Tom's office when the phone rang.

He'd been going through Tom's desk and making sure the analysts had looked for fingerprints in every square inch of the office.

Everyone froze and then turned in unison to stare at the office telephone. Karl got it on the third ring. He lifted the receiver to his ear but didn't say anything.

"Hello?" someone said.

"Yes?"

"Um...I think I have the wrong number."

"This is Tom Blake's desk. May I help you?"

"Would you let him know I have some more reports that arrived today?"

"Of course," Karl said. "Which reports are those again?"

A pause. "Just please tell him to come by."

"Okay. I'm actually supposed to meet him. Could you give me your address?"

Karl was surprised and also somehow not surprised when the person he was speaking to gave him the address of the building he was standing in. Once they were downstairs, in fifty words or less, Karl terrorized the lab tech into immediate compliance.

"The samples came from all over Europe," the tech said. "British police, German police, Interpol, other agency people. We got our first match a few weeks ago."

"Who was that?"

"Alan Sarmad was the guy's name."

Karl got a falling sensation in his stomach. "And who came afterward?"

"Benjamin Kotesh."

"Paris police found him half-dead less than seventy-two hours ago, you know that?"

The tech looked from Karl to James and back. "Wait, you don't think *I* knew—"

"What were you matching these guys' DNA against?"

The tech went over to a small refrigerator and pulled out a paper pouch. He laid it on the table, then picked up a Starbucks cup and backed away like the whole thing was out of his hands now.

Inside the pouch was a blue-and-gray flannel shirt. Drops of blood dangled off the fibers like little berries. Other places, where there was more of it, the blood had smeared. Karl noticed a fist-size stain on the front.

He looked at the tech, who finished his sip of coffee and then raised both arms.

"I don't know who it belonged to," he said.

Karl remained expressionless. "What if I said it was your job to know?"

"But that's not—"

"But it is now." Karl reached over and gently pulled the coffee cup out of the tech's hand. He placed it on the table, just out of reach.

The tech was silent, but Karl knew he was going to talk. People in his situation always talked.

"He never really told me anything," the tech said. "He just brought me the shirt and told me to identify the people who'd come in contact with it. I found the DNA of five men. One of them had clearly been wearing the shirt, but Agent Blake wasn't interested in him, so we—"

"Who was the man who'd been wearing it?" Karl turned to the shirt. Whoever it was, it looked like he'd died in it.

"I don't know," the tech said. Karl stared at him. "I swear to God, he never told me."

"So when someone hands you an article of clothing literally soaked in another person's blood, it's your policy to set aside the personal value judgments and not risk pushing any emotional boundaries by asking a question?"

"It wasn't my place to—"

"Something like 'Holy shit, there's a *fucking* liter of blood on this shirt. Dear god, who in the fuck does it belong to?'"

The tech's face hardened. "I don't ask questions. You know that."

Karl thought a moment. All this non-information told him something indirectly. Tom hadn't asked the tech to identify the man who'd been wearing the shirt, which meant Tom already knew who that was.

"I need you to ID whoever died wearing the shirt."

"That's going to take a while."

"What does that mean?"

"Weeks. Assuming I'm only going to be checking US databases."

Karl sighed. "Okay. Get started. Now tell me about the other men."

"We got Ben Kotesh's DNA report from the Germans. He was an exact match. However, with Jonathan Nast, we didn't get a match."

"So how did you know he left the DNA on the shirt?"

"We received a DNA report for a man who'd been arrested in the UK and forced to give the police a DNA sample. His DNA matched one from the shirt around 20 percent, which meant they're relatives, first cousins. Jonathan Nast was the only one we could find that remotely fit."

"How did you know who Nast's cousins were?"

"It was in the system."

"And how did it get in the system?"

"Honestly? I don't know, but Agent Blake was spending a lot of time on Facebook."

"Jesus."

"It actually wasn't that hard—"

"You said there were four men. Sarmad, Nast, and Kotesh makes three. What about the other one?"

"The last sample was never identified."

Karl pounded down the hallway with James jogging behind him.

"Get me everything on Alan Sarmad," Karl said. "*Every. Little. Thing*. He's Tom's next target, so finding him may be our last chance to find Tom. Comb through his contacts. Start with people in France, then expand. Get it started, and then call me. You and I are going to Blake's apartment."

"I'll get Agent Blake's address."

Karl stopped. "Don't call him that. He's not Agent Blake."

"What do I call him then?"

"Just don't call him that."

Tom lived on a gloomy little street in the eighteenth district that gentrification had passed by. When they got the door to his apartment open, the inside looked like it had been empty for years. There was nothing on the yellowed walls, which pushed in claustrophobically on what little space there was. When Karl saw the bed had a frame, he was relieved not to find a mattress with a rifle next to it. The room screamed *lone gunman* as it was.

"It's like he never moved in," James said.

Karl nodded. He didn't like that their target lived like this. Everywhere he looked, he saw signs of a life lived in the dead end of isolation. It was easy to picture Tom sitting in here by himself on weekends—so quiet and alone, he almost didn't exist.

The bookcase actually had a few books on it, and Karl's eyes stopped on a worn copy of *The Count of Monte Cristo*, which was interesting because it was probably the most famous revenge story ever written. Karl opened it up.

A photo fell out.

It was of two smiling boys, their skinny arms wrapped around each other. The younger one had to be Tom. He was maybe ten, but it was definitely him. The boy next to him was very different, but the resemblance was there. Karl was looking at Tom's brother. He was older, maybe fifteen, with disheveled hair. Something about him was familiar, but Karl couldn't place it. He was full-on belly laughing like whoever snapped the photo had just uttered the most perfect, hilarious thing he'd ever heard in his life. Tom was also smiling, like he didn't quite get the joke but could enjoy it through his brother, secondhand.

Karl smiled—but it died halfway up his face.

Eric Reese.

The boy standing next to Tom is Eric Reese.

Whatever Tom was doing, it wasn't for money or politics or state secrets. It was for his brother.

Karl felt James's presence behind him. "Give me a minute, will you?"

"Okay."

Karl heard him walk out of the apartment and close the door. He stood still, trying to stay calm. Eric Reese had finished undergrad at Johns Hopkins and his master's in molecular biology a few years after that. He was searching for the next thing, and Karl gave it to him. He recruited him for Prometheus.

The night the chimp got out of its enclosure and killed everyone in the lab, Eric had come to work late. When he saw Weaver had locked everyone in, he fled. A week later Karl tracked him down to a little motel on the outskirts of Paris. When Eric opened the door, he didn't seem all that surprised. He just nodded, looking ancient, like he'd seen it all and was now utterly exhausted by it.

"Come get a drink with me," Karl said.

Eric sighed. "How could you want a drink right now?"

"Jesus, how could you not?"

There was a time when Eric would have laughed at that. He was one of those people who was always ready to laugh at everyone's jokes.

At the bar, they sat alone on one end. It was 11:00 AM, and old men sipped drinks in silence.

"It's time to come back," Karl said.

Eric took a drink and stared into the glass.

"I don't think you understand. People are getting scared."

It took Eric a minute to say anything. When he did, it was just four words:

"You lied to me."

They'd told him the same thing they told Dr. Nast, that the stem cells were being developed to cure neuromuscular disease. It had made Karl sick every time Eric told him how grateful he was to be working on something so important to people's lives.

In some small way, he and Eric had been friends. That was when Karl realized he was not in any way this young man's friend. And he never had been.

They talked, and Eric had come back because that's what people in his position always did. He served out another couple of months as Dr. Nast's assistant and went home. Or so Karl had thought.

CHAPTER 15

100 BOULEVARD Gén Leclerc was Beaujon Hospital. A wing off the main building was only two stories high. Bogasian ran two steps up the side of it and jumped and caught a gutter pipe that extended roof-to-ground. He climbed hand over hand up to the seventh floor.

The windows were large and indented into the face of the building. Bogasian set his feet and lunged for the closest one. He caught the ledge with both hands and hung there until his weight settled. Then he let go.

He dropped to the window ledge below—the sixth floor, his real destination. When he landed, there was a moment when he could have lost his balance. His body started to drift away from the building, but he grabbed the wood frame around the window-panes with his fingertips and pulled himself back.

He peered into an unlit room with two rows of bed-ridden people. Cream-colored machines ran wires into their bodies.

He rocked a twelve-inch strip of wood side-to-side until it snapped off, then slipped two fingers over the glass pane and worked it free. He tucked the pane under his arm and reached in to unlock the window. After climbing into the room, he slid the glass back into the frame. Soundlessly he moved out of the light from the window and listened, but there was just the sucking and ticking of the machines.

He moved back into the light, which he didn't like, and toward the door to the hall. Midway, he had the vague feeling of being seen. He turned—

Someone on the bed was staring at him.

The body faced the ceiling, but the eyes were stretched in their sockets. They were fixed right on him.

As he moved closer, he could make out the decaying old person they belonged to. The teeth were missing, and the mouth hung open. Chunks of hair rotted on the scalp. He wasn't sure they were even attached to it.

Disgust slid up and down in his throat.

Gently he took the emergency-call cord between his forefinger and thumb and dropped it off the side of the bed. The eyes had seen him. He touched the throat, then put his other hand on it and started applying pressure.

He looked around the room at the others. All of them were motionless, in various stages of decomposition. He looked back at the one he had hold of—

The eyes were shut.

And they had been the whole time. He knew that now, just as he knew the hallucinations were getting worse.

The man resumed breathing as Bogasian eased his head back down on the pillow and pulled the sheet up to his chest.

He went to the door and peered down the hall. One cop was sitting outside Kotesh's door. Another was planted outside the nurses' station, chatting up a woman who was way too young for him. The rest of the hallway was relatively dark to help the patients sleep.

Bogasian glided down the hallway and seized the first guard. He clamped one hand over his mouth and another over the base of his skull and hoisted him in the air by the head. Then he backed into Kotesh's room and elbowed the door shut.

*   *   *

Bogasian left the lights off, so it was still dark as he watched the door swing open. The second guard shuffled in a little but didn't break the plane of the doorway. Only his head poked through.

It was quiet except for the clicks of Kotesh's machines.

"Louie?" the guard said. His head craned around, blind in the darkness.

The guard made his way into the bathroom, feeling around for a light switch. After a couple swipes, he hit it and froze. He stared at something in the bathroom mirror.

Then he whirled around and saw Louie folded into the corner of the room. Louie's face had turned dark purple.

The guard's eyes flicked to Kotesh. He was reclined on the bed with the right side of his face caved in. All the features stretched and pulled toward the low point, now his right eye.

Bogasian was standing by the window, exposed in silhouette. He merged back into the darkness.

The guard fumbled with his radio. By the time he got it to his mouth, he saw Bogasian. He tried to get away, but Bogasian caught him by the collar and punched him in the side of the head. He could feel the surprise running through the man's body like a current.

He pulled the fist with the collar down to the floor, pinning the guard's head against the linoleum. This time when he hit it, the head stayed in place. The second time, he felt the guard's skull give a little. Then it gave a lot.

CHAPTER 16

KARL'S EYES shot open.

He'd fallen asleep in his clothes on the bed at the Hotel Lotti. His heart was pounding, and he was trying to figure out why when he heard the phone ring again. He picked it up.

The deputy director of the CIA—a career politician—was already on his way to Paris. Marty had gotten the call with only an hour's notice, which itself was telling. The meeting would be at 9:00 AM.

Like all people in Special Activities, like all people who actually do something for a living, Karl hated politicians. He hated everything about them, from their creepy-perfect haircuts to the way there was something vaguely unreal about each one. Like someone had broken into a wax museum and, through some incantation, given one of the wax dummies a law degree and a vampiric bloodlust for "networking" and "thought leadership" and "horseshit." Since he'd joined the CIA, this petty hatred had metastasized into whatever hatred becomes after fear of losing one's job is added to it. Whenever the politicians arrived, work would cease, and questions had to be answered in this vague corporate-speak which Karl couldn't pull off without breaking down like Rain Man.

The fact they were here so quickly meant someone within the Beltway had an inkling of what was going on—and was shitting a brick.

Karl and Marty were in the hallway, almost to the conference room, when Marty stopped and turned to him. "They're going to pretend this is routine. Keep your answers short."

Karl nodded.

"You ready for this?"

Karl nodded again.

"Are you sure?" Marty said, as if to say, *I personally am not sure.*

"I was thinking I'd open with a joke about non-organic food. You know, let them know I share their concerns about what children today are putting in their bodies."

Marty sighed angrily, like he'd been expecting this. "Well, you'd only have to make amends for it later. Isn't that step five for you people?"

"Are you implying something?" Karl said. He sniffed his cup of coffee.

"Karl, I was speaking counterfactually. Are you telling me that today of all days, you put booze in your morning cup of…" Marty paused and glanced at the coffee as if there was a finger in it. Like most teetotalers, he was suspicious of alcohol and regarded other people's attraction to it as a disease ranking somewhere between smoking-related lung cancer and pedophilia.

"Do you have a mint?" Karl said.

"You know, you don't instill some confidence in these people, and they'll appoint their own team of investigators here. And once they find Prometheus, they'll go through our personal email, even our homes, to gather evidence against us." Marty turned around to walk into the conference room.

"I got something yesterday," Karl said.

Marty looked over to the conference room door to make sure no one was listening.

"I went to our John Doe's apartment, and I found a picture of him with someone we know. Eric Reese. We checked, and they're brothers, Marty."

Marty's face went blank. He looked away. "Why would Eric's brother come here?"

"You don't have a theory?"

Marty froze. "Are you working me, Karl?"

"I'm collaborating."

"That's nice. No, to answer your question, I don't have a theory. But you better get one, quick."

They watched each other for a moment. Then Marty backed into the conference room.

Karl took a few deep breaths and went over what he would say. Five minutes later he walked into the conference room. A dozen blank faces turned and looked at him, waiting to be impressed. There were two desk heads, their subordinates, a middle-aged woman Karl couldn't place, and the deputy director from the director of the CIA's office. No one introduced themselves.

Karl went to the front of the room. "I was brought in to find out who moved against Benjamin Kotesh and who ordered it. But we've had another development—"

"You mean in addition to a man who remains unidentified infiltrating, then busting out of, our embassy?" the director said.

"Yes, sir."

Everyone just stared at him.

Karl went on. "Another man, Alan Sarmad, also tied to organized crime, has turned up in the mix. Our people have discovered that Sarmad has financial ties to Kotesh and to Jonathan Nast. Which is why we think that at this point we're only seeing the pieces of a much-greater whole."

"There isn't time for this," the director said. "Marty brought you in—over my objections, I might add—to find the man who jumped that roof and killed Kotesh, not to blow this investigation out to include anyone who's ever done business with Kotesh."

"I know that, sir. But I found something better to do."

The director turned and looked at Marty—who, Karl knew,

was in a delicate situation. The director didn't outrank Marty morally, only formally, but he whispered in the ear of the man who did.

"Perhaps, sir," Karl said, "you should hear the voicemails left for the John Doe who was posing as our agent." He took out his phone and hit PLAY. "The voice you're about to hear is Maximilian Winter. He's a counterterrorism analyst for the German Federal Intelligence Service."

In the voice people use with someone they've spoken to a hundred times, a man said:

"Tom, Max here, just following up. We assume you received those reports, and that all was in order. I know we discussed getting the imaging in the next quarter, but we're wondering if we could move that up a month or two. Thank you. By the way, Gregor and I finally pulled the trigger! We'll be in Washington in…oh…three months— I'll get you the exact date!—and we're really looking forward to meeting everyone. Talk soon. Ciao."

"Just what the hell is that supposed to mean, 'imaging'?" the director said.

"He's referring to our satellite over Russia. In exchange for DNA reports on certain criminals, our John Doe promised the Germans access to images from our birds."

Every face in the room got a stricken look.

"What?" the director said.

"He's been doing this everywhere—using this office and posing as an agent of the Central Intelligence Agency to enter into agreements with police departments and intelligence services throughout Europe. They gave him DNA reports on people they've arrested who meet a certain profile, and he promised them access to our resources."

No one was able to speak. Probably they were all busy imagining the moment when some well-meaning foreign bureaucrat showed up, having done his part, now expecting them to do theirs.

Would they explain that technically there'd never been a deal because John Doe didn't work for them or would they just give the man what he wanted because this was one of those things where *anything* is better than the truth?

"And what does this Max guy mean when he says he's 'looking forward to meeting everyone'?" the director asked.

"As additional incentive, John Doe has been promising people meetings with high-level US government officials. I have a voice-mail from someone in the UK telling him he's looking forward to visiting the White House next month and playing racquetball with the president."

Someone in the room gasped.

"What in God's name is going on?" the director said.

"John Doe used those DNA reports to identify three people who left DNA on a shirt in our possession. Those three people are Alan Sarmad, Jonathan Nast, and Benjamin Kotesh. All three guys we've connected financially."

"What's the upshot?"

"John Doe's trying to find them for a reason, and the reason isn't just them. It's because they're connected to something bigger than them."

Karl didn't elaborate on that. He just stood there, waiting for Marty to take the reins. He'd always enjoyed watching Marty negotiate the "society" part of the job.

"In light of what happened at the embassy," Marty said, "we decided to task Karl exclusively with finding John Doe. But prior to that, Karl thought Alan Sarmad's involvement was a loose string, so he pulled on it. Now he has reason to believe investigating Sarmad will lead him full-circle — to John Doe."

"Then we should have been apprised of that," the director said. "How close are you to getting something definitive?"

Marty thought a moment, like giving this man the most exact, most thorough answer was a matter of life or death. All eyes in the room turned to him. It was so quiet Karl could hear the air-conditioning.

"Close," Marty said, and then he exhaled as though the thought that had gone into even this non-answer had exerted an almost physical toll on him.

"Can we expect something within forty-eight hours?"

Another pause, this one even more pregnant than the first. "Absolutely."

And the deeply sincere way Marty said this told Karl that this man wouldn't be getting a fucking thing from Marty in forty-eight hours. And probably not ever.

The director turned back to Karl. "Do we have any way of getting someone in to talk to Benjamin Kotesh?"

"He's dead," Marty said.

"What?"

"It just came out. He was found beaten to death in his hospital room. A nurse leaked it to a tabloid, and they were forced to confirm."

Karl remembered Tom's fight with the Marines. Beating a man to death didn't sound like his MO.

So who does it sound like?

Bogasian.

" 'Beaten to death,' " the director said. "Who would do such a thing?"

This is just the tip of the iceberg, Karl thought. *If I were to explain to you what this someone is capable of, I can money-back guarantee one of you freaking people would make pee-pee in your pants.*

The director snapped out of his thoughts and turned to Karl. "All right, so Kotesh is off the board. Let's go back to one. What kind of ties are we talking about between Sarmad and the others?"

"Our analysts have linked them to companies we believe are under common control," Karl said. "And the controlling entity, we believe, is Schroder-Sands."

"The pharma company?" the woman Karl didn't know said.

Karl nodded.

"They're a public company."

The director rocked up in his chair. "Schroder needs to go on the watch list immediately."

Marty bunched his napkin up and pushed it as far out of his vicinity as was socially acceptable. He kept staring at it. Now the whole room was watching the napkin. Marty leaned forward and, with the very tip of his finger, pushed the napkin exactly two inches farther away.

"I think we should do the opposite," he said without looking up.

The director swiveled his chair to look directly at him.

"Schroder is a perennial troublemaker," Marty said. "Two years ago they were caught loading banned chemicals on an Iranian freighter sailing under a false Hong Kong flag. Of course everyone is sailing under a false Hong Kong flag, and what everyone in this room would love to know is whether Hong Kong is the pimp or the prostitute in these situations."

Everyone chuckled knowingly.

"A few days ago," Marty continued, "the federal prosecutor in Berlin launched an undisclosed investigation into Schroder and several of its subsidiaries. According to my source, it's being co-ordinated with the tax authorities, which means it's major and they're looking for a conviction."

Karl's heartbeat picked up a couple beats. Marty hadn't mentioned an investigation.

"Now suddenly Schroder shows up in the mix with a body count approaching double digits." Marty looked up, engaged his audience. "Schroder is a go-between. Whatever they're doing, they're in the middle, same as Sarmad and the other men. Now the scary part: there's a primary mover behind all this, and we still have no idea who that is."

Marty shut up.

This, Karl knew, was one of Marty's unwritten rules: never explain enough to be completely understood. The willingness to believe something increases with the fear one has already somehow missed it.

The director looked deep in thought. "What are you proposing?"

"That Schroder be treated as a source of intelligence, not as a hostile. And that we allow Karl to swim through this maze of subsidiaries and see where he surfaces. That means making contact with Alan Sarmad and using his absolute discretion to get the information we need."

Karl was impressed—Marty didn't even glance at him. Schroder-Sands was the company Marty had partnered with to keep Prometheus's costs under the radar of congressional budget appropriators. They both knew more about that firm than they would ever let on this side of a courtroom.

The director looked at the woman. This was the second time he'd done it, and that told Karl who she was. She must work for the director of National Intelligence, the head of the entire US intelligence community. Even the director's boss reported to her boss. And since her boss reported directly to the president, this meant that Marty's quiet little investigation had drawn the interest of the White House.

"What are you going to tell the French?" the director asked.

"Nothing," Marty said.

"They're going to want something in exchange for operating in their country."

"At this point we haven't even told them Karl is in-country."

The woman and the director both winced.

Marty didn't seem to notice. "Europe is bankrupt," he said. "The Europeans just don't know it yet. They're not going to like us doing anything that threatens the lifeblood of a major employer.

And we can't trust our counterparts in the intelligence community. The bureaucratic class here has grown into one of those morbidly obese shut-ins who require 500 calories an hour or they will pass out. And now that the neighbors are starving to death, fatty is desperate to justify each and every calorie. If we tell our counterparts here about this, they are going to create so much work for us it would make a Teamster blush."

Everyone smiled at this except Karl. He was just watching everything unfold in mild awe.

The director was nodding. "But how do you use Karl in a way that keeps us off the front page of the *New York Times*?"

"If he resigns, that's too easy to see through. I think we should terminate him for performance effective nine months ago. Then I want him hired retroactively as a Chinese-walled-up-to-his-colon contractor providing training for my group. And I want to know right now if anyone objects to it."

No one said anything. And with that, Marty had sealed off whatever Karl reported to him from the rest of the CIA, the rest of the intelligence community, even from the president. And the son of a bitch had done it in the name of *advancing* everyone's knowledge.

"Karl, I assume you're on board with this?" Marty said.

Karl was quiet a moment. Marty asked for permission to do this, set him up to be disowned if needed, almost as an afterthought. *Karl, if we encounter the wolves, I'm going to need to trip you, so they take you first. I assume you're on board with this?*

"Oh, I'm sure I'll be like a pig in shit. Thank you for asking, Marty," Karl said.

Marty stared at him for a moment and then cleared his throat. "Is there anything else?"

Karl opened his briefcase and took out photos he'd gotten late last night. He handed them to Marty, who passed them to the others.

"This is a shipping container leased to Schroder-Sands by a company associated with Alan Sarmad," Karl said. "Someone at the company misplaced some customs paper, and they had to search inside."

Karl waited for the director to get to the last picture and see what looked like a pair of shop-made leg irons. The irons had chains attached to them, and the chains snaked out of the light from the flash and disappeared into the unseen depths of the container.

"Jonathan Nast, the man whose body we just found in Paris, worked for Sarmad's company. When customs asked him about this a month ago, he claimed to be a Schroder-Sands representative and said these chains were used to secure loose equipment. The port authority bought his story, but not before an employee snapped a picture with a cell phone."

The director looked at the woman, then back at Karl. "What the hell are these people up to?"

"It appears they're trying to move something—people—throughout Europe. And whatever they're doing, it's probably the reason our John Doe is killing them."

He left out the last part.

There's only one reason you use leg irons like those, and that's to restrain someone who's a danger to his handlers.

"When in the hell did you find out the Germans were investigating Schroder?" Karl asked Marty as they left the conference room.

"A few hours ago."

"Is that why all these people are turning up dead? Is someone at Schroder trying to cover their tracks?"

"Schroder's a public company now. They don't have the balls to do something like this. I meant what I said: they're just a middleman. It's their principal that scares me."

"Shit."

"Yes."

"But they don't have anything that implicates the CIA. The people at Schroder only knew us, not the agency. There's no connection for the investigators to find, right?"

"That's the way it starts out."

Marty's phone buzzed. He checked it quickly, but then he stayed there, staring at the screen. He looked up. "Come over here."

They went to another conference room. Marty shut the door and turned on the TV to the BBC. A newswoman sat behind a desk, looking into the camera as she spoke. In the corner of the screen, there were stills from black-and-white security cameras. Karl recognized the man in them: Benjamin Kotesh.

"Again the stills you're seeing are from video taken three years ago at a Paris hospital. It appears Benjamin Kotesh, recently deceased, was seen here stealing the bodies of fetuses that had been aborted, some as recently as fifteen minutes before he arrived to take their remains."

A new picture came up. This one showed Kotesh in a parking lot with a second man, whose face was hidden by a baseball cap. Karl was looking at himself three years ago. He remembered everything, the parking lot, the car he'd driven there, even the heartburn he'd had from some gruesome German street meat he'd eaten beforehand.

Marty leaned toward the screen. "Is that... is that you?"

"Of course not."

Anchor: "Authorities are looking for two suspected accomplices. One of them is this man seen here in the parking lot with Kotesh, and the other is a man named Alan Sarmad. Sarmad is believed to have employed Kotesh over the last three years."

Marty turned to Karl. "This is cancer." He shook his head. "Never mind what you told those compliance monkeys in there. Where are you really with finding Tom Reese or Bogasian?"

"We're making progress."

"'Making progress' is what weak, stupid people say they're doing when really they're just playing house. Tell me you have a lead
that's tangible."

I have nothing remotely tangible, Karl thought.

"We're searching Nast's hard drive," he said.

"And that's it? *Jesus Christ.*"

"You haven't really given me much to go on here."

"If you can't find Bogasian or Tom Reese, then you need to find
Alan Sarmad or Dr. Nast." Marty started to walk away, then circled back. "I don't care what you have to do, or who you have
to lean on, but these people need to be dealt with. This is why
I brought you back. I don't want some dickless, well-intentioned
analyst trying to do his best. I want *you* to do *your thing.*"

Marty walked out.

Karl went back to his office, thinking. The news report was terrible, but it wasn't without intelligence value.

*Now we know why Kotesh had all that security with him and why
Nast was holed up in his house. They must have gotten wind of the
fact the authorities were searching for them. And they'd known how
well it'd go down with their new employer, whoever that was.*

Now Sarmad is next. After they see this, they have to kill him.

As Karl walked over to his desk, James was waiting in his office.

"We got something," he said. "I found some receipts on Nast's
hard drive, sir. They're for a place in London—Ravi's Self-Storage."

Karl sat down and rocked steadily in his chair.

"You told us to flag Schroder-Sands if it came up in anything,"
James said. "Well, a subsidiary of Schroder leases a warehouse
right down the street. The warehouse burned down yesterday."

Karl stopped rocking.

He'd flagged Schroder not because he wanted to find anything
more but because he didn't. Schroder-Sands had no reason to
continue showing up because it shouldn't still be connected to
Prometheus three years after the program had been liquidated.

And yet Jonathan Nast had claimed to be a representative of the company just a month ago.

"Look," James said, "I know the connection between Schroder and this self-storage place is thin—"

"Everything we do is thin."

"You want to know what the London police think about the warehouse fire?"

"Not really. Cops are just janitors with guns."

"Cops don't carry firearms in England."

"You're not exactly raising my opinion of them."

"They think it was the work of animal rights activists, protesting Schroder's testing on rhesus monkeys."

Karl smiled. If he were a cop, he'd probably have thought the same thing.

"Where'd you get this?" he said.

"A friend from my Cambridge semester abroad. We used to play squash. Want me to go to London?"

"No, but send me the address for the storage place." Karl picked up the phone. "Nice work."

James excused himself.

Karl deleted the video file of Tom's engagement with the Marines. Then he took a pair of scissors and destroyed the hard drive the file had been on.

A few hours later he headed out to catch the 6:13 PM train to London.

CHAPTER 17

TOM WAITED for Silvana by his car, alternately looking at the yachts going into Le Port and the women on Nice's stone beach. He could never in his life have imagined a place like this. French-women aged seven to seventy were sunning themselves wearing only string-bikini bottoms. Everywhere he looked, he saw breasts—breasts beginning to rise, breasts beginning to fall. Just minutes ago, at a stoplight, he'd noticed a bronze woman adjusting her bikini straps, perfectly unaware of her almost total nudity. And he'd felt like a pervert twice over—first when Silvana caught him and then a moment later when he realized the woman was the same age his mother would have been.

To his other side was an endless row of cafés, bars, and luxury shops. They were like the rest of the city: no matter how bright it was outside, they looked dark, like they were hiding something.

Outside the shops, there was a line of Mercedes. No BMWs, no Jaguars, just Mercedes. These belonged either to bored-looking old men surrounded by angry-looking young men or to Arab families without a single article of clothing not marked G for "Gucci." At one point Tom guessed that everyone within thirty yards of him was a participant in the offshore banking system.

He looked over at Silvana, chatting with a man at a newsstand. The man had a map open for her and was smiling at something she'd said. He stood watching her. He couldn't imagine what it must be like, to be so comfortable, to be your best self, around other people.

He looked away, and when he turned back, Silvana was standing next to him. She opened the map and pointed to Rue Olivier de Serres outside Nice.

"Sarmad has this huge mansion. It's along here somewhere."

According to the scale of the map, she was pointing to a 10-kilometer stretch of real estate near the water.

"Okay," he said. "Now, you're sure you don't remember any part of the address? Even a number or two—"

She batted this away. "I'll know it when I see it."

Over the next few hours, he heard this line a lot. When he pressed her for a description of the property, when he asked if anything looked familiar, when he asked her anything at all: "I'll know it when I see it."

Twenty minutes later they were outside Nice, high in the jagged cliffs overlooking the Mediterranean. Eventually they wound their way to a flat remote area about 500 feet above sea level. He noticed Silvana staring at a set of thick iron gates, the kind that seemed like they should have the owner's initials on them.

Trying not to break her concentration, Tom pulled onto the shoulder so gently Silvana didn't seem to notice.

Her feet were on the gravel before he'd completely come to a stop. She walked a little closer to the gates, then turned.

"Yeah." She started nodding. "Yeah, this is it."

"You're sure, you're—"

"I think." The nodding stopped. "I think."

She was looking at the next estate, which also had thick iron gates.

"Just take a minute," he said.

"Damn it."

"One minute."

"It's one of these two, I can't remember which."

He had to be sure, so they walked to the intercom box. Silvana pressed the buzzer. She waited four seconds, then hit it again.

The intercom clicked. U2 was playing in the background.

"Allô?"

Silvana hit TALK. "Hello?"

"Allô?"

Tom intercepted Silvana's hand on the way to the TALK button.

"This isn't the place," he said.

They walked over to the second mansion's gates and continued along the stone wall surrounding the property. Tom grabbed the top of the wall and pulled himself up high enough to look over. A man was on the roof, looking in their direction. As Tom was about to drop back down, he noticed motion sensors in the top of the wall. He ran his hand over one.

Two more men, bodyguards like the first one, appeared outside. Tom let go and motioned Silvana back to the car.

"That's it?" she said.

"It is for now."

CHAPTER 18

ALL TRAINS rock back and forth, even the Eurostar, which was approaching 200 miles per hour. The rocking put Karl to sleep. Always did. That was his last thought as he let his eyelids close and smiled to himself like a boy with a secret.

When he woke up and looked out the window, the train was whipping past a gap in the forest. It was flat with bushes the size of a Buick. The moonlight made it all glow with the cold burn of silver. He could never go on a train ride without passing at least one spot where he'd have liked to hit PAUSE and stay—suspended—until he was ready to move on.

This one reminded him of home, of the brute flatness of the prairie. Either South Dakota called to something ancient in you or it didn't. It did this at random times in his life, like when he was nineteen, home from an East Coast college, and all his friends—even their parents—were a little unsure around him, so everyone drank to compensate. That night he walked home alone, carrying his shoes, and even though he was on a street with houses, there was nothing beyond them. And he liked that. He liked that if society's control over you ever got too much, or if the shit simply hit the fan, you could opt out. You could always run out there into all that wilderness and just disappear.

He wondered suddenly why he'd left. He knew the reasons at the time: opportunity, career, a one-time chance to do a truly worthwhile thing. He remembered the time he told his dad he wasn't coming home. For a second he'd seen it in his dad's face, how much he wanted him back. But then his dad said in a soft voice, *You'll always have a bed here. You should know that.*

After that, every time Karl came home to his family, he was more and more of a stranger to them. Everyone started to get polite. That was the death rattle: good manners.

Now here he was, on the other side of the planet, about to do ugly things to stop something far uglier from getting into the hands of the wrong people. And the fact was he'd helped make this ugly thing. Being here, he wasn't doing the world a favor. He was cleaning up his own mess.

When he was younger, he believed something that turned out to be a lie. He thought that if he did good things, that goodness would last him forever. Before Prometheus, he even felt he'd done some of those things—in Iraq, in Afghanistan, in Europe. But it was the classic soldier's trap. You went away. You did something at great risk to yourself, thinking what you'd done would become a kind of permanent capital, a 401(k) of character, that would carry you through the victory lap that was to be the rest of your life. But then you came home, and a week later—not even a freaking month—as you once again became a job applicant, a father, number 16 in the line at the deli, you realized you were right where you started. You were just like everyone else. And everything you'd done was very nice and very impressive, but it was the past. And the past is never enough to power a life.

As Karl's eyes slid shut and his thoughts began to dissolve into nothing, something else occurred to him. If the charges against him were dropped, he could finally go home. But the house in Maryland was in foreclosure and his wife was dead, so he didn't know where that was anymore.

* * *

Karl jerked awake in his seat. For a second, he didn't know where he was. There were commands in mid-sentence over a loudspeaker. Door chimes sounded over and over, more urgently each time. People outside were rushing away from the train. No one was inside except him.

As he got up, he saw he'd sweated through his clothes. He gathered his things, found a cab, and gave the driver the address for Ravi's Self-Storage.

The taxi hadn't passed another car in a mile when the wind and rain started. It was already overcast, but in seconds the world had changed. Turned against them.

The neighborhoods went from working class to underclass, and the driver stopped braking at yield signs. And as they drove past a dripping swastika spray-painted on a wall, even Karl got a little uneasy—even when he remembered he was white and nominally Christian and technically in the clear on that one.

Ravi's Self-Storage was miles deep in an industrial park where all the businesses had closed, some for the night, most forever. And the farther they went, the more it felt like they were leaving the world, not going to a point within it.

As they passed an alley, Karl saw a trashcan burning. No one was standing around it.

The driver hunched forward, trying to see through the rain. Row after row of buses and trucks lined the road, their grilles watching it like faces. The only sound over the rain was the timed whine of the windshield wipers. So when the driver said something, Karl didn't really catch it. He only looked up when the car stopped suddenly.

"How much farther?" the driver said. He sounded nervous.

The plexiglass that protected him from his customers was so dirty and ruined with sticker marks that Karl couldn't see a man in the front seat, only a set of eyes watching him in the rearview.

He looked at the map on his phone. "About a mile."

The driver didn't say anything. Karl waited him out. They sat there for half a minute before the cab started to creep forward again.

When they reached Ravi's, as soon as Karl cracked the door, the wind pinned it open. He got out and hauled back on it until he could stuff it closed. Then he crossed the street looking for an office. The wind was bending a white piece of paper inside a plastic sleeve tied to a chain-link fence. Karl straightened it and read: RAVI'S SELF-STORAGE IS CLOSING. THERE IS NO LONGER CASH OR ANYTHING OF VALUE IN THE OFFICE. ☺

He slid back into the taxi and heard a beep. A touch screen facing his seat lit up and flashed: AMOUNT OWED: £74.67.

He slipped two £50 notes into a change holder in the plexiglass divider. There was a pause, and then two cigarette-stained fingers fished them out.

"I'll give you another hundred when I get back," Karl said.

Ducking his head, he ran across the street.

Ravi's was a maze of hundreds of purple garage doors and blacktop in between. Karl stopped under an overhang before his clothes could soak through and looked for the management office. When he glanced back at the street, the cab was pulling away. He watched until its taillights disappeared in the distance behind a rise in the road.

He looked around the area for a gas station, something to indicate the presence of other people. But the only lights were the ones lining the road and the red warning bulbs running up a skeletal tower on the horizon. For a moment he felt how alone he was.

He kept walking.

To recap, four men left their DNA on the shirt at the lab. One had been killed in his home. Another had been beaten to death in a French hospital. Now only two remained. One was a man who'd never been identified, and the other was Alan Sarmad. Sarmad was Tom's only lead, which meant he was Karl's only lead.

Bogasian was another story. It was unclear how he fit in. Certainly he was being used under the new program to kill off players from the old program. But why? Why bother to kill such dangerous people? Yes, there was the investigation into Schroder, and, yes, it would lead to Kotesh and Sarmad, but so what? That was Karl and Marty's problem, not Bogasian's new principal's.

Unless Nast, Kotesh, and Sarmad had helped steal Bogasian from Marty.

In that case, the Schroder investigation would lead right to the new owners because Nast and the others knew who they were.

So what does that tell you?

Whoever was running the new program had something to do with the old program. There was no other way they could have infiltrated it so completely.

But who could have done that?

He didn't know.

He found himself wondering what Bogasian was up to right now. He told himself to withhold speculation on this, not let his mind run like it wanted to at unsafe speeds. But he didn't like it, the thought of Bogasian out there—somewhere. He imagined what Bogasian would do to him if he happened to show up here and find himself alone with the man who'd recruited him. Karl knew he wouldn't even have the right to protest his innocence— because that was the thing: he wasn't innocent.

He looked around suddenly.

Ravi's Self-Storage stretched out in front of him like a ghost town. The row he stood in led up a couple hundred feet where it split. He put his head down and ran. At the intersection, he looked both ways and saw a mirror image of what he'd seen before: each road was lined with purple garage doors.

He chose left just to make a decision and get moving. The

pounding of the rain made it impossible to hear anything, and Karl kept glancing over his shoulder. At the end of the next row, he found a graffiti-covered trailer that looked like it'd been dropped on the pavement from the sky.

He tried the door. Locked. He went around to the side. The graffiti there was eerily frank:

> Help me
> *The Lord helps those who help themselves, friend*
> *I lost my job and my wife*
> *Then kill yourself*

The metal grate on one of the windows was loose. So he worked it back and forth until he could pull it off and smash the window with his elbow.

Once he climbed inside, he hit the light switch. Desks lined the walls, and lopsided stacks of paper teetered on top of everything. In the center of the room, there was one telephone that everyone could face and compete for. The desks seemed to be comprised of wood composite and snot, and the wood paneling surrounding them was of the same technology as cardboard. The room resembled the office of a real business the way sea monkeys resemble those primates who play chess with researchers at Yale.

Karl was gratefully surprised, however, when the filing cabinet still had files inside. There were receipts going back to the time Nast started renting a locker, two years ago. But when Karl glanced at the name of the person who'd initially opened the account, it wasn't Jonathan Nast. It was an alias used by Alan Sarmad.

Karl found a key and a foot-long flashlight and went to the unit number on the forms. It was at the end of the complex, facing a field, and it was bigger than the others. There was a regular door next to a twenty-foot loading bay. He unlocked it.

The wind whistled through the doorway and went silent in the dark.

He stepped in and moved along the wall, out of the light from outside. He stood there listening.

A gust of wind sent a faint scream through the doorway. The door creaked on its hinges.

He clicked on the flashlight. The beam was narrow and tight. He swept it around the room, carving the darkness. He was standing in a storage bay with fifty-foot ceilings. Stairs led up to an office with windows overlooking the bay. As his flashlight moved across them, shadows of office equipment stretched across the ceiling like fingers reaching for something.

He found a light switch, and as he walked over to it, the sound of his steps expanded through the room, announcing his presence.

When he flipped the switch, no lights came on. He shined his flashlight up on the ceiling and saw the panels for fluorescent lights were empty. Someone didn't want to make it easy to poke around here, day or night.

He swept the flashlight around again. The room was empty except for a large white chest freezer. It sat against the middle of the far wall, perfectly centered, like an altar. He noticed a large padlock on it. When he walked closer, he heard the hum of a motor.

He stood there watching it, then went to the office and found a hammer. On his way back, he kept looking behind him and down the corridors of purple doors he passed. His heart was slamming in his chest.

In the unit, he put the flashlight on the ground behind him, facing the freezer, so he could see his work. The light threw his shadow on the wall. And as he jimmied the lock, he kept seeing the shadow and thinking there was a man walking up to him from behind.

As he was prying the last bolt out of the freezer, there was a metallic crash outside. He froze, waiting for another sound. Then he clicked off the flashlight and walked across the room in the dark. When he opened the door and looked out, he found an over-turned trashcan blowing around on the pavement. He closed the door. Locked it this time.

He finished working the last bolt out. When he opened the freezer, he didn't know what he was looking at until he saw the face.

Karl lurched back, and the freezer lid slammed shut. The sound echoed around him. He took a few breaths, then opened the lid and looked in again.

A young man was hunched over in the compartment.

Ice grew over half his head like moss. He looked as though he'd snuck in and nodded off. And as Karl reached in, for a moment he felt like he would lightly slap him awake and tell him everything was going to be okay.

But then Karl leaned in farther. Now he saw the rest of the man's face.

The man's mouth hung open, twisted in fear and pain, like he'd died not just scared, but scared of something incomprehensible to him. His eyes stared out of the tight flesh-mask that was his face. It was a look unlike any Karl had ever seen. When most people died, even from violence, they died gently. The rest offered by death became easier than the fight offered by life, and they accepted it.

This man rejected it. He'd died resisting and uncomprehending and rejecting it all.

There was no body. The young man's head was frozen into the side of a pile of ice and clothes. When Karl lifted a flap of cloth, he saw the back and sides of the skull had been surgically re-moved.

He stepped back and let the freezer door drop shut. In the si-lence, the sound was startling.

They're trying to inject people. They've failed with this one, but eventually they'll get it right.

He opened the lid again, sat on the edge of the freezer, and kicked apart the ice and pulled out the clothes that had been wadded up inside. They were too stiff for him to rifle the pockets, so he dumped them on the floor and waited for them to thaw. He stood there for fifteen minutes, alternately watching the pants and going outside to check the road.

When they were soft enough, he went through the shirt pockets first and then the pants. No wallet, only some change. He turned the pants inside out and noticed a little pocket accessible only from the inside. It was on the thigh, where no one would touch it during a pat down. Inside, a torn corner of stationery with an address: Bella Vista Hotel, 2567 Olivier. No city, no country.

He plugged it into his phone. The Bella Vista Hotel came up outside Nice, France. But it was exactly one mile down the road from 2567 Olivier. Karl knew this trick: if anyone found the paper and checked the address, they'd think the man had simply written it down wrong. But the address wasn't for the Bella Vista.

His phone rang. James.

"Sir, I'm just checking in—"

"I need you to scramble a charter in London to fly me to Nice. And I need you to meet me down there."

James clicked off. Karl called a taxi and waited in a shadow by the road.

Three years ago.

They were two days into the procedures before one of the chimps picked the lock to its cage and killed two people outside Paris. Afterward, when Karl came to visit Bogasian, he was recuperating from two eight-hour operations that had traumatized every major muscle in his body, his spine, his adrenal glands, and his brain.

His brain. It was all Karl could think about.

When Karl appeared in the glass window looking into Bogasian's room, Bogasian had perked up at the familiar face and somehow lifted his arm enough to wave. Karl waved back. He stayed even after Bogasian fell back asleep—as if being there could stop what would happen.

Months later, Bogasian changed. First, it was his muscles. Before the injections, Bogasian could bench 275 pounds. After them, he could bench 645. That is, he could bench at least that much. At that point they'd run out of plates to add to the barbell.

When he arrived, Bogasian could run at a top speed of 23 miles per hour. Usain Bolt, the world record holder in the 100-meter sprint, maxed out at 28 miles per hour. By the time Bogasian left, they clocked him at 37 miles per hour.

Timothy McVeigh, the Oklahoma City bomber, once said, "Science is my religion." Karl had always thought that was the batshit-crazy nonsense of a mass murderer who'd wasted 168 innocent people. But the more Karl watched Bogasian, the more he understood Bogasian had a power that had only existed in imagination. And even then, even if you stopped to think about it, it was something that should only belong to a god.

The project had been named after Prometheus, the Titan who according to Greek mythology had taught man to hunt, farm, and read. But when he gave man fire, the gods felt he'd gone too far. Zeus chained him to a rock where each day an eagle came and ate his liver, which would grow back because he was immortal, only to be eaten again the next day.

Everyone thought the man they'd created was a miracle. For a while, Karl thought what happened to the chimps might not happen to the man.

Then Bogasian said his brain felt different.

For weeks, his eyes were red. Karl thought he'd been crying.

One day he told Karl about the body of a boy he'd seen in Iraq. The boy had been hit by a truck and left on the side of the road. Bogasian said the way the boy was lying there, he looked the same way his college girlfriend did when she was sleeping.

He was lucky, Bogasian said. *He got out before he suffered, and for everyone else it was the other way around.*

He was crazy. That much became obvious to Karl. But what was scary was how good he was at it. Even though everyone else was becoming suspicious, Bogasian made sure not to do anything that might harden those suspicions into action. And once Karl brought up his concern about the things he said, Bogasian never mentioned them again.

The more disturbed a person is, the fewer mistakes he is allowed. Soon Bogasian removed all error from his life and work.

Meanwhile he was in a private hell that Karl couldn't even begin to imagine. And a horror would be set in motion. If a person can be defined as what he has done rather than what he will do, then Bogasian, as Karl knew him, wouldn't come out the other side.

Neither would two women in St. Petersburg.

A mother and her little girl. They were relatives staying the night with a target. Bogasian said they'd seen him. The newspaper said they were still asleep in their beds. It also said the fractures to their spines were consistent with a head-on collision at fifty miles per hour.

CHAPTER 19

AFTER TOM and Silvana left Sarmad's compound, Tom drove them to their motel. On the way back, he stopped at a little grocery, so they could get food for the night.

"How much money do we have left?" Silvana said. "I'm almost afraid to ask."

He counted it out and placed the bills on the center console. "215 euros."

She sucked air through her teeth. They sat looking at the stack of bright red, orange, and blue bills.

"That's our nest egg," she said. "Looks kind of sad, doesn't it?"

"I'm American. No matter how hard I try, this stuff looks like it goes with a child's board game."

"I think it's pretty."

"It looks like it's about to go to a rave."

She got out of the car and looked back at him through the open window. "So what's our food budget for the next twelve hours?"

"Fifteen euros."

"Each?"

"For both of us."

"Fifteen euros...fuck me." She thought about it. "You realize we're going to run out of money. What about shoplifting? I mean, is that on the table?"

He stared at her. "Would you like to shoplift?"

"No, I'm too scared."

"But it's okay for me to do it for you."

She grinned. "Like most people, I would never drive drunk, but if it's late and I'm hungry, I have no problem whatsoever getting in a car with someone who is." She put her hands on top of the car and leaned in, so their faces were close. "Don't look at me like that."

"Like what?"

"Like it pleases you that I'm beneath you morally. You know what? Almost all the money we have you took from me."

"I feel terrible about that."

"Clearly. I suppose if you decided to rape me, you'd expect me to stop thinking only of myself and start thinking about how we can work together to get it done."

He smiled. "You've been very helpful. I'd never deny that."

She leaned back, assessing him. "You're kind of a strange guy, you know that? You're silent *for hours*. And when I ask you something, half your answers aren't even in actual words. 'When are we stopping for food?' *'Mmmm, an hour.'* 'Where are you from originally?' *'Mmmm, America.'* It's like talking to Billy Bob Thornton in *Sling Blade*." She imitated his voice in Frankenstein monotone and her own in sweet, blameless falsetto. "But then out of the blue, you just suddenly hatch into this social butterfly and won't stop talking."

"Technically butterflies don't hatch. They pupate."

"Yeah, I think we've isolated our problem right there."

It was awkward to look directly at each other with their faces just three feet apart. For a moment they both watched an old man in a white T-shirt work under the hood of a car.

"Are you doing okay?" Tom looked at her. "With everything?"

She thought about it, softened. "Yeah..."

He turned back to the old man. "I could watch him all day. I don't know why."

"He's engaged in his work."

Tom nodded.

"Or maybe you like it because he's doing it without anyone else's help."

He laughed. "Maybe."

They watched the old man wipe his hands and squint at the sun.

"Thank you," Tom said. "For working with me and everything. I don't know where I'd be without you."

She seemed surprised, even flattered. And yet there was a sadness there as well. Like she wished more of life involved doing things that meant something to somebody.

"You really aren't like most other guys I know." She'd stopped smiling.

"How's that?"

"You seem like the kind of guy who goes home for Christmas break and then gets a job at the mall, so he can afford presents on his own."

She looked at the old man a bit longer and then held out her hand. He gave her the money, and she went inside.

He watched her through the window. And when she took her time picking everything out, he took it as a sign that she wouldn't run off and instead actually intended to stay and cook her dinner.

While she was in the store, he took some cash he hadn't told her about and went into a corner phone mart and bought two prepaid SIM cards and two Motorola phones with GPS. The man behind the counter asked for an ID and an address. Tom gave him Adrien Michel's national identity card.

When he got back to the car, Silvana was still in the grocery store.

On one of the phones, he downloaded a GPS program designed to locate the phone in case it got lost.

As soon as they got back to the motel, Silvana headed for the bathroom. While she washed her hands, Tom buried the phone with the tracking program in the depths of her purse.

When she came out, she sat at the table and methodically consumed a slab of smoked Gouda cheese and 75 percent of a box of crackers. Tom ate a pre-made sandwich. They talked only when she stopped for air.

Then Tom stood up and went to the door.

"I'll be back in a couple hours," he said.

"Are you going to do something—I don't know—wrong?"

"I don't think so," he said.

"What does that mean?"

"It means I don't think it's wrong."

They caught each other's eyes.

"You're not bringing anyone else back here, are you?" she said. "That's not what we—"

"I don't know anyone here, much less someone I'd bring back."

"What do you want with Alan Sarmad?"

He just looked at her. Her eyes dropped down to the table, and she hunched forward, making her shoulders look tiny. It was awful, watching her sit like that.

"What if you don't come back?" she asked.

"I left all our money in my bag. Well, your money."

She managed a small laugh.

"I realize you could just take off with it. I'm really hoping you give me at least four hours before you do that."

She laughed quietly again. "I will."

"That's what you'd say even if you weren't." He smiled.

"Yeah, probably."

"I should be back in an hour or two." He said it like it was something that would cheer her up.

She nodded without looking at him.

He left and closed the door behind him, softly, as though he didn't want to disturb her.

CHAPTER 20

KARL SAT on the charter plane, waiting for takeoff to Nice—to the address he'd found in the freezer.

The tarmac was empty. The boarding area had been too. He hadn't even seen the pilot when he got on the plane. People said the ocean was the last desert. But they were missing what was right in front of them. The last desert was what it had always been: the dead of night.

It had been a long day, and he was boozing. Not a lot. Nothing crazy, but some. An old-fashioned of redneck vintage. Lots of ice, lots of bitters, and half a packet of sugar. It looked like pruno, the stuff prison inmates brewed in their toilets.

He'd never been a regular drinker. He didn't have beer after work or wine with dinner. But every so often the clouds parted and the moon got too close. Episodic drinking—that was what AA would call it. Shedding his inhibitions and doing exactly what he'd always wanted—that was what his father would call it.

He smiled at that. Then in honor of his dad's memory, he jimmied open the locked snack cabinet on the plane and emptied the enormous basket of pretzels and cookies into his bag and began pulling them out and eating them, one by one.

His phone buzzed.

"There's something you should see," James said.

"What is it?"

"While Nast was in Morocco three years ago, an American was murdered there. The thing is: I think it could be the guy from the photo in John Doe's apartment."

Eric Reese, Tom's brother. Karl hadn't said anything to James yet.

"Tell me you got a name for him," he said.

"He was never identified."

"Then how do you know he was American?"

"I'm sending you the link. There was a video..."

The clip was simply titled *American Shot in Tangier*. The young man in it looked about twenty-five years old. Though he was blindfolded and the video was grainy, Karl knew immediately that it was Eric Reese.

The camera moved over him. Close in on the nose. Pan over to the cheek, which had a welt on it. Pull back to reveal that he was on his knees, caked with sweat. He was swaying back and forth a little, his hands tied behind him, and Karl guessed he had a high-grade fever.

Karl's eyes stopped on his shirt. Blue-and-gray flannel. It was the one the tech had shown him.

Eric lost his balance, and a hand reached into frame and righted him gently. The camera moved in on Eric's face. It held this angle without moving. For a moment Karl thought the camera was going to be turned off.

The barrel of a gun entered the frame.

It stopped six inches from Eric's head. The hand holding the gun turned slightly, and Karl saw a scar: two raised, pinkish zippers crossing each other, the result of a crude field dressing. Something about the hand turn seemed purposeful, like the scar was meant to be seen.

A shot.

Eric collapsed and was still. Karl put the phone down and sat without moving for a long time.

Then he picked up the phone, zoomed in on the murderer's scar, and saved it as a picture. He rewound the video until he could see Eric's face. He sat there, staring at it, out of breath even though he hadn't moved.

He dialed the office in Paris. Henry answered.

"Of all the guys who've been body-bagged, did any of them have a scar on his hand?"

Silence on the other end as Henry searched through their photos.

"Which hand?" Henry asked.

"The left."

"I don't think so. The scar, what's it mean for us?"

"It means our guy isn't finished."

Karl hung up.

There was an empty glass on the glossy wood table next to him. He raked his hand across it. The glass hit the wall of the plane with a thud but didn't break. He'd wanted it to shatter into a thousand pieces.

The video is over two years old, which means Eric had never gone home after Prometheus liquidated. Which means if he'd never met you, he'd still be on the East Coast, taking care of his little brother.

He wondered if Tom knew he'd just spent two days with the man who'd recruited his brother and involved him in the very thing that got him killed. He remembered Tom during the car ride after finding Jonathan Nast's body. He'd been too eager to hear about Karl's wife and laughed too appreciatively at Karl's jokes about Osama's taste in porn. Like he was happy to be having a conversation with someone. Happy just to be included.

Karl knew Tom and Eric's parents were dead, and he thought of Tom cut loose in the world, cocooned in some apartment he never left, surrounded by other young people who were starting careers, putting down roots, moving forward. While they were entering the future, Tom had both feet in the past.

Karl wasn't sure how long he stayed slumped in his seat, but eventually something his dad once said came to him: *There comes a point in every person's life where he's forced to confront the fact that what he's been is all he's ever going to be. He can accept it and maybe for the first time in his life become aware of his soul. Or he can get angry.*

Karl got angry. And eventually an idea came to him.

You're responsible for one boy's death. And yet even though you don't deserve it, you've been given a gift. He has a brother who's going to get himself killed, and you can help him.

What he couldn't do for Bogasian, he maybe could do for Tom. He could get him to a doctor or a specialist. Maybe they could take the stem cells out, or at least do something to alleviate the symptoms.

And what about the CIA?

He had no answer to that one.

But there was another problem. If Tom was anything like Bogasian, he was a ticking time bomb. And as Karl cataloged what he knew about Tom, what he came up with was pretty much nothing. He knew Tom's family was from Bozeman, Montana, one of the states which produced the most soldiers per capita. He knew Tom's father did something with computers, and his mother taught Sunday school. He knew—from Eric—that the elderly couple next door paid kids to shovel their driveway and mow their lawn, but Tom and Eric always did it for free because their parents told them to.

Really he didn't know anything about Tom Reese.

What do you call a young man with nothing, who's willing to go all the way for a cause? You call him a radical—if you disagree with him. And if you think he's right?

Then there isn't even a word for what he is. In the eyes of society, there is only order and disorder, and order is better.

All Karl really knew was that Tom was a little person, some nothing in the grand scheme of things, who'd risen up and done the impossible. He'd come from another continent and systematically hunted down the people who'd killed his brother, and he was willing to sacrifice himself to do it.

It was something that people just didn't do. No matter how much, in their sadness, they wished they could. And anyone who could do such a thing was not alive, at least not the way most people are. Because they weren't doing what living things do. They weren't clinging to life. They were imposing terms on it.

These are the most dangerous people in the world.

CHAPTER 21

TOM TURNED up into the bluffs. As the black presence of the ocean fell away, he could feel a charge in his chest. It collected in him like static.

He pulled up near the mansion gates and parked on the opposite side of the road. There were guards moving around outside. While he waited for the clouds to cut across the moon, he walked to the edge of a cliff and stared down at the Mediterranean. His hands started shaking again, and he let them shake.

Looking out over this corner of the world, he felt the smallness of his life, but in a good way. He imagined other people had stood here decades before him and thought of their problems the way he was now, and he could feel how circular life was and how for a moment his life had converged with theirs at the same point on the arc. He remembered Eric's shirt suddenly. He hadn't been able to go for it when he was breaking out of the embassy.

After he'd left Paris, days without hearing from Eric turned into a week. A week into two. He called the Paris police. He called Interpol. He thought of people who the authorities had given up on, who were saved only because a loved one never had. So he flew back. But Eric's apartment was occupied by someone else, and when he met the landlord, there was no history of a tenant named Eric Reese. He looked up the company that Eric worked for, but there was no record of its existence in any country in the world.

That was when he got the call from the FBI. There was no record of someone named Eric Reese entering Europe within the last two years.

He spent the next six months on the internet. It was the one resource he couldn't seem to exhaust. Then one day he found a video on marcosworld.com. The site was a virtual red-light district. Sneering men in pop-up ads exposed themselves and hated you for looking. Women arched their backs under dialogue bubbles that said, *Yes, master?* There was a clip of a Czech man cutting off his own penis.

The video showed a young man being executed in Tangier. Tom clicked PLAY.

After it was over and the screen faded to black, he just sat there.

Later, after the FBI dismissed what he'd seen, he tracked Eric's shirt to an evidence bag in a Tangier police station. The remains of the man who had died wearing it, someone the report referred to as Eric Wilke, a British ex-pat from Hong Kong, had already been cremated. Tom was able to buy the shirt because this was Tangier and things were for sale in Tangier.

He paid everything he had—and got everything he wanted. The FBI and Interpol said they couldn't use it to solve a crime that took place in Africa, so he took it to a private lab, which discovered the shirt contained DNA from four unidentified men. At that moment, the shirt made everything else possible. The shirt would lead him to his brother's killers. The shirt would take him to where he stood right now.

Waves slapped and sucked at the rocks below. Cliffs surrounded them, cutting them off from the rest of the shore. Probably no one in the last fifty years had stood on the sliver of beach he was watching. He liked that. These places weren't even forgotten. They were never known in the first place. No one had a reason to look.

But if you did have a reason, you saw them: not just hidden places but hidden possibilities.

After he found the shirt, he saw what it might—just might—be possible to do. He wanted to rise up, above the smallness and powerlessness of his life, just for a moment. And be, for that moment, better than he actually was and higher than he had any right to be. He knew it wouldn't last, just as he knew he wouldn't be coming back. But the possibilities were so great they would scare you—they would ache in your heart—when you made that decision: save nothing for the fall down.

Tom turned his back on the water and faced Sarmad's house. It was powerful, this proximity to the man he was looking for. It pulled in his chest like a magnet.

He got in his car, drove 200 yards down the road, and turned around. Sarmad's estate was largely treeless and wide-open. He couldn't sneak up. He'd have to punch his way through.

He re-gripped the steering wheel a couple times and accelerated up the road. The mansion gates grew in his windshield.

His car knocked the gates off their hinges. The car tires bit into the fat of the lawn.

Bullets pecked at the car exterior. Panic fire.

Tom kept going.

He scanned the length of the house for a weak spot. He had maybe five seconds to find one—he couldn't slow down or the panic fire would lose the panic quality. Four seconds. The whole first floor was fortified with brick. Three seconds.

The front door.

The brick ended five feet from either side of it. He turned the wheel lightly, but his tires spun on the wet grass anyway. Now his car was aimed at the brick corner to the left of the door. In terms of structural soundness, this was the part of the house most likely to kill him on impact.

Delicately—so he wouldn't spin out completely—he turned the wheel a few degrees to the right. It didn't take. The car slid, still aimed at the corner. So he did the last thing he wanted to do while speeding toward a brick wall: he hit the accelerator.

The tires tore through the grass and gripped the dirt underneath. This time the car turned when he yanked the wheel to the right. The door swung into view. He must have hit it going forty miles per hour.

Dust and wood fragments blasted the windshield.

The crash threw his body forward. Everything went quiet and sightless, even though he could still hear and see.

The next thing he knew, he was flopping out the driver's-side window. His car had chewed a quarter way up a majestic staircase. Rubble crunched under his shoes as he got to his feet. He didn't actually hear this so much as know, in some distant part of his mind, that a sound was produced.

He'd brought the gun he pulled on Karl in the embassy. He grabbed it out of his waistband. There were so many hallways he couldn't know where the response would come from. He turned around and around, kept his eyes from focusing on any one thing in order to preserve the wide-angle view.

Ten seconds. Twenty seconds. No one came running.

He picked a hallway and made his way to it. A man popped around the corner and raised his sidearm. No time to run for cover, so Tom closed the distance between them—so fast all the man could do was flinch as Tom drove his fist into his solar plexus.

He swung the hand with the gun into the man's temple, and the man went unconscious on his feet. Tom turned for the stairs—

Footsteps.

A second armed man was coming toward him from another hallway.

There was a sound behind him.

He whirled around and saw a third man had run into the living room. The man froze when his eyes, wide and urgent, found him.

Tom turned back as the man in the hallway rotated his arm

around the corner, already leveling his gun at him. Tom grabbed him by the lapels and swung him into the wall. The wood paneling split with a shriek. The other man appeared at the mouth of the hallway. As he raised his gun, Tom grabbed the man lodged in the wall by the hips and swung him like a baseball bat, hitting the second man with the first. Their heads collided, and when their bodies smacked the wood floor, neither one moved.

Tom glided up the stairs, his feet on the edge of each one, stressing the wood as quietly as possible. The second floor was silent. No sign of resistance. No sign of anything.

The paneling behind his head exploded.

He dropped—just in time to avoid the follow-up—and rolled right into another guy's sight line. There was a shot. Then another.

It was controlled firing: the guy had a lock and was releasing with intent.

Tom scrambled across the hall out of fish-in-a-barrel range. He landed in a room with a fireplace and slammed two contoured double doors shut behind him. His fingers clawed at the antique bolt lock. It had been partially painted over. The bolt resisted. But then he felt something in the lock. It wasn't quite movement, maybe the intention of it. He rocked the lock back and forth with increasing desperation—

Click.

People on the other side of the door were shaking the handles. He looked around. He was in a study. A large bookcase ran wall to wall. Hunter-green wallpaper stretched floor to ceiling. The chair in the corner had legs carved to look like a griffin's feet.

It would have to do. He smashed the chair, snapped off one of its legs, and wedged it through the handles of the double doors.

There was a cracking sound.

The doors heaved inward painfully, like they were holding in a sneeze. They would hold two minutes, maybe three. Tom scoured the room, saw glass doors leading to a balcony. He went out. There was no one on the lawn thirty feet below. He turned: the chair leg in the double doors was starting to split.

He went back inside and tore another leg off the chair. Then he dropped over the ledge. He hit the grass and slipped but caught himself by going out on all fours. He looped back around to the front of the house, then through the hole where the front door had been and up the stairs again.

He peered around the corner. Four armed guards stood, swinging the stocks of their rifles into the study doors. Tom waited until the chair leg inside gave out and the men streamed into the room. Then he crept up the stairs and yanked the double doors closed. He slipped the other leg of the chair through the door handles.

He made his way down the second-floor hallway and stopped at a thick door at the end. Inside, the room was dark with the blue-green glow of twenty or so little TV screens showing live feeds from different parts of the house.

He noticed movement on one of them—

A man running across the screen labeled GARAGE 3. He fumbled his keys into the lock of a large Mercedes. Then right before he dropped into the car, he stopped and looked into the camera, like he sensed Tom was there.

And Tom knew this was the man he'd come for.

He was down the hallway in a second, down the stairs in another. He slipped on the powdery rubble surrounding his car, righted himself, jumped onto the hood of his car, and ran over the top of it. When he landed on the lawn, he saw the Mercedes turn for the gates. It accelerated so hard it almost spun out. The driver slowed for a moment, allowing the car and its momentum to swing back to unity. Then the Mercedes sped toward the road.

Tom was already halfway across the lawn. He pumped his arms and went at the car in a dead sprint.

The Mercedes crashed through what was left of the mansion gates but still had to make a sharp turn onto the road. The car fishtailed and swung to a stop for a second.

Tom hurled himself at it in that second.

He sank his fingertips into the space between the trunk and the rear windshield and almost skidded off the back of the car. As he pulled his gun to shoot out the rear window, the Mercedes accelerated and turned toward the stone wall surrounding the property. A few feet from the wall, the driver jerked the wheel left. Tom didn't realize he was flying off the back of the car until he was already six feet away from it. He managed to tuck his head as his body torpedoed into the wall.

The impact knocked the wind out of him. His ribs were on fire. When he stood up, he was woozy and his lungs wouldn't inflate. He gasped on his way back to the house, holding his arms so they wouldn't jiggle against his rib cage.

He could breathe again by the time he staggered through what had been the front door. As he came into the foyer, he felt something warm and wet on his arm. He turned.

Blood.

He turned farther.

A man in a navy-blue suit was cocking a knife back. His other hand, a fist, connected with Tom's nose. Everything went white. When Tom slipped on the pieces of the wall scattered on the marble, the man punched him a second time, chopping him down to the floor.

Through little blurs, Tom could see the man's legs. As soon as he saw the right foot pivot, he slammed his heel into the ankle bone just above it. The ankle seemed to shoot off the top of the man's foot as it twisted.

Tom rose up.

The man lunged at him, carving the air around his face. Tom feinted back and shot his hand up. He caught the man's wrist in mid-air. The man looked at Tom's hand like he couldn't understand how it had gotten there.

Tom grabbed the man and raised him high above him. When he slammed him down, the floor seemed to rise up around the man's body. Afterward the man just lay there, buried three inches deep in the wood.

Tom stood for a moment, trying to catch his breath. When he staggered over to his car, he saw the rear tires were off the ground. He went to the rear bumper, lifted the back of the car, and walked it out from the house. The tires hadn't popped—he'd gotten lucky—and when he tapped the wires together, the engine sputtered to life.

He drove after Sarmad, who had a minute on him. The road was narrow and winding. Sarmad would top out at sixty miles per hour in that big sedan.

Tom went eighty. He zapped through sleeping villages, black expanses. He skidded onto the shoulder a few times but never touched the brakes. He figured the differential in their speeds was twenty miles per hour, so every minute he was gaining a third of a mile.

He shot for three minutes. It took him four and a half, but when he caught up with the Mercedes on Avenue Tourre, it was going sixty-five, not sixty.

Tom punched it to 100 miles per hour on the downslope of a hill and hit the back of Sarmad's car in what felt like a dead fall. Sarmad's tires slipped left, then right, before he regained control of the car. Tom rammed it again, and the tires slipped—but less this time. Sarmad was learning. He turned onto a deserted service road that intersected with Diables Bleus. He was taking them away from the settlements dotting the shore and going higher into the hills.

Sarmad took a right on an unmarked road. Tom made the turn and almost spun out. Sarmad took another turn, and the new road regressed under them quickly—pavement to gravel to dirt. Then it narrowed. Tom tried to maneuver to Sarmad's side to hit his car and put his rear tires in a slide, but there wasn't room.

They came up on a large hill jutting into the night. The road wrapped around it. As the Mercedes disappeared around the side, Tom turned right—straight up the hill. He crashed through a wire fence. It caught on his fender, and he had to shake the wheel to ditch it.

The hill was steep, and as he accelerated up, he lost sight of everything except the sky. He gripped the wheel, bracing for whatever he might run into.

The world swung back into view.

As he crested the hill, he could see Sarmad's car down below. He coasted down, gaining speed. His line on Sarmad was perfect. They were going to meet.

Seconds before impact became a certainty—

Sarmad looked to the right.

He threw his hands up as Tom T-boned his car.

There was no single distinguishable sound. Except for a second, the whole world was sound. It filled Tom's head until he couldn't see. Vibrated his body until he couldn't feel.

Tom was staring at the hillside through what used to be the windshield. He wasn't sure how long he'd been doing this. He tried to move, but his intentions couldn't seem to connect with any part of his body. He waited until the tickle in his leg grew into mild agony. Inch by inch, his body came back to him. Five minutes later he slipped out of the car onto damp grass.

He picked himself up and limped over to the Mercedes, which had somehow landed on its tires.

Sarmad was fine. His car was on fire and he was woozy, but he was fine. Then he saw Tom.

He shot up in his seat and yanked the door handle. Then he saw the gun in Tom's hands and sunk back in his seat. He made a point of not looking at Tom's face.

Tom stopped in the shadows. "What's in the bag?" He nodded at the thin black leather laptop bag on the passenger seat.

Sarmad seemed confused by this.

"You know what it is," he said. "Just take it."

When Tom didn't, Sarmad reached down for it with both hands.

"Don't do that," Tom said.

Both Sarmad's hands flipped up into the air. He waited. When Tom didn't say anything, he turned in Tom's direction, still careful not to look directly at him.

"Why don't you tell me who sent you and what this is all about?" he said.

"No one sent me."

"Then what do you want the bag for?"

"I'm not here for the bag."

There was a long silence. Sarmad's breaths became quick and shallow.

"What do you want from me?" he said finally.

"I found your DNA on the shirt Eric Reese died in. I want you to tell me who shot him, and then I want you to go to the police and tell them what your role was, and then I want you to die in prison."

Sarmad smiled a little. Now he turned completely toward Tom and squinted, trying to make him out. His hand moved off his lap.

"Tell me what's in the bag," Tom said.

"My car's on fire. If it blows up, it'll kill us both."

"No, just you."

Sarmad didn't say anything.

"I asked you what's in the bag."

"Pictures."

Sarmad's hand was now past his groin and en route to the hand-gun probably stored in the car door.

"Pictures of what?" Tom stepped closer to Sarmad, into the glow of the flames.

When Sarmad got a good look at him, suddenly he was animated.

He clawed at the wreckage, trying to get out, but two tons of twisted metal caged him. His eyes never left Tom's face.

"It's not possible," Sarmad said. "I saw you..."

"What did you see?"

"It's not possible."

Sarmad's eyes never moved. Even as he started shaking his head, his skull rotated around two immobile white balls. Tom walked closer. Each step he took amplified Sarmad's shaking.

"What's not—"

"We killed you," Sarmad said, and he actually sounded sad.

"Eric. You killed Eric Reese."

"We killed *you.*"

It wasn't said in response to Tom or in response to anything. It was just said.

"I watched you die on an operating table three years ago."

"Stop saying that."

"I saw your body..."

Tom flashed on himself waking up on a gurney, surrounded by people in paper surgical masks. He was looking around, trying to understand, and that was when he heard the sound of something metallic.

"What operating table?" Tom said. "What operation?"

Sarmad wouldn't answer, and Tom flashed on Eric in Paris, watching him like he was looking at a dead man. Then he was standing outside Eric's door on the way to the airport, listening to him cry.

"Did Eric know?" Tom could barely get the words out. "Did my brother do this to me?"

"...Nast..."

"Alexander Nast?"

Sarmad didn't answer.

"What did he do?" Tom walked closer, and Sarmad got very still. *What did he do to me?*

"He told us to get you. And then he gave you the stem cell injections until you died."

Stem cell injections?

He couldn't believe Eric would be involved with people who would do such a thing.

"What do they do?" Tom said. "The stem cells?"

Sarmad looked at him. "You know what they do."

"Why me?" Tom's throat tightened, and he felt wetness sting his eyes. "I was a kid..."

"Eric was threatening to go to the police. Please—just kill me. Whatever they told you to do to me—please just kill me."

"I didn't come here to kill you," Tom said. The stinging in his eyes got worse, and he willed himself not to cry in front of this man of all people. "Just tell me how much my brother knew. I have to know."

Sarmad spoke in a whisper. "I have money, more than you could ever spend in a lifetime. Please."

"Did Nast kill my brother?"

Sarmad's hand shot across his lap. Almost instantly he was leveling a gun out the car window. Tom felt a shock in the air as he swung himself down and out of the path of the first burst. He collapsed against the car body.

Another burst.

Tom raised his gun into the window and fired two rounds blindly.

Movement inside the car stopped. When Tom stood up, he saw he'd shot Sarmad in the chest.

Sarmad was still conscious, mouthing something over and over without producing any words. He struggled weakly against his seat, like a baby fighting sleep. It took him almost a minute to die. Then he just went slack, and his body leaned against the steering wheel.

Tom didn't move for a few minutes.

Flames bounced on top of the corpse of Sarmad's car. The way it burned against the blackened sky, the colors, it was beautiful in a sense. And Tom thought it was one of the most beautiful things he'd ever seen. In a sense.

He thought of the space where Eric died. Like that dark room, the countryside around him was a place where no one was looking, and nothing mattered unless you made it matter.

Three years ago Sarmad had taken an action. But here tonight there had been an equal and opposite reaction. And a principle had been asserted: even though Eric was dead and no one had done anything, his death still made a sound. And if you were responsible, the vibrations from it would find you.

They found Sarmad.

The fires were getting smaller, and the scene was getting darker. It was time to move.

Tom leaned into the car and lifted Sarmad's hands. They were warm and smooth. He could feel the tiny ridges on the palms. Carefully he turned each hand over. There was no scar. Gently he pushed Sarmad's body back against the seat and reached across for the black bag. He opened it, but it was full of papers, and there wasn't enough light to read.

He was almost too tired to stand, but he had to keep moving. There was now only one man out there he wanted to see dead. But this wasn't him.

CHAPTER 22

TOM LIMPED toward town. When headlights appeared in the distance, he laid out in a ditch until they passed. Two miles later, as the rain started, he reached an old Toyota with mud caked on the sides. It took longer than usual, but finally he wired it. On the way back to the mansion, he tried to think of a story in case the police were already there. But when he arrived, there were no flashing blue lights. There was no crime scene yet.

The driveway was so perfectly demolished there was an unreality about it, like a movie set. He righted the gates. They balanced poorly on their twisted hinges, but from the road they appeared intact. There was a light in each pillar supporting the gate. He unscrewed both bulbs to hide the tire burns on the pavement. The lawn was torn up with tread marks. There was no hiding that, so he just parked his car in front of the front door and went inside with Sarmad's bag over his shoulder.

Upstairs, the door to the study was smashed. Whoever had been inside had taken off. He decided to keep his search simple and start from the ground up.

The home didn't have a wine cellar—he was expecting one—but it did have a finished basement. He went from room to room, but they were so bare there was hardly anything to search. He stood for a moment. He had this weird feeling the space down here was different from the space upstairs.

Almost as if the basement was smaller than it should be.

Using the staircase as his reference point, he went upstairs and confirmed that the stairway to the basement was in the middle of the house width-wise. Then he got a pen and paper from the kitchen and went back downstairs. From the bottom of the stairwell, he walked ninety degrees right, counting the steps until he reached the wall.

Ninety-six steps.

Each step was about a foot and a half, he guessed, which meant that half of the basement was about 150 feet. He went back to the foot of the stairs. This time he walked the width of the basement in the opposite direction.

Seventy-four steps.

He didn't bother to calculate the footage. There was no way the foundation of a home wouldn't have the exact dimensions of the house it kept standing. He made a diagram on the paper:

74 steps   96 steps

Stairwell

There had to be a hidden room. He cleared what little furniture there was away from the wall and felt around for a switch or a button.

He found nothing, so he went to Plan B and ripped the shade off a floor lamp. He swung the base of the lamp into the wall and kept swinging. The drywall cracked. Then it crumbled. As pieces started falling out, he hit something. There was a funny sound. He swung the lamp again. Same sound. He tore down the loose part of the wall to see what was behind it.

Steel.

An entire wall of it.

And he didn't see any way around. It was now almost 10:00 PM. He knew it was stupid to stay this long. He went back to the stairwell and sat on the bottom stair, thinking. Then something occurred to him. He counted the steps to the front of the house.

Thirty-eight steps.

Then he counted the steps to the back of the house.

Only thirty-four.

There was another space unaccounted for in the basement. He updated the diagram:

It was possible this new unaccounted-for space could lead him to the original one.

He found a closet in the basement that was against the back wall of the house. It was tiny, four feet by four feet, and filled with winter clothes. He felt around, banged on the walls. None of them sounded hollow, and there were no latches or knobs on them, so he turned to the wall facing what he hoped was the hidden room and shoved.

The wall capsized into darkness.

It slapped on a concrete floor. He froze, waiting for something to move in response to the noise.

He was looking into a tunnel. The light from the closet only penetrated a few feet. He didn't like standing there, exposed in the light but blind to the dark, so he forced himself to walk right in.

His head hit something. He felt around until he found the lightbulb. Then he ran his fingers along the wall until they found a switch. He flipped it.

A 100-foot row of lightbulbs came on.

The passageway had a low ceiling, and he had to stoop to make his way down it. At the end, there was a galvanized steel door, newer than everything else in the basement. It had the largest bolt lock he'd ever seen in his life. That made him pause.

Whatever was on the other side was meant to be kept in.

With his fingertips, he rolled the bolt in the barrel. It squeaked loud enough to be heard on the other side of the door.

The door opened on a kitchen.

It looked like one from the 1950s, except there were fluorescent lights and no windows. He realized now why he hadn't been able to smash through the wall. Judging from the width of the room, it had to be almost five feet thick.

The kitchen opened into a living room, which looked like the hand-me-down living rooms people set up in basements for their teenagers. Behind the living room was a bedroom.

There was something shiny in the carpet. He knelt down and noticed a floor anchor. It was large enough to hold a decent-size chain. He ripped up carpeting and saw the anchor had been secured by expansion bolts with a strange feature: the tops were smoothed over. It'd be impossible to remove them without ripping up a block of concrete floor.

Sarmad had been keeping people down here.

They would have been chained up, with just enough slack to get from the bedroom to the living room, maybe the kitchen too.

But why?

Tom unslung Sarmad's black bag and stared at it in his fist. He almost didn't want to open it.

He placed the bag on the kitchen table and unzipped it. Inside were profiles on various men, bills of lading, travel receipts. Like the Prometheus files, they provided a lot of data but little actual information. He stopped on a stack of 8.5-by-11 photographs.

The first few were tight shots of a man's hands, feet, and arms. He looked like a bodybuilder. In the photos of his feet, there were purple shackle marks around one ankle. Each photo of the man had a stamped number in the corner: 57618443152121735. Tom kept flipping through the photos until he reached one where the man was on a gurney. The way he was splayed out, Tom could tell he was dead. He noticed the Marine haircut: short hair on top, shaved to the skin on the sides.

He kept going through the stack. There was a series of photos for another man, Asian, short hair, perfect posture, also military-looking, except there was a different number stamped at the bottom: 20865228106670380. He too had a purple ring mark around his ankle. Tom kept flipping through the photos and then stopped—

The last photo in the stack was of the first man, number 57618443152121735. He was standing against a wall painted institutional green. Tom glanced up and saw he was standing opposite the same wall. But what disturbed him was the man in the photo. He was smiling this all-American grin, and he wasn't chained up. In fact he looked like someone who'd made it right to where he wanted to be.

It almost seemed like this chamber served as some sort of processing center.

Tom gathered up all the photos and went back upstairs.

He finished his search of the house in the study. Then he sat down at the 400-pound mahogany desk and rummaged through it. After finding nothing, he got up to leave, then changed his mind and pulled out the Prometheus files he'd brought with him. He took a magnifying lens from the desk and ran the glass over the hands of the people in the photos.

When he found it, he almost didn't believe what he was seeing. He checked it again. The zipper scar. The same one from his brother's video. It was on the hand of Dr. Alexander Nast.

The man who shot Eric was Silvana's father.

The phone rang.

Tom stared at the antique-looking telephone for three more rings before he put the receiver to his ear.

"There is a man on his way to you," a voice said. It was the deepest Tom had ever heard, and it was mechanical. Like an engine that could talk. "Move everything immediately. Do not leave it in the safe."

Tom looked at Sarmad's bag and then over to the door of a floor safe. It was wide open. He hadn't noticed it until now.

"Do not make contact. I will engage this individual personally."

"You're too late," Tom said.

He waited. There was only the buzz of static somewhere deep in the phone line. He thought the other person had hung up—

"Who are you?" the voice said. The tone was exactly the same.

"I have everything now."

"Do you?"

"That's right."

"You must want something."

Tom looked at the picture in front of him. "Alexander Nast. I'll only deal with him."

No reply.

"Are you Alexander Nast?"

No reply.

"Do you work for him?"

"We want the girl," the voice said.

Tom froze. "What girl?"

"Who are you?" the voice said.

"Someone you took something from."

"And you want it back?"

"It's not something you can give back."

"And?"

Tom stood there sweating through his clothes. He knew he should hang up—nothing good would come from this conversation.

"You could walk away from this," the voice said. "Think of your family."

"See, there's your problem right there. You take everything from someone, and now you've got nothing to scare him with."

"So what we have here is a failure of tactics."

Tom's grip on the phone tightened. "I don't know how many people you've murdered, how many families you've ruined, you piece of shit, but you people finally killed the wrong person. And right now—what you did—it's on its way back to you."

Silence on the other end.

"And you know what?"

"What?"

"It's going to blow up in your face."

Tom slammed the phone down so hard the bell inside was still ringing when he left the room.

The line went dead. Bogasian stood there. That was the longest conversation he'd had with another human being in probably nine months. He found himself wanting to know more about the person on the other end.

But now he had a location. The man would be gone by the time he got there, but now he also knew where this man was going. The girl had family in Berlin. At times like this, people always went for family.

So he knew where the targets were now and where they were soon to be. This gave him the chance he needed to locate them. He sat down and mapped several routes between Nice and Berlin. There was one that started close to Sarmad's house.

He opened a new window and mapped the cheap motels, all the places unlikely to have surveillance cameras. All the places he would have stayed.

CHAPTER 23

EVERYTHING WAS swollen with water as Tom pulled into the motel. There were currents pushing trash down the streets, and water bled off the gutters in thick viscous clumps. It rained like it would rain forever.

When he let himself into the room, Silvana was curled up on the bed facing the corner, and the lights were off. Water running down the window cast shadows over the room. They circled the wall above her body like ghosts over their victim.

He shut the door—gently but loud enough for her to hear. She didn't move, but he heard a sniffle. It was quiet, like she didn't want him to know she'd been crying.

As he passed the television, he brushed his hand along it. Static. She must have had it on. He went over to the phone and hit REDIAL. It rang twice and went to voicemail for a Café Frita. Despite the fact that she ate like there was a small demon inside her, it was unlikely she'd called a restaurant. The call had probably been made by the previous guest, which meant she'd stayed off the phone like he'd asked.

Another sniffle.

Wetter than the one before it.

She must have been trying to hold it in. Tom grabbed a towel from the bathroom to stem the bleeding from his arm. A little blood clipped the edge of his shirt and tumbled into the carpet as he walked back into the room.

"Are you okay?" he said softly.

She didn't move. He stayed there, waiting her out.

"My brother," she said. Her throat caught and cut off the last syllable.

He lowered himself carefully onto the edge of the bed.

"It was on the news," she said. "Someone shot him in his house two days ago, and they just reported that they found his..." She trailed off. "They found him."

Tom felt himself nod in sympathy. For a moment he wasn't the man who sat outside Nast's house, imagining what it'd be like to kick down the door and stare into Nast's face as he squeezed the life out of him. Mucus ran down his throat. He needed to cough, but he didn't want to make a sound. He let it choke him.

"They think it's related to the murders of all those men in Paris." Now she turned and looked at him.

"Why do they think that?"

"A reporter just said the killings were similar." She hesitated. "That and my brother knew some of the men who were killed."

Silence.

"Do you know anything about it?"

"No, I don't."

He thought now would be the perfect time to ask her about her father, then got angry at himself for thinking that.

"I don't know why I'm crying," she said. "He wasn't a good person, I guess. I mean the things he did, the people he knew..."

He watched her eyes squeeze closed. The skin around them shook, trying to hold something in.

When some people cried, they did it without reference to themselves. They just cried. And no matter who was with them, they were alone. Tom could only stand there and look at her. It was like watching someone drown—without being able to stick out your hand.

She reached for a glass of water, and when she returned it to the nightstand, he saw the blood on it.

"Your hand's bleeding again," he said.

"It probably needs more duct tape." She tried to give him that crooked little smile of hers.

"I got some gauze. Maybe you want a proper dressing..."

She didn't say anything, but she gave him a look like it was her birthday and he was the only person who'd remembered.

They went into the bathroom. Rain pelted the window, and wet leaves stuck to the glass, twitching like fish spilled on the ground, drowning in oxygen.

Silvana flicked on the light and hopped up on the counter. In unison they both paused to take in the state of the room. The porcelain tub and sink were chipped and blackish around the edges. Everything else was white and covered with mystery stains, except for the pink bath mat.

She nodded at the mat. "What color would you say that is?"

"Pepto-Bismol."

"I think..." She regarded the bathroom. "Yeah, this is the worst bathroom I've ever seen in my life."

"Once, I saw a bathroom in the New York subway."

"Oh my god."

"Yeah."

"You saw it in real life? Or, like, in a documentary?"

"I used it."

"Oh my god." Now she put a hand on her chest like she was going to be sick.

He stared off. "It was like a fresh crime scene that existed on top of other, older crime scenes. It was one of those things that's so ugly it's almost beautiful, you know?"

She shook her head. "So you pretty much have Ebola now?"

"I do, yes. And since I've touched your hand, you do too."

She laughed. It was involuntary. Then she, like him, seemed to remember the circumstances that had brought them here. Immediately it was quiet like they'd never spoken in the first place.

She watched him through eyes swollen from crying as he placed her injured hand on her thigh.

"So do you have any family?" she said.

"No."

Silence.

"Do you have anyone who's like family?" she asked.

"No...I guess I don't."

She didn't say anything at first. Then she looked him in the eye and said like she actually meant it, "I'm sorry to hear that."

He dabbed at her cut. Even though he wasn't looking at her face, he knew she was in pain. He could feel it in her hand.

"Oh my god," she said, pulling his shirtsleeve back to reveal the cut on his arm. Then she noticed something on his neck and pulled his collar back. In the mirror, he saw the top of a black bruise.

"What the hell happened?" she said.

"It looks worse than it is."

"Are you okay?"

"Yeah."

He needed the gauze behind her on the counter, so he pointed at it to warn her he was about to come closer. She nodded as if to say he didn't need to ask. But when he leaned in and reached around her waist, their arms touched. She flinched.

She froze, blushing hard, and tried to laugh it off. But no sound came out, so she was left smiling painfully as she tried to hold an awkward lean away from him. Her shirt had ridden up, and his eyes instinctively ticked down to the flat of her stomach. As if sensing this nakedness—and his interest in it—she pushed the shirt down and resumed her awkward pose on the edge of the counter.

Suddenly he felt intensely aware of just how close they were, how alone. They were about to spend the night together in this room—something he'd never done with anyone before, even though he was twenty-two.

"You okay?" he said.

"It's funny. My brother was a lot older than me. But I keep thinking of the boy I grew up with. Then I think about the first time he was arrested. It's weird. I loved him, we all did, but there was always something wrong with him."

She waited for him to say something, but he just couldn't think of anything normal to say about the death of a man who deserved exactly what he'd gotten. Then he thought about Alexander Nast and his connection to the voice on the other end of the phone.

We want the girl.

"Do you have family other than your brother?" he asked.

She nodded. "My mom."

"Are you close?"

"Yeah." She hesitated. "I mean we don't see each other much. But that'll change at some point."

"And your dad?"

She looked away. "I haven't seen him in a long time."

He was about to ask more, but stopped himself.

It's not right to do this now.

He tucked the end of the gauze into a fold. When he looked at her, Silvana was tearing up again. She waved a hand over her eyes the way women do when they don't want their makeup to run.

"Sorry," she said. "I think this is the last of it."

She shimmied her butt toward the edge of the counter, like she was about to jump down.

"You want a hand?" he said. "You're kind of . . ." He pointed at her bandage.

"Um, yeah, do you mind if I . . ." She raised her hands toward his shoulders.

"Sure."

"Okay."

She put her arms around him. He slid his hands under her arms and pressed his fingertips into her skin. After looking at her for so long, it was almost startling to actually touch her. As he lifted her up, he could feel her breath on his neck.

Once she was back on her feet, she gave him a half-smile, and for the second time, he wondered if he'd made a mistake going after her.

"We should get some sleep." He said it casually, sensibly, like they weren't two strangers clinging to each other in a motel off the highway.

"I'm already there, but I need to kick you out first."

She locked the bathroom door behind him. A minute later the toilet flushed, and she appeared, eyes at half-mast. She paused when she saw him sitting on a sheet on the floor, then went over to the bed and slid onto it.

As she bent over, the top of a black thong with white dots poked up from the back of her jeans. He could see the tension in the fabric. It was so girly, unlike the rest of her outfit, that for a second it embarrassed him to know she'd been wearing something so sexual that close to him, nearly touching him, this whole time.

The thong disappeared. She tugged the jeans up a little, and he could see the curves and muscles in her legs flex and let go through the denim. He stayed still, letting his desire wash over him until all that was left was a dull empty ache. He sat in the ache.

Silvana gator-rolled around and around in the bedsheets until magically she was underneath them and they were no longer pinned to the bed. She turned to him.

"Thank you," she said.

"For what?"

"For being kind."

He was vaguely aware of nodding an acknowledgment.

"Good night," she said.

And before she rolled over and fell immediately to sleep, he saw it again: that crooked little smile wrinkling her face.

CHAPTER 24

BOGASIAN REACHED Sarmad's mansion a few hours before daybreak. He stopped his car at the gates, which looked ready to collapse. He didn't want to risk knocking them down and having some nosy cop come up to the house, so he left them in place and scaled the wall.

The house was quiet, and all the lights were off. Tire marks on the lawn led to a fifteen-foot hole where the front door used to be. With one step, he went from grass to foyer. He walked upstairs. The wood on the massive doors to the study was split.

Inside, the floor safe was open.

When he went back downstairs, there was a man in a suit flopping around, trying to work himself out of the floor.

Bogasian allowed him to finish standing up, giving him a clear shot.

Then he fired twice into the man's chest.

He found two other men on the ground floor. They looked like they'd been thrown into each other. He could hear them breathing. They were both still alive. By the time he left, they no longer were.

Outside he got back in his vehicle and turned down the road. In the distance, he saw a car moving toward him. He pulled off into the darkness of a tree canopy and killed the engine. The car got louder. When it passed, the pressure in the air rocked his car gently.

In the rearview mirror, he watched the car brake at Sarmad's gates. The driver parked off to the side of the road, the way Bogasian had, and two men got out. Bogasian uncapped a pair of binoculars from the backseat and watched them. One, he didn't recognize. The other was Karl Lyons.

A man he'd last seen looking at him through the window to his recovery room.

He didn't know whether Karl was after Sarmad or Tom, but he suspected it was both. When Karl disappeared from view, Bogasian put his car in neutral and let it coast down the hill. At the bottom, he keyed the ignition and went looking for Tom and the girl.

CHAPTER 25

THE FIRST thing Karl noticed was the fifteen-foot hole in the front of the house. Then he saw the gates looked like they'd crush anyone who tried to move them, so he and James climbed the stone wall.

As they crossed the lawn, wind gusted against the leaves with the ebb and flow of ocean waves. He didn't like approaching the house like this, out in the open. Whatever was waiting in the house could see them, but they couldn't see it.

With rubble popping underfoot, they went in through the hole and stood in the landing, listening. Wind hissed through the entrance. In a hallway they found the bodies of two men. In the darkness, the men almost didn't even look out of place. Karl checked the casings with a flashlight. They'd been shot with a 9mm.

There was another body in the foyer, right where they'd come in. The man was splayed out in a shadow that covered the corner of the room like a web. Flecks of blood dotted the backs of his hands, which meant he'd had his arms raised when he was shot. He'd seen it coming.

Karl thought about Tom's reluctance to harm the Marines in the embassy. He'd had a gun, and yet he hadn't used it. Maybe he'd gotten over that reluctance. Or maybe someone had been here after him.

Bogasian, was this you?

They went through the rest of the house, but they didn't find Alan Sarmad.

There were fourteen parking spaces in the garage. Only thirteen cars.

They went to the empty space at the end of the row and looked around. Karl noticed a phone by the wall. Someone had dropped it. He picked up the phone and looked at the last numbers called. There was only one.

He dialed it. The phone kept ringing. No pick-up. No voicemail. James used his phone to do a reverse lookup for the number. There was no name, but the line went to a farmhouse five miles away. Google Satellite showed the house had been torn down. All that was left was a barn.

Karl didn't like that.

He turned to James. "I'm going to drop you off in town. Go to the airport. Get the plane ready."

James looked like he was going to say something, but he just nodded.

Karl drove him into the sleeping town and then headed for the farmhouse.

They were already high above the ocean, but the directions took him even higher. The hills off the coast in that part of France were steep, and the road had to wind back and forth to make it up them.

At the top, the ground leveled off. He took another road that curved, parallel to the water. He couldn't see the ocean, could only sense that it was there, existing in the emptiness beyond the hills.

The road was little used. No headlights or streetlamps warmed the gray countryside. Telephone poles lined the crumbling pavement. They didn't seem to connect to anything.

The road split. One fork led deeper into the countryside, away from the ocean, and the other straight ahead, into a forest. Karl took the second. The road turned into a dirt path and began to snake through the trees. It was impossible to see more than thirty feet ahead. He wouldn't know what he was coming up on, so he rolled down his window, hoping he could make up in hearing what he'd lost in vision.

The path straightened and then narrowed. It became a hallway of trees. Leaves slapped the windshield. Branches scraped the sides of the car like fingernails.

He came out of the woods onto another open stretch of country. There were no telephone poles. No street signs. He didn't hear any birds, not even crickets. The other area looked abandoned. This one looked like no one had ever taken an interest in the first place. As he approached a thicket of trees, for some reason he thought of the story about ancient Spartans driving the Argives into the sacred grove, then setting it on fire and watching in silence as a thousand men burned alive.

He didn't see the barn until he was about to pass it.

It sat at the edge of the trees overlooking the hills below. He braked gently and looked around for some sign of people. Then slowly, with rocks and twigs popping under his tires, he drove to within a hundred feet of the barn and got out with his gun.

His shoes were loud on the gravel as he circled around trying to find a window. There wasn't one, so he put his ear up against the wall of the barn and listened. If there were any sounds being made inside, he couldn't hear them.

He stood, thinking. The wind whipped his clothes tight against his skin.

He walked around to the main door and got down in the dirt to see if there was any light under it. Nothing. He tried the door. Locked.

He got back in his car and drove down to the front of the barn. Then he turned the car around, put it in reverse, and backed into the barn door. He heard the wood shriek as the collision knocked him forward, harder than he liked. He climbed out. There was a huge rip in the door where his car had hit it, leaving a triangle of black space all the way to the ground.

He stood watching the triangle, waiting for something to come out.

It started to rain, and he pulled his collar tight around his neck. The wind picked up again, moaning softly from places he couldn't see. He clicked on his flashlight and squatted in front of the opening, shining the light around the entrance. His heartbeat was in his throat. He waited for a face to pop out at him in the dark.

A gust of wind rushed through the opening and whistled over something inside.

It startled him. He almost broke off and went back to the car, but he waited out the urge. From outside, his flashlight was too weak to penetrate the darkness, so he got on his hands and knees and crawled into the barn blind. Once he was in, he stood up and listened.

The only sound was his breathing. He didn't like that, being the loudest thing in a room he couldn't see.

He clicked on the flashlight. Saw a desk chair, then the desk itself. He swept the flashlight around the room and stopped cold when he saw it.

Ten feet from the front door, there was a plexiglass wall.

It sealed off the rest of the barn.

The wall diffused the beam from his flashlight into a milky glow. He moved the beam along the length of it, waiting for something to see the light and slam against the glass. The wind rocked the front door against its twisted hinges, and he wished it would shut up already.

He wanted very badly to see what was on the other side of the plexiglass, but that meant he'd have to go near it. He clicked off the flashlight and listened. After a minute of silence, he crept up to the glass, hands out until he touched it. Then he pressed the flashlight against it and clicked it on.

He was looking into a lab. It had been emptied out, but it looked almost exactly like the one outside Paris had.

The skin crawled across his back and arms.

He turned around and swept the light behind him, looking for a light switch. Something else caught his eye. Three metal cans of acetone. Acetone was one of the most common accelerants used in arson. They were planning to burn the place down.

He found the light switch, but when he tried it, nothing happened. He checked the lock on the door. Manual, not electronic. He could get in if he wanted to.

Do you want to?

He shined the light into the far end of the lab, trying to make out what was back there. Shadows moved in the opposite direction of the light, and he kept stopping because he thought he saw something. The room was filled with medical equipment. IV stands littered the floor. Hospital gurneys were shoved together in a corner like bumper cars.

There was something at the far end of the room that he couldn't quite see—something large and wrapped in clear plastic.

He unlocked the door. The bolt shot out of the lock, and the sound cracked through the room. Karl froze, ready to throw the lock back. But the lab was as it had been: completely still.

Gently he eased the door open. His hearing was so intense it became a kind of vision. He took a step inside. The acoustics of the room not only magnified each sound but moved it as well. He heard a footstep to his left and whirled around on empty space.

The lab was cold, almost freezing. His body wanted to shiver. Before he went farther, he checked the corners of the room with the flashlight. The thought of anything getting between him and the door was too terrible to think about.

He took a few more steps inside, and his footsteps followed him in echo. He walked around a red biohazard bag. Syringes poured out of it, hundreds of them. A few feet away, there was a pile of black hoods. He noticed blood on the floor.

As he approached the clear plastic on the ground, he saw a head of hair. Then he saw more.

There was a moment where fear almost had him.

They'd all been packaged together in clear plastic sheets like sausages. The bodies of thirteen men. They'd been stacked so each one leaned on the one behind him. Some of their faces were bloated. Others watched him. Their mouths hung open, like they had a secret to tell.

A gust of wind hit the barn, and the front door shook on its hinges.

Some of the men's arms and legs were missing. One man had a butcher's cut up his back where his spine had been removed. The skin puckered in around the incision. To a man, they were perfectly cut up.

Whatever they're doing, it's bigger than you thought.

He knew why they'd been killed. The stem cells hadn't worked, at least not as intended. And they'd been cut up so that someone could figure out what had gone wrong. Karl stood there, watching the men, wondering whether they were innocent. Whether he should feel anything for them.

The death of thirteen people should always be a tragedy, he thought. But he knew better than that.

He looked down and saw outlines on the floor where large machines had been recently removed. All of the men had condensation on them.

They were thawing.

He saw there was still one refrigerator left. Someone would be on his way back here for it, and whoever it was, he was going to burn the men along with the barn.

After locking the lab, Karl stopped at the desk and rifled through the drawers. There were armfuls of papers. He took his time, flipping through them all. At the bottom of one drawer, he found a prescription pad. The name on it was Dr. Alexander Nast. He almost wasn't surprised, or maybe he was too tired to be.

Afterward he sat in the dark with his gun on his lap, waiting for the sound of someone pulling into the driveway. He sat for an hour, maybe two, listening to his breaths.

When he left, he stopped and looked at the acetone cans. No one could ever find this place.

From a quarter mile away, he watched the burning orange structure collapse under the tree line. He waited for hours for someone to come. But no one ever did.

CHAPTER 26

PEOPLE IN surgical masks and gowns were standing around him. Tom tried to move, but he was on his back, restrained on something. When he realized what it was, the horror set in. He was on an operating table.

He'd just woken up, but he got the feeling that wasn't supposed to happen. One of the people in the masks was staring at him.

Then he saw the drill.

It was tiny but also seemed huge attached to a massive machine, and it was pointed straight at him. He fought the restraints and tried to crane his head to see the tip of the drill. For some reason he had to know where it would go into his body.

He started screaming.

Or maybe he had been the whole time and only now was becoming aware of it.

The people in the surgical masks were moving quickly but with professional calm. He screamed for them to stop, but his voice was so alien-sounding even he couldn't make out the words.

They weren't listening, so he started negotiating.

—Will you wait a minute?

—Why can't one of you just talk to me?

—Sir, I'll do whatever you want. Just wait one minute. One minute.

Why was he saying sir?

—What do you want? I'll give you anything. Please.

Then he felt a prick on his arm, and the world around him snuffed out.

Tom realized he was standing in his motel room. For a second he thought he'd just yelled out, but the room was quiet.

The dream had started two years ago and become more detailed each time. This one had been the worst.

He turned. Someone was sitting on the dresser, feet hanging over the edge, gently bumping the drawers.

The feet froze.

Tom looked up, and there was Eric. He was barely fifteen feet away but still somehow too far to approach. His face twisted. It wasn't a continuous movement. Each change snapped onto his face, like he was under a strobe light. Then Tom recognized the expression on his brother's face.

He was worried.

Something shifted in the mirror behind Eric's shoulder. Tom spun around. A man was leaning on one knee over the bed. His hands were around Silvana's neck, and he was putting all his weight onto them.

Tom started for him. But the man stopped, cocked his head in the air. Tom froze. He didn't know why, but he was terrified. The man started turning toward him, and when he was halfway around, Tom saw there were no whites in his eyes. They were all black—

He was looking at himself.

He looked back at Eric, but he was gone. And when he turned back to the bed, there was no one leaning over it. Bile swam up his throat. He looked at his hands. They were beyond shaking. His fingers arched and clenched. He tried to will them to be still before he went over and touched Silvana's arm.

Still warm.

He went into the bathroom and filled a glass of water. His hands were still going. He calmed them by making fists and taking deep breaths. After he drank the water, he stared into the mirror and watched Silvana on the bed. She'd kicked the covers down to her ankles and spread her legs half the length of the bed, so her body formed a big Y. He tried to smile. Because it was kind of funny the way she imposed herself on the bed.

He hadn't been dreaming earlier, he realized, because he hadn't been asleep. He'd been standing up when he came to. Which meant he'd been hallucinating.

He'd started seeing things two years ago, little things he knew a second later hadn't been there. He'd pass someone he suspected was watching him, but when he turned around, there was nothing—just an old man walking his dog. He'd never had a hallucination where he hurt someone before, though.

He wondered why someone had done this to him. Then he thought about how Eric might fit in and had to close his eyes. Most of the time when his thoughts turned to his brother, he was fine. But sometimes this sick feeling jagged up his face and emptied around his eyes. He didn't move until it went away. Then he looked at himself in the mirror.

He shut off the light. Because he didn't like how bright it was.

And he told himself that whatever other changes happened, he'd just have to deal with them. Because this was his life now.

Bogasian woke with a start.

His hands were going again. For a second, through the grogginess, they didn't seem like actual extensions of his body. The fingers flexed and curled like insects. They disgusted him.

He thought he was going to throw up.

He lunged for a glass of water and knocked it onto the floor. He rolled off the bed and padded into the bathroom and filled another glass. As he drained it, he studied himself in the mirror. He ran his fingers over the face that studied him back. He'd had a face women found attractive once. Unlike most large men's, it had fine features, not the broad slopes of a car windshield. There was still a trace of his old self in there, but now the skin was so thickened it looked like it'd been slapped on his face and massaged over his skull like raw hamburger.

Several months ago he'd been shopping for clothes and had made a mildly suggestive joke to a saleswoman. In his old life, it might have resulted in a drink together or at worst a conversation that went nowhere. But she looked at him as though he'd just jiggled a pair of handcuffs and suggested a drive to the woods.

Then she smiled so hard he could feel the effort it must have taken, and she escaped to the back room. Five minutes later, in men's coats, he felt the eyes of the other salespeople on him. Every pair of eyes seemed to raise his body temperature a degree, and his hands started shaking. He wasn't aware of being embarrassed. He told himself he couldn't possibly be uncomfortable about something like this. But he left and never went back.

Never went out again unless he had to.

Sometimes he imagined there was a signal everyone else could hear. And due to what had been done to him, he could no longer hear it. And because he'd lost it, there was no way to reach out to anyone. No way to get it back.

He turned off the light. The glare hurt his eyes.

And he stopped thinking about the way things used to be. Because those things weren't his anymore.

CHAPTER 27

KARL WAS on the dirt road on his way back into town when he saw headlights through the trees. He kept driving toward them and then realized they were no longer moving. He pulled to a stop and listened. Generic sounds of the forest. Crickets chirped, wind blew, and unseen animals made noises.

He crept out of his car.

The other car still hadn't moved. Its headlights shot beams of light out from around the tree trunks. Karl ran deeper into the forest and then circled around to the side of the car. As he got close, he could hear the engine. He tried to see if there was someone behind the wheel, but it was too dark. In situations like this, situations where someone might be trying to use uncertainty to kill him, Karl found it useful to try to figure out what the other person wanted him to do, and then not do it. In this case, the only way to see if someone was sitting in the car was to get closer, where Karl would make himself a better target. That was what the other person wanted, and so Karl started to turn around.

There was motion in his peripheral vision.

He didn't waste time by trying to turn and look. He just dove behind a tree. Something that sounded like a fist-size mosquito went screaming past his ear. Then he heard the gun itself as the shooter kept firing.

Karl spun around the other side of the tree and fired at the area where he thought the shooter was. His rounds hit nothing. They just disappeared soundlessly into the dark. He turned and fired into the front tire of the car. The right side sank. He shot out the nearside headlight too.

Then he walked in the direction the shooting had come from. The woods were quiet. Only the sound of the car engine covered his approach. He thought he heard something. When he turned, he saw a man kneeling out from behind a tree trunk. He aimed a handgun at Karl and started firing. Karl ducked behind another tree and fired back.

Through the strobing from the muzzle flashes, Karl watched the man stand up and retreat behind the tree and begin firing from around the other side. Karl kept shooting. For ten seconds, the only sound was their weapons.

Then there was darkness and silence.

Karl heard breathing. It sounded like air being sucked through a wound. He walked toward it and saw the man lying faceup. There was a bullet hole right below his trachea where his collarbone had been shattered. A combination of bone and blood seemed to be obstructing his airway. Another bullet had torn through the man's mouth and exited out his cheek. Half of one of his molars was stuck on the outside of the hole like a piece of food.

"Who are you?" Karl asked.

The man would die soon, but his eyes hadn't glossed yet. They watched Karl with a brain still functioning on the other side of them. There was another wound on the man's thigh. Karl stepped on it.

"Who are you?"

The man whimpered. It was a horrible sound. Wet. Like he'd swallowed a tablespoon of water and it was drowning him to death. He couldn't speak if he wanted to. Karl trained his gun on the man's face and then looked to see what his answer was. The man nodded, and Karl shot him through the forehead.

The man's face snapped from life to death so fast it was hard for Karl to believe he was looking at the same person. One moment, the face was flesh. The next, wax. Karl stood watching him. It was one of those things you almost couldn't help but do.

He searched the man for ID. He found a Swiss passport, probably a fake, and pocketed it. There was nothing else of value on the man. He checked the car. Nothing there either. He went back to the man's body and used the fingerprint scanner on his phone to take all ten of his fingerprints. Then he sent them to James and asked him to run them through all the databases.

12 hours, James wrote back.

Karl looked once more at the man on the ground. He was well dressed and had an intelligent face. Some people were criminals because they were stupid or because they lacked the impulse control to do anything else. But this man looked like he had options, which in turn meant he'd chosen this. Whatever this was.

Karl opened the man's wallet again and thumbed through the cash inside. There were euros, British pounds, Swiss francs, and US dollars. None of the bills were new, but they were reasonably crisp. All except for a twenty-dollar bill in the back. It was older than the others and frayed. Like it'd been in the wallet for a long time. Karl looked over the dead body and frowned because he didn't want it to be true.

You're an American.

CHAPTER 28

THE ALARM on the phone started bleating, gently at first, but the intensity would rise. Tom reached over and poked the keypad before the sound could run jagged through the room. Then he rolled onto his stomach and looked out the window. The horizon was purpling. The threat of day.

Silvana was lying on the bed like she'd been dropped on it from the ceiling. As Tom picked himself up off the floor, he was hit by how exhausted he was. Everything was sore, and his body was so stiff it hurt to move.

He took Sarmad's black bag and slipped into the bathroom. He pulled out more pictures of men who had that military look. He saw maps and invoices from medical equipment companies. There was too much to sort through before 6:00 AM.

He stopped on a surgical atlas. Some of its pages were dog-eared. The first page showed a procedure called a craniotomy. On the diagrams of the human brain, someone had penciled in notes. They were unreadable. Doctor's handwriting.

He went to another dog-eared page. This one showed a skull with dots made in red ink: two on top and one several inches above the right ear. He checked the front and back covers to see if a surgeon had written his name on them. According to a buddy of Eric's who was in med school, surgeons liked to sign their names on everything, even their anesthetized patients. Not here, though.

He picked up the photos of the man with the Marine haircut. In the ones where he was smiling for the camera, the "before" pictures, there didn't seem to be any marks on his scalp. Tom flipped to the photo of him lying on a gurney. A few inches above his ear, where his head was shaved to the scalp, there was a small purplish mark.

Tom ran his fingers over his scalp, pulling the hair apart. His fingers were shaking. Somehow he knew he would find it right away.

And he did.

A little knot of thickened purplish skin sat two inches above his right ear.

He clamped his jaw shut and gritted his teeth and started shaking. There was a moment where he imagined himself smashing everything in the room until the cops came. He stood there breathing, trying not to tap into what he actually felt—because if he let in even just a little bit of that, he'd go to pieces. He knew in some distant academic sense he ought to find out what had been done to those men, because it had also been done to him. But what he'd seen was horrifying in a way he'd never experienced before. It was like looking at your own dead body.

That led him to the other thing he knew.

He could never look at those photos ever again.

Bogasian only slept an hour or so, but it was enough to reset. He showered, brushed his teeth, did everything to start a new day and not just continue the one before it.

Tom and the girl were most likely bedded down along the highways leading north to Germany. They wouldn't be within the city limits because they'd want to be able to leave quickly, which meant not driving all the way through Nice. And so, starting at 5:00 AM, Bogasian stopped in motels along the way, flashed his Interpol ID, and then showed the pictures of Tom and Silvana.

An hour into it, he pulled into a place called Le Grande. The main office was lit up, but no one was inside. He hit the bell on the front desk and waited. Finally a woman came out of a dark office, straightening her clothes.

"We're closed," she said in French.

He opened his wallet to the Interpol ID and slid it across the counter. "You speak English?"

She nodded.

He pushed the pictures of Tom and Silvana across the counter.

"Are they in trouble?" she said.

He smiled. "I hope not. They may be witnesses to an incident in Paris."

"You mean the pile of bodies?"

"You know I can't comment on that."

She nodded, sure that he just had.

"They checked in last night," she said. "Asked for a cot."

"I'm going to need the key to their room."

She opened a drawer under the counter and started fishing through it.

He picked up a business card off a stack and read it. "Louna Laurent. That you?"

She nodded as he placed her business card in his breast pocket.

"You run this place all on your own?"

"Yes."

"That's wonderful."

She held up a set of keys and tried to hand it to him.

"I'm afraid I'm going to need you to come with me," he said.

When Tom came out of the bathroom, Silvana still hadn't moved. He was about to wake her up, but first he went over and took the phone with the GPS out of her purse. Once he'd pocketed it, he leaned over her and lightly shook her awake. She rolled onto her back and for a moment looked at him and then the room like they ought to have been just a dream.

"What time is it?" she said.

"Six."

She looked outside. It was still dark. "At night?"

"In the morning."

She moaned a little and kicked the covers down to her ankles. Tom was ready to go, so he grabbed a washcloth and started wiping any surface that would render a fingerprint. When he turned around, Silvana had already packed and was wiping down the table with a tissue.

"Am I doing it right?" she said.

"Yeah." He grinned at her.

She nodded and offered to do the bathroom while he went outside to put their things in the car. Once he was finished, he stood by the car and watched as she closed the door to their room and then wiped it clean.

On the way to the car, she paused by a trashcan but didn't put the tissue in it, which would leave behind evidence. Instead she glanced at him, aware he'd been watching, and winked as she tucked the tissue into her purse.

As Silvana crossed the parking lot, she stopped abruptly when a car passed between them. While she waited—it was less than a second—she looked at him, and he looked at her. She smiled. He smiled back.

She stopped at the car and looked at it. "What happened to our car?"

"I crashed it, left it in the middle of nowhere, and stole another one. Get in. Let's go."

"Oh, okay."

And they were over the Italian border in less than an hour.

The owner of the motel stopped at room 234 and looked at Bogasian. He motioned with the back of his hand for her to proceed.

She knocked on the door. "Mr. Michel."

There was no answer. She turned to him. Again he motioned for her to go on. As she unlocked the door, he put his hand in his jacket and positioned himself behind her.

The room was empty, but it smelled like people had just slept the night in it. Bogasian went over to the bed. Only the pillows on one side had been wrinkled. He picked a long black hair off one. There were sheets folded neatly on the floor across the room. He knew if he unfolded them he would not find long black hairs but short brown ones.

He turned to the owner. "What name did you say when you knocked on the door?"

"Michel. Adrien Michel."

"Did you get the woman's name?"

"No. Why? Isn't that the name you have on file?"

Bogasian moved toward the door.

"Can I see your ID again?" The woman was watching him like it was him she'd been staring at the whole time, not the room.

Bogasian stopped and stared at her. "Why would you ask me that?"

She took a shallow breath and glanced out into the parking lot, but it was empty.

"I just let you in a guest's room," she said.

He kept staring at her.

"I should confirm you are who you say you are."

"But why would you ask me if you weren't sure?"

She hesitated.

"If I wasn't an Interpol agent and you asked me that, right here, right now, what do you think would happen?"

She was shaking her head. Her mouth traced words that weren't there.

He walked up to her. When he reached into his pocket, the

muscles on her neck flexed, and she got a sad look. He pulled out his wallet and flipped it open for her.

"Next time make an excuse and call the police."

She looked up from the ID and nodded.

"Now if I have any more questions," he said, "I know where to find you."

He patted the business card over his heart.

CHAPTER 29

NORTH OF Milan, Tom kept looking around for snow-covered peaks and picturesque villages, but it was all flat and bare.

"I know, it's like you died and went to New Jersey," Silvana said.

The Alps finally came into view as they approached Lake Como. Then they hit Switzerland and were instantly transported to a rolling paradise of gentle hills and tree-lined mountains. Everything looked like it was meant to be hiked or skied on. Little cottages domesticated the landscape, which was so shock green you had to keep looking at it to fully believe it. For the first time in years, Tom was reminded of Montana, his home. It was a lot like his state—but without the wilderness. Without the *wildness*.

They passed Zurich and Stuttgart. Outside Heidenheim, they pulled into an autohof, the German equivalent of a truck stop. Tom parked the car in back, and Silvana rushed inside to the bathroom. When he watched her head toward the main door, then stop and take a longer route to a side entrance that didn't face the A7 highway, he smiled for the third time that day at how careful she was being.

Before he followed her in, he took out the phone with the GPS. He found the auto on-off feature and set the phone to turn on for five minutes every day, then automatically turn off. Next he disabled every feature he could think of to extend the battery life.

Then he switched off the phone and smashed the screen until it wouldn't light up even when it was on.

He took files out of a large ziplock Baggie in Sarmad's black bag and replaced them with the phone. If someone took the briefcase he'd stolen from the embassy, he wanted that person to assume (a) the phone didn't work and (b) it had been preserved because there was information on it. He put the ziplock bag and Sarmad's black bag in the briefcase and snapped it shut. Then he went into the autohof to find Silvana.

It was controlled chaos inside. There was a double line outside both bathrooms, and there were five lines of unnaturally patient-looking people in front of the Wienerwald and the McDonald's. Everything else had fallen to the children: what could be climbed on was being climbed on. Silvana hadn't even tried to get to the bathroom. She was just standing by the entrance, taking it all in.

Without turning, she said, "I'm thinking of just going on the floor at this point."

"If you wait in line, we'll be here for an hour."

"I know, I know."

"Can you hold it?"

"I don't know."

He thought a moment. "Can I ask you something? Is it, you know, number two?"

She stared at him. "Girls don't shit. They make flowers."

"Um, okay. But so long as we're not dealing with a flower situation here, you could just go in the woods."

"And what, squat?"

"Yes."

"Like a dog?"

"Yes."

She was quiet as they crossed the parking lot.

At the edge of the woods, she started to peel back some branches, then stopped. "This is, like, okay, right?"

"Well, I don't think a SWAT team is sitting in a van, waiting for us to pull our pants down."

She went in a few feet, then stopped again. "Do you have to go too?"

"No."

"Are you *sure?*"

That got him thinking about it, and of course whenever you thought about it, you had to go.

"Thank you for that," he said, and she grinned.

"All right," she said, clapping her hands. "So this is actually happening."

He walked twenty feet in and waited as she made her way out of view. Then he unzipped and relieved himself on a tree, enjoying how dark and cool it was under the canopy. For a moment, he felt normal. Nothing else mattered right now except this ridiculous little adventure of theirs.

He zipped up and headed back to the car. Two minutes later Silvana came out.

"You hungry?" he said.

"Ravenous."

Shoulder to shoulder, they crossed the parking lot. And it was kind of nice because when he looked around, he noticed everyone there was with family or friends. Everyone had someone. And right now, so did he.

"Can I tell you something?" Silvana said.

"Sure."

"Have you ever gone on a road trip where you almost didn't want to get to where you were going?"

"No, but I know what you mean."

"You know how I told you I have kind of a not-good relationship with my dad?"

"Yes."

"He's in Berlin, or at least that's where my mom goes to visit him. She's there right now. I haven't seen her in six months, and I haven't seen him in almost three years."

She watched him to see what he made of this. He had wanted to find Nast for so long, even before he knew it was Nast he was looking for, that he almost didn't believe what he was hearing. Now he knew where the man was. His heart beat faster.

"It's funny," she said, "I want to see him so bad, but I'm nervous. I keep thinking of all this stuff I can say so it isn't weird, but even in my imagination it's not working."

They stopped by the side door to the autohof. They were so close he could have put his arm around her, but then a large family started pushing past them, and he and Silvana spread to opposite sides of the walkway to let them through.

"He must miss you," he said.

"Yeah..."

Tom remained quiet.

"Something happened three years ago."

Three years ago, around the time Eric disappeared.

"My dad took a job in Paris. It changed him. He and my brother never really spoke, but I remember they got into these huge arguments. I overheard my dad once. He said, 'They're going to kill you too.' Then my dad...he just never came home, and he said he couldn't see us for a while. And the years went by." She shook her head.

"That's all you know?"

She nodded.

More people walked between them, and Silvana seemed to notice the autohof again.

"Let's eat," she said.

"Wait, don't do that."

She watched him for a moment and then smiled as she looked down. "I'm not used to people asking me so many questions. I get embarrassed." When he didn't say anything, she tipped her head in the direction of the food.

That didn't feel right, Tom thought as they walked in. *Using her dad like that.*

They found a little diner away from the bulk of the crowd. It seemed like the least-worst option.

Silvana motioned to a newsstand. "I need to get some Zantac." She tapped her chest. "Acid reflux."

Tom waited for a seat to open up. Other people, also tired and hungry, had the same idea. When someone left a table, he didn't wait for it to be cleared. He slid into the booth.

A couple had gone for the same table. Tom didn't think anything of them standing over him until the woman said something in German. He just looked at them, no idea what to say, but the woman began raising her voice when he didn't get up.

Her boyfriend or husband started gesturing at him and saying something to the people around them. Tom wasn't aware of feeling nervous, but then all of a sudden warmth stung its way across his cheeks, like he'd been slapped. Almost immediately he got the panicky feeling he'd had when he woke up in the motel. His hands were shaking a little. He wasn't sure what was happening. He looked around, trying to find Silvana. He shouldn't have done that—

All eyes were on him.

People were staring.

He thought he was going to be sick. Now his hands were flat-out shaking.

"I didn't see you waiting near this table," he said.

The man grinned and said something that ended with "American." He reached over and gave Tom's shirt a little tug. "Thirty minutes waiting. Get up, man."

"I'm sorry, but I didn't see you anywhere near this table."

"Stop talking. Do the right thing, man."

The man tugged on Tom's shirt again, a little harder this time.

"Why don't we wait for my friend, okay?" Tom said, eyes on the tabletop. He couldn't even look at the couple anymore.

"Don't tell me to wait, man."

No table was worth this. But Tom couldn't get himself to move. The fear he felt was unlike any in his adult life. Nothing about it was specific. It was the terror he'd get as a kid when the house was empty and the wind blew a door shut.

When he finally forced himself to look up, the man's face was distorted with hatred. His eyes were black, like two wet marbles had been slipped into his eye sockets. There was a bullet hole in his chest. Same as Sarmad had. Tom couldn't stop staring at it, even as he bit down on his fist and sank the fingers of his other hand into the heavy metal napkin dispenser. He was picking out a spot to aim for on the man's temple as he started to raise the dispenser.

Silvana appeared in a streak, which ended right between the couple, where she planted herself and began scolding them in German. The next thing Tom knew, the couple was walking away, and the boyfriend was looking back and pointing at Silvana, saying, "Bitch, bitch." And Silvana was pointing back and saying in the same tone, "Eurotard, eurotard."

Tom let the napkin dispenser drop underneath the table as Silvana slid next to him. She stopped as close as possible without actually touching him. He felt her hand on his back as she glared at people until they stuck their faces back in their food.

"Okay, what the hell was that?" she said.

"I don't know."

"You okay?"

He nodded.

"Really? It's all right if you're not."

"I'm good."

"I think I should take you to a doctor." She glanced at the bruises at the bottom of his neck.

"I'm fine."

"My dad says the person who's sick should never be the one to make the diagnosis."

"What did you say to those people?"

She tried not to smile. "I told them that you were my brother and you were special."

Tom looked away.

"Does that amuse you?" she said.

"We should leave."

He'd never had a woman stand up for him before. As she shimmied out of the booth, he just sat, watching her.

"I want to call my dad," she said. "Now that we're going there, I just want to . . . make sure it's okay. I assume that's all right?"

"Use a landline."

"Okay. Meet me at the car?" She waited until he nodded. "I'm not going to come back here and find you arguing with your hand and drinking your own urine, am I?"

He shook his head.

She headed across the atrium, disappearing momentarily behind people until she rocked out of view and never came back into it. He sat there, trying to make the connection between what had just happened and what he'd discovered that morning in the bathroom. He'd had hallucinations before, but what he'd been about to do to that man was real.

The hallucinations were dangerous. And they were getting worse.

Feeling the eyes on him again, he got up and made his way through the atrium—then stopped.

Silvana.

She was in the middle of the crowd, staring at him through it. Her eyes tilted up to a flat-screen television high on the wall. There were shots of Sarmad's mansion. Bodies coming out in bags.

He looked back. There was no blame on her face. She just watched him with shock-wide eyes and began moving backward, slowly putting more people between them until only strips of her were visible, then strips of those strips, then nothing at all.

Tom ran through the parking lot, toward the car, turning in every direction. He saw the car but not her.

A woman slipped around the other side of the truck stop. He ran in her direction.

As he got closer, he could see she was shaking. The wind had whipped her hair into a black nest. When she saw him, she took off for the woods. She ran the way people run when they're screaming, except she was silent.

He grabbed her before she could crash full-speed into the branches. But then she fought him so hard that he would have hurt her if he didn't let go.

She yanked free, almost toppling over. Then she walked back the way she'd come, toward the car. He caught up to her again as she rounded the corner of the building. As soon as she saw him, she did a 180 and almost walked into an old Coke machine.

As she reeled back, there was a sound like a quarter plinking against a metal sheet.

Then he saw the hole in the machine.

He ran at her and tackled her, flattening her against the concrete.

Now she started screaming. She hit him with fists and elbows as he rolled them around the corner of the building. He wound up on top of her and pressed his bodyweight into her as she struggled to stand up. She was facedown, and he pinned her arms to her sides, so he could get his mouth against her ear.

"Someone just tried to shoot you in the head."

From the angle, he guessed the shooter was right by their car, at the back of the parking lot. The shooter wouldn't be able to see them here, but they wouldn't be able to see him either.

The side of the building they were against was angled on the woods and an empty weeded stretch of tarmac. They couldn't go for the forest because that would bring them right back into the shooter's sight line. But they couldn't go the other way around the building: it was 200 feet of wide-open blacktop. If the shooter closed in, he'd have them in open shot.

Fifty feet away, there were doors to a men's room and a women's room, both long forsaken and scarred over with rust. Tom grabbed Silvana's hand and led her toward the women's room. He had to hit the door a few times to shake off the decay sealing it shut. The next time he hit it, the door burst open.

Bogasian was sitting in the driver's seat with his legs on the passenger door. He put the rifle down, swallowed a mouthful of Egg McMuffin, and rolled up the window.

He'd caught up to them on the road outside the motel, heading into Germany. When they went into the autohof, he'd followed them in.

The parking lot was clear, so he screwed the silencer on his .38 and picked up the Egg McMuffin. The silencer was special-made out of an oil can and was about the length and width of a woman's forearm. He nudged the car door open with his foot and went around the truck stop in the opposite direction Tom and Silvana had taken—in case they were trying to sneak around the other side.

Holding the McMuffin gave him a natural-looking reason to pin his arm against his side, which kept the .38 from poking through his jacket. On the walk over, he took a couple more bites.

He stopped at the back corner of the truck stop and peered around it. Nothing but empty blacktop.

He didn't think they'd doubled back and gone for their car, and he was pretty sure they wouldn't have crossed the original line of fire and tried for the woods. So he walked the length of the building and stopped at a men's room and women's room. One was caked with crud and looked as though it hadn't been disturbed in fifteen years. The other was also caked...but not around the outline of the door.

He pushed the door open.

It was dark. The only light came from slats in the windows by the ceiling. He closed the door behind him and bent the doorknob down against the frame. Turning, he paused and listened for the sound of breathing.

In the middle of the bathroom, there were chipped sinks with black holes rotting out like cavities. He went over to them and stooped down and checked under the stalls.

He kicked the first stall door.

Empty.

He kicked the second. Also empty. By the third, he was beginning to think they'd actually hidden in the last stall. But when he kicked it open, it was empty. The toilet was missing. There was a hole in the wall where it had been shoved through.

Bogasian hunched down and crawled through himself. There was about five feet of space behind the wall to allow a repairman access to the pipes for each toilet on the other side.

As they ran out, Tom heard someone kicking the stall doors. The crawl space led to a concrete corridor that ended at a door with daylight glowing through the vents. They pushed the door open and found themselves back on the same side of the building they'd gone in. Tom slammed the door and gripped the doorknob and bent it down against the frame. Silvana looked at him, not comprehending, but then they were running for the car.

They got in, and Tom grabbed the mess of wires hanging under the steering column and touched two of them together. The engine whined but wouldn't turn. He reknotted the power wires and then held the starter wire against them. The engine shook without starting, but he kept holding it. He was looking for another car to steal when the engine finally fired.

The shortest route to the highway was the narrow strip of blacktop that passed near the bathrooms. He decided to risk it. As he drove past the women's room, a dent materialized in the center of the door they'd come out. It was so deep it made the sides of the door buckle inward.

Tom couldn't believe what he was seeing. If he'd tried the same thing, it would have broken his arm.

Seconds later the door burst out of its frame, and a man stepped into daylight.

In the rearview mirror, Tom saw the man stop and watch them merge onto the A7. There was something about the way he stood there. The calm of it.

Tom kept glancing at the figure behind them until the distance made it disappear.

CHAPTER 30

THE G-FORCES rocked Karl to sleep on the flight back to Paris. But his head kept falling forward, startling him. He'd be drifting off, the nervous energy draining off him, and then there'd be a falling sensation, and he'd jerk wide-awake. After ten minutes of this, he was wound too tight to sleep, so he gave in and stayed in that in-between state where he wasn't awake but wasn't in control of his thoughts either. When those thoughts led to Tom, he followed. But then Tom led him to his father. And his father led him back to Bell.

Bell, South Dakota.

Karl was a teenager. The economy had wet the bed, and the town wanted to condemn a piece of his father's property, a little tract of bush and bird shit, and give it to some developer promising jobs. They were going to have a town hall meeting to approve it. People asked his dad not to go, begged him. They said there'd be trouble, and besides the project might not pass.

But his father was going to that meeting. *And Karl,* he'd said, *you are going to that meeting.*

Why, Karl asked.

To see something.

They didn't talk in the car ride over, but Karl told himself that whatever happened he'd go down with his dad. He took pride in that, the kind of pride that somehow made him love his dad even more.

When they pushed through the double doors, men set on them. The whole town was in there. Al Fincher, who owned a farm equipment distributorship and hadn't had a down year in two decades, said in his withering, never-miss-church way: "Quality people don't do this." A neighbor who coached middle school basketball stepped forward. The man spoke softly, but he put his hand on Karl's dad's arm. He asked him to do the right thing and not speak, but he wasn't really asking.

You're takin' my property, you're gettin' my words. That was what his dad said.

Then he broke for the lectern. Suddenly everyone was shoving each other. Some old guy pushed Karl, and Karl pushed him back. Even someone's wife got in on it. Then he saw a kid hurl a Coke bottle, and the next thing he knew, his dad was on the ground, cupping his face. His nose was broken.

The kid was maybe two years older than Karl. A man had his hands on his back, soothing him as though he was the one who needed soothing. No one said a word to him.

Karl helped his dad up, and as they walked out in stone silence, he thought: *This is what a rebel looks like. It's not James Dean or rock 'n' roll. It's a man without friends who's in the way. It's someone who everyone wants to just recognize his own unimportance, but who won't. Something in him just can't.*

As Karl realized this, he wasn't proud. He was scared, because there was no right or wrong in those people's eyes, just need, a need that was bigger than his dad's need, that was bigger than his dad himself. It was something he never wanted to be on the wrong side of ever again.

Now Tom was on the wrong side of it. There wasn't a nation in the world that wouldn't take his life if it knew what he could do. And he was about to learn how alone he really was. He wasn't just a man without a friend. He was a man without a country. And after last night, it wasn't just the US government who wanted him dead. Karl remembered the lab, those men staring at him from their packaging. Whoever had done that would be looking for Tom, and when they found him, it wouldn't be a Coke bottle that smashed his face.

Karl thought of the look Tom had before he hit the water, the indifference of it. Then he thought about the events that could cause a young man to do such a thing, and he knew he wasn't just going to get Tom medical help. He was going to help him escape, no matter who he'd killed or how sick he turned out to be.

No peace came over him with this decision, though. Not like he hoped. Because he knew the truth: when you helped a man without friends, you became one too.

Two days after that town hall meeting, his dog had gone missing. She was a little mutt he'd adopted who looked like a golden retriever puppy even though she was full-grown. He went door-to-door to the neighbors, but no one knew anything. They found her three weeks later. She'd been hung by her plaid collar from a little maple tree.

Back in Paris, Karl walked right through Marty's reception area and into his office.

"Excuse me, *sir?* You *cannot* just go in there," the assistant said.

Karl slammed Marty's office doors shut and twisted the bolt.

Marty looked up at him from a massive computer screen. "They just found Sarmad's body."

There was some feeble tapping on the other side of the door. Karl banged his fist on the door, and the tapping stopped.

"I found the lab," Karl said.

Marty just stared at him.

Karl searched his face for a reaction. "It was just like ours."

"Was?"

"I burned it."

"How did you find it?"

"There were thirteen men inside. They'd been butchered."

"My god," Marty said after a little too long.

"You know anything about it?"

"I'm a career politician, Karl, which means I'm a weasel, but I'm not a butcher."

"I'm going to ask you something, and I hope you can make me believe you. Did you know Eric Reese is dead?"

"No."

Karl held up a still of Eric from the execution video. "I pulled this from a video on the internet. *On the internet.* How come no one at State ever asked us to ID him?"

"Do you know how many videos there are like this? Too many." Marty thought a moment. "How could Eric be connected here?"

"These people we're looking for, they didn't just take Nast and the others. They went after everyone. And why would they do that? Because they've restarted their own version of Prometheus."

"We shut it down. We shut it way down. And we kept the pieces separate, so they couldn't ever unite against the whole."

"These people got to Eric Reese and tried to make him continue his work. There's only one reason they'd do that. They didn't just want Bogasian. They wanted to create more of him." Karl pointed out the window. "Our own program has been running for three years without our knowing it. And right now it's out there somewhere, firing on all cylinders, controlled by people whose intentions we don't understand because we don't even know who the fuck they are."

Marty watched him a moment. "What is it, Karl?" His voice was soft suddenly, father-like.

"I found a prescription pad in the lab. It had Dr. Nast's name on it."

"You waited to tell me?"

"You were the one who knew him. Was he really the type?"

"When the sun goes down and the wolfsbane blooms, everybody's the type."

"He was already a wealthy man. He doesn't need the money."

Marty got up and went to the window. "People are greedy for far more than money. Need I remind you of Dr. Bull?"

Dr. Gerald Bull was the Canadian engineer who developed a "supergun" for Saddam Hussein. It was basically what a howitzer would become if you kept it in a cage and tube-fed it male enhancement pills. It had a range of 600 miles and could fire a satellite into space. Like all the best scientists, Dr. Bull was obsessed with possibility—right up until it got him shot five times in the head. No one knew who'd done it, because pretty much the whole world wanted him dead. But it was a reminder that today's hopeless romantic is tomorrow's supplier of sarin gas.

"Anyone who'd take a job like that has a touch of mad scientist in him," Marty said. "You ever wonder why a guy like Nast would come work for us in the first place?"

"Every time I saw him."

"His brother had early onset Alzheimer's, and his old man spent ten years in a home with it. What offers the best chance of a cure? Stem cell research."

Karl didn't say anything.

"People from Prometheus are dying, and the only one left is Dr. Nast. Reminds me of the movie *Ten Little Indians*. You know how to tell who the murderer is? You wait until everyone else is dead."

"Only one problem with that: once everybody's dead, it doesn't really matter anymore who the killer is."

Marty smiled. "Ah, but you're assuming the people in question don't all deserve to die."

Karl went quiet. Then he said, "I won't lie. Opening that file and seeing Ben Kotesh in a pile of his friends, it almost felt a little bit like…Christmas morning."

Marty burst out laughing. "See, this is why I missed you. You're the only person I can talk to about these things! I mean if you can't dance on the grave of some piece of shit, then I'm sorry, but you're just not having *fun* anymore."

"You know what I love about the CIA? It's really the place for you if you're a people person."

Marty burst out laughing again.

"Nast does fit," he said after they'd both gone quiet. "Who else could have performed the operation on Tom? Who else could have developed some remedial treatment for Bogasian, keep him civil enough to do their uncivil things? And his son had contacts with Alan Sarmad and Ben Kotesh. My god, he could have plugged his father right in."

"We need to be sure."

"I've never been sure of anything in my life." Marty stood still in the window. "In the thirteenth century, did you know it was common to torture all the suspects in a criminal investigation? They believed if you failed to live a life above suspicion, then you weren't entirely innocent. And you deserved to be punished for who you were as much as what you did or didn't do."

"Sounds like the thirteenth century pretty much sucked. And I don't want to kill an innocent man."

"Point is it's easier to find out the truth about a man than it is about something he's done. A lifetime provides decades of evidence. A specific action provides only a few seconds of it. Nast's son was a bad man, doing bad things for bad people. Someone who raises a man like that might not be provably guilty, but he isn't really innocent either."

Karl didn't know whether he agreed—or couldn't have disagreed more.

Marty went back to his desk and sat down. "What about Tom?" he asked.

"Three of the men Tom matched to his brother's shirt are dead.

That leaves one, and it could be Dr. Nast. Tom will be going for him. I have to get there first."

"I mean what are you going to do when you find him?"

"Find out if he's actually Eric's brother."

Marty's eyes searched Karl's face. "Someone that dangerous can't be allowed to just walk the streets."

Karl didn't say anything.

"If someone turned him, imagine what he could do. Even if he is Eric Reese's brother, he's Pandora's box, and we need to close the lid. Kill one, save a thousand. That's the math."

"But for once, the one is innocent."

Marty was quiet for a moment. "Does it matter?"

They looked at each other.

"Your problem is your concept of guilt. He may not be guilty in his heart. But he is in his effect."

They kept watching each other.

Karl leaned forward slowly. "We got his brother killed, and now we're going to kill him for doing something about it? If we do this, we're nothing. We're shit."

"Right now you're having an emotional reaction."

"Don't you ever get tired of it, gambling with your chance to be a somewhat decent person?"

"No, that's what it takes to stand for something."

Karl stood up and headed for the door. "This is going to end badly."

"Not for us, it won't. The agency is covered."

Karl turned back.

"According to my records," Marty said, "Tom Blake is an operative who finishes a rotation in a week or so. Now, as for the young man causing all this trouble, no one seems to have any way to identify him. And I have no idea who he is."

"Jesus Christ."

"Doubtful."

Karl yanked the door open so hard it shook when it hit the doorstop.

"Karl," Marty said, "kill him. There's no option here that doesn't end in that young man's death. I'm sorry, but we don't get to feel good about this one."

Karl walked back to his office. He wasn't so upset that he couldn't read between the lines. Tom's very existence would point people to a technology no one was ever supposed to know about. And that was unacceptable. For Marty. For the CIA.

And if Karl was honest, for him too.

CHAPTER 31

THEY'D BEEN driving for twenty miles or so. Silvana's eyes were glued to the road behind the car, but no one came up on them.

The panicky sensation Tom had never went down. His fingers weren't shaking—he was gripping the steering wheel too hard for that—but they wanted to.

How had that man found them so fast?

How did he do that to the door?

There was a desperate childish voice in his head that wanted to call a time-out, so he could have a minute—*just one minute*—to think things through. He tried to tell himself he just needed a little while to calm down, but this wasn't nerves. It was the feeling you got when you were outmatched.

It was horrifying how young this made him feel. He wanted to say to that man or to Karl or anyone else coming for him: *You can't really kill me. I'm still practically a kid. Four years ago I was in high school. I was a mathlete.*

Karl's voice answered him: *They're going to do a lot more than find you.*

He looked at Silvana again. She'd been quiet for a solid twenty minutes, her body shaking against the pleather car seat.

"Who the hell are you?" she said suddenly. "No, *what* the hell are you?"

He looked at her.

"What are you going to do to me?" she said.

"Take you to Berlin."

"Is something going to happen to me there?"

He started to answer her—

"Who would hurt me?" She swallowed. "Who the hell would want to hurt me?"

"I don't know. But I'll get you to a safe place, and then we can be done."

"A strange man at a truck stop just tried to kill us in a public *bathroom*. So please—pretty please—tell me what me being here with you means."

She watched him. She was scared of him before, when she thought he was just a guy who'd killed a bunch of people outside Nice. But now it wasn't the fear in her eyes that worried him.

"I'm in more danger now, being here with you, than I ever was before. You knew that, didn't you?"

"Yes." He started to say something else.

"And what? You're sorry."

"No."

Her eyes widened at this, and the look of hatred on her face deepened.

"I can't be sorry because the truth is: I'd do it all over again. I can only tell you that I hated doing this to you, and whatever you think of me, I deserve it." There was a part of him that wanted to tell her everything, but he couldn't do that.

"How did that man do that to the door?" she said. "That was impossible, you know?"

"I know." Tom checked the rearview mirror again.

"So how did you do it? I saw what you did to the doorknob."

He didn't say anything.

"Pull over."

"We need to put as much distance between us and—"

"Pull over."

He looked at her. "You know I can't."

"How. Did. You. Do. That?"

"Look, I don't know, okay?"

"Bullshit."

She unlocked her door and shoved it open. They were going eighty miles per hour. Wind hit Silvana's face and whipped her hair back. Tom pulled off the highway and, once they couldn't be seen from it, stopped the car.

She got out and walked off, never looking back.

"Wait." He said it over and over until she got so far away he was shouting. She stopped at the top of a small rise and stood without turning around.

He looked back down the road. There were no cars, but he watched the horizon, knowing something was coming for them. He waited for it to solidify out of the blur.

Eventually she came down the hill.

"You're not telling me everything," she said.

We want the girl.

"Are you telling me everything?" he asked.

"I am." She looked down at her feet. "I mean, I even told you about my brother."

Watching her stand like that, all he wanted was to put his arm around her.

"Okay," he said. "What do you want to know?"

"Why did you kill those men?"

He looked away.

"I deserve to know." She fixed her eyes on him and slowly nodded her head. And the way she did it, the dignity of it, left him with no choice, at least not one he wanted any part of.

"A few years ago I visited my brother in Paris," he said. "The night before I flew home, he and I went out. The next morning, I had no memory of how I got back to his place. He was acting like something was wrong. By the time I got home, he'd just vanished. Six months later he was dead."

She searched his face, deciding whether to believe him. Whether to feel for him.

"After a few months, I noticed something was different. I was different."

"Different how?"

"I was stronger, faster, different." He looked at her. "But there are side effects. I see things sometimes. And it's getting worse."

"That man at the autohof, is he like you?"

"Sarmad told me there'd been a stem cell experiment. But I think whatever was done to me isn't as...it's a light version of whatever they did to the other people, and I think that man back there was the only one to survive."

"What are you going to do if he finds us again?"

"I don't know."

Silvana looked away. "Do you think your brother did this to you?"

"No, he would never."

She got closer. "Can you really know?"

He looked down. "Eric...was just one of those people. He could never have done something like this."

"Okay," Silvana said, and the way she said it was soft, like she understood.

They both watched each other.

"And what are you here for?" she said.

"Four men killed my brother, and one of them is still out there."

He checked the horizon again. Now that his adrenaline had dumped, he could feel his exhaustion. It hung on him, pulling down with the ceaselessness of gravity.

He noticed a drainage pipe in a ditch. For a second he had an insane urge to crawl inside it with Silvana and sleep for a day.

"Did you kill those men in Paris?" Silvana asked.

"No."

"Was it you I saw at my brother's house that night?"

"Yes."

"Did you...did you kill my brother?"

"No." Now he fixed his eyes on hers. "But I wanted to."

She watched him for a long time and then slipped back into the passenger seat. He got behind the wheel.

"Let me take you to Berlin," he said. "I'll get you to your parents."

He put his hand on her forearm.

She recoiled.

Not much. Maybe half an inch.

Silvana's eyes went to his, like she hadn't meant to do it. And he realized now he'd been right: it wasn't her fear that should worry him.

It was uncanny valley.

Uncanny valley was a robotics theory Eric had told him about. People prefer objects similar to people. They will feel affection for something that has a face, like a teddy bear, but not for something that doesn't, like a rock. As an object becomes more human-like, people's positive feelings toward it spike. But there's a dead zone where if something becomes too human-like without actually being human, those positive feelings suddenly reverse and crash—into uncanny valley. It was why nobody in middle school wanted to sit next to the kid with the prosthetic hand.

Tom didn't look any different, but he was different. And he was sure he'd seen it in her face, that nanosecond of revulsion.

He looked away and started the car, ending the moment between them. He had to. The part of him that was still normal—still only recently a teenager—would have died a little if he'd stayed in that moment.

"Tom . . ."

It was the first time she'd ever used his name. But all she did was shake her head and look out the window.

CHAPTER 32

THE SKIN had bruised immediately after he hit the door at the truck stop. Now it was almost black.

Bogasian sank back in the motel tub, down to his nostrils, to let it soak. Every once in a while, he poked at the bruise, and a thin worm of blood was birthed into the water. After a few minutes, he stood up. He poured rubbing alcohol down his arm where the skin had split and shook from the pain. After he got dressed, he sat at his computer.

He should have known better than to sit still like that.

They crept up on him. First, darkness seeped into his eyes. Then a white streak blotted out his vision, so bright it hurt. It was gone in less than a second.

Another white splice lit up his eyes, hitting them like lightning.

More splices. They joined together into images. Then the images expanded into scenes. It was never people he'd killed, but people he'd seen on his way to kill.

—The woman in Moscow who glanced at him from a nearby taxi and froze. Time marched on, but she was paused, expressionless, as her whole body pointed at him. And he was scared because it wasn't the woman looking at him but something else using her eyes to see.

—The boy who almost hit him with a bike. The boy cowered on the ground and put his hands up as Bogasian stood over him.

But underneath those shaking arms, there was a face that wasn't afraid, that saw him for what he was.

—The waitress from the last restaurant he'd ever been to. As she took his order, a bullet hole in her forehead dribbled blood onto her uniform, and she just stood there with an apple-pie smile while blood ran into her eyes and mouth.

In the lab, they'd told him about the attacks he'd get during long periods of downtime. A doctor explained that his increased metabolism seemed to cause a "slight increase" in anxiety, and that without something productive to "crowd it out," he'd have a problem.

And the little dickhead had been right.

Once tasked, Bogasian could keep the splices and the darkness on the edges. But in moments like this, they gained on him. They were always gaining on him.

As a kid, he and a friend had gone on an amusement park ride called the Teacup. People spun around in gigantic cups and saucers that rotated on a carousel. Except he and his friend found they could get their cup to spin faster by twisting the stationary wheel bolted into the middle of it. So they twisted and twisted. It was slow at first. Then they really got it going. And still they twisted and twisted—until they'd gone too far. It wasn't ordinary dizziness that they felt. They were past that inside of five seconds. Then the g-forces had them.

They both grabbed at the wheel.

Then they were clawing at it.

But the Teacup weighed a couple hundred pounds. They couldn't slow down. His friend was sobbing. He'd deflated in his seat, eyes to the sky. Prone, like an offering to God. But Bogasian realized if he kept his eyes closed, the dizziness was tolerable. He just couldn't ever open them. As soon as he did, everything turned and turned—up, down, left, right—until the world was carving itself to pieces right in front of his eyes. Until he would have done anything to make it stop.

Now he had the same problem. Eventually the splices would never stop or the darkness would snap across his eyes like a curtain. And then—

He'd be back on the Teacup.

And he didn't know how long he could stay on. Or what things he would do to get off.

Tom and Silvana.

They were his lifeline. He'd spent the previous hour dialing hotels, trying to find a reservation under Adrien Michel. He would spend the next hour doing the same.

Tom had been a surprise. The way he'd been able to bend the knob on the door, it was obvious he'd been worked on. Other than himself, Bogasian had never known of anyone who had gotten injected and survived.

He went to the window and watched the lights dotting the horizon. At this safe distance, this late hour, he could finally look directly at them.

After two long hours, a message came. His computer screen went dark, and white letters emerged:

—*You were to follow, not engage.*

Bogasian typed: *He has Sarmad's files.*

—*We need him alive.*

Suddenly he understood. Whatever had been done to Tom wasn't as bad as what they'd done to him. And now that they'd seen Tom, they just had to have him.

—*Find, follow, and await tasking. Berlin is now the priority. There's a new target.*

Bogasian went to get up. But another message appeared.

—You're zero fail on this.

And Bogasian could breathe again. He was back in motion. He was one step ahead of the Teacup.

CHAPTER 33

TOM STOOD outside a little market in the dim area between the streetlights. Silvana was inside. He watched her dump an armful of groceries on the checkout counter, then run back for a few more things. She kept turning around and making comments to the clerk, and whatever she was saying, it was cracking him up.

For now, what happened at the truck stop almost seemed behind her. Or at least, for a moment, it didn't have her by the throat. She was alive in that moment.

She came out of the market cradling a bloated grocery bag. As soon as she saw him, she cocked her head at the bag, indicating the feast they were going to have, and smiled. She was too far away for him to say something but too close not to look at.

He liked that, waiting for her like this.

Back in the motel room, booked with the Sorbonne student's ID, they sat at the desk and ate their dinner. In between dangerously enormous bites of food, Silvana told him stories about her friends and asked him at least twenty questions about what he did for fun. (At least ten of these took some form of: "Well, there must be *something?*") He asked her about her brother, and all she said was, "There's nothing really there to talk about, I guess." She didn't bring up the rest stop, but she asked him more about his brother. *What was he like?* Then she perked up. "No, tell me something weird about him."

"You want to hear something weird about Eric?"

"Yes."

He thought about all the things Eric had given up to take care of him, how much time and energy it took to include your kid brother in every single thing you ever did as a twenty-two-year-old. Still, at times, Tom got a glimpse of the young man Eric would have been under different circumstances.

"He had a thing about doll hair," Tom said.

"Doll hair?"

"It disgusted him. Like he couldn't eat if there was anything with doll hair in the room."

"What?" She was grinning.

"And feathers too. If a feather came out of a cushion and he was eating, you could actually see the moment where he'd stop chewing and just sit there, staring at it."

"Tell me you used this against him in some way."

"Well, naturally his college friends found out. One night he goes on a date with this girl Sarah Patino, who everybody was in love with. Before Eric went out, his buddies are asking him how he got a date with her, and this devolves into him giving everyone this lecture on the importance of personal hygiene and actually listening when a girl is speaking. Then he mentioned he'd probably be bringing her back, and he'd appreciate it if there was no leering at or attempted touching of his date. And, you know, everyone was sort of suspiciously accepting of all this. They're all like: *Of course we'll behave. In fact we'll even clean up a little.*"

"Oh god."

"So, by the time Eric comes back with her, we're all outside looking in the windows, and there's feathers *everywhere*. It was like someone had thrown a chicken coop into an industrial fan. He tries to laugh it off, but after a few seconds we see he's sweating. And every time Sarah isn't looking at him, he starts sneaking this tissue out of his pocket and wiping his forehead.

"They walk to the kitchen to get to Eric's room in the back, so we all run to the other window, and we see Eric is just standing there, staring at it: on the counter, there's a raw steak with doll hair sprinkled on top. This thing… it was like something an artist in Germany came up with. I mean it made *me* sick. Sarah asks him about it, except Eric isn't really saying much at this point. He's just planted there, looking at it like it's a human head."

"What happened?"

"He puked. And then she puked. And then she *never* went out with him again." Tom started laughing.

Silvana stared at him. "Men are animals. I really mean that. You're like crocodiles with a human face."

"That was a week before he graduated," Tom said, and he got quiet. "He left for Europe two years later, almost to the day."

For the rest of the evening, he sat talking and listening but mostly watching her. He'd never thought or cared about a life after finding the men he was looking for. It would be unreasonable to expect to survive this. But if he did somehow get a life, and if that life was filled with things half as nice as the woman across from him, it would be a good one.

He was brushing his teeth when she appeared outside the bathroom door. She was in her underwear, her legs barely covered by an extra-large T-shirt she'd bought at the convenience store.

She held up her toothbrush, and he made room for her. As she bent over the sink to wet her toothbrush, the shirt hitched up to the area where her legs turned into hips. Then they stood together, mouths open, their brushing the only sound in the room. He sensed she was watching him.

"So what does it feel like?" she asked.

"What?"

"You said your body wasn't the same. What's it feel like?"

He didn't know what to make of her question, not after what had happened in the car.

"Do you feel things more?"

"I don't think so."

She bobbed her head, satisfied. He lost his concentration for a second, and his eyes ticked down to her legs. He never would have guessed they'd be that tan.

Her toothbrush stopped.

When he looked up, she was watching him again. She reached across his body to get a tissue, and her hip brushed against his. He waited until she was done and went to rinse his toothbrush. She spat a mouthful of toothpaste right as his hand moved under the faucet. The gob of blue yolk slid off the back of his hand.

They looked at each other.

"You didn't give me any warning," she said.

He rinsed it off.

"I'm sorry about what happened in the car earlier."

He nodded.

"It's just that, you know, what you did was..."

He kept nodding, hoping she would drop it.

"Not normal," she said. "I mean I was scared of you *before* you bent a doorknob like that. So..."

"You don't have to explain yourself."

"But I want to."

He dried his hands for what seemed like a long time.

"Look," he said. "I know what I am is...I mean I guess I'd feel the same way if I were in your position."

A funny look flashed across her face.

"I think you're underestimating me," she said.

To avoid her stare, he took his time folding the hand towel until it was perfectly symmetrical.

"I don't know what it is, but something about you keeps telling me you're a good person even though I hardly know you and"—she laughed sadly—"I really have no reason to trust you."

He went to walk past her. She shifted her bodyweight, leaning in his way.

They were about a foot apart. Now he couldn't help but look into her concerned blue eyes. On their own, they were nice. But as the epicenter of the wounded look on her face, they were too much for him to look at.

Remember her father.

She was still staring him down.

Except now something about her was open. He moved toward her. He didn't know why. He just did it.

She didn't flinch this time. Her mouth opened a little, and he kissed her. Then they were pressed together, and his hands were running over her body and hers over his. And he couldn't stop cupping and re-cupping her thighs and her butt because they were so smooth and tight and like the surface of a ball he couldn't quite get hold of.

Silvana hopped up on the counter with her knees apart. She curled one leg behind his, guiding him between her thighs. Their pelvises bumped lightly, and he felt her other leg wrap around him, locking him in place. His body fit perfectly, like it'd always been meant to be there.

The bathroom rug slipped underneath his feet. They fell halfway to the tile, laughed into each other's mouths, and went over to the bed. They dropped themselves down side by side, and he squeezed her chest against his until he felt the bend in her sternum. She pulled him on top of her.

And there was nowhere else to go. No next step. For the first time since Eric died, he found something that didn't lead him somewhere else. Except deeper into the place where he already was.

CHAPTER 34

KARL WALKED into the war room. Everyone was either talking on the phone or typing in front of a laptop. They looked like a bunch of MBA students doing a group project to hunt down and kill enemies of the state while simultaneously rationalizing a company's supply chain. He sat between Henry and James.

"Silvana Nast. Have you gotten anything new about where she might be taking him?"

"We got something else—an incident at a truck stop near Heidenheim," James said. "Two couples got into a screaming match of some sort, and somebody called the cops. Description of one of the couples: an American male in his twenties, brown hair, brown eyes, six feet, and a female with black hair and 'light-colored' eyes."

"They released all that over a little argument?"

"Apparently someone saw them go behind the building. When an employee went back there, she saw that two doors had been completely destroyed, and there were bullet holes in a soda machine. The Heidenheim police just put out a press release on their website."

"Map the route from Nice to Heidenheim."

James pulled up the map and turned his computer so Karl could see it. Tom and Silvana—if these two people at the truck stop were actually them—were well into Germany. They could be going anywhere within it.

Karl was relieved Tom still had the girl with him. She was his acid test. He didn't think she was involved in any of this, so if her body turned up in a ditch, he'd have to revisit this whole idea of helping Tom.

"Write down her address for me," Karl said.

James wrote it down on a piece of paper and handed it to him. "There's one other thing," he said. "Those fingerprints came back a few minutes ago."

He typed something on his laptop and brought up a picture of the man who Karl had killed last night.

"His name's Dorian McKittrick."

"American?"

James looked over. "He works for us."

With great effort, Karl pushed the words out. "What was that?"

"He's an employee of the CIA. He's in the National Clandestine Service in counterintel."

Karl pictured Dorian McKittrick kneeling at the base of a tree, trying to shoot a half-inch slug through his face at 1500 miles per hour.

At the bottom of the bio page, Karl looked under "Family." McKittrick was married with two children: Elizabeth and Lindsay. They lived in Virginia. The girls were probably on their way to school right now. Probably they were rushing to catch the school bus or taking too long in the bathroom or swapping horror stories about some boy who could make his arm fart the alphabet.

James was staring at him, trying to read his reaction. "What's the significance of this guy?" he said.

"Nothing yet. Just a theory I'm working on." Karl walked out. He dialed Marty.

The man whose teeth you blew out the side of his mouth was not only an American, he was your coworker.

Marty's voicemail told him to leave a message, and he hung up.

*   *   *

Karl looked at Silvana Nast's address. Then he did something he probably shouldn't have and actually went to it. It was stupid, going to the apartment of the girl they'd tried to grab off a public street. But he needed to find out if she knew her father's location.

He broke into the building with a bump key, which he used only because he refused to walk around foreign countries with a pick and a tension wrench. Upstairs he saw a notice from the police on her door. He knocked and waited ten seconds. Then let himself into the apartment with the bump key and went right to her MacBook.

He opened the lid, and the operating system started up. A password prompt stopped it cold.

He opened the top drawer of her desk to look for something with a password scribbled on it. To begin with, the drawer was so jammed full of stuff he almost had to rip it out just to get it open. Then he saw the exact nature of what he was dealing with. There were about a hundred scraps of paper with to-do lists on them, a fistful of parking tickets, thirty loose Altoids breath mints, a tampon wrapper (ripped open in seeming haste), a Gordian knot of old cell phone power cords, a piece of chocolate (melted, tooth marks), a three-carat yellow diamond ring, and two tubes of hand lotion, each of which was crusted with and yet still leaking moisturizer out the nozzle like some sort of ceaseless, alien ejaculate.

The thing was a fucking petri dish.

He gave up immediately on finding a password written down in there and went to step 2. Years ago someone at the agency had put together a list of the most statistically common passwords. Apparently without knowing much of anything about a person, you had about a 90 percent chance of guessing their password—sort of like when you ask people to choose a number between one and ten, almost everyone chooses seven.

Karl tried *123456*. He found something with a phone number on it—presumably hers—and tried that. Then he tried *qwer1234*.

The computer started loading. She hadn't even tried to be sneaky by capitalizing the *Q*.

He went to Settings, then to Passwords. This new page showed a list of websites she used frequently and the username and password she used to log in automatically to each one. He went to a travel booking website. Under Past Trips, he saw she'd booked seven flights to Tegel Airport in Berlin in the past three years but canceled them all last-minute. He sat back.

She would only do that if there was someone in Berlin she was desperate to see—but couldn't.

Her father?

Karl brought up her browsing history and searched for "Berlin" to see if she'd looked up an address before any of her canceled trips. One came up. It was for a Motel One near Charlottenburg. She'd want to stay somewhat near her father, so there was a good chance he was in the vicinity.

Charlottenburg. There was something familiar about the name.

He remembered Dr. Nast telling him about a brother-in-law who was making a killing through a minority interest in a friend's property development firm. It had been selling properties around some high-rent part of town. Charlottenburg?

He logged in to Facebook and scrolled through Silvana's Facebook friends, looking for family. She had about two thousand friends, which was just astonishing to him, so it took a while to find an aunt and an uncle who lived in Berlin. Elisabeta and Stephen Strasburg.

Elisabeta resembled Dr. Nast, so Strasburg must have been the brother-in-law. Karl clicked on Strasburg's profile. But Strasburg was too old for Facebook. There wasn't much there. Karl tried googling him. Not much there either. But an image search online showed pictures of Strasburg at various charity events with the names of the people he was standing with in captions below. Karl started plugging all of their names into Google to see where they worked. It took him almost half an hour. Then he found a man who was the CEO of the Charlottenburg Group.

That was it. The name of the company had Charlottenburg in it.

Karl googled property sales in the area and looked at the names of the companies selling them. The Charlottenburg Group was the first one to pop up. He went to their website and looked at a list of properties they'd sold in the last three years near Charlottenburg. There were two. And Karl bet there was a unit in one of those buildings that had never been sold and was still on their books. He wrote both addresses down.

As he got in a cab, he called James.

"Meet me at the airport."

CHAPTER 35

BOGASIAN'S EYES flipped open, and he shot into consciousness. It wasn't day yet, but there was a little light leaking in around the curtains. With his heart hammering in his chest, he slid off the bed. His arm was still swollen, and the skin was raised tight. He unwrapped the motel's bar of French-milled cocoa butter soap in the tub and massaged it over the area. When he was done, he flossed and brushed his teeth.

The truck stop where he'd found Tom and Silvana was only six hours from Berlin, but he was certain they hadn't reached it yet. After what happened, they'd move to back roads, which would turn a six-hour drive into a much-longer one. And once the shock of everything wore off, they'd crash.

They were probably going to the nice part of Berlin, which meant West Berlin. There were two routes there from where he'd last seen them: the A2 and the A9. Both led to the Berliner Ring, which surrounded the city like a beltway and could get them reasonably close to any place within it. He decided to focus on the Ring, which was a natural choke point.

Once they reached it, though, he couldn't know which way they'd go: east or west. Not unless he helped make the decision for them.

He sat in his car at a truck stop, eating a McToast Schinken-Käse with a side of fruit and yogurt. A trucker driving a MAN flat-nose with a trailer pulled in and headed for the men's room on the side of the building.

Bogasian got out.

Inside, the man stood in front of one of ten urinals, hips forward, bodyweight rocked back on his heels. Bogasian turned the lock on the door and walked over to him, checking the stalls on his way. They were all empty except for one with a piece of paper taped to it that said: KAPUTT!

When he was close, the man started shaking out the last few drops. Bogasian stopped four feet away and glanced around the room until he heard the zipper go up. The trucker turned, noticing him, and offered what sounded like a greeting.

Bogasian grabbed him. The man tried to resist, the whole time staring at him, wide-eyed— *Why are you doing this?* Bogasian pulled down until the man's head was trapped under his armpit. Then he wrapped an arm around his throat. Their bodies faced each other. Once he walked them backward into one of the stalls, he locked his fists and strained upward.

The trucker's feet came off the ground. With his eyes turned up to the ceiling, Bogasian cut off the man's air supply using his own bodyweight. He held this position until the man stopped moving. Neither one of them made a sound.

Bogasian took the keys out of the trucker's pocket, locked the stall, and climbed out over the top. Then he took the KAPUTT! sign and stuck it to the stall door.

He got in the semi and turned onto the A9.

At the junction, he merged onto the Berlin beltway going eastbound. And at the six-mile mark, he accelerated. The chug of the engine rose into a high spinning noise like the scream of a dentist's drill. He swung the rig from the center lane to the far-right lane. Twelve tires liquefied on the asphalt, and the smell burned the air. As the momentum of the rig caught up and swung it to the right, Bogasian twisted the steering wheel left.

The rig cut across four lanes of traffic. The valves were shrieking, and the trailer started to jackknife as he collided with the center divider. When the whole thing rolled, he extended one arm against the steering wheel and the other against the back of the seat and held himself suspended over the pavement spinning and stripping everything in the window below.

It took 200 feet of friction to stop all the momentum.

By the time he slipped out the door, there was already a pileup eight cars deep. It would take at least a day to clear the wreckage. Since the cars were on the other side of the rig, no one saw him once he jumped out of the cab. He walked to the closest truck stop, smashed the window of a parked car, and drove it back to his car.

He switched vehicles and drove to the junction of the A9 and the beltway. This time he merged westbound—which wouldn't be clogged with stopped cars—and found a place where he could see the Berlin-bound traffic and parked. While he waited, he thought about his life.

For three years, he had worked for people he didn't really know or understand because he depended on them for medical treatment. They kept him alive for a price, and he found that price acceptable.

It was the same life Tom would have after they caught him. Once the side effects escalated, he would do anything just to make them stop.

Bogasian sat in the car for a long time, imagining this.

And he decided that once he killed the target in Berlin, he'd kill Tom too.

CHAPTER 36

TOM WOKE up and looked around for Silvana. She was sitting at the table wearing nothing except for a silver wax-seal pendant around her neck. Somehow it made her look even more naked. There was a large blue box in front of her, and she was chewing a donut with her legs crossed.

"There was a Kamps around the corner," she said. "It thought it could hide from me, but I still found it." She grinned.

He just looked at her, and she looked down like she too was just noticing she didn't have clothes on.

"I was about to get in the shower, but the bear claw was calling my name." She grinned again.

"How much cash do we have left?"

She sorted through her purse with her unglazed hand, paused for a second, and laughed. "We have one euro." She held it up.

"Well, if we run out of gas, I guess we'll just have to steal another car."

"Why don't we just steal some gas?"

"It's easier to steal the whole car."

She sat taking huge bites of the bear claw.

He watched her for a moment. "Why don't you just unhinge your jaw?"

She started laughing, but her mouth was full, so it came out as little sniffs through her nose. She held up a hand to stop him from making any more comments until she'd swallowed.

Then she kicked out a chair for him. "Sit down."

He didn't move.

"Am I making you uncomfortable?"

"Eating like this . . . is this something you do?"

"Uh-huh. Now sit down." She kicked the chair again.

He walked over and fished out a chocolate donut, and they ate facing each other. The only sound was their chewing. It was nice, doing this with someone he'd just spent the night with. He remembered Eric and his friends always seemed to have more fun together the morning after their nights out than they did on the nights themselves. He understood now.

They sat, talking about nothing in particular. Then Silvana stopped smiling.

"Can I ask you a question?" she said, and he got the sense she was working up to something.

"Sure."

"What you're doing could get you in some pretty bad trouble. You don't seem that worried about it."

"That's not a question."

"No, I guess not."

She kept watching him.

"So why aren't you worried about it?"

"What is this?"

She shook her head. "Nothing. I was just—it's nothing."

He took a small bite of a donut. He didn't know why, but he was getting angry. He tossed the donut on the table. "I can practically hear you thinking over there. If you have something to say, you can say it."

"Have you ever wondered whether your brother would want you to risk your life like this if it meant you never got to have a life of your own?"

He spoke in a low voice. "Some people murdered my brother,

filmed it, and uploaded it on the internet. And I'm supposed to—what—turn the other cheek?"

"That's not what I'm—"

"Or maybe we can sit down with Dr. Phil, and I can talk about my feelings, and they can talk about theirs, and we can see that there's an 'emotional truth' here, and really what we all need to do is *listen first.*"

She stared at her bear claw with a look of utter sorrow.

"Of all people, I thought maybe you'd understand. My brother disappeared, and nobody would help me. Not the State Department, not the FBI. It was like he never even existed in the first place." He could see he was hurting her, but he couldn't stop. "Well, if my brother's life mattered so little that nobody would do a damn thing, then you know what? I'm going to *find* the people responsible, and I'm going to *make* his life matter."

"Why?"

"Because I have to, okay? I have to."

Silvana kept watching him, then looked out the window. Her eyes were wet. For a moment he didn't think she was going to say anything.

"Your life matters too, you know," she said. "Maybe you're too sad to realize that or you don't have anyone to tell you that, but I'm telling you...right now."

Her face screwed up, and the wetness grew in her eyes. "My brother's dead. I haven't seen my dad in years. And you, you—" She caught herself before she could say what she really thought about his situation. "Sometimes I think there's just so much sad, incomprehensible shit in this world that the most you can hope for is to sit naked with some girl in a shitty motel and eat crappy, mildly chemical-tasting donuts together." She looked down. "And it doesn't have to be with me, okay? But when something nice comes along, you should take it. At the very least, do that."

He was quiet for a minute.

Then he got up and walked to the bathroom. When he came out after his shower, he started packing his things. Silvana was already dressed and packed. She sat on the same chair where she'd been naked fifteen minutes ago and stared at the floor.

When he was done, she grabbed her stuff and walked to the car. Before he left, he stopped and looked at the teardrops she'd left on the table.

He wiped them up.

They crossed into the Berlin city limits after two hours of silence. Silvana had barely looked in his direction.

There was a pileup on the eastbound beltway, so they went west. Once they turned off the highway, there were people outside, families walking around, the signs of everyday life. Back at the motel, it'd felt like he and Silvana were the only people in the world. Now surrounded by this, they seemed like what they were—two people who barely knew each other.

Before stopping outside the address she gave him, Tom braked at one end of the street and looked around. Silvana turned toward him, but when she saw he was looking at the street and not her, she turned away again.

Everything seemed normal, so he idled up to the curb in front of the building. He noticed the door to the main entrance was protected by a thick metal gate with a security camera next to it.

Silvana waited for a good ten seconds. When he didn't say anything, she hopped out of the car and yanked a grocery bag with her things out of the backseat. Then she leaned into the passenger window.

He started to say something right as she started to say something.

"Sorry, go ahead," he said.

"I just wanted to say... thank you. For getting me here and everything."

"Least I could do."

Her arm was on the window. He could touch it if he wanted to.

"Where are you going from here?" she said.

"I don't really know yet."

"I hope you find..." She stopped herself. "I hope things work out."

"I hope they work out for you too."

She smiled, but it was polite, like they had already parted ways.

"I suppose I should..." She turned and looked back at the apartment building.

He nodded, already agreeing.

"I should let you go," he said.

"Yeah..."

"All right."

"Okay."

"Okay."

"Drive safe."

"Like I did in Paris."

She laughed.

"All right."

"All right."

Half-wave.

Half-wave.

And she was gone.

Tom turned the corner and pulled to a stop. He looked at the passenger seat, then around the rest of the car. When she was in it, the car had been this little world. Now he saw it for what it was: a stolen piece of crap.

He rested his head on the steering wheel. Two things floated up inside him. Already he missed her. And in a couple of hours, he was going to kill her father.

CHAPTER 37

BOGASIAN WATCHED Silvana go into an apartment building. Tom waited until she'd disappeared inside, then turned the corner and pulled over suddenly. His head sank against the steering wheel. *He must be exhausted,* Bogasian thought.

When Tom drove off, Bogasian didn't follow.

Tom needed a rifle. Plan A had been to go to one of the local shooting clubs, which were to Germans what Elks Lodges used to be to Americans, and request a lesson. He'd ask for something bigger than a .22 and then just run out with it. But this would involve the police, not to mention stealing from people who shot guns for the hell of it.

The gun show in Magdeburg, however, would not.

Still he needed a permit, which was a problem. And he wouldn't be able to buy the gun right then and there, only order it for future delivery, which was an even-bigger one.

It took him an hour trawling the comments section of gun websites before he found a way around this. And a couple hours after that, in the conference wing of the Best Western in Magdeburg, he arranged an order for a Blaser 30-ought-6 from a private seller. And this private seller arranged for Tom's future delivery to take place fifteen minutes later in the parking lot. The issue of a permit didn't come up.

On the drive back, he got off the highway and trudged through some woods until he found a clearing. He marked a tree and fired at it a few times, each time correcting the sights. The gunshots were loud, but no one came to check them out.

Back in Berlin, he scoped out the building Silvana had gone into. It had eight stories, and there was a nine-story office building across the street. It was now 5:35, and since in Germany, when the work day ends at five, the work day *ends at five,* the office building was probably empty.

Tom waited twenty minutes. No one came out. He checked the front of the office building. There was a security station in the lobby. No guard. He tried the door. Locked.

He went back to his car and got the rifle case and the briefcase with the files. In the alley behind the building, he threw both over the security fence and then scaled it. He found a fire door to the office building that required a key card for entry. The door handle didn't have latches, so he guessed the door was locked shut with two large magnets.

He put both hands through the handle and yanked so hard the door twisted. It was a trick he'd learned at Johns Hopkins while Eric was there. So long as the magnets touched directly, they could withstand anything, but when you bent the door, you bent the magnet—and took the magnetic fields out of alignment.

The door popped open, vibrating in his hands.

He walked into a hallway lined with fluorescent lights. He passed by the elevator. It would likely have a security camera, and there was the off-chance some workaholic was still in the building. So he lugged everything up the stairs to the roof.

The sun was low, and the sky had flipped—blue to orange. As he looked over the neighborhood, he saw long triangles of shadow and sunlight that interlocked like a gigantic backgammon board.

Silvana's family's building was, as best as he could tell, made up of luxury condos with one unit per floor. The part of the building he faced was basically floor-to-ceiling window, so he was able to see the living room and kitchen of each unit as the lights came on. There was no sign of Silvana.

He opened the CIA files and flipped through the pictures of Alan Sarmad and the other men responsible for Eric's death. He ended on Dr. Nast. He would have traded all the others for Nast.

He shot Eric. Point-blank. In the head.

And Tom didn't really give a shit why.

He knew he should ask about what had been done to him. He was sick and getting worse. But he didn't want the man who shot Eric to ever give him anything, not even the truth.

And anyway from what he'd seen in the photos, the prognosis was obvious.

More lights came on in Silvana's building. There was a family with a cat on the fourth floor and another with a small child on the fifth. The lights on the top floor came on. An attractive older woman stood paused on the edge of the living room with her fingertips still on the switch. Something on her mind.

The resemblance was obvious, even through the scope of a hunting rifle.

Silvana walked out of a hallway that fed into the living room. She was about ten feet below eye level with him. Her mother followed her into the kitchen, and while Silvana dug around inside a box of crackers, her mother pulled ingredients out of the cupboards. Tom could see their lips moving as they talked.

Every time the older woman walked past Silvana to get something, she trailed her hand across Silvana's back until the distance pulled it off. Silvana was hunched over her crackers, shy almost. She didn't notice when her mother stopped whatever she was doing to watch her.

He leaned against the ledge and waited.

*   *   *

The sun still hadn't set. It loitered on the horizon. Inside the penthouse, a man came in the front door. Silvana saw him and stopped.

He stopped too.

Neither one of them said anything. Tom couldn't see Silvana's face, but when the man moved part of the distance toward her, she was already covering the balance.

They hugged hard. No patting or swaying—just her face pressed into his shoulder. Silvana's mother came over. The man looked at her over Silvana's shoulder, and they both stood watching each other.

As the sky flipped back—orange to dark blue—Tom looked at Nast's photo. He ran a fingernail over the twisted scar on Nast's hand. Then he popped a magazine in place.

German law only allowed two cartridges per magazine, so he chambered a third round. Next he shouldered the rifle and placed one elbow on the ledge. He used eyesight alone—the poor man's approach—to determine distance. At 100 meters, you could see another person's eyes. At 200 meters, facial detail was still recognizable. Only at 300 meters did the target's face become blurred.

Tom had unusually good eyesight—always had—and could see Silvana's face as well as her mother's. He estimated he was a little over 150 meters away. He erred on the aggressive side because underestimation meant the wind would have more time to act on the bullet. Since he didn't have a wind instrument, he looked up the wind speed in the area on his phone. Twenty-four kilometers per hour, which he converted to fifteen miles per hour. But it was picking up. Already he could hear nothing of the city below. He made a few lateral corrections.

Now he put his eye to the scope and Alexander Nast in his crosshairs. Nast was standing, listening to someone. Tom panned over to Silvana, who seemed to be in the middle of a story. She was talking with her hands.

The wind picked up even more. Tom made another lateral correction and waited for a clear shot. Through his scope, he stared at Nast.

From a world away, I came from nothing.

And I found you.

Nast walked into the kitchen and then back into his sights. He was only three meters from the window. Tom took a deep pull of air, held it, and let it out slowly. He was more accurate on the exhale. His hand flexed. He thought it was the chill of the wind, so he waited a moment and then put the hand back on the rifle. But it flexed again, harder this time. It was starting to shake, not a lot yet, but he knew it was going to be bad.

He unshouldered the weapon and leaned against the concrete ledge. He started breathing and balling his hand up, breathing and balling up. He squeezed his eyes closed. When he opened them, his hands were calm. He looked at them. Dead calm.

He got back in position. But when he looked through the scope this time, he saw Eric. Eric was watching Silvana and her family. Tom jerked his eye off the scope. When he looked again, Eric was still there. Only now he'd turned and was staring back at him.

Like he was trying to tell him something.

CHAPTER 38

KARL MET James at the airport, and they were able to take off within the hour. It was a short flight: the plane had barely leveled before it began descending. On the ground, they got in the car James had arranged, and since they were armed and had no right to be, they obeyed the advisory speed limit all the way to the penthouse.

Taking aim with the rifle, Tom knelt with his elbows resting on the ledge. He breathed gently against the wood stock, feeling it rise and fall with his body, until the rifle became an extension of him.

Looking through the scope, he panned to Nast, but a curtain had been pulled partway closed. He could still see into the apartment, but now he could only get a twenty-foot view of a sixty-foot scene.

A shadow would float across the length of the curtain, and Silvana would pop out, pick something up, and disappear. Sometimes two shadows would converge. Then one would head toward the open part of the window, and he'd follow it in the scope, waiting for Dr. Nast to appear in the window. But he never did.

So Tom flipped the strategy. He left the rifle pointed at the uncurtained part of the window and waited for Nast to come to him. It took almost twenty minutes, but finally Nast rocked into and back out of view. He scooped up two dirty glasses on the coffee table, too fast for Tom to react.

But there was still one glass left.

Tom set his finger on the trigger and the crosshairs on the approximate area where Nast's head would be as he reached for the glass. A shadow sped along the curtain. Tom took a deep breath and exhaled. And as he did, he put a few pounds of pressure on the trigger.

The shadow got closer to the edge of the curtain. There was the streak of a person in motion. At the table, the streak stopped, and the motion lines ran together into the shape of Nast's head. Tom put a little pressure on the trigger. He could feel the bone in his finger against the metal—

He thought of Silvana sitting naked on the chair, her bare leg so smooth it almost looked wet. He thought of her smiling as she talked to the street vendor in Nice.

He couldn't do it.

Nast wiped lipstick off the glass.

Looking at him, Tom just couldn't do it. He took his eye off the scope and collapsed against the ledge. He sat still. After a minute, he picked up the rifle and looked through the scope again—

There was a little red dot.

On a black power box above the window Nast stood in, there was a piece of black tape that had come loose in the wind. A red light flickered through it. It hadn't been there a second ago.

What he was looking at wasn't a power box.

Raising the rifle, he turned and searched the adjacent buildings through the crosshairs. On a building across from Nast's and two buildings down from his own, he saw something and froze.

There was a figure on the roof, the man from the autohof.

The man was aiming in his direction. There was a lighter-size flash from the gun in his hands, and then Tom's neck was wet. He fell to his knees and dropped his rifle on a mound of gravel, expanding it. He ran his fingers along his neck, feeling for a hole to plug. But all he found was a gash through the side of his neck. He grabbed the rifle and scrambled behind a vent as the man started rapid-firing.

Staying as low as he could, Tom aimed at Silvana's building until he found the black box again. It was held in place by staples. Tom put the crosshairs of his scope on one of them and squeezed the trigger. The box jumped a little, like it wanted to fall, but the staple held. He shot again, and again the box jumped. But still the staple held.

He reloaded twice and fired as fast as he could until he had only one cartridge left. This was his last chance. He took dead aim. He was going into his exhale when the box exploded.

There was a crack in the air like the sky had split down the middle. When he took his eye off the scope, the corner of Silvana's building was scarred with black char. Wind was bending the tower of smoke coming off it, and a fire was burning at the sky.

Suddenly he got a warm soup feeling across his stomach. When he looked down, he saw blood running from his midsection into his crotch. The next thing he saw was the sky—he'd collapsed on his back.

In the time it took for him to lift his head up, the man from the autohof was landing on the rooftop of the building next door. He'd left the rifle and opened fire with a handgun. He didn't break stride as he ran right off the side of that building and onto Tom's roof.

Tom clawed at the briefcase and crab-walked behind the roof entrance, out of the bullet spray.

The action on the man's gun snapped open with a metallic echo. He must have been empty because Tom heard him drop the gun on the gravel.

Blood was dripping off the corners of Tom's clothes and disappearing into the little gravel rocks. He balled up part of his shirt and tried pushing it into the wound. But it was taking a lot of energy to do this, and his arms felt like bags of fat hanging off his shoulders.

He wasn't sure what to focus on: the man coming to kill him or the blood loss that was going to anyway. He'd collapsed on the gravel with his back against the roof access door, and he couldn't see the rest of the roof. He realized he hadn't heard any movement from the man since he'd dropped the gun. Delicately he twisted around to try to see where he'd gone.

The man was standing over him.

He was still—like he'd been watching him for some time. Tom's eyes dropped to the knife he was holding. The blade was stubby and wide and stuck out of his fist like a chrome fin. Tom tried to rock to his feet, but he couldn't even get within the ballpark of standing up. He raised his legs to protect himself, but the man kicked them out of the way. It was like getting hit in the thigh with a baseball bat.

Instantly the man was on top of him. He kept his right hand, which held the knife, high and out of reach. With his left forearm, he mashed Tom's face into the gravel. Tom squirmed, shaking his head *no, no, no* over and over until he could get his eyes back on the knife. Then he weakly wrapped his arms around the man to stop him from repositioning.

The man's eyes never seemed to move. They just pointed at him with insectile blankness.

Suddenly the man stood up, taking Tom with him. Two centers of gravity went up. The man sent them both crashing back down. Tom's head was already bouncing off the ground when an elbow rammed it back down.

He felt the man's weight shift. He knew what was coming. He raised his knee and lowered his elbow to protect his side. He braced for the stab—

At the same time both Tom and the man turned to see the knife was in Tom's forearm at a shallow angle and not one of his internal organs. It twisted under the skin, stretching the surface of it. But when the man tried to yank it out, Tom wouldn't let him—

because he didn't want to be stabbed again, because leaving the blade inside him seemed like the only way to stop it from going in somewhere else.

Wrapping both hands around the handle and leaning back with all his weight, the man was finally able to pull it out. And as he did, Tom saw the scar with two zippers twisting up the back of his hand.

It didn't really register at first. He was so woozy all he could think was: *Oh, this is the man whose life I actually want to take.*

The man stopped and watched him looking at the scar. Except he hadn't really stopped. His face stayed in place—curious—but the rest of him feinted toward Tom's ribs with the knife. As soon as Tom went to cover them up, the man feinted back and came right over the top. With both of his hands around the handle, he knelt over Tom like he was a human sacrifice. As he plunged the knife into Tom's stomach, Tom only got his hands up enough to absorb some of the thrust.

The first inch hurt the most. Tom pushed and clawed at the man's hands, but the blade kept slipping in. There was enough blood now that the man's fingers were slithering through his. All Tom could see was wet silver pouring in.

There was a gunshot.

They froze.

A second gunshot.

They turned in unison. The man's hands were still covering the handle, so Tom placed his fingers on the flat sides of the blade, delicately, and started pulling it out. Whatever friction held his fingers against the blade came from the ridges of his fingertips and the viscosity of his blood.

He saw the outline of a man on the fire escape. The man raised a handgun, to show he was armed, and leveled it at them.

The man from the autohof raked his hand through the gravel and came up with Tom's briefcase. Trying to make it to the stairs would have brought him within range of the man on the fire escape, so he fled across the roof toward the office building next door. He threw himself over the edge.

"No, don't," the man on the fire escape shouted.

But it was too late. Tom watched the other man arc up a little and descend out of sight. There was the sound of breaking glass from the window he'd thrown himself through.

While the man on the fire escape was yelling, Tom hobbled over to the roof entrance and somehow made it down the stairs to the ground floor. He had barely managed to open the double doors to the alley when he heard a car engine. It was accelerating—in his direction.

He hobbled across the alley and saw a little Renault slide to a stop at the double doors he'd just come through. The car door was being thrown open as he turned the corner and cut down another alley. Blood was running into his shoes, and the soles started to suck at his feet. It was the only sound in the alley.

The scar on the man's hand flashed in his mind. Then he saw the hand entering frame in the video.

He noticed how drowsy he was, but even through the drowsiness, he could feel the branches of the nerves in his body, splitting the pain, spreading it. He needed medical attention or he'd bleed out.

He saw the scar on the man's hand. Then he saw the hand enter the frame.

He turned down another alley, looking for a doctor's office. Some lights came on, and when he looked down, he realized his steps were shaking little drops of blood off his clothes. He rested for a moment and tried to catch his breath.

You lied. You didn't get her to her family safely.

He imagined Silvana trapped in the rubble, waiting for help, unable to comprehend what had just happened.

Even if she isn't dead, you couldn't do anything.

He saw the scar, then the hand enter frame.

He approached a fork in the alley. The alley to the left was dark except for the bluish-white light over a door. He went left and wiped his hand over the wettest part of his clothes and smeared his blood on the stucco under the light. Then he squeezed his shirt and pants to wring out as much blood as possible on the pavement. When he looked back, the fork seemed so far away he wasn't sure he could make it back. But he concentrated on each step, willing the pavement to turn under him.

If you trip, soon you'll see your brother.

He saw the scar, then the gun coming toward his brother's head.

Finally he retraced his steps back to the fork and stood there out of breath. Then he staggered down the alley to the right. He didn't know how far he would get, but all he could think was: he'd finally found the man who killed Eric, and now he couldn't do anything about it because he was about to die.

CHAPTER 39

MARTY'S BEEN *lying to you.*

That thought raced on a continuous loop through Karl's head as he watched Bogasian hurl himself off the side of a building and through an office window. Bogasian was supposed to be working with Dr. Nast, and yet he'd just blown up the roof of Nast's home. And if Marty was lying to him about that, he would only be doing it for a good reason. Marty never took a risk unless there was a proportionate reward on the other side of it.

When Karl turned toward Tom, he was gone too. Karl jumped off the fire escape onto the roof and lifted his radio. "He's on foot. Cover the west entrance. I'll go east."

"Copy," James said.

Karl flew down the stairs and crashed out the double doors into an alley, so fast he almost ran into James's parked Renault. The car was empty—James was probably already searching the alleys. Since Tom had to be close, Karl exhaled halfway before he spoke, to take the volume off his whisper.

"Do you have eyes on him?"

"Negative," James said.

"Forget Tom Reese. I need you to go up to Nast's apartment and see if there are any survivors. If they're in critical condition, take them to a hospital. Otherwise put them in my car."

A pause. "What?"

"Just do it."

"Copy."

Four alleys emptied into the one he stood in. Karl figured he had one shot at this.

He's scared. He has maybe thirty minutes before he bleeds out—

Karl leaned over and scanned the pavement.

Blood. A little dollop of it.

The next one he found was just a dot. But once he found it, he had two points, and when he connected them, he had a line. And the line was pointing down alley number two. Karl followed the red dots like a trail of bread crumbs.

Then the alley split. He stared down one alley and saw a cat licking at something on the ground. He went over, picked the cat up and raised it into the streetlight. There was blood on the white fur around its mouth. He patted it on the head and put it back down.

He followed the alley to another fork. This time both branches curved out of view, and there were no cats to bail him out. So he walked up the alley to the left, illuminating the ground with the light on his phone. He was about thirty feet in, about to turn around, when he saw blood smeared on the stucco exterior of a building, right under a security light.

He looked around. It was the only light for fifty feet.

He stood there, not liking his shit luck.

Then he doubled back to the fork and took the alley to the right. His steps got quick—he knew he was close—and he pointed the light on his phone at the pavement as he walked. Tom would have cupped his hands under the bleeding to put the biggest gap he could in the blood trail, but eventually it would spill over.

Finally Karl found what he was looking for—a big streak of blood.

He was running now.

As he came out of the alley, he saw the green cross of a pharmacy. It shared the same building with a doctor's office. The glass doors were locked, so he went around back. The rear door was ajar, the doorknob ripped out.

He nudged the door open and stood, listening. Deep inside, someone was yanking drawers open and swiping their contents onto the floor.

Tom was so cold he could feel where the nerves in his teeth rooted into his face. It took him a long time—a minute almost—to realize what this meant:

Shock.

He wasn't sure at what point he'd pass out. He'd never been so aware of his heart pumping with so much thrust. It was pumping minutes of his life out of his body and all over the Chiclet-white tile. He could feel himself getting sleepy.

You're going into shock.

He lurched forward and tore through the cabinets until he found an emergency-care manual in English. His fingers were so sticky with blood that a page ripped off and stuck to his thumb. He licked and sucked where the paper met his thumb until the page slipped off.

The table of contents—like most tables of contents—was useless. He flipped to the index.

Blood loss.
—Rapid.

Soon you'll see your brother.

The next thing he knew, he was at the bottom of a paragraph with no idea how he'd gotten there. He caught himself looking around for a place to lie down and had to look at the blood on the floor to scare himself back into action.

He went around ripping out drawers, searching for suture needles. Eventually he found some. They came pre-threaded, so he sat down, stripped, and then disinfected.

He started with his stomach, but pushing the sides of the wound together was like shaping Cream of Wheat.

He gave up and jabbed the needle into one flap, pushing it inward until a sharp little metallic head was birthed into the inner wall of the wound. Then he pushed it through the opposite wall and turned it upward until it came out his stomach. He yanked both ends of the suture upward, which pulled the wound closed. But as soon as he let go to put in another stitch, the whole thing fell apart.

One of the doctor's offices was being renovated, and there were a bunch of tools in the hallway. He got up and rooted around until he found a soldering iron.

Surgeons had been using hot metal to stop bleeding for thousands of years, and he told himself the soldering iron was just a primitive version of the same thing. He plugged the iron in and rolled onto the gurney. Once it was hot, he stared at it and took a breath—then another breath. He pinched the hole in his stomach shut as best he could and let the iron go down toward it.

He smelled it before he felt it. The pain whited everything else out. The smell was hard to describe. It just smelled *wrong*. He lifted his head and saw two pieces of flesh being melted into a swollen mass on his belly. But the hole was nowhere close to being sealed. He dipped the iron back down. The smell hit him again. But when he looked, he saw he was pushing the iron down in an area three inches from his wound.

The soldering iron fell to the floor. This he knew not because he felt it slip out of his fingers but because he heard it thud, far away, like someone else had dropped it.

Eric was sitting on the counter.

"I'm sorry," Tom said.

He saw blood everywhere. It was someone else's blood now, someone else's mess.

A shadow on the floor moved. He looked up. A figure stood in the doorway.

Tom slapped his hand into a tray full of instruments by the table. He came up with a bunch of things and dropped them all except for a scalpel. The figure walked up and took it out of his hand.

"You're bleeding out," the figure said.

It was Karl's voice. Except he wasn't talking, he was shouting. In Tom's face. Still Tom couldn't quite hear him.

"Do. They. Have. Blood. Here?" Karl was enunciating like this was the tenth time he'd asked.

"Don't take me to the hospital."

"You need help."

Tom thought of the pictures of those men. For a moment he wasn't scared he was going to die. He was scared of what they'd make him do if he lived.

"Wake up." Karl slapped him and then put his phone to his ear.

"Leave me. Please. Just leave me."

"I'm going to move you."

Tom's head lolled to the side. Everything he carried inside him, everything that existed only because he remembered it, began to go dark. His mother dropping herself into the Volvo for the last time. His dad waving goodbye through the windshield. Eric grinning as he gave him his first beer.

Tom looked at the room, then at Karl. He tried to speak, but the words died in his throat.

I don't care what you people do to me. I still have my family. I belong somewhere. And I'll never belong to you.

CHAPTER 40

BOGASIAN CRASHED through the window, hit a desk, and rolled onto the floor. When he came to, for a moment he didn't remember how he'd gotten there. He rocked back and forth a few times and worked his way to his feet. There was a maze of deserted cubicles outside the office. It was quiet except for a copy machine beeping for maintenance. It was the kind of place he'd always imagined his messages went on nights when there was no response.

As he made his way down the hall, he saw someone poke her head out of an office and disappear back into it.

He paused outside the room, his heart seizing in his chest. Then he forced himself to look inside. It was dark, but he didn't turn the light on. He could make out photos on the walls of a family smiling, their heads nuzzled together. The room was empty.

He heard footsteps behind him on the other side of the cubicles. He whirled around and caught a glimpse of a woman holding a little girl's hand. They disappeared down a hallway.

Sweat dampened his back. He knew them. Three years ago he'd murdered them in their sleep.

He let himself out the back door of the building, got in his car, and drove to a motel. He rolled onto the bed in his room. It was easy to sleep because he didn't want to be awake.

*　*　*

Bogasian's eyes flipped open in the dark. He saw movement in the corners of the room. He bolted up in bed and swung his head back and forth, searching every inch of every shadow. His heart thudded in his chest.

More movement.

He whipped around.

Movement to the left.

Now to the right.

Whatever it was, it was just out of view. And he knew no matter how fast he moved or how still he stayed, it would always be there, pulsing on the edges, threatening to become visible.

There was movement on all sides of him now.

He bowed his head and let the dark crawl over him. He bit his lip and held his breath as it seeped through his eyelids and floated up his nose. He waited for all the images of everything he'd done to catch up to him.

He wondered how Tom dealt with it.

The memory of Tom on the roof came to him. He'd never seen a dying person fight like that. People didn't fight to the end. People fought until they saw the end. And once they'd seen that, it had them. The sadness had them.

But it didn't have Tom. And he had almost a pint of blood smeared all over the roof before Bogasian even got there. Bogasian wondered why, and then he remembered Tom staring at his scar. There was only one place he could have seen it before.

The resemblance was obvious now that he thought about it. They could be brothers, which meant they probably were. Eric was the one who came to him weeks after the surgery and said, *We can take these things out of you.* And Bogasian had just stared at him, knowing he could choose to care or not care. Meanwhile Eric stood there repeating himself, begging, eventually walking away.

Eric came to the lab less and less after that. And the few other times he was there, he argued with the others. He threatened to go to the police unless they did a procedure to mitigate the side effects.

Now Bogasian understood why they'd injected Tom. It was a way to motivate Eric to stay on and keep his mouth shut. Besides, when they were done with Eric, they were just going to kill him anyway. They had to now.

He and the others made the decision to record what they'd done to Eric. They did it as leverage in case their employers decided to do the same thing to them. They never should have done that. Bogasian went on to do worse things, but they would never exist for him the way the video did. He spent months thinking about it, never watching it, before he decided to do something.

The recording showed Eric's face pretty clearly. It also showed that his death was a planned execution, not a mugging gone wrong. That would kick the investigation up to Interpol. From there, they'd figure out Eric entered Tangier under a false identity, and then using work visas, they'd track that identity to a company connected to Schroder-Sands. It wouldn't take long to discover the stem cell labs after that.

He uploaded the video at 2:00 AM on a Friday night, wearing only his boxer shorts.

When he killed Eric, he put a large wet cut between himself and the world. But when he posted the video and no one did anything, he realized there was nothing out there keeping track, no one to whom any of it mattered. And the cut healed—which meant he never would.

CHAPTER 41

TOM DIDN'T want to wake up ever again, but eventually his eyes opened. He might have been staring at the room for hours, maybe days, before he realized this was a bedroom and he was the person in it.

There was nothing on the walls. No furniture other than a dresser, a table, and the bed he was on. The curtains were closed, but judging from the little triangle of light on the windowsill, it was sunny out. He preferred it dark and had a feeling that whoever set up the room for him knew that.

He started to sit up.

There was a noise in the hallway.

He dropped back down and closed his eyes. The door opened. He didn't hear a lock.

Someone came in. Tom opened his eyes a few degrees, but his eyelashes and the dimness of the room clouded his view of a face. Whoever it was moved down against the floorboards rather than over them, and he guessed it was a man. The man slid a tray onto the table by Tom's head, and his upper body shifted out of view. Tom sensed he was being watched and hoped his eyes appeared closed.

The man moved back into sight and bent over him. Tom waited until he could smell him—

He shot up, pulled the man onto the bed by his collar, and

locked him in a sleeper hold. His mouth was right next to the man's ear.

"How long have I been here?"

"Two weeks."

"Where am I?"

"You're in my safe house."

"Who are you?"

"He's my father."

Tom's head spun toward the doorway, the direction of the voice. Silvana.

She stood watching them. Little nicks and cuts dotted her face. A purple hand-size bruise covered her right eye and ran across her face until it disappeared in her hairline. Tom let the man go and saw for himself it was Dr. Nast. Nast looked back at him and then walked out, favoring one leg.

Silvana came over and set a bowl down on the table next to him. Tom could feel her proximity on his arms and chest. But she didn't come closer. She stirred something on the tray and walked out.

He had that feeling of warm soup on his stomach again.

Tom jerked awake and sat up on his elbows. Dr. Nast waited until he settled back down, then continued wiping something over the wounds on his stomach.

"These burns, you did them yourself?" Nast said.

Tom didn't say anything.

"Whatever you used, it stopped most of the bleeding. Probably saved your life."

Tom watched Nast's hand move over his sternum.

"This is going to hurt a bit."

Nast tweezed at his stitches, and Tom looked at his hands. No scars on either one.

"I think you know I'm not who you're looking for," Nast said, eyes on his work. "I worked with your brother at a subsidiary of Schroder-Sands. We were 'recruited' to work with the Americans to develop stem cell treatments for disease. We performed the procedure on the man who did this to you."

Nast tried to smile, but it came off as a wince.

"They told us he had a latent form of muscular dystrophy. He was actually healthy, of course—though he didn't stay that way for long."

Nast swabbed the skin that had swollen up around the scar under the stitches.

"What went wrong with him?" Tom said.

"Paranoia, eventually paranoid psychosis. Nightmares, hallucinations, increased propensity for violence and diminished remorse when he acted on that propensity."

"Why did he try to kill you?"

Nast smiled his wincing smile again. "I doubt it is he who wants me dead. I doubt at this point he's capable of wanting anything in the sense that you or I would use the term."

"So who does want you dead?"

"I found out what my principals were really up to. After I left, I met with a reporter. His body was found in the Thames. A suicide, they ruled it. Then my brother died. They've been looking for me for years. My son..." He swallowed, dropping the word. "My son worked for them, and they used him many times to try to find me."

"There must be other witnesses."

"There were. You killed them."

Nast placed some gauze over Tom's wound and began taping it.

"I know it was you who killed my son." His throat squeezed the words down to a whisper. "I do not think he deserved that. He was not an unredeemable person. But I understand why you did it..." His fingers never stopped applying tape.

"I found four men's DNA on the shirt my brother died in. I had reason to believe your son was one of them. I didn't kill him, but I wanted to."

"Then who did?"

"The same man who tried to kill you."

Nast stared at him for what felt like a long time and then touched him on the arm.

"I failed my son as a father," Nast said. "Karl told me the CIA has a word for the consequences others face as a result of our actions."

"Blowback."

Nast nodded. "Do you think you could ever forgive me for the blowback I caused?"

Tom couldn't say anything. His thoughts couldn't turn the corner into actual words.

Nast finished with the wound.

He touched Tom on the chest as he stood up. "I liked your brother very much. He was everything my son was not."

Nast gathered his things and left, gently pulling the door closed behind him.

CHAPTER 42

KARL STOOD in the hallway outside Tom's room because he wasn't ready to go in. He looked out the window over the gray empty of East Berlin. One in every six buildings in this area was vacant, including the one he stood in. Another kilometer out, and it was like standing outside time in an infinite parking lot. The only things jutting from the pavement were the weeds and the casino-size pours of concrete that used to warehouse people.

It had been easy to vanish here, because this place was itself vanishing.

Two million human beings disappeared after the Wall came down. Now those who stayed were choosing to disappear. Everywhere across the former Soviet bloc, birth rates were down. Suicide was up. In many places, alcoholism was the most common cause of death for men. The UN estimated that by 2050 the population of Russia would fall by 25 percent, and the population of Ukraine *by half.* Russians now had more abortions than live births. Russian women were looking around, seeing what their children would become, and saying, *Uh-uh, no way.* And East Germany was right there with them.

The East Germans survived secret police, neighbors who informed, and the mass collective potty-training of their children. But they wouldn't survive their freedom. Fascism had killed twenty-five million people. Communism killed another seventy-five million. These people had worshipped the wrong thing, crushed each other body and soul in the name of it, and now they'd learned the price of being wrong. They'd lost something out there in the great big wash. And whatever it was, it took their faith in the idea that something about life was special. Something about it mattered. And so now all they got was reality, the facts.

It turned out people didn't live on those.

Maybe saving Tom was an expression of faith in the face of fact. Maybe it was a chance to do something for someone he admired in a way. Do something beyond himself, better than he was. Or maybe it was just dumb. He'd go to jail for it, and no matter what he did, someone would come for Tom.

But he was his father's son. He'd done dumber things. Apparently he was going to keep on doing them.

When Karl walked in, Tom's shoulder was weeping a little blood. Tom picked off part of a bandage and tossed it in a garbage can with a misshapen tower of bloody gauze rising out of it.

"Why were you on that roof?" Karl asked.

"What do you want with me?"

"I want to know something. How did you get here? How the hell did you do all this?"

"I don't know. I just did."

"Bullshit. People don't just do this."

"That's exactly what every system depends on: everyone being who they say they are and no one doing the unthinkable."

"I think it's because most people care about their futures. Don't you care about yours?"

"I care."

"Let me tell you something. It doesn't matter how right or how noble what you're doing is. There are things the world just won't let you get away with. Because it *can't*. You stole a CIA officer's identity. You stole state secrets and made deals with other countries. You even killed someone. Explain to me in what way your life isn't over."

"People always say, 'Think of your future.' But what they really mean is do what you're told and accept what you're given. Well, I knew the odds when I went into this, and I thought they were good enough. So I jumped. And you know what? That's what it takes to care about something."

Karl couldn't think of anything to say to that.

"You're here to arrest me, aren't you?"

Tom was still defiant, but as all defiant people eventually find out, defiance is exhausting. That's why it's so rare. Karl stared at Tom and saw the exhaustion in his eyes. For a moment Tom looked like Karl had just said yes, he was here to arrest him, and now it was all over.

"What are they going to do with me?" Tom asked.

"I'm not going to arrest you."

After a while, Tom said, "You want to know what got me on that roof? There was a picture of Nast in the files. He had the scar from the video."

"He was in here earlier. You look at his hand?"

"Nast said he worked with the people behind this. You know anything about that?"

"Nast was our asset. Marty recruited him."

"Did he know he was an asset?"

"No, and that made him the best kind."

"He said he worked with my brother. Did Marty recruit Eric too?"

"No. I did."

Karl waited for the reaction, the explosion at what he had done. But Tom just sat there.

"We called it Prometheus," Karl said. "It was an experimental program to inject stem cells into operators in order to augment motor-nervous function."

Tom's face tightened. "And Eric did this? He did this to people?"

"He did it to one person, Ian Bogasian, our only test subject. He thought he was saving his life."

Tom's eyes were unfocused, like he was listening to another conversation. "Where did you get the stem cells?" he asked.

"From human embryos and fetuses that had been aborted."

"Someone put those in me."

Tom stared at him, his eyes anchored as his face contorted around them. He was trying to resist it, look normal, but the contortions went deep. They didn't just change his expression. They changed his face.

"When did you have the surgery?" Karl said. "Do you even know?"

"Three years ago."

That would have been shortly before Eric turned up dead. Which made sense. Doing the first stage of the operation on Tom would ensure that Eric stayed on to fix whatever had gone wrong with Bogasian—because whatever it was would soon happen to his brother. But of course Eric hadn't been able to fix Bogasian.

"Nast told me about Bogasian, what happened to him," Tom said. "I don't have symptoms as bad as that."

"You will. Silvana told us about the episode you had in Heidenheim."

Tom crossed his arms over his chest and stared at the floor. He nodded slowly, already agreeing with what he had no choice but to agree with. Karl imagined him getting angry or shouting or crying. But Tom did none of those things. He just sat there.

"I'm sorry," Karl said.

Tom looked up for a second, nodded an acknowledgment, and looked back down.

"Nast thinks there might be something he can do for you," Karl said. "But he isn't sure yet."

"Is there anything I can do for Nast and Silvana, you know, while I still can?"

The question surprised Karl. He looked at Tom and suddenly saw what had always been in front of him. It was something he'd seen in every corner of the earth, no matter how rich it was, or how poor. He saw a young man without a place in the world. He saw someone who was desperate to be needed—but wasn't.

"How old are you?" Karl said.

"Twenty-two."

Karl shook his head, felt a stab in his chest. "God, I loved being twenty-two."

He imagined himself at that age, getting wasted with his friends and chasing girls like they were proof God loved him and wanted him to be happy. Then he imagined Tom sitting at home by himself watching a movie, which if it was any good would be the highlight of his weekend.

"Don't you have somewhere else you can be? Aren't there things you want to do?"

Tom said nothing.

"I mean you ought to be tear-assing around with your buddies, breaking the law and upsetting old people with your loose morals and strong language."

Tom cracked a faint smile. Karl waited for him to say something, anything. But the silence was so complete it hurt.

"Nast has to be able to threaten to go public," Karl said finally. "Unless he has leverage, he won't be safe. But there's no hard evidence. It was burned in his apartment."

"In Sarmad's basement, I found pictures of men who may have had the procedure done to them. On each picture, there was a number."

"Do you still have them?"

"Bogasian got them, along with the Prometheus files and everything else."

"Do you remember the numbers?"

"I saved them on a phone. Give me your number. I'll forward them."

"I don't have a phone."

Tom stared at him. "Why not?"

Karl shrugged.

"Why aren't you carrying your work phone?"

"Just write the numbers down."

Tom searched his face and then got his prepaid phone and copied the numbers down. There were two of them. 20865228106670380, 57618443152121735.

"What about the briefcase?" Tom said.

"You need to forget about the briefcase."

"You said Nast needed evidence—"

"Bogasian has it."

"But—"

"You need to understand something. Whatever they did to you, it's nothing compared to what they did to him."

"Those people turned my brother into an internet video, and they turned me into...*this*," Tom said. "I can get the briefcase, and I can deal with what comes of it."

"'What comes of it' killed Dr. Nast's wife last week."

Tom froze.

"He didn't tell you, did he? She died in the blast."

Tom's eyes were wet, but the surface tension never broke. No tears came.

"Take me," Tom said. "Nast could use me as the proof he needs to go public."

"You think once governments find out what you are, they're just going to let you walk around?" Karl watched his hand go out and touch Tom on the shoulder. "No one can ever find out about you, okay?"

"Why are you doing all this for me?"

"I liked your brother. And if we don't figure out a way to treat whatever's happening to you, I don't think he'd like what you'll become."

Karl was on his way into the kitchen when he overheard Silvana and Dr. Nast.

"Why are you helping him?" Silvana said.

Dr. Nast sighed. There was the sound of bodyweight releasing into an old chair. Karl was about to walk in—

"I've never told anyone this because it wasn't what I wanted."

"Dad, what are you talking about?"

"They talked to me... three years ago."

Karl could hear the strangle in Nast's voice.

"They came to me. I wouldn't agree, not after what happened the first time, but they mentioned you and your mother. So I went with them to the lab. There was a boy strapped to one of the tables. He was drugged, but his head kept moving. I performed the operation on him. They were in a rush. They didn't even give me an anesthesiologist, so I flatlined him on the table and told the nurses he didn't survive. I thought that was his only chance. I'd only performed one stage of the series of operations I did on Bogasian. After the nurses left, I sutured the bone flaps and called Eric Reese. When he showed up, he said the boy was his brother." Nast's voice dropped to a whisper. "We carried him to Eric's apartment. That was the last I saw of either of them."

There was a heavy sigh.

"And I think that boy is the young man lying in the bedroom over there."

Quiet.

Then a sniffle. It was coming from Silvana, Karl realized.

"Dad..." Silvana said the word softly, like it was a fragile, important thing.

When Karl walked into the kitchen, Silvana had bent down and was holding her father in his chair. She was rocking him back and forth a little, and he was letting her.

CHAPTER 43

THERE'S NO victory in revenge, someone once said. Tom didn't think what he was after was revenge. Still he didn't see the victory in it. Only the dead. Only Silvana's mother.

He stared at the ceiling, wishing he could explain to Eric that justice was a dead virtue. It didn't create anything. And it could never give him what he really wanted.

He knew Bogasian was the man he'd dreamed of finding, and he didn't see how he'd ever be able to kill him. Whatever they'd done to Bogasian, it was far worse than what they'd done to him. He knew that now, just as he knew it would never be enough to kill him. He'd still have to find whoever put Bogasian up to it and whoever put that person up to that. So there could be no justice for Eric. Not because it wasn't right. But because it wasn't practical. It was just too hard.

He thought of the files Bogasian had taken. If they meant Dr. Nast and Silvana could be safe, he could get them back. He couldn't kill Bogasian, but he could maybe evade him.

Tom rolled onto his feet. Immediately his hands went to his ribs. The pain surprised him. His eyes stopped on a couple rolls of medical tape. He started wrapping it around his torso, tight, holding everything in place. He pressed on his side. Pain. But low enough to make do.

He started the GPS program on his phone. After the map

loaded, he saw that the briefcase—or at least the smashed phone he'd left in it—was still in Berlin. About five kilometers away.

He paused with one foot on the windowsill and the other on the fire escape. It was dark in the neighborhood, but he could see the lights of West Berlin in the distance. He stood watching them, imagining the life taking place within their glow, the life that was still possible for Silvana and her father. And maybe for himself too.

CHAPTER 44

KARL WATCHED through the raindrops on the car window as the taxi drove past Checkpoint Charlie in Berlin.

When the Berlin Wall was still up, the checkpoint was famous for being the easiest way to escape from East Berlin into the West. Even so, people died trying. One teenager who tried to make a run for it in the sixties was shot through the pelvis. The guards left the boy tangled in the barbed wire for an hour before he finally died. Now it was a wholesome tourist destination. It was amazing, that a place like this could one day be boring.

The cab dropped Karl off at an empty office building. As the elevator smoothed upward, the thought crossed his mind that Marty might kill him right then and there—not for stashing Tom and Dr. Nast but for knowing about them at all.

At the top floor, Karl headed into an empty office suite. Five men he didn't recognize took him to the conference room. He got the sense they were assets, not agents.

He and Marty sat across from each other.

"He told me about the file," Karl said.

Marty turned to the others, and they walked out of the room.

"He told me about the scar you photoshopped onto Dr. Nast's hand." Karl shook his head, exhaled. "I want to believe there's some logic here in service of a good intention. But I don't see any logic. Or any good intention."

Marty sighed. "Karl, please. I don't have the energy for another conversation about our feelings."

Marty leaned back, crossed his legs, and swept something off the tabletop.

"Tom shows up here three years after Dr. Nast had convinced me he was dead, and he does a search on Ben Kotesh, which I've flagged, so I have someone follow him. A week later Kotesh turns up in a hospital, and all his men are dead. So I connected the dots, and the line that resulted pointed at some other people...people who presented an issue and who Tom could help us find."

"You knew the whole time?"

"No, I suspected the whole time. Was it illegal? Yes. Was it a crisis? You bet your ass. And guess what? I didn't let it go to waste." Marty stood up and started pacing.

"How did you know he'd move on the Prometheus files?"

"I gave it one chance in three." Marty shrugged. "It's a probabilistic world."

"Nast isn't involved. You could let him go."

"It's a little late for him to choose his level of involvement. Do I need to remind you of the officials taking a hard look into Schroder-Sands and what will happen if they catch even a whiff of the CIA? And after what's happened to his wife, I don't think we should rely on any outpouring of goodwill from this man."

"Were you behind that?"

Marty didn't say anything.

"Tom has to walk."

"Where are they?"

Karl stared at the dark shine on the tabletop. It was like looking down a bottomless well.

Marty stopped pacing and sat back down, right next to him. "He impersonated a CIA agent and broke out of an embassy. He's embarrassed a lot of people. But I don't want to kill him." Marty was quiet for a moment. "I want him to work for us."

Somehow that scared Karl more than Marty wanting him dead.

"He's not a threat," Karl said.

"He's perfect is what he is. He's a cutting instrument wrapped in skin."

"He's sick, and it's getting worse."

"Then we'll treat him. Nast could even handle it. We've had our differences, but I'm willing to mend fences."

Without looking up, Karl said in a quiet voice, "Marty, to be honest, sometimes I wonder whether you were pushed from your mother's loins or whether you somehow ate your way out."

Marty chuckled, like Karl had conceded something. "We're working on something big, bigger than Prometheus."

Now Karl knew for sure. The lab outside Sarmad's didn't belong to someone else. *And that man you executed, he was also one of Marty's.*

"Tom has tolerated the stem cells better than any living thing we've ever observed," Marty said. "There's so much we can learn from him."

"I thought he was Pandora's box."

"You know the funny thing? I still believe all that. I just have no intention of actually following it."

"When you're done with him, we both know what you'll do to him."

Marty stared out the window. When he spoke, his words were soft but emphatic: "It's a fraction of a fraction of the human population that inflicts all the misery on the rest. A third of all Muslims, 500 million people, sympathize with terror groups, yet only a tiny percentage actually join one. Violent repeat felons comprise less than .25 percent of the population, and yet they inflict almost all the most serious crime on it. Civilization is doomed because it takes a thousand men to build a bridge and only one to blow it up. *And we have a technology that completely turns that on its head.* With Tom, we have a way to cull the worst of the worst from humanity and never get caught. Isn't that the reason you joined the CIA?"

"He's a nice kid, you know that? I actually think you'd like him."

"I didn't realize you were one of those people who value something based on how warm and cuddly it is. So that's your morality? Puppies?"

Marty got a sad look.

"How many kids did you kill in Iraq, Karl?"

Karl just stared at him.

"How many died because of a strike you called in? I bet you don't know. I bet you made a point of not knowing. Now think of all the children who *won't* die from our bombs because we have Tom. We'd be taking one life and redistributing it to thousands."

Karl folded his hands, unfolded them. "You're probably right— he is only one kid. I mean, look, I'd love to put a sack over his head and give him to you and all. It's just that, well, I'm afraid I like the little rascal too much to do that."

"As it is, he's so dangerous we can't let him go, so I think this is a pretty sweet compromise. Now if you don't like that, if you think it tramples a tad hard on the traitor's *rights,* then I'm sure there are some wonderful anarchists in California who'll let you join them in their world without compromise, but you're going to have to worship Sheba the moon goddess and renounce all toilet paper. *Now tell me where the fuck Tom is.*"

Karl didn't say anything. He just hit Marty so hard he felt the bend in the bones of his hand.

Marty grabbed his collar and punched him back. They stood up together, swinging. It was messy and silly, like a hockey fight. The door banged open. Four men ran at them and peeled them off each other. One pinned Karl against the wall with his forearm on Karl's windpipe.

Marty nodded at Karl's hand. Another man grabbed it and,

with Karl resisting the whole way, spread it against the wall. A third man took out a large Glock and leveled it so the barrel hovered about three inches from Karl's index finger.

"The bullet won't shoot your finger off," Marty said. "It will blow it apart." When Karl didn't say anything: "It's your index finger, Karl, and then it will be your thumb. And frankly I just ate, so let's not put ourselves through this lightly."

The man with the Glock cocked the hammer.

Karl choked out an address. "Heinze 55, 6B."

One of the men plugged it into his phone and showed it to Marty.

"East Berlin," Marty said, still huffing as he straightened his shirt and smoothed his tie. "I love it." Then he picked up his phone and dialed. When someone answered: "We already have an address, but just in case, I need you to run a utilities search within a three-mile radius of Heinze 55 in East Berlin. Check for any places where the water usage is up over 100 percent this period. On second thought, they've been taking care of a wounded man. Make it 200 percent."

This was an old tactic of the East German secret police, checking water usage to see if someone was hiding another person.

"That kind of hurts my feelings," Karl said.

"I like to think I know you pretty well. If they're not at Heinze, they'll be nearby. The funny thing about East Berlin: even twenty-five years after the Wall came down, it's still a wonderful place to disappear."

"This really isn't necessary."

Marty stared at him sadly. "Let's hope not. Otherwise you owe me a finger, Karl."

CHAPTER 45

TEENAGERS DANCED on the poles of the U-Bahn subway car, which was painted school-bus yellow. They were dressed in uniforms of drab green with the words WORKER RAGS and CITIZENS OF HUMANITY scrawled on them in blood-red. The clothes were vacuum-sealed to their waifish bodies. And for a few minutes the car was a commune Dance Dance Revolution on wheels, complete with a greasy long-haired man who smelled of patchouli and never took his eyes off Tom's crotch.

The rest of the passengers watched the kids or didn't watch them, but either one, they did with utter blankness.

Nothing can climb very far above the everyday, Tom thought. *Not for long anyway. This is how you go to face the person who took everything. You take the six train.*

Tom sat, looking at the floor. He thought of Silvana's mother for a moment without meaning to.

One of the girls on the train was dancing in front of him. This went on for a minute before he realized she was dancing *to* him. She motioned for him to get up and join in. Her friends were giggling. He looked up at her and tried to manage a polite smile as he shook his head. But as soon as she saw his face, her hips lost the beat.

"Sorry," she said in a British accent. "Sorry."

She danced, now with no enthusiasm, back to her friends.

The car pulled into the station. Tom got off and walked through a cavern slathered in cartoon-green paint to the nearest exit. The map on the phone took him to a two-story brick apartment building surrounded by houses. He walked around to the backyard.

In the window of the front unit, a woman was pointing a carving knife at a tall man who was keeping himself between her and a massive glistening ham. She was going for the ham. He was going for the knife. The guests around the dinner table were laughing and cheering as the man made a little show out of holding the ham high, like a waiter, out of the woman's reach.

He passed another apartment. In one window, a woman was standing in a dark room, her face inches from the glass. Her eyes were cataract-filmed and white, like a corpse pulled out of a river. She wasn't looking at him, but she was pointed in his direction. Like she knew he was there.

He pressed himself against the side of building, unsure what he'd just seen. When he went back, the window was empty. And he knew it had been the entire time.

He looked up to the second-floor apartment. Dishwater-gray light from the unit barely pushed out into the night. He worked his fingers into tiny holds in the brick latticework and climbed up.

The first thing that struck him was how much the place resembled his apartment in Paris. There was nothing on the walls. No television. The only furniture was a Formica kitchen table and a couch that looked like it rented with the place. And the only sign that a human being had actually been here was the broken glass on the kitchen counter.

Droplets of condensation were still stuck to its sides.

The window was locked. Tom dropped back down into the yard, where he'd noticed a small shed. He found a trowel inside and thought he could use it to pick away at the windowpanes.

Then he saw the duct tape.

He tossed the trowel.

Back at the window, he worked a coin out of his pocket and ran the edge of it over the glass. Slowly—and thus quietly—he peeled off strips of tape and pressed them against the windowpane. Then he molded one of the strips into a handle and hit the glass with his palm until it broke. The shards stuck to the tape, and the tape dampened the sound.

Tom pulled out the glass, reached in, and flipped the lock. He guided the window up and slipped into the apartment. He knew it was a good idea to close the window, but he still got a tight, trapped feeling when he did.

The briefcase wasn't in the living room or the kitchen—if it was here at all. The only way into the rest of the apartment was through a long unlit hallway. He wasn't sure just how far back the hallway went because the light from the kitchen died ten feet down.

The apartment was the absence of noise or movement. And he was disturbing it. As he waded deeper and deeper into the unit, the absence played tricks on him. He kept spinning to see things that he never got eyes on and freezing to hear sounds that never repeated.

A noise from the kitchen.

It ran jagged through the silence. He ducked into a bathroom and listened for footsteps. There weren't any, only the noise he now recognized as the refrigerator cycling on.

Click. Whir. Click. Whir.

He became aware that his back was to the rest of the bathroom. Little hairs tingled on his neck, waiting for a disturbance in the air. He turned around, holding his breath, preparing for a face mixed with the shadows.

The shower curtain was halfway closed.

He crept up to it. Slowly he reached out and with his fingertips nudged the curtain open.

Click. Whir. Click. Whir-r-r-r-r-r-r.

No one there.

He eased back into the hallway. The refrigerator noise would cover the sound of someone coming for him. He kept going. It was like walking into the ink of a Polaroid. As his eyes adjusted, the darkness moved into the vague shape of a hallway. He tried to stick to his peripheral vision. Since the eye's rods were more sensitive to light than the eye's cones and since the rods were concentrated on the edges of the retina, the best way to see in the dark wasn't to look directly at something but toward a point near it.

At the end of the hall, he reached the master bedroom. The door was half-open, and across the large room he could see the dead neutral light of a laptop screen. As he walked closer, he noticed two multicolored lines were chasing each other around the black screen saver. And within their glow, he saw the briefcase.

Air moved across the hairs on his neck.

A line dropped from the top of his vision. It was colorless, a bend in the light. He flinched, putting his hand up to protect his face. He only realized the line was a wire when it cut into his throat, trapping his hand in the process. He smelled something metallic. When the person behind him worked the garrote back and forth, he realized it was the iron in his blood.

The wire stopped only when it hit the bone in his hand. Tom went soft and allowed himself to be pulled backward, which took some of the pressure off.

Then he swung his elbow behind him.

It connected with something hard but with a little give. The garrote loosened enough that he broke for the hallway. He got close. His free hand was clamping on to the door frame—

Then he seemed to run into a clothesline.

The garrote was again yanked tight. An object in motion stays in motion, and his legs ran out from under him and scissored into the air. As soon as he landed, gasping, flat on his back, he realized he was being dragged by the garrote farther into the bedroom. He could feel the loops in the carpet under his fingernails.

When he came to a stop, he started to work his fingers under the wire, but it just dropped off his neck. He shot up and went to take the first step of a flat-out sprint to the hallway.

Then the door shut, and the room went pitch-black.

Tom froze. He needed the light from the laptop to orient himself, but Bogasian must have shut the lid. The room was so dark that Tom's sense of space was wasted. He couldn't tell whether he was facing a corner of the room or the center of it. He strained to hear. And he didn't move. He didn't even think about moving.

A drawer slid open.

One second stretched into two, two into five. Then along with his sense of space, his sense of time was wasted too. He could have been standing there twenty seconds or two minutes.

Something grazed his arm.

There was the intricate sound that movable pieces of metal make against one another. He clawed in front of his face until one hand hit something. He grabbed it and pushed it to the side. Light shot out around his fingers. The silencer of the handgun wasn't even a foot from his face. He'd pushed it just enough to direct the barrel away from his chest. The muzzle flash lit up the room.

As Tom went for the gun, Bogasian shook him off. Tom hit the floor and rolled through the dark.

Another muzzle flash.

Bogasian fired randomly into a tiny chair in the corner. The room went dark again. There was a moment of quiet, and then another flash lit up the room. Bogasian had moved. Now he was in the next corner, firing into a closet door.

This was the process of elimination. And Bogasian had just ruled out half the room.

Bogasian fired again, this time into the wall Tom was a few feet from. As the light expanded past them, their eyes snapped together. And as everything faded to black, Bogasian was already swinging the gun on him.

Tom dove out of the path of the light. He rolled on the floor—didn't stop—and bounced up to his feet. The room lit up again, and a hole appeared in the spot on the carpet where he'd just been.

He stayed in motion while Bogasian fired. The quick succession of muzzle flashes had the effect of a strobe light—each flash revealed the two of them in a new pose. Tom saw a heavy-looking green ceramic lamp. The room went dark. By the time it lit back up, he had it in his hands.

Bogasian stopped shooting and listened for him. Tom floated in his direction.

Bogasian fired again.

Only this time, Tom was right there. As the muzzle flash stretched out around them, he raised the lamp in both hands over Bogasian's head. And as the whiteness snapped back like a rubber band, he brought the lamp down.

And Bogasian turned.

With a look that said: ?

The shock of the lamp against Bogasian's skull vibrated the bones in Tom's arms all the way up to his teeth. Tom hit him with the lamp again and again. Until it broke into pieces. Then he beat him with the pieces.

As the ceramic broke away, Tom looped the electric cord around Bogasian's neck, turned, and threw him around his body. Bogasian hit the bedroom door so hard that both he and the door seemed to have been pressure-sucked into the hallway.

And Tom was on him.

He was punching and kneeing and elbowing and using every annex of his body that was hard, bony, and flat. He dug one hand into Bogasian's neck, so he could hit him with the other hand. He could feel it with each impact, that he was beating the life out of someone. Just knocking it right out. And he wasn't scared this time. And the feeling he'd wanted back on the rooftop, he now had. He had found the solution to his problems, and it was this man's face.

The skin on it jiggled with each blow. Bogasian's eyes were open, but they didn't see. It was quiet as Tom leaned over him. Except for the wet packing sound of his fist on Bogasian's face, there was only the mild hiss of room tone.

Bogasian's eyes shut gently, a millimeter at a time. Not like a man losing his life but like someone achieving the rest he so badly wanted. Then he was no longer moving. Tom stopped.

And he couldn't do it. He couldn't beat this man to death.

He noticed his finger was dislocated and made a fist to try to pop it back in place. When he looked back down, Bogasian's eyes were on him. Actually seeing him.

Bogasian rose to his feet. They were toe-to-toe. Tom feinted to the left and swiped at Bogasian's head with his right fist. Bogasian dropped a foot, just in time, and when he popped up, he swung the edge of his hand into Tom's windpipe.

Then he stood there and watched Tom choke.

Tom couldn't follow what happened next. He had no idea how fast Bogasian really was. Tom went to take another swing. Suddenly he was looking at Bogasian from three feet farther away, like he'd been teleported backward. And his cheek was bleeding where Bogasian had split the skin.

A fist hit his stomach, and Tom felt a pop in his abdominal wall. The next thing he knew, he was on his back and trying again to inhale, but his chest was so deflated he didn't have the physics to open it back up.

As Tom flopped around on the floor, Bogasian disappeared into the bedroom and reappeared with the briefcase and the gun. The action on the gun was open, but once he got back into the hall light and pointed it at Tom, he saw it was empty and tossed it. As Bogasian stepped past him, Tom got to his hands and knees and slapped the briefcase, sending it end over end down the hallway into the living room.

Bogasian crouched and swung at Tom's head. Tom ducked, and Bogasian's fist disappeared into the wall up to his shoulder. The impact coughed plaster into the air. Both of them squinted and choked on it. Tom rolled to his feet, wrapped his arms around Bogasian's torso, and swung him like an axe into the wall.

The drywall caved more than a foot, into a jagged outline of Bogasian's head and shoulders. But somehow Bogasian was already on his feet when Tom came at him again. As Tom grabbed him, Bogasian used his momentum to spin him into the wall so hard the back of Tom's head disappeared into it. White dust shot into the hall in thick clouds. They took turns coughing on it.

Tom rocked back and forth, pulling himself out of the plaster. Then they were punching each other so fast Tom couldn't follow what was happening.

Suddenly Bogasian grabbed him, spun around, and drove him back-first into the wall on the other side of the hallway. Tom's body hit a stud. Bogasian grabbed him again and slammed him back several times in succession. When Tom doubled over, Bogasian cupped his skull and hurled it against the wall. As Tom collapsed to his hands and knees, he saw ropes of bloody snot coming off his nose.

Bogasian picked him up. Tom kicked him in the knee and punched him in the face. He went to throw a bigger punch. His torso twisted and then released with his fist at the end of it. Bogasian caught his wrist, plucked it right out of the air. Tom went to hit him with his other hand. Bogasian caught that one even more easily than the first.

He started to twist Tom's arms past the limits of each joint.

They stood with their faces a foot apart, straining for position. Tom dropped his eyes to the scar on Bogasian's hand. When he looked up, Bogasian was staring at him. Like he wanted to ask him something.

Tom found his footing and tried to drive Bogasian backward, but Bogasian flipped him over his hip and threw him, face-first, into the other wall. Tom didn't just hit the wall this time. He crashed through it and collided with the floor. Immediately he vomited. Facedown, unable to move, he told himself, *Get up, come on, get up*. That was when he heard the police siren.

A window broke somewhere in the apartment.

When he staggered into the living room, he saw the entire window structure was missing. There was no sign of Bogasian—or the briefcase—in the yard.

CHAPTER 46

BOGASIAN TURNED onto Heinze Street and headed for the rendezvous point. When he was close, he slowed the car. Three black sedans were parked outside. He reversed into a connecting alley and rolled the driver's seat back so his face would be out of the glow from the streetlights. Then he texted *Here* on his phone.

Almost immediately a car door opened. Marty got out, and Bogasian rolled the window down. Marty didn't make eye contact as he came over. He just pointed to the briefcase on the passenger seat.

Bogasian handed it to him and watched him place it on the hood and open it to verify that all the files were inside. Satisfied, Marty snapped the case shut and stood looking around in every direction but Bogasian's.

"Is everything else in order?" he said.

"He came to the apartment."

"How would he do that?"

"He put a tracking device in the briefcase."

Marty's eyes moved to the case.

"I got rid of it."

"We're searching the building now. We need you when he returns." Marty stood there a moment, still looking around, then went back and stood by his SUV. Bogasian got out of his car and waited near him.

THE PROMETHEUS MAN

A group of men streamed out of the front entrance of Heinze 55 and walked to the black cars.

"The building is empty, sir," one of them said.

Marty snapped his phone open. "This is Martin Litvak. Code-in is..." He patted himself. Searched his inside pockets. "I need to request an override. I can't find my device."

A pause on the other end.

"You know what? Just connect me to 316."

Another pause as they transferred him.

When someone else picked up, Marty said, "Karl gave us a bad address. Shoot him."

He was quiet for a moment.

"What were the results of the utilities search?" He listened and then said loud enough for everyone to hear. "Schleizer 77. Apartment 8D."

Karl saw the man Marty had left behind walk past the conference room window and look in on him.

He'd be coming in with a gun once Marty realized the address was bad. What was unclear was whether he'd be coming for Karl's life or just one of his fingers. Karl stared at his index finger.

Then he looked at his barely there reflection in the window. The figure staring back at him looked haunted. He thought of how his dad, in some grim, back-alley, Irish way, would be amused by what he was about to do, and even though the thought did nothing to increase his odds of survival, it made him feel a little better.

By now Marty would have reached Heinze.

Karl stood up and pressed himself against the wall next to the door.

A minute later he saw a shadow on the conference room window as the guard looked in again. When the man threw open the door and rushed in, Karl clotheslined him. The man's face went slack momentarily as the back of his head hit the carpet. Then suddenly he was conscious again, and his hand shot to his hip and extended with his sidearm. Karl dropped to his knees and grabbed both of the man's hands.

Slowly he was able to use his bodyweight to push the gun up over the man's head. Once the man's arms were out of the way, Karl released one hand and dropped an elbow on the man's jaw with all his might. He did it over and over until the man went limp.

The other men must have gone with Marty because the suite was empty. Karl let himself into Marty's office.

The sun had set, but still he left the lights off. He took out Marty's remote-access security device, which he'd palmed while Marty was punching him in the face. There was a string of ten numbers on the key card that changed every thirty seconds. Marty was still logged onto his computer, but when Karl went to access the system, he got a coded challenge. He entered the number that flashed on the card.

Once he was in, he saw two things: the Prometheus files were not hard copy only, as Marty had claimed, and they were a shell of what they should have been. If someone were to look them over, they would guess that as far as Marty knew, the project had never gotten off the ground. But there was something else.

A reprimand from Marty to Karl. It even had Karl's signature, forged to acknowledge receipt. In the letter, which was dated three years ago, Marty directed Karl to confine his work to actionable projects and stop making off-market purchases of stem-cell-rich "body parts." Also per "numerous requests," Karl was to end the experimental program testing stem cells on lab animals. Finally he was to end contact with the three men he'd been using to acquire the stem cells: Benjamin Kotesh, Jonathan Nast, and Alan Sarmad.

There they were—all the men who killed Eric except for Bogasian.

Now Karl knew why Marty had brought him back. Oversight committees, the inspector general, prosecutors—they weren't stupid. When something went wrong, the senior person on a team would do absolutely anything to pin it on the junior person. If any of this came to light, the people asking questions would expect Marty to swear up and down that it had all been Karl's doing, that Karl had acted without his knowledge.

But Marty wouldn't do that.

Karl could almost picture the interview. Marty would insist—*insist*—that Karl was one of the agency's best operatives. He'd get angry on Karl's behalf. They would take out the reprimand—Marty would never point to it himself, the bastard was too smart for that—and Marty would say of course Karl stopped screwing around with stem cells when asked to.

And they would believe him, because only one thing explained why he'd stick his neck out to bring Karl back: he was Karl's victim too. And the more they thought about it, the more they'd wonder: *If Marty Litvak were the one running an illegal stem cell experiment, why in the hell would he mention its existence in an on-the-record document?*

Karl had one of those out-of-body moments where a person can look back and see his situation with almost total objectivity. And what he saw was the perfect person for Marty to pin this on. The casting was so good he kind of admired it.

Almost as an afterthought, he entered the two seventeen-digit numbers Tom had shown him into an online GPS program. He'd known as soon as Tom had given them to him that these were GPS coordinates. He had to play around with the decimal points, but eventually he figured out that the first number was for Haiphong, a port in Vietnam.

From there, it was a short drive to China.

The second number was for Kodiak Island in Alaska.

From there, it was a couple hundred miles to Russia.

Karl sat there a moment, not believing what was right in front of him. Marty had not only kept the Prometheus technology from the CIA, he was now selling it to the Chinese, the Russians, and God knows who else. And he was using Bogasian to kill off the people who'd helped him.

Except his plan hadn't been working. The men in the barn were dead. Which explained why he wanted Tom so badly.

CHAPTER 47

BOGASIAN PULLED to a stop along with the other cars outside Schleizer 77 and rolled down his window. The men got out of their cars and glanced at him. Quick glances that lasted only as long as they needed to.

Marty's window went down, and the others came to it like flies.

"This building is empty except for 8D," Marty said. "Cut the power."

"What if we can't locate them?" one of the men said.

"Then burn it down."

Bogasian looked up at the eighth floor. He thought he saw two blinds being held apart snap back together.

The men went to their vehicles, pulled out rifles and night-vision goggles, and filed into the building. When Bogasian got out of his car, Marty was already on the phone. His window was still open. Either he didn't know Bogasian could hear him or he just didn't care anymore.

"We've found Nast. We'll have Tom soon," Marty said. "Is the lab ready?"

The voice on the other end said something about Karl.

"Then he'll be on his way here. That's fine. Bogasian is in play." Marty snapped the phone shut and noticed Bogasian. "Tom and Karl will be here any minute," he said.

Bogasian nodded and went to turn around.

"I want Tom, but otherwise your tasking is broad. That means everyone else in the building."

Bogasian looked at the front door, thinking about the men they'd just sent inside. He looked back at Marty, who nodded.

"Everyone."

Bogasian crossed the street and walked into the building. If it really was abandoned, it had only recently been given up on. The fixtures hadn't been vandalized much, and there were no desperate manifestos spray-painted on the walls.

The stairwell was massive. Twenty feet of open space with a staircase winding around it. A heap of smashed furniture sat at the bottom. When he reached the eighth floor, he saw dark shapes darting in and out of rooms. He took out his sidearm and tapped it on the railing. Four men materialized in the doorways, rifles trained on him. Bogasian lowered his gun and pointed to 8D.

"We already checked it," one said.

Bogasian didn't reply. He just walked into the apartment.

The one who'd spoken led the others in. His hand went up to his earpiece, and he listened for a moment.

"Okay," he said, and looked over at Bogasian. "He says to search the neighborhood."

"No," Bogasian said, "go to infrared."

The man hesitated.

"Do it right now."

Reluctantly he toggled the infrared.

"Scan the couches and chairs."

Bogasian stared at the man until he complied.

The man went around the room and stopped by the couch. "It's still a little warm," he said.

"Then they're still here." Bogasian turned to two of the others. "You're bottom up. The rest of us are top down."

They went to the roof, which was clear with no escape to adjacent buildings. Then they began to work their way down, floor by floor.

CHAPTER 48

THERE WERE no lights in the apartment, and Tom noticed the shiny, unusually clean cars by the curb. They didn't fit the neighborhood. Someone would be watching the front of the building, so he went around back and yanked on a double door until it opened. He wanted to tear straight up to the eighth floor, but it was quiet inside and that told him: *Maybe you want to be careful.*

He moved silently up the stairs, staying close to the wall. If anyone took a quick peek down the stairwell, he wouldn't pop from the background.

When he reached the seventh floor, he heard two creaks. They were close together. He slipped into a hallway and waited. And when he wanted to go—felt he had to go—he made himself wait just a little longer.

A shadow moved at the end of the hallway.

He saw the movement more than the shadow.

It stopped.

Then it crossed the hallway. Darkness domed over the other side of the hall like a hole in the building. The shadow merged into it.

Tom heard feet scuff the floor. The sound was coming from an apartment down the hall.

A thud.

Someone cried out.

Tom was already halfway down the hall when he heard a voice: "Where is she?"

Dr. Nast was standing with his arms up. Tom careened into the bedroom right as Silvana stepped out of the closet and swung a closet rod at the gunman. She knocked the three-inch-thick goggles off his face, seemed to like it, and wound up to hit him again. But the gunman stepped backward, creating space, and trained the rifle on her head.

Tom reached over the man's shoulder and shoved the stock of the rifle down. The muzzle swung up, away from Silvana, and the stock slid out of the man's hands.

The gunman got over this very quickly. The rifle had barely left his grip before one hand dropped to his waist and came up pointing a handgun. He turned the gun on Tom.

But Tom turned with him. Then Tom grabbed him by his shirt and whipped him against the wall. The man's head slapped off it. Somehow he stayed on his feet and staggered back in the direction he'd come, the gun still in hand. He was leveling it when Tom punched him so hard his jaw caved an inch into his face. The concussion left him on his feet. His gun paused on Tom's chest, and for a half-second Tom could only look down the barrel, waiting for the light at the end of it.

The man collapsed on the floor.

Tom picked up his rifle and pistol. When he turned to Silvana, she was staring at him.

"You came back," she said.

When she saw his face, her lips formed a gasp, though she didn't make a sound.

He surveyed Dr. Nast's chest, looking for the bullet wound. But Nast pointed down to his thigh. There was a tiny harmless-looking rip in his pants. As delicately as possible, Tom rolled him over and found another small rip.

He nodded at Nast, relieved. "It went through."

He tore the arm off Nast's shirt and tied it around his leg. With his hands clamped on Tom's wrists, Nast fought his way to his feet. Once he was up, he didn't let go. He looked at Tom and touched him on the forearm and smiled. His eyes were wet.

Tom handed the pistol to Silvana, and the three of them slipped out of the room and made their way to the stairwell.

Footsteps.

They froze. The footsteps were coming up the stairs. The hallway was too open to fight from, so Tom steered them into the closest apartment.

But the shooter must have seen them.

Slugs gouged through the walls right where they'd been standing. Tom shoved Nast and Silvana to the floor. Wood split. Windows shattered. A chunk of plaster dropped out ten feet from Tom's face.

The shooting stopped. Then the shooter jammed his gun into one of the holes he'd created. There was only room for the muzzle of the rifle, so he fired blindly at them. Tom dove out of the way as bullets punched into the floor.

The shooting stopped again. Tom heard the metal chuckle of a reload. He watched the shot-out hole in the wall and saw the shooter's shoulder move down on the other side. The man was lowering himself to look through and check the damage.

Tom picked himself up and ran as hard as he could at the wall. It was so rotted it looked like papier-mâché. He'd already covered half the distance before he saw a man's chin appear in the hole. And as he lowered his shoulder and hit the wall, he saw an eye. It was looking at him—and widening.

The entire wall shook as he crashed through it and landed on top of the shooter. He was still skidding as he grabbed the man and hammer-fisted his face until he stopped moving.

Tom took the man's radio and put the headset on. He shouldered the automatic rifle and went back for Silvana and her father.

They helped Dr. Nast to his feet, and the three of them rushed over to the staircase. They would be easy targets while they were on the stairwell, so Tom slowed them down before they came to it. They waited for sounds—voices, footsteps, something. Tom inched closer to the railing, so he could get eyes or ears on anything there. Once he confirmed everything was clear, he motioned Silvana and Nast over.

A wood plank creaked on the floor directly above.

Tom pointed his rifle at the ceiling and waited for another sound.

After a moment, he took a step back—he could feel the stress in the floorboard and tried to put his foot down as slowly as possible.

It creaked anyway.

Ping.

Ping.

He looked down. There were two tiny holes in the floor where he'd been standing. He looked up. There were two holes in the ceiling, similarly spaced.

Ping.

A divot materialized an inch from his foot. There were three holes in the ceiling spaced equally—three feet apart. Now he knew where to aim. He trained the automatic on the next spot in the trail and fired a burst.

He waited.

No sound.

Then blood ran from the holes in the ceiling in strands.

He realized he couldn't lead them out of here the way he'd thought. He didn't even know how many people were in the building. He motioned Dr. Nast and Silvana back into the apartment, gave them time to find a hiding space, and then pressed the TALK button on the radio.

"Requesting assistance," he said. "Northwest corner of the seventh floor."

A long silence. Then: "Rendezvous northwest corner. Seventh floor. I'm approaching from the southwest stairwell."

"Copy," Tom said.

He found the door to the southwest stairwell and hid around the corner and waited. He heard the door to the stairwell swing open and shut. He stood with his rifle trained on the doorway and counted ten seconds, his pulse jumping in his throat.

No one came.

Sweat ran down his face and stung his eyes. He tried to wipe it with his shoulder. His hands were so sweaty they felt slippery against the rifle. He wiped them on his pants and re-gripped.

No one came.

He whipped around to make sure someone wasn't already behind him.

There was another small stairwell opposite the one he crouched near. To cover one, he had to turn his back on the other. He was trapped. He stood there, looking back and forth, straining to hear someone's approach. He wanted to move, but he didn't want to make a sound.

His eyes searched the darkness of the first stairwell, trying to make out a boot or the outline of a person moving toward him. For one insane moment, he wondered if he'd somehow missed someone in the half-second that he'd turned around.

Something moved in his peripheral vision.

When he whipped around, Bogasian was on the fire escape. Tom lurched backward as the wall beside his face exploded. From the other side of the window, through the falling glass, Bogasian was already sighting the follow-up.

The wall exploded a second time. Shots boomed through the hallway, echoing over one another. As Tom collapsed behind a corner, he fired a burst and saw Bogasian was already barging through the broken window.

Tom scrambled down the hallway and ducked through the doorway of an apartment missing its front door. Two walls had been knocked down completely, allowing him to see into the adjacent apartments. There were several six-foot holes at chest level in the remaining walls, which were spray-painted and marked for demolition. He crept to the other side of one of the holes and waited for Bogasian.

Forty feet away a pair of eyes looked right at him.

Silvana.

Her lips parted to whisper something, but Tom shook his head. She raised one of her hands, but he couldn't see what was on it until she stuck it in the light. It glistened—slick with her father's blood. He was bleeding out.

Tom nodded, trying to exude calm, like they'd figure it out. Silvana stepped back from the hole in the wall, and her face faded to black.

He checked his magazine. Empty. When he slid the chamber open, he found a round. He waited with his gun trained on the missing front door. But he didn't like it, just leaving the two of them out there, so he made his way through the shadows, stepping around diagonal strips of light from the street.

A floorboard compressed.

He froze in a crouch. Sweat pooled in his shoes and on the back of his shirt. His legs were so tired they started to shake.

The floorboard made another sound as a large weight came off it.

There was a thin band of light thirty feet to his left. It had nothing solid to reflect off of, so he only noticed it when Bogasian's arm swept through. A handgun winked in the light. He heard Silvana say "You don't have to do this" as Bogasian leveled the gun in her direction. Bogasian took another step, out of the light.

Tom only had a second, so he aimed for the spot in the darkness where he thought Bogasian was and fired.

He heard the gunshot from his weapon—followed instantly by one from Bogasian's.

He rushed blindly to where Bogasian had been standing. Silvana was on the floor, cradling her unconscious father. She didn't say anything when she saw him. She just shifted her eyes to a door across the room, and he understood. He noticed Bogasian's gun lying on the floor. There was blood on it.

The door led him into the main hallway, back by the stairwell. When he turned, he saw Bogasian. His left hand was dripping blood with the regularity of a leaky faucet.

Tom put the rifle on him and motioned for him to put his hands up.

Bogasian saw him, took a few steps in his direction, and stopped. His hands went up as an afterthought, barely above waist level. The bleeding flicked red droplets down his wrist, and he stood there indifferent to it.

"You're not going to have me arrested, are you?" he said.

"You're a murderer."

"Of who exactly?"

They looked at each other, and they both knew of who exactly.

"You don't have the briefcase, you don't have anything."

"I have you."

Bogasian shook his head like he was disappointed. "You'll need more than that."

"The proof is in your skull. And you can bet they'll open you up to get it."

"I've noticed people aren't shy about that."

"I saw the pictures. Are there others?"

"They tried."

"We're the only ones?"

Bogasian smiled.

They stood there awkwardly. Now that Tom had found the man

who shot his brother, he realized they didn't really have anything to talk about. There was just...nothing to say.

"You killed Alan Sarmad," Bogasian said.

Tom didn't say anything.

"That's how it starts. First, you kill the guilty."

Tom wondered if Bogasian knew he was empty.

"You look like your brother," Bogasian said. "Eric, right?" He took a half-step in Tom's direction. "I can't remember his name sometimes. You get so you can't remember a lot of things."

Another half-step.

"He tried to help me. After the operation. You deserve to know that."

"He felt bad for you."

Bogasian laughed a little. "He did this to me."

Tom thought he had never seen such sorrow in another person's eyes.

"He didn't know," Tom said.

"That doesn't matter. That never matters."

"It matters to me."

"Anything that matters to you and no one else doesn't really matter."

"We'll see."

Bogasian smiled again. "You're one of those people. You think what you do actually says something about the world."

Another half-step.

"I wish you hadn't come here." Bogasian froze, and his eyes turned sad. "I know you had to, but I really wish you hadn't come."

Tom tightened his grip on the gun. "Get down on the floor."

Bogasian kept gliding toward him. When he stopped, he leaned forward. "You're empty."

He lunged, knocking Tom off-balance, and pinned him against the railing. Immediately Tom's cuts were open and flowing. Bogasian wrapped his arm around Tom's neck and squeezed.

Tom couldn't pry him off him. So while he choked, he went for the stairwell railing. He pivoted as much as he could around Bogasian and threw them both into it.

The railing bent for a second and then ripped out of the floor. They paused over the edge of the stairwell as they both fought for balance. Tom went over the edge first. He managed to twist as he dropped and jam his hand at the rail, which was still attached to the floor above at one end. His fingers closed around it, and all of a sudden he'd stopped falling.

He could see the blur of Bogasian falling after him.

His other hand shot out. He reached for Bogasian's wrist, and Bogasian must have also reached for his because their hands snapped around each other. They looked at each other in shock.

Another anchor ripped out of the railing. They dropped three feet and swung into the wall. Tom's grip on Bogasian slipped a half-inch. His left hand got smashed between the railing and the wall and went numb. The gash on it drooled fresh blood down his arm and into his face, but he didn't let go. Something inside him just wouldn't do that.

He glanced down.

Bogasian was watching him.

Bogasian couldn't understand why Tom didn't just let go of him. He watched him start to shake, knew he wouldn't be able to hold them both for long, not with his middle finger broken.

Bogasian sensed they were getting lower and lower. Whatever was still keeping the railing attached to the floor was bending. Metal was lengthening. And the math was simple: there was too much weight.

The only thing Bogasian ever really knew about Eric was

that he'd tried to help him. And Tom was here because of Eric.

He let go.

Tom tried to hold him, but Bogasian's hand started to slip. Bogasian was looking at him and nodding *It's okay, let me go, it's okay.*

They were both still looking at each other when Bogasian fell. Tom watched him fall forty feet before he disappeared into the darkness. There was the slapping sound of something filled with liquid colliding with the ground.

Tom hung there and listened for a sound he knew he wouldn't hear. A gasp or a moan. Then he started climbing back up the railing.

When he was halfway, Karl appeared on the seventh floor and looked down at him. He was shouting and pointing at something Tom couldn't quite see. Tom was too exhausted to understand. He just kept trying to climb up the rail. But as he got closer, he saw the section he was holding on to had split from the rest. There were only a few bolts left holding it, and Karl was hauling back on the railing to take some of the weight off.

Tom's hand was on the seventh floor when there was a series of sounds. Something creaked, and something else snapped. Tom looked at Karl for help. Then his hand clawed at the floor, and he fell six stories.

Karl watched Tom fall until he disappeared in the shadows. He heard him hit the floor. Then he rushed down the stairs.

At the bottom, he found Bogasian's body. It had been crushed by its own weight against the ground. Blood sprayed the tile and painted the wall. There was a stack of decaying furniture a couple feet from him. When Karl climbed up it, there was some blood, but he couldn't find Tom's body.

He ran into the street and then the alley behind the building.

They were empty.

CHAPTER 49

(Three months later)

SCHRODER-SANDS was hosting its first annual Muscular Dystrophy Hope Gala at the Mayflower Hotel in Washington, DC. According to the press release, it was an event you didn't want to miss.

Karl couldn't have agreed more.

He arrived early, and it was still photo call outside the hotel. A famous actor and a senator were gripping each other in one of these "We did it!" holds while flashbulbs strobed out half a city block. The actor flashed a peace sign, and the senator, like a good Texan, wasn't going within a mile of that one. He just hefted his fist.

Karl tried to slink along the perimeter of the lobby, but a waiter thrust a glass of champagne into his hand. The lobby was lit up in red, which diffused along the walls into princess pink. A man nearby leaned over to his lady friend and whispered, "It's quite vaginal." And they both started laughing. Karl laughed too, and when the couple stopped and looked at him, he raised his glass. They both smiled uncomfortably and fled to the other side of the room, and all of a sudden Karl was having a whale of a time.

He choked down his champagne as he looked for Marty. He didn't see him anywhere, so the first thing he did was get a real drink. Then he ordered two more because the bar looked busy and he didn't like any nonsense between rounds. After that, he filled a jacket pocket with some butter mints and planted himself at a small table in the corner. He sat there, sipping beer and sucking on mints even after everyone else had filed into the ballroom.

His phone vibrated.

The message said: *We're ready.*

As he approached the Grand Ballroom, he could hear—and feel in the back of his throat—four hundred people applauding, really slapping their hands together. He opened the door and saw Fritz Lang, CEO of Schroder-Sands, taking the stage.

Then he spotted Marty.

He was seated at a table of people like him, not the beautiful people but the politicians—who proved what some guy once said about Washington being Hollywood for ugly people.

Lang raised his arms to hush the audience. But they wouldn't wind it down. Some people cheered louder, not about to let him rain on this, their parade for him. He managed a patient smile. Karl had never known who Marty's contact was at Schroder-Sands. He'd figured it must have been someone pretty high up, but he'd never imagined it would be the CEO himself.

Lang dipped his head toward the mic. "Now I think we all know who this event is really about. And if you know their story, you know there isn't time to keep them waiting."

The clapping died off instantly.

Lang stared over the audience. "Since Schroder-Sands began Project Hope three years ago, annual deaths of children from neuromuscular disease have fallen 5 percent. We have saved the lives of literally thousands of children—"

Clapping from one of the tables.

Lang turned on them. "No," he said. "Don't clap."

A hush fell over the audience. This was his second scolding, and he was going to lose them with a third.

"Our innovations went to eight thousand children last year. It's given hope to thousands of others, and you know what?" He pounded the podium with each of his next words. "That's. Not. Good. Enough."

Thunderous applause.

"We. Will. Not. Stop." He was still pounding. "Ever."

Even more thunderous applause.

Lang stood beaming.

Karl looked at Marty, and Marty glanced over and did a double-take. Then he smiled. Karl smiled back. And as he did, he took his phone out of his pocket and held it up so Marty could see it.

He took the draft email with a video attached and hit SEND.

Marty's phone lit up. He pressed something on the screen and sat watching the video.

Two hours earlier, Karl had met privately with the director and the deputy director of the CIA and shown them the video of Dr. Nast. Nast sat in one of those spaceless, blacked-out interview rooms across from an unseen interviewer.

"So you used stem cells to enhance a person physically?" the interviewer asked.

Dr. Nast nodded.

"And you had no idea about the actual purpose of what you were working on?"

"They told us it was a life-saving treatment for a man with a rare neuromuscular disease."

"What was the actual purpose?"

"To weaponize a human being. Basically."

"Eric Reese," she said. "Why was he was killed?"

"The principals chose not to reveal the program to the US government. Instead they developed it for sale to other governments. Once substantial sales had been made, everyone involved in the development or distribution of this technology was killed."

"Except you?"

Nast nodded. "Except me."

"You presented physical evidence to us. Can you please explain for those watching what that evidence is?"

"I have tissue samples from the body of the man we augmented."

"The test subject?"

"Yes."

"Do you know his name?"

"Ian Bogasian."

"You said 'body.' That means he isn't alive?"

"Correct."

"How valuable is the program Mr. Bogasian was associated with? Do you have any idea of the dollar amounts involved?"

"A biotechnology firm just licensed a far less advanced stem cell technology for $120 million a year. I assume comparable amounts were transferred to the executive overseeing our project."

"And that man's name?"

"Martin Litvak."

Karl had stopped the video at this point and told both directors they could keep this copy because he had more of them. They asked what the fuck he wanted.

He asked for immunity for himself and the guaranteed safety of Dr. Nast and Silvana. They were to receive US citizenship as a show of good faith. In exchange, the tape would never get out and Martin Litvak had to be arrested. That night.

They asked about Tom, and he repeated what he'd already told them: Tom was dead. They said he'd have an answer in two hours.

When the men and women from the CIA walked into the ballroom, they didn't look like they were there to arrest someone. Three of them went over to Marty's table and stopped beside it. People turned and looked at what was going on. Marty smiled at them and then whispered something to one of the agents. The agent whispered something back, and Marty's smile died.

Marty looked around, saw even more people looking at him, and waved the agents away.

None of them moved.

"I would like to thank our colleagues at the United Nations for making this program possible," Lang said. "Hopefully with the passage of new legislation in the EU, we can enter even more markets, particularly those that do not happen to be in the good graces of the United States."

Knowing laughter from the crowd.

One of the agents put his hand on Marty's arm. Marty jerked it free. A woman two seats away gasped. Now everyone in the vicinity was staring.

"Excuse me," Lang said from the podium. "If those causing the interruption would please cease doing so, I'm sure I speak for everyone when I say—"

As soon as Lang saw the agents, his voice choked off. He managed a smile and continued his speech, now in monotone.

But no one was listening. The eyes were on Marty. He looked naked somehow. Or at least the rest of the room seemed like it was looking at a naked man.

When the agents stood Marty up, the forces animating his face had quit. He looked straight ahead, staring at something only he could see.

Karl headed toward the lobby along with the rest of the dinner guests.

That was when he saw Tom.

The expression on his face suggested he'd been watching Karl for a while. He was smiling. Not like in the photograph, not like when he was a kid next to his brother. But it was a good smile, the kind you see on another person, and even though you have no idea what that person is thinking, it makes you smile too.

Dr. Nast had performed a series of operations on him, removing tissue where he could. Tom would never be like he was before, but there was a chance he'd live a normal life.

He was arm-in-arm with Silvana. Even though they were fifty feet away, somehow the distance was impossible to cross, and Karl felt like he was looking into an old photograph in the attic. The two of them were young and beautiful—and normal.

Tom looked so normal Karl could feel it in his chest.

He was just a twenty-two-year-old with a girl on his arm.

And then—just like that—he was gone, carried away forever by the tide of tuxedos and ball gowns.

ACKNOWLEDGMENTS

First of all, I'd like to thank my wife, Lindsay. I don't know how to put this delicately, but the amount of crap she put herself through so I could finish this book was pretty substantial. It was also, now that I think about it, a kind of love. She's a first reader, a co-conspirator, and for some reason she had this conviction, based on little initial validation from the outside world, that I was a good writer.

Zee, *thank you*.

I'd also like to thank my parents for their love and support, as well as my sisters and my brother. My sister Courtney not only gave feedback on the book but also liked it enough to attempt several times to acquire a 10 percent ownership interest in it (at lowball, vulture rates).

I'd also like to thank Renni Browne, Shannon Roberts, and John Marlow, who edited the book before it sold. Their edits helped me land an agent. I also received valuable feedback from first readers Toby Carlisle, Jama Young, David Hardy, Joe Cantwell, Jon Blake, and Sarah Hardoby.

I'd like to thank Emily Giglierano, Josh Kendall, Wes Miller, Reagan Arthur, and Ruth Tross for both purchasing the book and believing in it. Copyeditors Betsy Uhrig and Sue Betz did incredibly valuable work enhancing the readability of the text and finding errors. Thank you also to Pamela Brown, Maggie Southard,

ACKNOWLEDGMENTS

Sabrina Callahan, and the rest of the marketing/publicity team at Mulholland.

This book wouldn't exist if it weren't for the work of Tony Gilroy, Raymond Chandler, and Stephen King. I owe a debt of gratitude to them.

Finally I'd like to thank my agent, Stacia Decker. I saved her for last for a reason. I pitched this book to every agent in the business, in some cases six or seven times. She was the only agent who wanted to represent me. And after she helped me streamline the story, we got multiple offers and ultimately wound up selling the book in a matter of days. It was a dream come true.

ABOUT THE AUTHOR

Scott Reardon is a graduate of Georgetown University and Northwestern Law. He currently runs an investment management firm in Los Angeles. *The Prometheus Man* is his first novel.

You've turned the last page.

But it doesn't have to end there . . .

If you're looking for more first-class, action-packed, nail-biting suspense, follow us on Twitter @**MulhollandUK** for:

- News
- Competitions
- Regular updates about our books and authors
- Insider info into the world of crime and thrillers
- Behind-the-scenes access to Mulholland Books

And much more!

There are many more twists to come.

MULHOLLAND:
You never know what's coming around the curve.